D1062678

*RIGHTS*

# *RIGHTS*

BY

LAWRENCE GOLDSTONE

THE PERMANENT PRESS

Sag Harbor, NY 11963

**Library of Congress Cataloging-in-Publication Data**

Goldstone, Lawrence, 1947–
Rights / Lawrence Goldstone.
p. cm.
ISBN 1-877946-13-3 : $21.95
I. Title.
PS3557.0426R54 1992
813′.54—dc20 91-36047
CIP



**Manufactured in MEXICO**

PERMANENT PRESS
Noyac Road
Sag Harbor, NY 11963

for Nancy

# PART I

# CHAPTER ONE

Clarissa Taylor blinked awake. The all-night call-in radio show, commonly referred to in New York as "Psycho Rap," was just signing off, to be immediately replaced by the soft music and softer talk of "Mornings with Milton." Clarissa stifled a groan. After fourteen years, she still had not become accustomed to waking up in the dark.

She swung her feet over the edge of the bed and placed her hands on her knees. Now came the hard part—pushing herself to a standing position and then making it into the bathroom to wash her face. This operation was performed in silence as the three Taylor children need not arise until after seven-thirty. As much as Clarissa wanted to spend time with her babies, she would never deprive school children of an extra ninety minutes of sleep.

After the bathroom, the next stop was the kitchen for a quick cup of instant coffee. One thing about the restaurant business—breakfast came with the job, even if it was only a toasted bagel. But breakfast for the kids was another matter and Clarissa made sure that the children's places were set at the little table in the dining alcove. She tore a piece of paper off the pad with the multicolored sheets (today's was pink) and wrote them a note. She did this every day, if nothing more than to say, "Study hard. I love you. See you for dinner. Mom."

She often imagined Matthew, so serious and responsible, shepherding the girls to their seats and supervising their corn flakes and milk, adorned by fresh banana or peach. She had been more than once tempted to get to work late in order to secretly observe the ritual. That was just a fantasy, of course . . . Clarissa Taylor had not been late for work in almost ten years, not on the day of the hurricane, during the transit strike or merely due to the vagaries of the New York transit system.

When all was prepared and she had dressed in her green blouse, dark skirt and low-heeled shoes, Clarissa paused outside the girls' room as she did each morning, then, whispering a prayer of thanks, quietly slipped out the door and headed for work.

Like the radio station switching from "Psycho Rap" to "Mornings With Milton," the subways were also undergoing their daily early morning transition from sanctuary for the criminal and derelict to conveyance for New York's working millions. The remains of the night's carnage were still evident but force of numbers was swinging the tide to first-wave Wall Streeters, construction workers and those in the service professions whose businesses must be up and running by the time the rush began in earnest during the next hour.

The trip on the 'E' train was better than most, the Queens run not being among the favored of the city's subway marauders as it ran exclusively through middle-class neighborhoods. After a short wait, Clarissa boarded the train and took the seat that was always available at six thirty-five and settled in to read her *Daily News*.

Twenty minutes later she exited onto the now-sunlit Third Avenue to wait for the bus and the ride to Seventy-seventh Street. This was the pleasant part of the trip, traffic flowing freely and the city still giving off the illusion of relative tranquility and cleanliness. She looked out of the window, watching Third Avenue drift by, filled with the expensive boutiques and high-rise apartment buildings that catered to Manhattan's obsessively upwardly mobile.

At the appointed stop, Clarissa Taylor got off the bus and walked briskly toward Lexington Avenue. Without breaking stride, she rushed past the homeless man just awakening in the next doorway and entered her place of business to begin another day of work.

Times were good for Clarissa Taylor.

Times had certainly changed for Fruitful Willis. Not since he was a young boy in North Carolina, the eighteenth of twenty-two children (Mrs. Willis named all her offspring from her favorite passages in the Bible) had Fruitful felt such a sense of privilege.

Privilege was a condition that had oft eluded Fruitful Willis these past two decades since, at age fourteen, no longer content to share a bed with three of his siblings, he had journeyed north to use what everyone in Cottontail Run had agreed was a remarkable way with people to make his place and secure his fortune. But the race for success was fiercely run and he was just one more country boy who had dragged dreams and ambitions to an unfriendly and impersonal city. Still, Fruitful Willis was no quitter and now, after a lifetime of struggle, he had finally made it to the Upper East Side.

He took a deep drag of the cool, early spring city air. What to most of the scurrying population was an acrid, lung-searing miasma, a textbook of pollutants mixed with just enough oxygen to maintain vital functions, was to Fruitful a pastoral bouquet. It all depended on what you were used to, really, and Fruitful Willis was used to the urine-drenched atmosphere of steam tunnels, public waiting rooms and other burrows that were the standard accommodations of the city's homeless.

Just the term 'homeless,' was an indication of how far Fruitful had come. Just three years ago he was a 'bum,' a 'vagrant,' a 'crazy,' treated with contempt and avoided with loathing by every person who had a choice in such matters. It was nothing for a cop to shove him along at the end of a nightstick, for a security guard to roust him out of a sound sleep, or for a shop owner to evict him from the front of a store or restaurant with the business end of a broom handle.

Three years ago, when Fruitful was a bum, he had no recourse against such treatment. If some distracted city official decreed that, 'for his own protection,' he was to be shipped off to a teeming, cramped city shelter (Fruitful hated crowds) and be exposed to beatings and the theft of his few possessions in order to extend some addict's habit for another few hours, off he went.

When Fruitful Willis was a bum, he had no rights.

But Fruitful Willis was no longer a bum. Not the shopkeepers, nor the city officials, nor the cops (at least publicly), nor the mayor himself dared to refer to Fruitful Willis as a bum. Without extending himself in the slightest, Fruitful had graduated from bum-dom to the far more prestigious position of a member of the homeless.

Now, like any other member of society, Fruitful Willis had

rights. He could finally get a good night's sleep in the bus station. Not only did the guards no longer roust him, they even protected him from the packs of roving drug addicts. By day, Fruitful was free to perch wherever he liked in order to entreat alms from passersby. True, the competition had increased—there was now another member of the homeless on virtually every street corner—but, to counteract the dilution of market share, Fruitful was now permitted to put that remarkable way with people to work in heretofore forbidden sales techniques.

Although he himself found nothing unusual in his appearance, Fruitful discovered that his torn plaid shirt and once-khaki pants, combined with the sneakers devoid of shoelaces and socks, all of which had acquired what could modestly be termed a 'lived-in' look, were useful tools in persuading the more conservatively attired members of the populace to part with some idle change. In contrast to when he was a bum and had no rights, Fruitful might now chat up members of his target population to make it more difficult for them to avoid the feared eye contact. The first axiom of his trade was that eye contact was *sine qua non* to a successful score.

A practiced and particularly effective maneuver saw Fruitful shuffle a few paces and place himself in the path of an oncoming elderly woman. He found that if he greeted the lady with some charming phrase regarding the weather or her attire, she almost invariably preferred giving him cash to continuing the discussion. In her haste to circumvent the pile of rags and unwashed human, occasionally one of these wide-eyed octogenarians even favored Fruitful with a piece of paper money.

These days, Fruitful was particularly pleased with himself. With cunning and guile, he had secured a spot directly outside a small but thriving delicatessen on Lexington Avenue in the high Seventies. He couldn't quite make out the name although he was sure it began with a 'P.' Of all the venues in his long career, this place of business was by far the most lucrative; what marketing people called a 'high traffic area.' Due to its proximity to the subway, his establishment got heavy commuter business morning and night, and the delicatessen was busy, breakfast, lunch and dinner.

Fruitful squinted and laughed to himself, although the laugh was audible the entire length of the block. He had most surely done it this time. They all knew it too. Competitors had attempted to seize his location by persuasion or by screaming at him or even, once or twice, by force. The deli owner had tried all the old tricks to get him to take his business elsewhere. None of it had worked. Fruitful had beaten back all attempts by his fellows to rob him of his good fortune. And as for the owner . . . Fruitful laughed again. The owner couldn't do shit. He don't own the sidewalk too. I can stay here as long as I like.

I got rights.

Fruitful checked the one pocket of his clothing that had yet to dissolve under the combined assault of age, wear and bodily fluids, the depository of the day's receipts. He shook the cache. Heavy, heavy, heavy. Fruitful tossed off another laugh as the pedestrians who had given him a wide berth jerked their heads reflexively in the direction of the sound.

Well, thought Fruitful Willis, another good day. This is my spot. I got a right to it.

Then, feeling nature's urge within him, Fruitful sauntered to the edge of the sidewalk and positioned himself between two parked cars. And, as those diners inside the restaurant who had been so unfortunate as to secure window tables looked on, Fruitful Willis dropped his pants, squatted, and peacefully defecated at the edge of the curb.

The second he heard the gagging and groaning from the front, Murray Plotkin knew exactly what was wrong.

It's that bum again.

Murray sped to the head of the store, futilely affecting nonchalance so as not to pique the curiosity of the two or three customers who were not yet aware something was amiss. He arrived to find what had become an all too familiar scene. His entire front section, carefully constructed to afford a view of the street so that his customers could feel the added cachet of gazing out upon strolling New York while ingesting their lean, center-cut Plotkin's Perfect, had degenerated into a frenzy of lost appetites and demands for the check.

Murray realized immediately that there was nothing he

could do to salvage the situation. In a perversion of killing the messenger that brings bad news, Murray's customers seemed to hold him responsible for the actions of the man squatting just outside the window. He also knew that not one person who was currently in the restaurant, nor any of the customers' friends, co-workers, members of their families or those whom they engaged in idle chatter would ever set foot in his establishment again.

Twenty minutes later, after surveying his empty delicatessen, Murray Plotkin retired to his office, a squirrelly room in the rear of the store with a tiny window which provided him little light but an unobstructed view of the debris-strewn alley that ran behind the building. As Murray often did in moments of strife, he gazed up at the wall and the two photographs that resided there, one of his father, Izzie, Plotkin's patriarch, and the other of John F. Kennedy, who had himself sampled a Plotkin's Perfect on a campaign swing through Brooklyn. Spurred by the image of his father advising a president-to-be to stand up to Khrushchev, Murray opened a bottle of Doctor Brown's Cel-Ray Tonic and reminisced.

When the old neighborhood in Brooklyn, the Flatbush of William Bendix, Barbra Streisand, Danny Kaye and Mae West had begun to acquire the festering sores of poverty, Murray had initially vowed to dig in his heels and stick it out. After all, Izzie Plotkin had established more than a delicatessen—Plotkin's was an institution, a tradition ("Come *plotz* at Plotkin's"), and Murray had been taught that traditions survived, in fact, had a responsibility to survive, despite whatever hardships fate or health food might throw in his path. (So reverent was Murray of tradition that he retained his father's Eastern European accent even though he himself had been born at Caledonian Hospital on Ocean Avenue.)

But as the deterioration continued, Murray Plotkin realized that sometimes for a tradition to survive, it has to relocate, so he found a new location, suitable for Plotkin's Perfect and now, twelve years later, Plotkin's of Flatbush was as much of a fixture on Lexington Avenue as it had previously been on Church Avenue.

But this time the photographs and memories did not have the desired effect. He was tired and for the first time since the family had set foot in the New World, a Plotkin considered defeat.

It was not that he hadn't tried. When the nameless wretch had first perched outside his door, harassing his customers and anyone else who happened by, urinating in the street and making occasional raving noises, Murray Plotkin had done what any good citizen would do. He sought help for the man from one of the myriad of city agencies whose very existence was predicated on aiding such people. After all, Murray Plotkin had reasoned at the time, the man was clearly disturbed and not responsible for his actions, and besides, there but for fortune . . .

The city agencies had arrived promptly in the person of three young men and one young woman who strode purposefully into Plotkin's of Flatbush between the breakfast and lunch hours. Each was wearing a gray suit, brown shoes and some variety of red-patterned tie. One of the young men, serious and dark skinned, with hair shining from tonic, stepped forward.

"Mr. Platkin, we are from the Department of Social Services." The young man spoke without smiling. He did not offer his hand but, rather, produced a business card.

'Arthur Jabbawallah,' it read, 'Senior Case Worker.'

"We are here, Mr. Platkin, to determine whether or not the subject of your complaint qualifies under Section Thirty-seven-point-four of the New York City Indigent Persons Law."

Murray nodded, grateful and impressed that New York would so quickly marshal four professionals to deal with his problem.

"First, Mr. Platkin," continued Arthur Jabbawallah, "we need some information."

A second young man stepped forward, holding a clipboard to which was fastened an official-looking form. For the next twenty minutes, Murray Plotkin gave the young man (who did not present a business card), a slew of information, including his social security number, his tax identification number, his food and beverage permit number, his liquor control number, the number of years he had been in business, his home address, the number of years he had lived there and a copy of his auto registration. As the young man entered the information on his form, the young woman punched the data into what looked like a television remote control device, but was actually a portable computer terminal, purchased with a federal grant from the Department of Defense.

During this process, Murray wondered only slightly why the city agencies needed so much information about him, when the problem was the man lounging outside his door. It was probably to protect him in case of dispute, he decided.

When the forms had been completed and the data entered, Arthur Jabbawallah read over the entries and nodded. "Now, may we speak to the subject of your complaint."

Murray indicated the front door and all four adjourned to the street. Murray watched through the window as the third young man leaned down and appeared to speak earnestly with the bum. Five minutes later, all four re-entered the store. Arthur Jabbawallah had passed beyond serious and now looked stern.

"Mr. Platkin," he began, "we have determined that the man outside does not qualify under Section Thirty-seven-point-four."

"Vot does zat mean?" ventured Murray, afraid of the answer.

"That means, Mr. Platkin," said Arthur Jabbawallah, "that, in our professional opinion, the man outside is not mentally ill in the legal sense, nor does he constitute a bodily threat to either himself or others."

"Vot are you talking about?" queried Murray, trying not to raise his voice and antagonize an official city emissary. "Look at him. You don't sink he's crazy? Vhich von of you is ze psychologist?"

Arthur Jabbawallah frowned. "None of us need be a psychologist, Mr. Platkin. Section One-eight-three of the Omnibus New York City Human Services Law states that four licensed social service professionals are all that is necessary to make a determination of mental competence provided one is a senior case worker."

"So, vot are you telling me?" asked Murray, his gratitude for the promptness and concern of the city agencies quickly eroding.

"I am telling you," the senior case worker explained patiently, "that Mr. Doe out there has a right to remain on the public street unless he violates the rights of others by harassment or by becoming a public nuisance. He might then be removed if an offended citizen lodges a formal complaint."

"Doe? Is zat his name?"

"We don't know his name. He doesn't have to tell us."

"But vot about me? I had to give you my name."

"You, Mr. Platkin, are the complainant."

Murray's head began to swim. "Vot happens if a citizen files a formal complaint?" he asked, although he had been under the impression that that was precisely what he had done.

Arthur Jabbawallah shrugged. "That would put Mr. Doe in violation of Section Six-nine-two of the Penal Code. For that he would receive a thirty-day sentence. But, I should tell you," the senior case worker added, "the jails are so crowded that Mr. Doe would probably be back on the street the following day."

"And free to come right back and *plotz* in front of my delicatessen?"

Arthur Jabbawallah did not reply.

Murray stuffed his hands in his pockets. "So vot if I chase him away vit a broomstick?"

"*That* is a violation of Section Three-eight-one of the Penal Code," responded the senior case worker.

"So vot?" growled Murray, his face now a bright shade of red, almost matching his scrupulously dyed hair. "Like you said . . . I'll be out the next day."

"I'm afraid Three-eight-one is a good deal more serious than Six-nine-two. You risk imprisonment for up to one year."

"So vot about my business? Vot do I do if zis . . . zis . . . thing drives away all my business?"

"I'm sorry," replied Arthur Jabbawallah, although not seeming so in the least, "there's nothing else we can do. He has rights too."

Murray began to speak, but Arthur Jabbawallah was not finished. "And by the way, Mr. Platkin," he continued, glancing at a small piece of paper, a print-out from the portable computer terminal, "our records show that you owe a fifty-dollar fine plus two hundred dollars in penalties for an overdue parking ticket. In compliance with Section Two-four-eight of the Motor Vehicle Code, we have been forced to make an entry suspending your driver's license until the ticket is paid."

Later, perplexed and two-hundred-fifty dollars poorer, Murray tried to make some sense of the situation. If a soft drink peddler or a hot dog vendor or even a ten-year-old with a lemonade stand had set up shop in front of his establishment, Murray had a perfect right to petition the authorities to have the interloper removed, fined or even eventually arrested. After all, that was what he paid his New York City Franchise Tax, New York State Franchise Tax, Commercial Rent Tax, Metropolitan Transportation Tax and Personal and Corporate Income Taxes for. Could it be possible that begging might occupy a higher rung on the ladder of protected commercial activities?

Murray realized, albeit too late, that he had been foolish to ask government to do something that he should have done himself. Since Murray Plotkin considered himself a humanitarian (wasn't he a regular contributor to the United Negro College Fund?), his next approach was to simply offer the man what he claimed to desire.

Since the man invariably asked his targets for "some change so's I can git somethin' to eat," Murray Plotkin, during a lull, went out to the man and offered him something to eat. Murray had decided that he was even willing to feed the man regularly since any restaurant was forced to discard a good deal of perfectly edible excess—bread, end cuts of meat, etc—useless to Murray, but a bonanza for the hungry man outside. All the man need do in return was receive his feast at the back door.

Murray congratulated himself for Solomonic wisdom. The best solution, after all, was the one that satisfied the needs of both parties.

His competitor, however, saw things a bit differently. When Murray presented his plan, the man screamed and leapt to his feet, suddenly bug-eyed and snarling. "What you mean, somethin' to eat? You tryin' to buy me off? Wassa matter . . . don't you like no black folks near yo' white Jew restaurant?"

The force of the words, as well as the assault on his nostrils, drove Murray back. As he retreated, he tried to tell the man that anyone who could pay the check could eat in his delicatessen and even tried to point out his many black employees but the words came out in a jumble.

Sensing his advantage, the man took two menacing steps forward, his remaining, idly placed teeth now fully bared. His adversary, now just inches away from his face, Murray Plotkin, whose concept of physical bravery consisted of vigorously wagging an index finger under the nose of Schneckel, the dairy man, who he had always suspected of misdating the sour cream, reached back, feeling for the wall of the building to keep from toppling over. He tried to find the door to his delicatessen while the street entrepreneur continued his assault.

"Thas what you white folks always do," the man screamed. "Throw us scraps to get us to move along. Jes like we was dogs. Who you think you foolin'?"

Then to solidify his hold on this precious piece of territory, the man spun around and addressed the crowd that had begun to gather to observe this bit of street theater.

"See dis man," the black man yelled, pointing the accusing finger of racism at Murray Plotkin. "Dis man tryin' to get me away from his lily white restaurant. I ain't botherin' nobody . . . jes tryin' to get a little somethin' to eat . . . but dis man . . . he don't like no *NIGGERS* here!"

As Murray escaped into the sanctuary of Plotkin's of Flatbush and headed for the back, he paused just long enough to see his competitor collect money from shocked onlookers, appalled that this pathetic discard of society was going hungry in front of a thriving eatery.

Murray Plotkin made it to his office and slumped in his chair. He realized his shirt was soaked with sweat and that his heart was beating so hard and fast that he could see the little arteries in his wrists jump and twitch. In a reaction common to all men over sixty, Murray thought he was having a coronary. He sat still and asked God to let the feeling pass. God obliged.

Fear was soon replaced by anger and Murray grabbed for the telephone and dialed the number of the local police precinct. To hell with trying to be a good samaritan. Who was he kidding? This was New York. Good samaritans get *schtupped* in New York.

A loyal contributor to the Police Athletic League for enough years to have a little ceremonial shield sticker in the window of his Lincoln Continental Mark III, Murray had no doubts that he would command better treatment from Sergeant Micluski than he had from the city agencies. After all, Sgt. Mac, as Murray and every other merchant in the area had called him for ten years, was a working man himself and had always protected the rights of the Murray Plotkins, sometimes by direct application of the law, sometimes by interpretive application.

Sgt. Mac listened sympathetically as his old friend Murray gave the details of his escalating war with the bum.

"Yeah, Murray, it's a bitch," commiserated Sgt. Mac. "I'm getting these calls from everyone in the precinct. These beggars are everywhere. Some of them even rent little kids, you know, babies, to get the sympathy vote."

"*Rent?*"

"Yep, that's what I said. They give some junkie with little kids a couple a bucks for the day and keep the kids to beg with." Micluski paused. "Tell me, Murray. Did he strike you? Touch you at all?"

"No, Sergeant. He just screamed at me like . . . like, a .. he just screamed."

"Shit, that's too bad. If he touched you we might a had somethin'."

Murray was surprised that Sgt. Mac was asking all these questions. Usually just the existence of a problem in his precinct was enough to get New York's Finest on the march.

"Sergeant," Murray began tentatively, his recent experiences leaving his confidence in government a bit shaken, "can't your people . . ." (a more appropriate phrase then 'cops') "just chase him away? Back to the Bowery or verever he came from?"

"I'm afraid it's not that easy, Murray," replied Sgt. Mac. "You see, ever since the Mayor tried to have the mentally ill homeless forcibly removed to shelters and was beaten in Court, we have been given very strict guidelines about what we may and may not do in these cases."

"Vot are you talking about, Sergeant?" Murray felt his neck getting red. "He doesn't bathe. His clothes stink. He urinates in the street. He bothers my customers and old women. He's killing my business. ARE YOU TELLING ME YOU CAN'T GET THIS *SCHWARTZE* OUT FROM IN FRONT OF MY STORE?"

As soon as the epithet was out of his mouth, Murray felt ashamed. He was generally painstaking in avoiding racial stereotypes, having been accused more than once of being one himself.

Sgt. Mac was not especially interested in the moral and philosophic issues but it pissed him off to feel his hands tied in the face of this attack on his territory, his precinct. That Sgt. Mac took as a personal affront.

"Look, Murray. Don't give yourself a heart attack. Let me see what I can do."

"Thanks, Sergeant," replied Murray, his faith in government cautiously restored. "I knew you could help."

Sgt. Mac was a man of his word and not thirty minutes after Murray hung up the telephone a uniformed officer appeared in front of the delicatessen. Murray sidled up to the front door to overhear the conversation.

Fruitful Willis had seen the cop two blocks away. Uniformed officers of any sort failed to inspire fear in Fruitful, a veteran of the streets. Uniformed officers were a regular fact of life, the guardians of the border between their world and his, the protectors of those who would be just as pleased to see Fruitful Willis rot.

The presence of a uniformed officer merely called for a shift in strategy. In the old days, when Fruitful Willis was a bum and had no rights, he scurried off at the sight of such men, aware that they had the power to arbitrarily question, manhandle or detain him. In fact, petty harassment had been the authorities' primary approach in those simpler times—a billy club none too gently in the ribs and a 'move along.'

Now that Fruitful Willis had elevated his station and become a member of the homeless, he need not hustle away at the sight of uniformed officers. Now that Fruitful had rights, he need only sit calmly against the wall of the building or stand casually on the sidewalk. Ten minutes earlier, he had noticed the old Jew with the ridiculous copper hair lurking just inside the doorway and realized that some sort of official visit was imminent. He decided that the upright position was appropriate to the occasion and pulled himself to his feet when he first spotted the cop.

As soon as the man in uniform crossed the street, Fruitful

knew he had been correct. The cop had indeed been sent to roust him. Fruitful Willis laughed at the prospect of the confrontation and ran his dirt-encrusted fingers through his long matted hair.

The cop stopped opposite Fruitful and placed his hands on his hips—the traditional police 'what do you think you're doing?' posture. Fruitful Willis, possessed of the dignity and pride incumbent in his new status, returned the officer's gaze.

"How you be dis afternoon, Officer?" Fruitful smiled, flashing his remaining teeth at the cop. No reason not to be sociable.

The officer did not return Fruitful's greeting. "You got some ID, fella?" he demanded with a frown, irritated that this bum had the gall to look him in the eye.

Fruitful laughed again, the cannon blast having the usual effect on the passing pedestrians. "Don't think so, Officer. I lef' my wallet in my othuh suit."

The cop's eyes narrowed. "That's very funny, fella. I'll tell you what. Why don't you take your comedy someplace else?"

Fruitful Willis, who could work a room with the best of them, noticed that once again the little playlet was drawing a crowd of the curious.

"What you mean? Why can' I stay right here? Ain't I good enough for dis neighborhood? What right you got to chase me?"

The police officer, who was, in fact, young and inexperienced, had been taught throughout his youth that civilians should respect the law. He had been taught in his three years on the force that civilians should fear the law. A more seasoned officer might have handled the situation with deftness and diplomacy, but the young officer was in no mood to be diplomatic.

"This says I have the right," he growled, brandishing his nightstick. He took a step closer and hissed at Fruitful through clenched teeth. "And I say that you are a public nuisance and that you should take your act elsewhere."

Fruitful was in a dilemma. In the old days a man with no rights must simply do what he was told. Now he had rights, but the cop had superior force. But would he dare to use it in the midst of the little crowd that had gathered to witness this example of modern law enforcement? Hell, concluded Fruitful Willis, what good are rights if you don't use them?

"Why's I got to move?" Fruitful whined, expertly breaking his voice for that extra added pathos. "I ain't botherin' nobody."

He left out the part about getting something to eat to avoid giving the impression that he might be pan-handling. He also left out the part about the cop being a racist. Unlike Murray Plotkin, who strained through life to be a reasonable man, the cop wouldn't care less about such an accusation.

His patience exhausted by the debate with this advocate of street rights, the young police officer jabbed his nightstick into Fruitful's ribs. (When in doubt, return to the tried-and-true.)

"You're bothering *me*. And you're bothering other people. So find some other place to do it." The young officer gave another short jab with the lead-lined club, almost unnoticeable to the crowd but enough to make Fruitful wince.

Fruitful Willis may have acquired rights, but this cop had not seemed to have gotten the message. A wily tactician, Fruitful decided to withdraw until he could improve the odds.

At the sight of the bum shuffling down the street, Murray Plotkin heaved a massive sigh. He had witnessed the entire confrontation, all the while asking God to let the policeman prevail. (After all, it had worked with the coronary.)

Murray popped out of the delicatessen as soon as the bum was out of view. Beaming, with copper hair reflecting the sunlight, Murray Plotkin appeared to the young policeman almost as ludicrous a spectacle as the bum he had just rousted. No matter. The Sergeant had said to clear the front of the deli and that is what he had done.

Jews take the cake, thought the young officer, himself an active and xenophobic member of the Shamrock Society. They always scream about equal rights and all that other liberal bullshit. But as soon as one of them gets the short end of those equal rights, they scream for the Irish cops to bail them out. How come Jews never fight their own battles?

Murray Plotkin, for his part, felt only a burst of gratitude coupled with that secure feeling that comes with the knowledge that the power structure is ally and not oppressor. He profusely thanked the young officer for a brilliant piece of police work and invited him in for a cup of coffee.

"No thanks, Mr. Plotkin," smiled the patrolman, ever polite to neighborhood merchants in keeping with one of the sergeant's strictest rules. "I've got to get back to the station."

That wasn't exactly true but the young Shamrock had no intention of enduring the old Jew's chatter which would only ruin the coffee anyway.

"Okay, I understand," replied Murray, almost unable to contain himself at the sight of the front of his establishment unadorned by the bum. He decided that this officer was most surely an example of the finest of New York's youth, a hope for the city in the face of the human wave assault being mounted by drop-outs, drug addicts and derelicts.

As the young man turned to leave, Murray called after him. "And Officer . . . please tell Sgt. Mac thanks for me."

The Shamrock turned back for a moment, smiled and touched his nightstick to the brim of his cap.

To celebrate his liberation, Murray filled a bucket with water and strong detergent, went outside and mopped the sidewalk in front of his restaurant.

# CHAPTER TWO

But a freshly mopped sidewalk did not mean the end of Fruitful Willis.

The following day, just after the rush hour, a beautiful, clear morning that found Murray Plotkin's spirits as bright as the sun itself, Fruitful Willis returned. Murray, although idling at the front window of the store admiring both the weather and the now-unobstructed view of the street, did not see his adversary through the glass until Fruitful was virtually upon him.

At the sight of his tormentor, Murray felt his morning onion bialy with a *schmear* turn hard in his stomach. Oh no, he thought, not again, (although, in truth, he had suspected that perhaps one lesson would not be sufficient to discourage the tenacious). He turned to head for the telephone, the link to Sgt. Mac, but then stopped.

The bum was not alone.

Arriving with the filthy, shuffling rag-pile was a short, well-groomed, conservative looking black man in a business suit and topcoat, and—Murray's stomach tightened another turn—a young, attractive white woman accompanied by a man in a windbreaker holding what most surely appeared to be a portable television camera.

Murray grabbed the back of the nearest chair while his mind raced. Should he go call the police anyway? What about his lawyer? Maybe he should go out in the street and tell them all to get the hell away from his store. What was happening to him? What had he done? Why were they persecuting him? Why did everyone pick on the Jews? What could he do?

Events moved too fast for Murray to make a decision. The attractive young woman moved toward the entrance to the delicatessen. (To Murray's view, she seemed to glide rather than walk which exacerbated the other-worldly feel of the event.)

Murray Plotkin realized with some chagrin that he was about to make his television debut, probably in an impromptu panel discussion with a vagrant, a newswoman and the still-unidentified black man. And his accent would paint him in the upcoming encounter as the archetypical foreigner, the money-grubbing Jew. Thus, when the woman strode into the delicatessen with her best 'you can trust me' smile, Murray relaxed not one whit.

"Mr. Plotkin?" crooned the young reporter, extending her hand in the modified macho style favored by today's professional women. "I'm Cornelia Pembroke. Might I have a few words with you?"

Murray stood frozen, eyeing Cornelia Pembroke. (Cornelia Pembroke? What kind of name is that? Couldn't be more *goyisheh*. Sounds like she came over on the Mayflower. What will I sound like to a Cornelia Pembroke?)

Cornelia Pembroke (whose real name was actually Karen Pzytriek and whose forebears were virtually identical to Murray's except for perhaps originating two hundred miles to the north) again cast her disarming smile at the copper-haired figure before her.

"Mr. Plotkin, I'm from WRCT News and I wish to ask you about that gentleman outside."

"Yes?" he asked, trying to keep his answers brief and hide the now hated accent.

Disarming fixed naturally on her face, Cornelia Pembroke tried to decide whether or not she had wasted her time by coming here. There was no story if all she got was a filthy lunatic and a petrified deli owner. Television demanded *conflict*. Whiffet had promised that this would be a good one, so she had grabbed the mini-cam technician and come to record the confrontation. Some confrontation, she thought. Oh well, I'm already here. Let's see what I can salvage.

"Mr. Plotkin," she continued demurely, "WRCT is here at the request of Herbert Whiffet. He's the gentleman outside . . ." Murray wondered if she was referring to the bum or the other one. "Mr. Whiffet is an attorney representing the Mobilization for the Homeless. He was approached by Mr. Willis there . . ." So that was the bum's name. Murray couldn't decide if that knowledge made the situation more personal or more ridiculous. "Mr. Willis has claimed that you have used strong-arm tactics and illegal means to prevent him from exercising his Constitutional right to remain on the street in the vicinity of your store, and that your motive for doing so was a stated hatred of black people."

"'Stated hatred of black people?'" Murray growled, feeling his face redden. (This is more like it, thought Cornelia Pembroke.) "Look around, lady. Vot do you see in here? More blacks and Puerto Ricans voik here than vhites."

Murray spun and pointed to the cashier. "Clarissa," he yelled, "do I hate black people?"

Clarissa smiled at the reporter. "No, Miss. I've worked for Mr. Plotkin for fourteen years and he doesn't hate anybody." She smiled at her employer.

"Yes, Mr. Plotkin, I see." Cornelia turned up her smile until the needle was on overload. "I've got an idea. Why don't you just step outside with me, and you can state your position on tape."

Murray found himself in another quandary. He had no wish to place himself at the mercy of this Cornelia Pembroke and her entourage, and certainly not outside the protected surroundings of Plotkin's of Flatbush. But he knew that if he refused the interview, his enemies would have the forum to themselves, able to accuse him of anything they liked. Perhaps he could achieve a compromise.

"Vhy don't you just do it in here?" he asked.

"Oh, I'm sorry, Mr. Plotkin," sighed Cornelia Pembroke, "I wish I could. But, you see, we came prepared for an outdoor shoot and the tape we have won't produce quality footage in artificial light. Just step out for a moment and we can get your position on tape."

My position, thought Murray Plotkin. As if he needed a 'position.' Wasn't it enough that he tried to be fair and to do the right thing? Did he need a 'position?' Even as he moved to the door, his stomach told him that this affair was not going to end well. But Murray went all the same, surrendering his fate to the modern authority of the media.

As he stepped into the sunlight, he noticed the camera aimed right at his face. Then the screech of Mr. Willis cut through the city din.

"Dat's him! Dat's de man who got de cops to beat me up. Jes for tryin' to get somethin' to eat. I wasn' botherin' nobody."

Murray looked to Cornelia Pembroke, ready to 'state his position,' but the reporter had turned her attention to the lawyer, Whiffet, and Murray was forced to endure the taunts of Mr. Willis as he waited for his turn.

"Why are you here today, Mr. Whiffet?" asked the reporter, shifting into the neutral beat and tone of the dispassionate seeker of the truth.

Herbert Whiffet spoke slowly and reasonably into Cornelia Pembroke's microphone as the camera swung around to close on his face.

"I am here today, Ms. Pembroke, to defend the rights of one homeless man against one other man's cruel and vicious attempt to deprive him of those rights. Perhaps this case, where one of society's rejected—homeless, friendless and penniless—is further battered and denied his only opportunity to obtain food and a few pennies for shelter by the greed and lack of compassion of one of society's favored sons, abetted by the local police who serve one segment of society at the expense of another . . . Perhaps this one case can serve to jab at the consciences of good people so that these injustices may be redressed for all disadvantaged people."

Murray listened to the reasonable man give his reasonable speech, (during which even the bum, Mr. Willis, fell silent, undoubtedly overcome by all that reasonableness.) Suddenly, Murray was petrified.

*Gott in Himmel*, he thought, this Whiffet sounds so good, *I* almost believe him.

And Murray Plotkin knew beyond doubt that he had been set up, tricked by the *goyisheh* Cornelia Pembroke into leaving the safe confines of his delicatessen to be confronted by a *bum's lawyer*.

Then, before he had a chance to gather his thoughts, the microphone was thrust into his face.

"Do you have any comment on these charges, Mr. Plotkin?" asked the neutral Cornelia Pembroke.

*Charges? Charges?* Murray heard himself speaking quickly, his accent more pronounced than ever.

"Vot are you talking about, disadvantaged? He bothers old ladies! He pees in the street in front of people who are eating! He intimidates my customers! I've had zis business for tventy-two years and I'm being ruined by zis BUM."

"Thank you, Mr. Plotkin," smiled Cornelia Pembroke. Well

what do you know, she thought. Herbert was right after all. This was going to look wonderful on the Six O'Clock.

Then, a product of an industry that preferred its neutral coverage of the day's events to have a little drama, Cornelia Pembroke offered her microphone to Mr. Willis, taking care not to get too close.

Fruitful made the most of his opportunity. Putting an extra measure of pathetic tremolo into his delivery (this was television, after all), he whined, "I don' know what he's talkin' 'bout. I don' bother nobody. Jes' tryin' to git somethin' to eat." Then Fruitful smiled. "Who knows, mebbe one dese days I might even git back on my feet so's I can git work."

Murray Plotkin watched the performance dumbly. He knew he had to say something else to make people understand, so that those watching the news that night would not see him as a ranting maniac. He reached for the microphone, but Cornelia Pembroke pulled away.

"Thank you, Mr. Plotkin," she smiled, as sweetly as before, "we've got all we need."

"But vot about 'stating my position?'" Murray protested. "Vhen do I get to do that?"

"Oh," replied the reporter, more the ingenue with every word, "you already did, Mr. Plotkin. I asked for your comments and you stated your piece—quite eloquently, I thought."

That night, Murray watched the Six O'Clock News on WRCT. Making an exception and leaving some of the early dinner customers solely to his staff, Murray borrowed a small portable television from Gino di Napoli, who owned the dry cleaner's down the street, and sat in his office and watched his performance. Maybe it wasn't as bad as he thought. Maybe he would be pleasantly surprised.

Murray Plotkin was not pleasantly surprised.

That night Murray came face-to-face with the first rule of television interviewing. In the least common denominator world of broadcast news, delivery beats content. Despite the weight of his arguments and their obvious truth in the face of the filthy Mr. Willis, the bilious manner in which they were presented neutralized their impact. Mr. Willis, on the other hand, despite his complete absence of social fitness, had an inherent feel for performing that the copper-haired, accented Murray Plotkin lacked.

As a result of his new celebrity status, enhanced by an eloquent statement by Herbert Whiffet regarding the rights of the disadvantaged, apparently taped after the camera crew had left Murray's store, Murray Plotkin was left with no doubt that further efforts to remove the bum would result in his sinking lower and lower in public esteem. All hope of securing the aid of any government agency, including that of the coveted Sgt. Mac, was now lost.

So, as he sat in his office two weeks later trying to understand how his rights had come to be inferior to those of a bum who defecated in the streets, Murray Plotkin knew that it was time to consider the unthinkable.

The unthinkable had some strong things going for it. Murray was a widower, his beloved Sarah gone five years hence. His children had been on him for years to ease up and enjoy life a little. (It was hard to make them understand that what Murray enjoyed most was his business.) His son, who had defied tradition but who nonetheless made a good living importing low-priced garments from the Far East, had even obtained an option on a condominium in Boca Raton (where the junior Plotkin had relocated) for when 'Dad was ready.' Getting to watch his grandchildren grow up was one major advantage of the unthinkable.

Another was the standing offer from his landlord to buy him out of his lease. Murray had had the foresight when the city had verged on bankruptcy to sign a thirty-year commercial lease at very favorable terms. As a result, his landlord was stuck with fifteen additional years of below-market rates in the still highly-prized Upper East Side real estate market.

The unthinkable began to lose its edge. Murray Plotkin, for the first time in his life, began to consider retirement.

What do I need this for? he wondered, thinking of the long hours, the wear and tear on his aging feet and back, the avalanche of city ordinances to be followed, the crippling taxes to be paid. For all this, I need to be a pariah in my own neighborhood, put on television and made to look ridiculous?

Murray Plotkin reached for the telephone.

"Eugene?" he asked when the man answered. "It's Murray. Tell me, Eugene . . . that offer, for my lease. Does it still stand?"

# CHAPTER THREE

Herbert Whiffet had not been nearly as impressed with the Fruitful Willis affair as had Murray Plotkin. For Herbert Whiffet, television was an integral part of his practice and any event that attracted the attention of only one local station was not sufficient to justify his participation. Herbert Whiffet was usually a four- or five-station man, unless for his own purposes he had leaked an exclusive to a favored reporter in return for an open-ended *quid pro quo* at a later date.

Fruitful Willis had actually been something of an embarrassment. Serves me right for going against my instincts, Herbert thought. When he had first seen the bum, referred by his contact at the Mobilization for the Homeless, who kept a lookout for such cases, he had had his doubts about how productive the story might prove to be. But he had given in and agreed to meet the victim. From the beginning of the discussion one thing was clear—this Fruitful Willis was one hell of a performer; just the right mix of pathos, sincerity, intelligence and stage presence to be a potential hit on the news. So Herbert had taken on Fruitful Willis and tried to drum up some interest in the case. Maybe the restaurant angle could do it. 'Hunger in the midst of plenty,' and all that.

But his first instincts had been correct; the story had been a washout. Fruitful, for all his talent, was not unique or even unusual—New York was a city packed with talent.

Herbert Whiffet surveyed his Lenox Terrace, seven-hundred-square-foot, one-bedroom apartment, much as Murray Plotkin had surveyed his office. It was an act that seemed to symbolize taking stock of one's business, of fitting together the past and the future. Things were not at all bad—Herbert Whiffet's destiny was moving within his power to control.

And Herbert was well aware that control of one's destiny was no small potatoes for a black man. Whites, for whom society's rules were formulated, took the luxury for granted. For many whites, their futures were ensured by the rule of perpetuation, the passing of opportunity from generation to generation; for others, merely doing a good job in their chosen professions ensured theirs. For a black man, however, the rule of perpetuation did not exist (unless one wanted to be a porter or janitor) and merely doing a good job in one's chosen profession was no guarantee of anything except frustrated ambitions and retarded advancement, both of which Herbert had experienced all too acutely.

A black man must make his own way and Herbert Whiffet had sought, located and now had claimed the most treasured gift that a capitalist society can bestow—the protected market. Although entry to most protected markets involve a patent or copyright, formal rules of entry, a government contract or favorable legislation, Herbert Whiffet's market was not protected by government or guild. Entry to his market was strictly controlled by that very trait that excluded him from other markets—race, specifically the suspicion within the black community that in every aspect of day-to-day living, in every rule and statute, in every arrest, in every real estate transaction, white society was motivated by and acting under a racist hatred and fear of blacks.

Most of Herbert's fellows lacked the schooling, the training or the public bent to lead their oppressed brothers and sisters to first-class citizenship. Thus, in order to ensure that his market remained protected and that he rise appropriately within it, Herbert Whiffet need do only two things. First, he must see to it that racism remained in the forefront of the community consciousness, and second, that he be viewed as a Champion of his people, leading the charge to dignity and equality, riding point, willing to stop the racial bullet.

Few who met Herbert Whiffet for the first time would have guessed him a Champion. Although both his father and mother were over six feet tall and his two brothers had formed a feared center-forward combination on both high school and college basketball teams, Herbert stood only five-four, a height he had reached at age eleven. Even now, at age thirty-five, he shaved only every other day.

But if fate was to rob him of height, athletic ability and a deep voice, Herbert Whiffet would merely use adversity to spur him to excellence in other areas. If he couldn't dunk, he would read; if he couldn't impress girls with speed and grace, he would impress them with erudition and diction; if he was hesitant in the locker room, he would be proud at the debating table.

Luckily for Herbert, the senior Whiffet was just the man to promote those attributes in his youngest. In fact, Calvin Whiffet found the athletics and general lack of seriousness in the eldest sons rather distasteful. This was not what he had spent a life of struggling to achieve.

Calvin Whiffet had founded and still maintained a law practice in Monroe, Louisiana, servicing a clientele that was totally rural and almost exclusively black, although the neo-populist explosion in the deep South had sent him a smattering of white-sharecropper business. Herbert's father (Mr. Whiffet to everyone, white and black) eked out a modest existence handling filings, simple probate, run-of-the-mill criminal cases and an occasional property dispute; standard general practitioner legal fare.

But Calvin Whiffet was no standard, run-of-the-mill man, with anything but a standard, run-of-the-mill mind. As everyone in Monroe was quite aware, had Calvin Whiffet the good fortune to be born blond with blue eyes, his talent might have carried him right to the governor's mansion. As it was, he had overcome being the son of a common laborer who had deserted Calvin's mother and nine siblings when Calvin was five years old and made his way through high school, no meager achievement, then college at Grambling, and then, astoundingly, through law school.

By the time Herbert had arrived, Calvin Whiffet was sufficiently established to have purchased a three-bedroom frame house on the edge of a black neighborhood abutting the more prosperous white section. The whites didn't mind the living arrangements; Calvin Whiffet was one of those blacks whose acceptance whites could point to as proof that they weren't prejudiced. They didn't go so far as to invite him to their homes or offer him membership in their clubs, of course, but nonetheless graciously accepted his proximity.

Hand-me-down acceptance neither fooled nor deluded Calvin Whiffet. He knew that men like himself, those who had risen out of serfdom, bore the responsibility to perpetuate their own progress in their progeny because only then would blacks develop the leader class that might enable them to move the entire race forward.

At his father's insistence, Herbert applied to Tulane. After years of being drilled in black pride and the inevitability of racial struggle, Herbert had thought to enroll in Tuskegee or Howard. But there was no arguing with Calvin Whiffet. Since his son would spend his adult life fighting the white power structure, feeling isolated and shunned amidst condescending smiles and insincere overtures of friendship, he might as well learn about his adversaries early on.

Ordinarily, a young man from Monroe, even with Herbert's excellent academic record, would have great difficulty in securing a place in the freshman class at Tulane, shoulder to shoulder with the cream of white Southern youth—and certainly not on full scholarship. But Calvin Whiffet attended the pre-admission interview with his son and then spoke privately with the president of the university.

Of course they were not prejudiced, the president assured Mr. Whiffet, of course they were always looking for qualified black students. Yes, financial aid was available to the exceptional and needy, but while young Herbert's record was excellent, there were others who merited the assistance more. Yes, most of them were white, but that was a matter of coincidence. No, Mr. Whiffet, that is not it at all—it is not a contrivance to keep Tulane 'racially pure.' We are looking for the best students, regardless of race.

After thirty minutes of discussion, it was decided that the resources of Tulane University would be mobilized to prove that the venerable institution was indeed color blind, and Herbert Whiffet got his scholarship.

As was common in the post-Martin Luther King South, white students went out of their way to make Herbert welcome, just as Calvin's white neighbors had made him welcome. With great sincerity, they chatted with him about classes and tests, showed curiosity about Herbert's background and sought common experiences with which to cement a bond. Unfortunately for Herbert, all this sincerity was confined to daylight hours, when students were thrown together going to class, but did not extend to the evenings when it was time to date or go to parties or even to go for a beer. An exception was made during exams, when Herbert's hard work during the semester made him an ideal study partner. Studying with Herbert Whiffet made even the most racially hardened white student feel liberal.

Thus, for fourteen of a semester's sixteen weeks Herbert was on his own or left to socialize with other members of Tulane's limited black student population. It was as if this group was a satellite, circling the main student body but held at a distance by forces of nature.

A 3.1 grade-point at such an academically respected institution as Tulane enabled Herbert to gain admission to law school at the University of Virginia. Law school was more of the same and Herbert graduated in the top third of his class, a ranking certain to gain him entry into one of New Orleans' better, if not quite top, law firms. But, for the first time, Herbert Whiffet went his own way. If he were really at the cutting edge of black progress and social change, he reasoned, why idle in a traditional Southern city like New Orleans? Surely the goal would be better served the closer Herbert got to the nation's centers of power. So, not unlike Fruitful Willis, with visions of moving and shaking, Herbert Whiffet headed for New York City.

But unlike Fruitful, who had never really succeeded in cracking New York's armor, Herbert's foray was an instant success. He secured employment at one of the city's most prestigious law firms, Gray, Steinford & Hodge, one of twenty new junior associates culled from only the best of the nation's law schools. As impressive as his credentials were, he ranked twentieth in this elite group.

But Gray et al was no different than any other large institution, always on the lookout for a Negro or two to demonstrate its equality in hiring, and this son of a lawyer from the deep South with his excellent manners and perfect diction could not be more ideal, particularly since he was less than imposing physically. Besides, Gray, Steinford & Hodge was one of New York's premier 'liberal' firms and it just wouldn't do not to have a reasonable percentage of black associates. Why, Gray et al even boasted a black partner (although he lived in Scarsdale, drove a BMW, sent his son to Choate and had never voted for a black candidate in his life).

Herbert's study habits stood him in good stead at Gray, where seventy-hour weeks for junior associates were considered vacations, but his peers, most from good white families, had study habits every bit as diligent. They were also every bit as ambitious and every bit as smart (or smarter). And, although Herbert Whiffet had a burning need to succeed in order to become a leader by example in the war for racial equality, each of his fellows at Gray et al also had a burning need to succeed for reasons of his or her own.

Despite the disadvantages, Herbert was not without weapons in the gladitorial contest that is life for junior associates in America's major law firms. Being one of the few black recruits at Gray, the partners did all they could to ensure that Herbert Whiffet did not wash out in the first round. After all, what was the point of employing token Negroes if they were gone in six months?

Consequently, Herbert got the easiest assignments on the most visible cases, and if a junior associate were needed to appear in court to give the Gray team that intimidating presence of legal numbers that is as important in litigation as force of fact, Herbert was sure to get the nod. With the help of this *de facto* equal opportunity program, Herbert became one of the stars of his class, or so it appeared to his nineteen competitors.

There was a good deal of grumbling in the bathrooms as a result, about preferential treatment and the like, some of which came to Herbert's attention. It's just racism, he sniffed to himself. I work as hard as anyone else and no one has handed me anything. They're all jealous, upset that a black man is a better lawyer.

But tokenism, like the statue of justice, wields a two-edged sword. As at Tulane, where the black students orbited the main student body, so it was at Gray. Black attorneys weren't really competing against whites; they were actually competing only against one another for the few upper echelon spots that the partners of the firm had allocated for such purposes. Not that senior management had an actual quota system, merely that the partners knew how many Negroes they felt comfortable with. Thus, if Gray, Steinford & Hodge was a giant pyramid with sixty partnerships and hundreds of associates, the black contingent was a much smaller pyramid with two partnerships and tens of associates. (The additional black partnership a concession to the changing times.)

Within this 'black group' was a lot of high-powered talent, young men and women who had graduated near the top of their classes at Harvard, Yale, Michigan and Stanford, high draft picks of previous recruiting years. In this heady competition, constricted by the numbers, Herbert Whiffet didn't have a chance.

"Oh, I don't know," he said one evening in response to a comment about the rigors of associatehood, "if you put in the hours and have the talent, making partner doesn't seem so difficult."

Annie Holdsworth got a big laugh out of that one. Annie was one of the ranking black associates, copper-skinned, impeccably groomed, the daughter of a local surgeon. Herbert thought she was about the most beautiful woman he had ever seen. It had taken six months for him to ask her out for a drink.

"What's so funny?" he asked to cover the wound.

"My poor, naive little Herbert," she sighed, "your chances of making partner within the millennium are about the same as my chances of flapping my wings and flying to the moon."

If the same comment had come from a white colleague, Herbert would have crossed it off to jealousy or racism. But coming from Annie, the tall, brilliant, utterly spectacular Annie . . .

"Why won't I make partner?" he challenged, a bit too shrilly. "I'm doing all right so far."

Annie Holdsworth shook her head patiently and sighed at the farm boy (an appellation that encompassed anyone raised below the Mason-Dixon line). For the next five minutes she gave Herbert a lesson in the workings of the modern American law firm. At the end of the lecture, Herbert Whiffet had drastically reduced expectations, but even worse, realized what a fool he appeared to his enemies.

"If all of this is true, it's nothing but racism. First they deny black people an opportunity to advance, then they blame them for their lack of advancement. They all might not be so successful in maintaining power if they had to go out and earn it all over again themselves."

"That's rich coming from you, Herbert," Annie smiled, speaking in a deceptively smooth courtroom manner. "You who haven't earned a damn thing since you walked in the door.

"And one more thing, Herbert, while we're about it," Annie continued, "all I hear from you, someone who has had all the breaks, is give me this and give me that. You want power, you want to be a leader of your race, Herbert? Go out and earn it. You know, Herbert, it's people like you that give the rest of us a bad name. As for me, I'll earn what I get. I don't want hand-outs from anyone."

Herbert Whiffet left Gray, Steinford & Hodge not six months later. It was not that he ran away. Quite the contrary. After some reflection, he realized that Annie had done him a favor. The path to power and equality lay not in diluting the power base in a futile attempt to infiltrate white institutions. That may be the path of opportunists like Annie Holdsworth, blacks who care only about their own futures and not one whit about their brothers and sisters.

No, the path to power lay in developing our own institutions, then, when the time was right, attacking the white power structure in strength and making their institutions ours.

And Herbert knew just which institution he intended to make his. He decided in those first contemplative days as an independent member of the New York Bar that before the age of forty he would become district attorney of New York County.

But district attorney was a public position and winning the prize demanded that Herbert Whiffet become a public figure. Following the sage advice of Annie Holdsworth, Herbert eschewed the traditional road, a tortuous and circuitous trail through the white-dominated political clubs, and opted instead for the much more direct approach of the protected market.

Herbert Whiffet would use his law practice as a springboard to public recognition and power, and if fortune did not bring to his door the type of inflammatory case that catapults an attorney to fame, Herbert would create them.

Now, seven years after that fateful decision, a full five years remaining in which to fulfill his goal, Herbert Whiffet was right on schedule.

# CHAPTER FOUR

Clarissa Taylor lacked Herbert Whiffet's grandiose ambitions, although she had developed some fairly advanced aspirations for her children. Her pride in Matthew grew with each year and it was now clear that the money she had saved to secure him admission to a good private high school had been a solid investment. Veronica and Jeanette, spaced at two-year intervals below her son, showed equal promise. It was not just the children's solid academic achievements which were the source of the mother's joy. It was the sight of three well-mannered, hard working, responsible children, each with a goal that far outstripped that of either of their parents.

For Clarissa Taylor, the trick had been escaping the projects and the quicksand of Bedford-Stuyvesant for the Land of Opportunity, Forest Hills. True, Clarissa Taylor did not live in the Forest Hills of the West Side Tennis Club or the sixteen-room private homes, merely in a two-bedroom apartment on the third floor of a forty-year-old apartment building near Union Boulevard, more Kew Gardens really. But a stock trader who made a windfall in the market and purchased one of those mansions could not have been any more pleased with his acquisition than was Clarissa Taylor with hers. For, if we measure success by the length of the journey, Clarissa's two-bedroom apartment in Forest Hills was by far the greater achievement.

Nine years ago, Freeman and Clarissa Taylor had just had their third child. Although it was a difficult delivery, Clarissa considered the time spent in the Medicare hospital as a vacation; a vacation from Freeman's screaming, alcohol-induced vitriol and violent sexual demands. The vacation was made complete by farming the other children out with trusted friends, thus easing the fear, Clarissa Taylor's biggest fear in a fear-filled life, that her husband might take out the loss of his manhood on the children. With the children elsewhere and their vermin-infested, city-owned, three-room urban shanty empty, he would most certainly spend the entire week in the bar with his cronies.

For a long time Clarissa had understood Freeman's drinking, his need for social anesthesia. A man can't feel like a man when he can't work, when he is forced to support his family by humiliating weekly trips to the welfare office or the food stamp office or the Medicare office, forced to wait in large open rooms in under-sized cracked plastic chairs with other of the humiliated, denied the opportunity to perform a father's most primal function.

For a time, Freeman had sought work regularly—and desperately. But in a city where most skilled and able workers find it difficult to maintain a decent standard of living, the mere willingness to work long hours at back-breaking labor for low wages was nothing more than a guarantee of life-long poverty. Lack of skills was the ghetto's most common ailment.

Like most of his peers, Freeman Taylor had not thought much of school when he was a boy; school was something the smart crowd steered clear of. School was for suckers and they didn't teach you nothin' anyway.

The crowd with which Freeman hung out, while avoiding what passed for the educational process in Bed-Stuy, supported itself by running numbers or peddling nickel bags of marijuana. The members assured one another that they would always be smart enough to live by their wits. After all, the streets were where the money was. But Freeman and his pals had forgotten, or had yet to learn, the first law of economics—supply and demand—and the supply of small-time street hustlers was enormous and the small shrinkage to the criminal justice system was more than replenished by younger and even more aggressive competition. Where Herbert Whiffet's was a protected market, Freeman's was the textbook open market, right out of *The Wealth of Nations*.

By the time Freeman Taylor absorbed his economics lesson it was too late, for nowhere else in society is the punishment for an adolescent misjudgement so severe as in the ghetto, and Freeman Taylor was among the city's adrift before his twentieth birthday.

Not that he was aware that he had floated loose of society's moorings. Ideals, even those sprung from a ghetto youth, rarely disappear without impetus. As he entered his third decade, newly married to the foxy Clarissa Burks, Freeman figured that all he needed was a break, and a smart energetic guy like him could surely make his own breaks. Freeman had taken to his marital responsibilities with enthusiasm—after all, you can't stay a kid forever. No more drugs or numbers. Freeman would take the straight world by storm.

So the newly-reformed Freeman Taylor, aburst with youthful energy, willing to start at the bottom, applied for whatever unskilled work was available: common laborer, stock boy or messenger.

With charm, enthusiasm and a child on the way, Freeman often succeeded in getting hired in that first year. See, he told his wife, all I needed was a break. Now watch me move up. Starting at the bottom was one thing, languishing there quite another, so Freeman Taylor took every opportunity to tell his supervisor, or maybe even his supervisor's supervisor of all the productive changes that could be made in the way things were done. Freeman then sat back and waited for the boss to take notice of such an obviously bright young man and reward him with enhanced responsibility and a raise in pay.

At first, Freeman was rather puzzled when this did not occur. Oh well, he assured his wife and now the mother of his son, I guess some places don't want to do things better. But don't worry, Mama, I'll just go somewhere else where they're not so afraid of brains and ambition.

But two years and one daughter later, Freeman Taylor finally realized that *everyone* seemed to be afraid of brains and ambition, at least the kind of brains and ambition that reside in a high school drop-out with an 'attitude.' ("What attitude's that?" he had asked with a scowl when the white bookstore assistant manager had first cast the aspersion.) That was when Freeman, heretofore ecumenical in his racial attitudes, decided that it wasn't that whites (and lick-spittle Uncle Toms) were afraid of brains and ambition, it was that they were afraid of blacks who stood up for themselves. It was racism, plain and simple, that was depriving him of his right to advancement.

Freeman lacked the resources to fight the pervasive disease and, with his childhood occupations also unavailable, he became increasingly bitter and morose. Bottom of the barrel jobs lost their appeal when Freeman realized that for him they were top of the line. Freeman's charm and energy gradually disappeared along with his illusions, and he was soon being rejected for even the menial jobs for which he was qualified. It was supply and demand again, as a new generation of charming, energetic young men (generations are only a year or two apart in the ghetto) moved in to take his place.

Clarissa's salary from her cashier's job was not enough to support the family at even a poverty level and with no work and no prospects Freeman Taylor took the only road left. He resorted to the public dole and a life of bowing and scraping to arrogant black clerks doing the dirty work for condescending white social workers. On the verge of his third child, Freeman Taylor, younger than was Herbert Whiffet on the day he graduated from law school, had run his life's course.

So, as Clarissa lay screaming in the delivery room, Freeman Taylor sat in Pappy's Bar on Nostrand Avenue playing with the little glass that contained his sixth (or was it seventh?) shot of rye, feeling the load of the new child as if its weight were measured in tons. Another child meant more lectures on family planning from the case worker, the gouging out of whatever minuscule dignity he might have developed since the last visit to the welfare office. As the dim ceiling lights reflected off the tiny pool of escape in the glass before him, Freeman Taylor realized that he could not take any more. He thought about what Willie Turner had said—that there was always work in non-union construction jobs outside the city. The pay wasn't enough to support a family, but maybe enough for one man who just needed a room in which to live and an occasional taste after work.

Although Pappy asked Freeman what was wrong when he noticed him crying, the philosophic proprietor wasn't too concerned. All the regulars got the blues every now and again. It was the booze and the life. When Freeman assured him everything was fine, Pappy returned to daydreaming while cleaning the beer glasses in the cloudy wash-water.

But everything wasn't fine with Freeman Taylor. Although he felt liberated by his decision, it didn't kill the pain. Even the hardest man feels a twinge when he realizes he will never see his wife or children again.

When Clarissa returned home from the hospital, she was

relieved that Freeman wasn't there. She assumed he was at Pappy's and that was fine. She placed the baby in the rickety crib that had served her previous offspring and strolled into the bedroom to change her clothes.

For an instant, Clarissa thought that perhaps they had been robbed. The bedroom was in total disarray, clothes and relics of the Taylors' five years of marriage everywhere. In most of the nation's households, a woman confronting such a scene, once robbery had been discounted, would be puzzled, forced to sort through the mess and determine what had happened. Among the urban poor, however, the answer is quick in coming because the occurrence is all too common.

Clarissa knew immediately that Freeman had abandoned his family. She hurried to the dresser, pulled out the top drawer and looked at the back of the frame. It was as she feared. The precious bankbook containing the few hundred dollars they had saved was gone. Clarissa stared for a few moments at the spot where their one valuable possession had been hidden, taped to the inside of the dilapidated piece of furniture that constituted the couple's bedroom set.

Each of us has a moment when life simply seems too overwhelming to continue. This was Clarissa's.

But Clarissa Taylor was a resilient woman and after one hour of sitting on her bed and staring, remembering her youth and her husband, both now disintegrated, she was taking steps to see that her family would survive. The loss, after all, was not that great. It was not as if Freeman was depriving the family of financial security. If anything, the now-departed Mr. Taylor had been a drain on the family's finances, good only to go to the welfare office while Clarissa worked. The appointments must now be rescheduled, but Clarissa was sure her employer would indulge her a few days to get her affairs in order. Mr. Plotkin was always understanding about family matters and had seemed pleased to give her all the time she needed in order to have the newly arrived Jeanette.

Day care arrangements must be made, of course, and Clarissa was distrustful of city agencies. Too many children had told terrible stories of sexual abuse at the hands of the staff, or of just plain neglect. Mrs. Taylor upstairs, unrelated to Freeman but claiming to be the children's 'name Grandma,' had always been all too happy to look in on the children during Freeman's frequent sojourns to Pappy's. Maybe Clarissa could formalize the arrangement. It wasn't fair to impose on Mrs. Taylor like that, but she seemed to like the kids and Clarissa was fighting for her life.

Clarissa's developmental years had not been much different from Freeman's—not much attention to school, running with a fast crowd and the pursuit of whatever glitz a ghetto adolescent could hope for. But children change things. Matthew's arrival had, as is the case in so many poor black families, inverted the parental roles, so now Clarissa was much more able to cope as a single parent than would have been her husband if fortune had been so unkind as to leave him to care alone for his progeny.

After securing additional time off, Clarissa spent those next few days making her arrangements. She visited all the public agencies with which the family had been forced to deal and alternately begged, cajoled, cried, yelled, reasoned, feigned nervous exhaustion, threatened to make a stink and charmed, all to secure approval to have reporting arrangements and other bureaucratic necessities conform to her family's new circumstances. As a member of the 'underemployed' or 'working poor,' Clarissa Taylor faced much more difficulty in making the system respond to her needs than if she had been destitute, but nonetheless succeeded in getting everything done satisfactorily.

The following Monday she had returned to work. She was not at the register ten minutes when Mr. Plotkin took her aside. He asked her to follow him into the back room. She hated that room; there was barely space for one person let alone two and Mr. Plotkin's hands always smelled of cold cuts.

This summons was particularly disquieting. Clarissa had taken a lot of time off recently, and everyone knew how the Jews were when they thought someone was beating them out of a little money. Please God, she asked, don't let him fire me. Just when I got everything arranged for my kids.

"Tell me, Clarissa," the copper-haired man began after they had both squeezed into the tiny office. (He pronounced her name with a guttural 'R,' leaving an impression of a soft growl.) "Vot happened at home?"

It was a strange question. How did he know anything had

happened? She had not given any specifics when she had spoken to him on the telephone. Did she look that bad?

Clarissa's first instinct was to slough off the question. No one wants to hear about other people's problems. If they can't avoid the problems they avoid the person and in this case avoidance might mean dismissal. And besides, it wasn't anybody's business but hers.

The deli man must have read her reaction. "Come, Clarissa, tell me. It helps to talk."

To the cashier, Plotkin had always been just a boss. She realized that despite working for him for three years she had never really looked at him except to create the caricature portrait we all develop of those whose features we do not study. Now she saw that Murray Plotkin had a rather kind face, or maybe Clarissa just needed him to have a kind face. She didn't even notice his hair.

Clarissa Taylor began to speak of her past weeks, of enduring the pain of childbirth alone, of the fear while in the hospital of a drunk and violent husband awaiting her at home, of the hollowness that came with the realization that she would now sleep alone and that three children must be raised without a father.

She was surprised at how good it felt to unburden herself. The only concession she would not make was tears. They were there, all right, pushing to come out. But Clarissa had sworn to herself in the first few moments in the devastated bedroom that no tears would be shed for Freeman Taylor.

Murray Plotkin listened, nodding periodically. When the cashier had finished, her employer sat silently, digesting the information. The nervous energy expelled, Clarissa had a moment of panic. What had she done? This moment of weakness would cost her. Weakness always does.

"Well, Clarissa," said the deli man, "here is vot I think ve should do . . ."

We? thought Clarissa Taylor.

"Ve should first make sure that your children are in good hands. This Mrs. Taylor . . . is she reliable?"

Clarissa was confused, caught somewhere between embarrassment and suspicion. She nodded and mumbled. "Yes, I think so."

"Good," said Murray Plotkin, "make sure she has the store

number. She should know to call vhenever there is any trouble."

Clarissa nodded again.

"Vot about the bills?" he continued. "Do you need any help?"

Clarissa cleared her throat and shook her head. "No, Mr. Plotkin, we'll make out."

"Murray," he replied with the same guttural 'R.' "Call me Murray. Anyvay, I'm going to give you $200." Clarissa started to shake her head. "Don't be silly," said Murray Plotkin. "Use it for food and to get settled. After everything gets sorted out, ve'll decide vot ve should do next."

During those next few months, what Murray Plotkin 'did next' was to virtually adopt Clarissa Taylor and her three children. He periodically gave her extra money for food, inquired regularly as to the children's welfare and gave Clarissa any time off she needed to solidify her new arrangements.

As time went on Clarissa became as much a fixture in Murray's restaurant as the Plotkin's Perfect and gradually she evolved into perhaps the highest paid deli cashier in New York as Murray used her salary to subsidize her children.

It was an odd relationship and, despite outward appearances of familiality, one with distinct limits. Although Murray's generosity knew no bounds and he was full of helpful advice on the children's education, he never ventured to visit his cashier at home or to make any attempt to see the family, even after her elevated pay had allowed Clarissa to escape Brooklyn and the slums. Nor were Clarissa and her children ever invited to the Plotkins. The only time Murray saw Matthew, Veronica and Jeanette Taylor was during the holidays when Clarissa brought them to the store. During those brief visits, the girls would present Mr. Plotkin with home-baked cookies and Mr. Plotkin would ask them about their grades.

Although from time to time Clarissa resented Murray's paternalism, the benefits for her children maintained her silence and outward good will. Not wanting to jinx the arrangement, Clarissa tried not to question her benefactor's motives, but some speculation was inevitable. Why her? she wondered. Certainly Murray Plotkin was no philanthropist. Why had he focused what seemed to be the sum total of his charity on her? Clarissa found no answers but was certainly grateful for the twist of fate. It should only continue.

Now Murray Plotkin was gone.

As a result of his war with the bum and being humiliated on television, Murray Plotkin had sold his store and would soon move to Florida. It had happened suddenly, about two weeks after the bum defecated in the street in front of the store. After the employees had arrived for work in the morning, Murray had locked the front door and called everyone into the back storeroom. (The office was out of the question.)

Murray Plotkin had looked grave as he addressed his staff. Whatever he felt, the situation would turn out to be far more grave for them.

"People," he began, unable to make eye contact, "after two generations, Plotkin's of Flatbush is closing its doors." The old man made it sound as if a great institution of state was passing away.

"I find," he continued, each member of his captive audience feeling the numbness of unemployment creeping over them, "zat I can no longer keep up with the rigors of ze business. I am going to retire."

Murray was looking at the floor now, unable to face the six people whose lives he had just disrupted. Now came the hardest part, and Murray recited the deli's last will and testament in just above a whisper.

"I have set aside a month's wages for each of you. I am sorry about . . . all of zis."

Then silently, looking up only to avoid bumping his head, Murray gave each employee an envelope.

There were some questions afterward and one man made a plea for Murray to reconsider, but there was nothing much to be said and within an hour everyone had left, leaving Murray Plotkin alone in the locked, empty delicatessen awaiting the second-hand men who would buy and dispose of his stock and fixtures.

Clarissa Taylor was in shock. It had been thirteen years since she had been out of work. Now at thirty-six, lacking a high school diploma, she would be forced to look for a new job. And, although Murray had secretly left three months pay in her envelope, what would happen to her after that money ran out?

Clarissa realized that she had grown soft after nine years of preferential treatment. How could he do this? How could he leave now, just like that? If only he would have left her alone she would still be tough enough to make her way. But now Clarissa realized she had to support three school-age children and a two-bedroom apartment in Forest Hills on three months severance pay. All because that old bastard wanted to play God with her and her family.

I hate you, you son-of-a-bitch.

# CHAPTER FIVE

Bingo!

People in any field of endeavor wait for that one opportunity, that one special chance to propel themselves out of the crowd, to make that explosive leap and escape the gravity of mediocrity and break free to the stars. Actors wait for that one part, writers wait for that one book, farmers wait for that one crop, horse breeders wait for that one colt—and lawyers wait for that one case.

Herbert Whiffet had his case.

When told of the particulars, Herbert had quaked down to his toenails. This case was everything that the Fruitful Willis affair was not. It had incendiary social implications, a recognizable villain, and although the victim was not exactly a heroic figure, alterations might easily be made. But what this case had that was special, that was unique, that was man bites dog, what this case had that set it apart was a *videotape*. The incident had been recorded by an uninvolved spectator on *videotape*.

Herbert Whiffet ran through the events for perhaps the twentieth time, although it had been but two hours since the incident had been brought to his attention.

Rock cocaine—crack—a cheap, insidious and immensely profitable variety of the highly addictive drug, had all but taken over the city's poor neighborhoods. It made the early scenes of such films as "Death Wish III" look like reality. Marauding gangs of drug dealers, themselves forbidden by superiors to touch the lethal substance (violation of the rule punishable by death) cruised through their fiefdoms in vans with darkened windows, spraying automatic gunfire at rivals or citizens who attempted to contest their control, particularly those who sought assistance from the authorities.

The killing or wounding of innocent bystanders during these disciplinary actions was merely considered bad aim and caused the offending marksman to be teased unmercifully by his fellows, although the details of some unfortunate twitching and bleeding on the sidewalk made for great conversation, a way to break up an otherwise tedious day.

To demonstrate absolute authority, this new breed of paramilitary dealers had no compunctions about including the police in their target practice, a heretofore unthinkable breach of etiquette. The police took an understandably dim view of this latest tactic and vowed retribution. This was the same police force that merely mouthed platitudes when innocent children were gunned down in the streets, in effect promising to round up twice the usual suspects. When their own came under fire, however, all the excuses about 'insufficient manpower,' or 'hands tied by the criminal justice system,' or 'lack of cooperation by the community' ceased.

As part of their attempt to demonstrate the folly of shooting at police officers, the department had begun sweeping crackdowns (an apt phrase, perfect for the newspaper headlines) whereby entire neighborhoods were cordoned off and a battalion of local, state and federal law enforcement officials descended on the target area armed with automatic weapons of their own and protected with body armor. Helicopters circled overhead, prepared to pick off any members of the opposing army who attempted to snipe from the rooftops, until the police could gain control of the high ground.

It was during one of these raids that Herbert got his case.

Loath to enter a building and chance a gun duel on twisting stairways or in darkened corridors, the invaders always attempted to flush their prey into the street. Since, following the age-old tradition, these raids were conducted at dawn, the result was that a good many residents were sent scurrying out of their homes in varying degrees of undress and early morning befuddlement. While the police attempted to act with surgical precision, adhering strictly to the terms and locations specified in the search warrants and only tossing those apartments or storefronts actually used for drug dealing, it was inevitable that some innocents were caught up in the dragnet.

Time of day, circumstances and the mix of the guilty and the not guilty created a good bit of confusion. Invariably, one upshot of these affairs was a hefty number of civilian complaints alleging police brutality and other forms of official misconduct, often pressed by the guiltiest in order to create the possibility of a court dismissal on the grounds of rights violations. These cases were a dime a dozen and rarely resulted in anything for the complainant's lawyer but a good deal of paperwork, useless court appearances and minimal fees. Certainly nothing to arouse the attention of a well-known activist lawyer.

But every so often there was a rights violation complaint with such obvious merit, and thus such obvious newsworthiness, that lawyers clawed and scraped to get the case, competing for the prize with a ruthlessness rarely seen outside the Roman arena.

On the morning of May 18, the authorities conducted a massive raid in Manhattan Valley, a small enclave of run-down tenements and gentrified minority brownstones abutting the western border of Central Park between 100th Street and 110th Street, stretching west to Amsterdam Avenue. Manhattan Valley is largely Hispanic, but an entrenched drug ring called the Ghosts, dominated by the area's remaining blacks, controlled some twenty percent of the turf.

Residing within this territory, in the top floor apartment of 73–75 West 107th Street, one of the locations named prominently in the search warrants, was Lawanda de Bourbon, consort to a number of higher level members of the gang. Lawanda was eighteen years old, with long thin legs and large breasts upon which gravity had yet to have an effect. She was generally referred to as 'Diana' because of a striking resemblance to Diana Ross.

When the raid began, at 6 AM, Lawanda de Bourbon evidently decided that she had no desire to meet the police at such an ungodly hour and headed for the roof rather than the street. Wearing just a teddy and a rather abbreviated pair of panties, Lawanda apparently sought to lose herself by ducking into one of the other buildings on the block accessible from a common roof.

But, either due to the early hour or an underestimation of the extent of the raid, Lawanda de Bourbon was unprepared to encounter two uniformed and body-armored New York City policemen running at her from one of those adjoining buildings.

It is unclear what ensued in the next few seconds but the long-legged, high-breasted, negligee-clad young woman found herself near the edge of the roof, her upper half visible to the residents of the tenements on the north side of 107th Street. One of these residents was Fernando Rios, just arrived home from the local social club, who, at the first sound of the commotion, had run to fetch his portable videotape camera to record the momentous event for his later viewing pleasure. While filming, he glanced upward to the woman on the roof.

"Ahhee, chihuahua," Fernando breathed in awe, "look at those *tietas*."

Fernando quickly swung the camera in the direction of the drama on the roof just in time to see one of the policemen fire at Lawanda de Bourbon from no more than six feet away. The viewfinder fixed to his eye, Fernando followed the woman as she slowly toppled over the edge of the roof and fell, teddy fluttering, four stories to the ground, landing unceremoniously on top of a row of garbage cans.

Fernando Rios had only a third-grade education but was sufficiently schooled in modern media to know that he had just struck gold.

Fernando's first instinct was to offer the tape, at an appropriate price, to one of the bevy of television reporters invited by the police commissioner to witness the latest attack on the city's drug dealers. (Terms such as 'significant setback,' 'major seizures,' 'key arrests,' and 'serious blow' were guaranteed to be included in each broadcast.) But Fernando Rios stopped himself from running out to the street and holding an impromptu auction. Instead he went to the refrigerator, grabbed a beer and pondered his position, never letting the precious tape, perhaps the most valuable thing that he had ever touched, out of his sight.

In the first place, he reasoned quite correctly, if the cops got wind of the existence of a videotape of one of their own putting a bullet through some unarmed black chick, especially one dressed like that, they would seize the tape as evidence before he could get close to a reporter and all

Fernando would get would be an illegible receipt scrawled on a piece of note paper. That would be followed by the disappearance of the tape, or its substitution with a blank and claims by the cops that Fernando had been shooting with the lens cap on.

Even if he did get to the press, how much should he ask for? How could he be sure he'd actually get the money? And then, even if he did get paid, they'd probably just run the tape on the news and he wouldn't even get to be on television. *Bull-shit.* No, concluded Fernando Rios, this calls for cleverness.

So, like anyone in America with a story to tell or a skill to market or a property to peddle, like any actor or writer or athlete or lecturer, Fernando Rios decided to get himself an agent. Inexperienced in these matters and with no listings in the Yellow Pages to consult, Fernando grabbed a second beer and tried to figure out who he could use as an agent.

Just as Fernando finished his fourth, an act which left his refrigerator denuded, the light went on over his head. Of course! Most agents are lawyers, aren't they? And what lawyers would be best to bargain with the reporters and the cops? One of those guys that are always on the news, screaming about police brutality and cover-ups and the like. Of course!

Feeling proud of his deductive processes, Fernando Rios let his mind work still more. His first thought was to get some *Latino* lawyer, but no, that wasn't right. This was a black case, a black chick. Ergo, a black lawyer. Why not that guy he saw on TV making a stink about the bum in front of the deli? That guy's always on the news, yelling about something. He'd know what to do.

Although Fernando Rios could not name a single public official save the President of the United States and the Mayor of the City of New York, media recognition being what it is, he had no trouble recalling the name of Herbert Whiffet.

So, unbeknownst to Herbert, Fruitful Willis had been instrumental in Providence dropping into his lap what, under less fortuitous circumstances, he might have been forced, jealously, to watch fall into the lap of another.

Upon hearing Rios' story, Herbert Whiffet had assured the

man who, even at 10 AM, smelled like decomposing beer, that he had indeed done the right thing and that it was an absolute necessity to have representation when dealing with such explosive material.

Herbert had offered to keep the tape for his client, so that the risk of theft or impounding was mitigated. Rios had balked at parting with the precious recording until his agent and legal representative assured him that, with the item in safe-keeping, they might realize as much as $5,000 for it. To cement the bond, Herbert renounced claim to any portion of the money. Herbert Whiffet was a Champion, merely interested in defending the rights of his people.

Fernando Rios, who had no interest in the lawyer's motives or the rights of anyone other than himself except insofar as it affected his share of the profits, reacted to the $5,000 figure with even greater awe than he had shown for Lawanda de Bourbon's *tietas*. As greed overcame caution, Fernando, who may have had his first stroke of genuine good fortune in an otherwise bleak and hopeless life, consented to entrust the prize to his new associate. In addition to the money, Herbert was forced to agree to make Fernando's appearance on television a part of the deal.

Herbert then had a condition of his own, that Fernando Rios say nothing to anyone until cleared to do so by his agent. Fernando consented easily to this discipline, but when his agent informed him that the deal was off if the condition was violated, the film-maker's consent became more grudging.

As soon as he could usher his client out of his office, Herbert Whiffet was on the telephone. Before doing anything with the media, the lawyer was savvy enough to get all the details of the event, both from the official version and from the grapevine. After all, since the police were as yet unaware of the existence of documentary evidence of the incident, they would most certainly be tempted to manufacture some story to deflect blame to the victim, standard procedure in this type of affair.

Let's have the cops make the first move, decided Herbert Whiffet. There's no need to be rash.

It was time for Herbert to put his ear to the ground. He arranged the meeting he wanted, then, sweating and glancing over his shoulder, hustled off to place the tape in his safe deposit box. All the way to the bank he felt like a diamond courier with the big shipment, unaware as to whether or not the bad guys had been tipped off.

But Rios had kept his word, at least for the first hour, and the tape was interred without incident. Herbert heaved an enormous sigh, dried his hands and without further delay set off for Grant's Tomb.

New York City is a notorious mare's nest of political intrigue and those in the forefront cannot exist without a network of spies and sympathizers intertwined in the fabric of city government. A Champion will attract any number of idealists and opportunists, the former risking their livelihoods to do the right thing, the latter waiting to jump on a new bandwagon if today's disenfranchised become tomorrow's power brokers. Herbert Whiffet preferred working with members of the first group for their services were offered out of conviction and therefore required no reciprocation.

For some time, Herbert had been cultivating the favor of his current rendezvous. Renee Lieberman-Smith was an assistant district attorney, thirty-two and single, despite the hyphen-Smith which she had appended to leave marital status indeterminate and add a dash of culture. She was one of those overweight women who talk of the perils of exercise and defend the rights of smokers while exhaling a thick cloud of tar and nicotine in a crowded restaurant. Renee was privy to Herbert's ambition to take over her boss's job and thus hoped, in addition to her genuine desire to help the disenfranchised, to benefit from a change in administration.

Renee Lieberman-Smith had been with the Manhattan DA for six years and during that time had grown increasingly disillusioned with the politics that pervaded that office, personal considerations that prevented the discharge of the DA's duty to protect all citizens equally. Unlike those who simply acquiesced to the pressure, Renee was doing something about it.

Herbert Whiffet, for his part, despised Renee's incessant smoking and constant chatter. But, he had to admit, her information was top drawer and she gave great head.

When Herbert arrived at the monument, Renee was already there, pacing about and taking quick little drags on her cigarette, indications that she had some tidbit of information that she could not wait to pass along. The lawyer took a deep breath to prepare himself for his performance.

"Renee!" he said as if greeting a long-lost friend. "Thank you for coming."

ADA Lieberman-Smith smiled and tossed her cigarette to the ground, leaving the butt smoldering on the sidewalk, a habit that Herbert, an extremely fastidious man, found particularly irritating. She advanced on her friend and sometime lover and took one of his hands in both of hers. Herbert steeled himself to her touch so that he would not flinch. That one involuntary gesture would cut him off from a fabulous source of information forever.

"I'm glad to see you, Herbert," said ADA Lieberman-Smith, introducing just enough breath into the remark to give it an additional level of meaning.

Herbert returned the smile but not the squeeze. "Me too," he said, walking the tightrope between sincerity and further enticement. He pulled his hand away in a 'not in public' manner.

At times such as these, Herbert kicked himself for ever sleeping with the overweight white woman. But she had been so insistent and had asked nothing in return. Or so it seemed at the time. Pleasing a black man in bed seemed to her to be a political statement, a sign of acceptance in the front lines of those fighting for the rights of the oppressed. He often wondered how a woman like that ended up working for the prosecution instead of the ACLU.

It was quite simple. Renee Lieberman-Smith, only child of a union organizer for the International Ladies' Garment Workers Union and an elementary school teacher from the Bronx, had decided upon graduation from New York University Law School, firmly in the middle of her class, that the DA's office was where the action was. Where better to protect the rights of the downtrodden than in the center of law enforcement for the City of New York? She was, in fact, one of a number of young idealists who opted for the prosecutorial side of the fence. She had envisioned herself prosecuting Mafiosi and drug kingpins, indicting slumlords and zealously pursuing cases of police misconduct, all activities that the interviewer had assured her were high priorities of the Office of the District Attorney of New York County.

Instead, she spent her days handling an unending series of petty felonies, over ninety percent of which ended in plea bargains, sending to prison those very people who she felt were society's victims.

Of course, the interviewer who had enticed her with promises of Robin Hood law knew perfectly well what the real world was like. Assistant district attorneys do not make very much money and few criminal lawyers with a wisp of talent spend a great deal of time on the People's payroll before seeking greener pastures (in every sense of the term). The interviewer was therefore charged with ensuring a continuing flow of grist for the prosecutorial mill, and what better allure was there than idealism?

So Herbert Whiffet, the embodiment of those ideals, endured some left-wing small talk, biding his time until he could ask ADA Lieberman-Smith what information she had that made her inhale her cigarette smoke in those little gasps.

When it was safe to do so without offense, Renee's continued commitment to the struggle re-established, Herbert took the plunge.

"Well, Renee, what've we got?" Herbert used the first person plural whenever possible, ever assuring the young woman that they were in the fight together.

ADA Lieberman-Smith grabbed the Champion's hand once more, squeezing it tight. It seemed all she could do to restrain herself from jumping up and down. This time Herbert did not pull away. Renee's excitement was so infectious that he didn't even mind that she had drawn out her moment.

"Herbert, it's dynamite." ADA Lieberman-Smith let go of her comrade and began to speak in a whisper. "It seems that the woman who was shot, this Lawanda de Bourbon . . . she was only eighteen, you know . . . this girl, I guess you would call her, was playing both sides. She was a high-level informant, working with the detectives at Manhattan North—they work out of the West 100th Street Station, you know, right in the neighborhood. The Manhattan North crew were the same guys who coordinated the raid from the NYPD side."

Herbert nodded, trying not to start jumping up and down himself. Renee didn't know about Rios and the tape, and he had no desire to share the image of the eighteen-year-old with the incredible body falling to her death on camera, lying virtually naked on a row of garbage cans, an unarmed narcotics informant executed (as she most certainly was) by the police.

But a glance at Renee told Herbert that there was more. Herbert cocked an eyebrow as Renee pawed the ground with her shoe.

"Also, there's a rumor," ADA Lieberman-Smith continued, looking up with a frown. Whatever it was had apparently piqued her sensibilities. "This de Bourbon girl was apparently quite good looking . . ." To say the least, thought Herbert Whiffet, trying to hold his deadpan expression. "And I've heard rumblings that some of the detectives were, you know, making it with her."

For a second, Herbert didn't know how to react. It was important to show the proper face to Renee. He didn't think he could pull off moral outrage, particularly since, as Renee had seemed to forget, she was making it with him, but clearly he had to show something to support Renee's disgust at the moral lassitude of the detectives in Manhattan North.

He decided to opt for the intellectual approach. "Of course," he said, eyes widening, pounding one hand in the other, fervently revealing the obvious, "of course. She must have had something on them so they took her out."

Time to move off the sex angle. "Tell me, Renee, who was the actual shooter, and what's the official story?"

For a moment, Renee's mind flashed to the preliminary police photos of Lawanda de Bourbon, her high breasts and long, thoroughbred lines, then to her own apartment, a cluttered studio in the East Eighties, and the many nights she spent alone. Maybe Herbert might be persuaded to come by later . . .

She snapped back to the subject at hand when the lawyer's question registered.

"Oh. Not shots, shot. One shot. Fired by a Patrolman Rodriguez, James Rodriguez. He's a rookie working out of the 24th. They're also on West 100th."

"Yes, I know," Herbert nodded. Rodriguez, huh? Too bad. Wish it had been Ryan or McCarthy or McDermott or something. And a rookie. It's always easier for the police to drum up sympathy for a fresh-faced young patrolman in order to sell an accidental death verdict.

"What did he say?" Herbert continued. "What was his story?"

"He's still being interviewed, you know," ADA Lieberman-Smith replied, "but from what I hear, he's claiming she had a gun."

"Was a gun found?"

"Not so far. But who knows? Maybe she dropped it when she fell." ADA Lieberman-Smith snorted, thinking again of Lawanda de Bourbon who, even in death, made Renee all too aware of her own lumpy thighs and sagging breasts. She reached in her bag for another cigarette. "She certainly wasn't concealing it on her person."

"Anything else?" asked Herbert, now impatient to get going and begin the preparations.

This was going to be a big one, all right. There was no organization that was more blatant and more arrogant about depriving people of their rights than the police. Clannishly inbred, policemen believed that they were not merely the enforcers of the law, but also its interpreters and sometimes its makers.

Herbert's musings were interrupted by a light touch on his arm. He looked up to see ADA Lieberman-Smith with *that* look on her face.

"Uh, Herbert," she said shyly, "maybe later I could help you plan your strategy. You know, after work . . . ?"

"Damn, Renee, I'd love to," he replied, with an expression that left no doubt that it was true, "but I've got to meet with a lot of people to set this one up. And you know . . ." Herbert smiled and winked, a gesture that made him feel singularly ridiculous, "it wouldn't do for us to be seen together."

Renee Lieberman-Smith was once again required to accept an anonymous (and unrequited) role in the war against injustice.

"Yeah, sure, Herbert," she said glumly, trying hard to accept the Champion's words at face value and not as the inevitable rejection, "I understand."

This was the hard part for Herbert. He hated dealing with that downcast, whipped dog look. Was he supposed to make a date for sometime in the future, say something to mitigate her hurt? What did these women want anyway?

He shifted from one foot to the other. "Look, Renee, as

soon as this settles down, we can get together again. But for now, people will be watching. You know how much the newspapers would like to get something on me. We're just going to have to cool it."

Herbert hated street talk, but that, combined with logic, always worked with honkies.

"Yeah, I guess you're right," Renee agreed, mollified by the soundness of the argument. "Okay, then. I'll let you know if I hear something else."

"Thanks, Renee. That would be great."

# CHAPTER SIX

Phil Gagliardi hated internal affairs work. What a shitty way to be rewarded for eighteen years of being an honest cop. Now, instead of being out on the streets he loved, using his skills and experience to catch crooks, he spent his time investigating other cops, forced to do his best to make cases against his brethren, all the time hoping that he would not be successful. But Phil knew he had no choice. If internal affairs didn't do its job and the bad cops were allowed to do whatever they goddamn well pleased, control of the investigative process might pass to civilians. To the New York City Police Department, there was no threat greater, no insult deeper, than being forced to submit to the authority of a civilian review board.

So Phil did his job, making him a feared and hated member of the department. Although only a detective first grade, Phil Gagliardi was far more powerful than most captains, able to go virtually wherever he pleased within the vast thirty-thousand-man army, sniffing and ferreting, all to protect the very men who despised him from the rule of the mob waiting just outside their doors.

Phil shuffled through the stack of papers in the file that had been handed him an hour ago. It didn't take a detective's instincts to know that this one really stank. A nervous rookie pops some drug bimbo dressed only in a nightie because he said he saw a gun. Unfortunately for this Rodriguez kid, no one else saw the gun and no gun was found at the scene. Phil read further and took a drag on the cigarette that was to be his last before quitting, the same status that had been accorded each of his previous thousand smokes. When he got to the part about Lawanda de Bourbon's activities as an informant and the confidential memo about her propensity for sleeping with detectives he almost moaned audibly. It was hard to imagine pursuing a more unpleasant series of coincidences, or not such coincidences.

Under most circumstances, detective work is a painstaking, linear process, in which the investigator's greatest ally is time. In fact, the cases that are solved after years of work are greater deterrents to crime than the ones solved in hours, for it leaves any criminal with the feeling that he is never safe, no matter how much time has passed, that the law may be just behind him, ready to gobble him up. Unfortunately, the same rules do not apply to internal investigations, particularly those that inspire public interest. In these circumstances, the police must be perceived as being swift and relentless in their zeal to keep their department pure and free of misconduct.

As this case was most certainly going to create a hue and cry, Detective First Grade Phillip Gagliardi was forced to abandon his favored 'one step at a time' approach and attack the problem from all angles. To this end, he had secured an interrogation room at Midtown North and had the whole crew lined up, ready to be interviewed. He nodded to Patrolman Wong, his stenographer and witness, to bring in the first victim.

Phil Gagliardi was immediately struck with how young and fresh-faced was Patrolman James Rodriguez. He didn't look the least bit Puerto Rican with his soft features and straight brown hair. Phil noticed the absence of a wedding ring and decided that Patrolman Rodriguez must be something with the ladies. At Gagliardi's request, the young man, who until just recently was merely another anonymous rookie who had cursed his fortune in getting the 24th instead of the 19th, slid into the metal institutional chair across the table from his interrogator.

Phil toyed with the remains of his last cigarette and smiled at the kid. Rookies were easier, thank God. They didn't know the tricks yet.

"Patrolman," Phil nodded curtly. Then, softer, "Jimmy, isn't it?"

"Yes, sir," replied Patrolman Rodriguez, just as scared as any civilian murder suspect.

Gagliardi smiled. "Relax, Jimmy. Nobody's here to railroad you. We're just trying to get the facts."

Patrolman Wong took everything down, the NYPD version

of the inscrutable Oriental, his stenographer's record a back-up to the tape being made by the recorder next to Gagliardi's left elbow.

Phil picked up his pack of cigarettes, containing only ten more of his last one and offered it to the Patrolman.

"Smoke?"

"No thank you, sir," replied the scared rookie, lightening up not one bit. Patrolman James Rodriguez might be new to the force, but was certainly not new to the police. Growing up in the *barrio* made anyone something of an expert in interrogation techniques, even those few kids who stayed clean and finished high school.

Phil frowned at the pack in his hand. "Yeah, it's a filthy habit, ain't it? This is my last pack."

The rookie smiled a bit at that one.

Time to shift to business. "Look, Jimmy," said Gagliardi, keeping the friendly tone, pronouncing the patrolman's name as if he were Irish, "I've got to read you your rights. You're not a suspect in anything, this is just an inquiry, but those are the rules."

The reading of rights, which Gagliardi did softly and slowly, rather than in the bored monotone he used for street felons, had originally been intended by the courts to inform the dumb and indigent that they didn't lose their citizenship when being questioned by the police. It had evolved into the ultimate red flag, assuring the silence of even the most potentially cooperative witness. Rodriguez, for whom silence meant dismissal from the force, had no such option.

When the formality was completed, Gagliardi began. This Rodriguez looked like a good kid, and, God knows, the department needed good Spanish cops. Too bad this one's going to end up in the shit-can.

"Now, Jimmy, tell me everything that happened. Be thorough so if there's anything to back up your story, we can find it." And anything to trip you up, added the detective to himself.

"Well, sir, we mustered at 5 AM. I was assigned with Officer Robert Blakemore. We were to use the staircase in 49 West 107th Street, which was not a building named in the warrants, to get to the roof and cut off anyone who was either trying to escape or maybe shoot from the rooftops. We did as ordered when the action commenced. I was in the lead. As I entered the rooftop area, I saw a black female, dressed only in, uh, evening wear . . ."

"What sort of evening wear, Patrolman?" If this damn case wasn't so damn serious, Gagliardi would have laughed his head off. 'Evening wear.' Shit.

"It was . . . a transparent negligee and a pair of underpants," replied the rookie, reflexively looking at the ground.

"Anything else? Was the woman wearing anything on her feet?"

"No, she was barefoot."

"Was being barefoot impeding her progress? Was it slowing her down, I mean?"

"No, sir," replied the patrolman emphatically. "She could really motor."

Until this point the interrogation was deadpan, but as the image began to form of this almost naked, barefoot black chick zipping across the rooftops, things loosened up a little. It was almost like two cops sitting around and shooting the shit. Even Patrolman Wong smiled a little, although it was hard to tell.

Everyone was relieved that the tension had lifted a bit, although it made life much more dangerous for Patrolman Rodriguez.

"Now, Jimmy," smiled the detective, "what did you and Officer Blakemore do next?"

"Well, sir, Officer Blakemore had pulled even with me. When this black female spotted us, she put on the brakes."

"Tell me, Jimmy, had either of you drawn your weapons at this point?"

Patrolman Rodriguez squirmed. Since the IAD man must already know the answer, the question was certainly a set-up.

"Yes, sir. Both of us. As soon as we reached the roof we had drawn our weapons. The operation was considered high-risk and we were following instructions."

"Of course," replied the detective. "And how far were you from the female when she 'put on the brakes?'"

"About fifty feet."

"And did you determine at this point if she was armed?"

Despite his plight, Patrolman Rodriguez smiled. "We didn't see a weapon, no sir."

"Do you recall something amusing, Jimmy?"

"Well, sir, you've seen the photographs. The black female was, well, really something. She turned and ran, and me and Blakemore, uh, Officer Blakemore, we stopped for a minute and looked at each other. It wasn't exactly what we'd expected to see up on the roof."

Gagliardi frowned. Blakemore was little more than a rookie himself. From such stopping and gawking are dead cops made. Whoever assigned two young guys like these to cover the roof on a narcotics raid should have his ass kicked to Staten Island. Probably the Feds.

"Go on."

"I yelled for the black female to halt and then when she didn't, Officer Blakemore and myself pursued."

"What do you mean pursued? Where did she go?"

"Across the roof," replied the young patrolman, puzzled at such an obvious question.

Gagliardi didn't know whether to yell at the rookie or pat him on the head. He was a nice kid, but totally out of his depth.

"Jimmy," asked the detective slowly, leading him where he should have gone on his own, "did either you or your partner have the female in sight at all times?"

Rodriguez looked up, finally getting it. "No, sir. She ran around one of the structures that holds the water tank. We figured she was making for the fire escape."

"And you followed her?"

"Yes, sir."

"Did you stop before turning the corner? Just to check?"

Gagliardi was angry with himself. He was leading this kid shamefully and anyone reading the transcript was bound to know it. But this was it. If the rookie didn't get it now, he was on his own.

"No, sir, we didn't stop. We had determined that the female was unarmed so there seemed to be no reason to proceed as if we were following an armed suspect."

"And?"

"We turned the corner, me first, Officer Blakemore backing me up, and when I saw the black female she was about to go on to one of the fire escapes. I yelled for her to stop and she spun around. When she did I saw a gun in her hand. I don't know how she got it but there it was. I fired one round hitting the woman in the chest. She crashed against the ledge and then fell over."

Gagliardi sighed. Even a twelve-year-old knows that a drug gang might hide a gun on the roof. This was too lame for words.

"What happened to the gun, Patrolman?"

Rodriguez looked at his interrogator, wide-eyed and innocent, inspiring Gagliardi's sympathy all over again. "I just don't know. I didn't see. Either did Blakemore. Maybe it went off the roof with her."

Gagliardi shook his head. "No gun was found near the body." He should have closed it there, but he had to ask. "Jimmy, how could you or your partner not see what happened to the gun?"

"Well . . . she was . . . shit, Detective, I never shot nobody before and this one, young and dressed like she was . . . after I shot her, I just couldn't take my eyes off her."

Gagliardi interrogated Blakemore and got full corroboration. Gagliardi was convinced they were telling the truth on the theory of who would make up such shit, but determining fact was not his job, thank God.

Next came the hard part. Gagliardi was always uncomfortable interviewing superior officers. (You interrogated inferiors but interviewed superiors.) This one would be particularly tough because Patrolman Phillip Gagliardi had once reported to Lieutenant, now Captain Vincent D'Angelo, who, to make matters worse, was a fellow Neapolitan.

Unlike Patrolman Rodriguez, who had shuffled into the room to face his accuser, Vince D'Angelo fairly swaggered in and addressed the internal affairs investigator like he was still his boss.

"*Ciao*, Phil," grinned the captain. D'Angelo glanced at the cigarettes on the table. "Still on your last pack?"

Gagliardi forced himself to return the smile. Just like I figured, he thought. D'Angelo is trying to turn the interview upside down. I gotta get control. Gagliardi reminded himself of the dead girl and the coming headlines.

"Captain," he nodded curtly.

D'Angelo cocked an eyebrow at his old patrolman but retained his affability. "Captain is it?" D'Angelo laughed. "Must be serious, hey Phil? Guess you got to read me my rights."

Gagliardi nodded again and droned out the required words. D'Angelo indicated his understanding. The lieutenant reached for his cigarettes and offered the pack to the captain.

"No thanks, Phil. I quit five years ago. Those things can be harmful to your health."

The detective smiled, lit up and tried to get started. He had thought about this interview since he had seen the file, but it hadn't made it easier. Department discipline runs deep and Phil Gagliardi couldn't shake the knowledge that he was interrogating his old commander.

"Captain," he began, the cop's monotone his defense against intimidation, "the file indicates that the dead girl, Lawanda de Bourbon, was an informant for one or more of the detectives reporting to you in Midtown North . . ."

As had become a habit through inertia, Renee Lieberman-Smith sat on the sofa and watched the 11 O'Clock News on WRCT. She hated the television, as much a symbol of her loneliness as the half-empty scotch and water in her lap. Renee had resisted acquiring a TV set for years, television being nothing but a series of mindless sitcoms geared at intellectual mediocrity, the quintessence of passing time rather than filling it. But, two years ago, citing the need to be informed, she had purchased a nineteen-inch color set manufactured by one of the interchangeable Far Eastern electronics companies. The infernal machine had slowly wormed its way into her life and now, upon reflection, she had to admit that "Roseanne" wasn't so bad after all.

Renee wasn't sure why she had chosen the news on WRCT from among the six or seven other options. Like the rest of the local news broadcasts, WRCT was merely an electronic tabloid, its purpose to titillate rather than inform. She decided that the network people were right. Viewers picked a news station by the personality of the anchor and the reporters, not the content of the broadcast.

Ordinarily, Renee watched the 11 O'Clock News with a drifting mind, an excuse to finish her drink and drag herself off to bed, but tonight was different. Tonight ADA Lieberman-Smith was awaiting the news with interest, especially the lead story.

As the show came on, Renee wondered which of WRCT's crew of intense young men and attractive young women would get the assignment. She ran through this exercise any time there was a story that interested her. For this plum, she already knew, of course, for that was the real reason she watched the show. With the morbid fascination of the self-perceived unattractive, Renee Lieberman-Smith awaited the inevitable appearance of the slim and lovely Cornelia Pembroke.

And in short order, just as she knew it would, the soft features of the sweetheart of WRCT filled the screen. The shooting of Lawanda de Bourbon was indeed the lead story and Cornelia's piece had been taped at the scene earlier in the day, at the conclusion of the raid. She stood in front of the row of garbage cans that had been Lawanda's resting place only hours before and recited the facts of the case, how the police had apparently shot, either by accident or as a part of some grand conspiracy, an unarmed eighteen-year-old beauty who had been on the police payroll and, according to rumors, may have been granting sexual favors to members of the force. The contrast between the soft, innocent features of the reporter and the sordid backdrop was a news director's dream.

The picture cut away to film shot earlier, film of Lawanda de Bourbon's magnificent eighteen-year-old virtually unclad body lying across the row of trash cans, then being loaded into a six-foot-long thick plastic bag, grotesquely reminiscent of the food storage variety.

It was only the publicity surrounding the narcotics raid, a grand exercise in police determination and efficiency, that had allowed the film crews to be present to get such fabulous footage. Although live bare breasts were strictly forbidden for family viewing, each and every news director had decided that dead bare breasts were not covered by the same prohibition, and Lawanda de Bourbon's final pose was transmitted on every news show in the city.

Renee Lieberman-Smith and millions of other fascinated New Yorkers watched the camera cut back to the lovely Cornelia Pembroke, who looked almost virginal by comparison. The reporter was detailing the day's later developments.

" . . . And stating that they were unwilling to trust the review procedures of the police department, the parents of Lawanda de Bourbon have reportedly retained legal counsel to ensure that justice is done for what they termed their daughter's 'cold-blooded murder,' and to take appropriate action as warranted by today's shooting. The de Bourbon family has informed WRCT that their attorney will hold a news conference tomorrow. Police officials said that the de Bourbon family has every right to obtain counsel, but its investigation will proceed regardless so that a swift determination may be made of the facts and whether or not internal or criminal charges will be filed."

Then the soft-featured young woman, the very picture of the serious news professional, looked directly into the camera and signed off.

"Cornelia Pembroke, WRCT News, reporting from West 107th Street."

As the picture cut to the anchor desk, Renee Lieberman-Smith purposefully punched the off button on the remote control that had come with the television. Three minutes of Cornelia Pembroke was all she could take.

Kicking off her clothes, the garments joining remnants of past days' attire scattered randomly about the apartment, Renee headed for bed, unmade since the sheets had been changed six days before. She paused, as she often did, at the full-length mirror that she had purchased five years ago when she had sworn to get into shape and once again surveyed her naked body. As she turned to profile, her least flattering angle, Renee wondered what Cornelia Pembroke was doing tonight to celebrate the coup.

I'll bet *she's* not alone, Renee thought, realizing that Cornelia was her sister in the Rodriguez case. *She's* probably out at some club with her latest boyfriend.

With visions of the laughing, not-a-care-in-the-world Cornelia Pembroke basking in the adulation of her newest, even more gorgeous, beau at one of New York's hottest night spots, Renee Lieberman-Smith turned out the light in her single occupancy apartment and tried to get some sleep.

# CHAPTER SEVEN

In what would most surely have pleased Renee Lieberman-Smith, Cornelia Pembroke did not spend the evening of her latest triumph out on the town. In fact, that night, Cornelia Pembroke was not even Cornelia Pembroke. She was Karen Pzytriek, having dinner at her parents' two-bedroom-with-a-terrace sixteenth-floor rent-stabilized apartment in Lincoln Towers on West End Avenue. The development, consisting of six buildings and over two-thousand apartments had converted to condominiums two years earlier, but Irwin Pzytriek had declined to purchase, a decision about which he increasingly gloated as New York real estate prices continued to soften. "Accountants aren't so dumb after all," had become a constant refrain.

"Are you still seeing that boy from the newspaper?"

Karen helped herself to another sliver of strudel. No matter how many times she asked, her mother insisted on buying four-thousand calorie desserts from L'Eclair. As everyone but her parents seemed to know, television made even the thinnest person look heavier. The wags were just waiting to note that Cornelia Pembroke seemed to be getting a little jowly.

"No, Mama," she frowned. "Not for a month now."

Betty Pzytriek played with her wedding ring. "Why not, Karen?" she asked. "I thought you liked him. You said he was intelligent with a sense of humor. That's not such a bad combination."

Irwin Pzytriek grunted. "I didn't like him . . . he never listened. A 'T.' Ask for a 'T.' Where do they get these people?"

"Daddy," said Karen, "do we have to watch television while we eat?"

The elder Pzytriek cocked an eyebrow in his daughter's

direction. "What's wrong with 'Wheel of Fortune'? Besides, you *work* on television. I'm sure you don't mind when people watch your news show while *they* eat."

"That's not the point," retorted Karen. She turned to her mother. "Ken was fine," she continued, trying to pick out the pieces of apple with her fork and avoid the crust, "it's just that we never got to see each other. And, well, it's hard to see someone who's in your business. It's too competitive."

"No? If it's not the point, why do you run the show at dinnertime?" challenged her father, eschewing further discussion of the young man who never listened. Betty Pzytriek coughed and stood up to get more coffee. "Oh, all right," he muttered and, pushing himself up from the table, walked to the little counter in the corner of the room that held the thirteen inch black-and-white dining companion and punched the 'off' button.

"Thank you, Irwin," said Betty.

"Tell me something, Karen," her father said as he resumed his seat. Irwin Pzytriek was still dressed in the suit that he had worn to work that day, tie still knotted at his throat. Karen had always thought her father had a vague resemblance to Richard Nixon. "Why is it your station always sides with the blacks?"

Karen took a forkful of strudel. Why did I have to come for dinner the day Lawanda de Bourbon was killed?

"We don't side with anybody," she replied evenly. "We report the news. We show the public what's going on and we try to do it honestly. When a civilian is shot by the police under questionable circumstances, the role of a free press is to keep the matter in the public eye so that official misconduct is not swept under the rug."

"You keep the matter in the public eye so your ratings won't be swept under the rug. But I wasn't talking about that girl." Karen waited. Her father never needed prompting. "I'm talking," he continued, voice rising, "about that story you did on the bum and the deli owner. You let the blacks walk you around like you had a ring in your nose."

Karen found herself pining for Vanna White. "The deli owner had no right to persecute somebody just because he was homeless."

"*Persecute? Persecute? Ha.*" Irwin Pzytriek shook his head. "Who was persecuting who? That bum made cocka in the street in front of the store. How come your honest station didn't report that?"

Karen stopped. "Where did you find that out?"

"It was in a letter to the editor in the *Post*. You're too involved with television. You don't read."

Karen withheld her impressions of the *New York Post* as an authoritative source. "That doesn't make any difference, Daddy." Had Willis really defecated in front of the store? "Whenever a homeless man is harassed just because he is disadvantaged, the news can play an important role in protecting his rights, which in turn helps protect the rights of those like him."

Irwin Pzytriek snorted. "Is that what they tell you to say to get around the fact that you people always go for the cheapest sensationalism you can find?"

"Nobody tells me to say anything."

"That's too bad. It's worse for me to think that my daughter made that up herself." Irwin paused. "And of course we know that some ordinary white person who's worked in a business all his life and is being ruined by some maniac . . . we know he's got no rights. Your station would never think of protecting him. That's not news."

Betty Pzytriek poured her husband a cup of coffee. "Irwin," she admonished. "Karen doesn't come for dinner that much. Don't have a fight."

Irwin Pzytriek threw up his hands. "Who's fighting? Don't I have a right to my opinion?"

Karen noticed that somehow her strudel had disappeared although she didn't remember eating the rest of it. She started to reach for the platter again but stopped and instead folded her hands in her lap. From here she would begin to count the minutes before she could leave without disturbing her father's view of the evening as a happy family get-together punctuated by spirited intellectual interchange. But she didn't have to get fat doing it.

"The station would defend anyone we think is being oppressed . . ."

"You *think*? Just who is it who decides who's oppressed and who isn't?"

"Well, Daddy, everyone in news has to make subjective judgments. Even the *Post*. And besides, we always give the subject of a story the chance to respond."

"And what was this response?"
"The deli owner claimed that the homeless man was driving away his business."
"And how was the homeless man doing this? Had he opened a competing delicatessen on the sidewalk?" Irwin Pzytriek's mouth had started to settle into that smug smile of triumph that Karen hated. It was a gesture that seemed to be reserved for those closest to him.
She dared an impatient look. "No, Daddy. The deli owner claimed that the homeless man was harassing passersby and that he urinated in the street in front of those eating in the restaurant, among other things."
"All lies, I suppose. A story concocted by the fellow to cover his own crimes."
Karen squirmed. "I don't know if they were lies. I suppose they were true."
"You mean you didn't know? Don't you investigate before you run a story?"
"Of course we do. But that's not the point. The man had a right to use the public streets. If he violated the law, Mr. Plotkin had legal recourse, but he had no right to try to take the law into his own hands."
"And this violation of the rights of the homeless came to your attention, no doubt, because of a public outcry about the shabby treatment to which this poor unfortunate had been subjected."
"Not exactly. I heard about it from a contact of mine. A lawyer. He defends people who have had their rights violated. After the homeless man had been forcibly evicted by the cops, he went to the Mobilization for the Homeless and complained. The lawyer called me and I went with him to the restaurant."
Irwin Pzytriek leaned forward. "You mean that this lawyer told you a story about the violation of someone's rights and, taking that story on face value, you brought a camera to a man's place of business and then subjected him to a media inquisition, but did not subject either the lawyer or the homeless man to the same process, and then just showed the piece on your show without even finding out if it was true?"
Karen Pzytriek realized that her blouse was soaked under the arms. "Yes, Father. I suppose that, as always, you are correct."

"So what happened next?"

"I don't know what happened. It wasn't the kind of story that demanded follow-up."

"Of course not," sneered her father. "Well, let me tell you what happened. The guy went out of business. Cornelia Pembroke ran a man out of his livelihood who had worked like a dog for his whole life. And I'll tell you one more thing. This man was completely honest. Do you know how I know he was honest, Miss Pembroke? I know he was honest because my accounting firm did the work for his restaurant."

Karen looked in the direction of the crumbs on her plate but saw only Murray Plotkin's comical expression as she allowed Herbert and that bum to vilify him.

"And there's more. You did such a good job at defending the rights of the oppressed that six people are now out of work."

Karen remembered the face at the cash register.

"But I suppose that's a fair price for upholding the rights of the downtrodden. By the way, I wonder what happened to the downtrodden. Wherever he is, I hope he appreciates the effort made by Cornelia Pembroke to guarantee his rights."

What *had* happened to Fruitful Willis?

After his brief turn in the spotlight of city street life, Fruitful Willis, the urban chameleon, had once again blended into his surroundings, indistinguishable from any other of the burgeoning number of homeless.

Fruitful had been rather shocked on the day that Murray Plotkin closed his doors. Of all the calamities that might befall him, having his gold mine disappear was the last thing that he had considered. Now Fruitful was left in front of a padlocked store, certainly not the optimum atmosphere in which to ply his trade. Fruitful Willis, a man for whom the ebbs and flows of daily life made barely a ripple, suddenly found that he was angry. Who did that red-haired old Jew think he was, to pull up and leave like that?

But Fruitful prided himself on resourcefulness, a quality that had allowed him to survive in the days before he had rights. Okay, he thought, just because one guy left doesn't mean the whole block had gone bad. The deli was the best place, sure, but the entire stretch of stores got the subway traffic. Where was the next best spot?

Unfortunately for Fruitful, the boundaries of his decision were not as wide as he would like. Being a member of the homeless had become rather popular as not only former bums, but a good many others from the vast population of the poor had rushed to join such an exalted and de-stigmatized group. Fruitful no longer had the option of simply sauntering over to another choice spot and taking up where he had left off. Most of the best places were occupied and it was becoming common for two or three members of the homeless to be found conducting their affairs within twenty feet of one another. Arguments as to land rights occurred regularly and occasionally resulted in the flailing of arms although blows were rarely struck.

So Fruitful Willis looked up and down the street that he had the right to walk freely, hoping to find a suitable location that did not require him to abandon his clientele. To his surprise and delight, Fruitful noticed a green-grocer on the corner at the end of the block, diagonally across from his current location.

Sizing up the grocery with his practiced eye, Fruitful could not believe his good fortune. The place was perfect, maybe even better than the restaurant. Corner location, always a plus; outdoor vegetable and fruit displays, sure to attract browsers as well as cut off a good deal of the sidewalk by which a pedestrian might elude Fruitful and make his escape; a subway entrance just off the corner; and, best of all, no competition in sight.

Fruitful blasted a laugh and began to shuffle up the street. He was already congratulating himself on his coup. There was nothing that a man with rights and a sharp eye could not accomplish.

If things were not good enough, as he neared the corner he saw that the proprietors of the green-grocer were a bunch of little foreigners, Chinks or something. Ha-ha. Fruitful stuck his hand in his receipts pocket imagining the wealth that would begin to accumulate there in the next few hours.

Fruitful shuffled across the street and fine-tuned his business plan. Just to the right of the store, between the vegetables and the subway entrance seemed the best place.

When he reached the desired spot, two or three of the little foreign men were watching. Fruitful smiled. He knew that foreigners were no match for someone with rights. Fruitful, playing it cagey, leaned against a lamp-post on the curb in front of the store.

One of the little foreigners suddenly wrinkled his nose.

"Ahyee, it smell here." He pointed to one of the others. "Kim, you hose down sidewalk. Get smell out."

Before Fruitful realized what was happening the second little man emerged from the store holding the end of a garden hose and began to wash down the sidewalk. Suddenly Fruitful felt his feet becoming wet as the flowing water made its way through the holes in his shoes. Although it was almost summer, feeling water on his body was the last sensation that Fruitful Willis wanted.

"What you doin', man?" he screamed suddenly. "You gittin' me wet!"

"Still smell," said the first man to the second. "Hose more."

The second man, careful to avoid aiming the hose directly at Fruitful, nonetheless managed to spray water up at him. Fruitful Willis was getting soaked. What kind of treatment was that for a man with rights?

For the second time that day, Fruitful found himself angry. It was not the roust that bothered him, it was the fact that it was being administered by *foreigners*. Surely he had more rights than they. Fruitful advanced two steps in the direction of the man with the hose. Although he had no immediate violent intent, Fruitful's appearance in itself conveyed a good deal of menace. By the time he had taken the second step the first foreigner had produced a club, seemingly from thin air.

"You bother us, I whack you good," he said, leaving no doubt he meant it.

Fruitful stopped in his tracks, sizing up his position while continuing to get wet. He had three choices: grab the hose from the man and risk getting hit with the club, stand there and get wet, or, unbelievably, withdraw. Before succumbing to the third alternative, Fruitful attempted a gambit.

"Why you doin' dat?" he wailed. "I's jes tryin' to git somethin' to eat." Since he had attracted his customary crowd of onlookers, although at a greater distance than usual due to the spray, Fruitful went for the move that had worked so well for him at the deli.

The second foreigner aimed the hose at the ground, suspending Fruitful's shower, but did not turn it off. The first foreigner grabbed some peaches, placed them in a plastic bag and put it on the ground in front of Fruitful Willis.

"There," he said, "I give you fruit to eat. Very healthy. Now you go."

Fruitful looked at the bag at his feet, trying to decide his next move when he heard a terrible sound.

Laughter.

The onlookers were laughing. At him. Fruitful's eyes bugged as he felt the blood rush to his face. How could the people laugh at him? How could they side with these foreigners, little Chinks who talked funny?

Fruitful was seized with indecision. He didn't want to give up such a prize location but, rights or not, he did not seem to have any choice. What was even worse to a performer, he had lost the sympathy of the audience.

As he was figuring out what he might do next, the second little foreigner began to slowly move the nozzle of the hose in his direction. Feeling the hated spray once more, Fruitful Willis turned and, leaving the bag of peaches on the sidewalk, began to shuffle down the street.

No wonder this corner had been unoccupied, he thought as he made his way in the first direction that had occurred to him. These little guys were crazy.

But Fruitful wasn't finished. He remembered what he had done the last time he was evicted. He remembered what a man with rights could do.

Fruitful Willis stopped and got his bearings. He strained his overworked memory. What was that address again?

# CHAPTER EIGHT

For as long as he could remember, Clovis Buckworth had hated the summer. It was not just his tendency to perspire, which necessitated multiple daily showers and liberal applications of deodorant—Clovis' antipathy to vacation season was rooted in tradition. Throughout his formative years, summer meant extended stays at the Buckworth family compound in Newport; repeated vainglorious exhibitions of a family tree that traced to Ethelred the Unready; interminable discussions about oil prices, oil exploration, oil regulation; jokes about crude oil, salad oil, suntan oil and musk oil; forced exposure to Uncle Ayler's llamas, who young Clovis thought smelled horribly and who had a tendency to bite when Uncle Ayler wasn't looking.

But the worst part of the summer was the almost ritualistic worship of wealth that the otherwise parsimonious Buckworth clan reserved for family get-togethers. Net worth was personal worth; money was morality. And the worst offender was his father, Clovis Buckworth II (the son having dropped the 'III' although each year at Christmas he received a dozen shirts emblazoned 'CB III' which Clovis gave away since they were the wrong size anyway). As seen by his son, CB II affected the smug superiority common to those who have inherited wealth while doing nothing to enhance it.

Clovis took off his glasses and wiped the sweat off the bridge of his nose. These days, although the younger Buckworth had chosen a calling which prevented him from travelling to Newport, and had, as the family accused, 'squandered' his trust fund, Clovis had an entirely new set of reasons for hating the summer. As any first year physics student knows, increased heat in an enclosed space causes expansion of the substances trapped inside until finally they begin to react violently. A city is not exempt from that law and the summer meant yelling, arguments, fist-fights, knifings and increased drug use with its inevitable side effects of vomiting, illness and death.

And, while it was only May, the madness was already in mid-season form. Things at the shelters were getting totally out of hand. Clovis Buckworth almost missed the days when heroin was the drug of choice. Heroin was expensive and those under its influence would merely nod out and not bother anyone. Strung out junkies were a problem, true, but those in need of a fix knew that they were unlikely to score enough by robbing those who were forced to resort to public shelters.

Crack, unfortunately, was another matter. The drug was so cheap and so addictive, that those in need of the price of a score could do quite well preying upon the concentrations of homeless that filled the armories where many were housed. In addition, those under the influence of the drug were apt to become irrationally violent, venting their fury on any man, woman or child that had the misfortune to happen into their vicinity. That, in turn, caused many of the homeless to eschew the shelters, preferring to take their chances on the streets. Thus the streets had become a repository of these unfortunates, and although there was no real decrease in his problems at the shelters, the territory that the executive director for The Mobilization for the Homeless was forced to cover was now more far-flung. And all of this had begun to get to Clovis Buckworth. Clovis had expected that his chosen career would have its frustrations but he had not expected futility.

So, after a day of trying to find temporary housing for burned-out families and battered wives, Clovis Buckworth was in no mood to deal with Fruitful Willis. He too had watched Cornelia Pembroke's report on the news. He always watched Cornelia Pembroke on the news. The darling of WRCT commanded his attention every bit as much as she did that of Renee Lieberman-Smith. He had even vowed to ask Herbert for an introduction as a *quid pro quo* but, at the last moment, lost his nerve.

Clovis remembered that Fruitful Willis was waiting and had, in fact, been staked out in the shabby anteroom for over an hour. He blew down his shirt front in a feeble attempt to create air currents, took a deep breath and beckoned the homeless man to come in.

"Mr. Willis," he nodded politely, politeness as much a part of his upbringing as prep school Latin, "please have a seat."

Clovis Buckworth casually pushed his chair as far as possible from the side of the desk where Fruitful took his seat. It was a reflex, an extension of his reaction in the llama pens.

"Now, Mr. Willis, what seems to be the problem?"

Equating politeness with subservience (as it had always been for him), Fruitful Willis shifted easily in his chair. When he addressed the man behind the desk the pathetic warble of his street voice was gone. Fruitful Willis had rights and this man was but a public servant, four-eyed and balding to boot.

"Ah be rousted again. Some guy turned a hose on me and another one made to hit me wit' a club."

Clovis Buckworth nodded and reached for a pad and pen. "Where did this happen, Mr. Willis?"

Fruitful shifted in his chair once more. Although the public servant was as outwardly polite as before, Fruitful's keen ear detected an almost indiscernible edge in the man's tone absent in the previous meeting.

"It was near de othuh place," he replied, some of the warble sneaking back into his voice. "Some li'l foreign guys sellin' fruit." Nothing wrong with introducing patriotism into the discussion. "They wasn't American," he added helpfully.

"Yes, Mr. Willis," Clovis replied, pen poised, "let's have the details."

Fruitful recounted his run-in with the Korean greengrocers, embellishing the story only slightly so as to imply that the Koreans were the equivalent of the bloodthirsty hordes that stormed across the Yalu River.

Clovis Buckworth listened to the recitation, moving Fruitful along when he got bogged down in describing the sneering, vicious foreigners who were denying an American somethin' to eat. (Fruitful did not see fit to include the part about the peaches—probably rotten anyway.)

When Fruitful had completed his story, Clovis Buckworth sat for a moment or two reviewing his notes. Then he looked up and shrugged.

"I'm sorry, Mr. Willis. I don't think we can help you."

Fruitful's eyes began to bug. "What you mean you can' help

me? Dem guys rousted me. Ain't I got a right to be on the street?"

"Of course you do," replied the executive director of the Mobilization for the Homeless. "Any citizen has a right to use the public thoroughfares. But the grocers also have a right to clean the sidewalk in front of their store. In fact, they are required to do so by the Board of Health."

Fruitful Willis, a man whose existence depended on his ability to detect the slightest change in his surroundings, immediately realized that to this man he was once again a bum.

"So what you tellin' me?" he growled.

"I'm telling you, Mr. Willis, that it sounds to me that you have no recourse through this agency for the incident at the grocer's. If you think that the proprietors broke the law in the way they treated you, file a complaint with the police like any other citizen. Your complaint will be investigated and, if found to have merit, appropriate action will be taken. I feel I should warn you, however, that filing a false complaint is a crime. Do you understand what I have just said?"

Clovis paused, allowing time for a reply. When there was none, he continued.

"Now, if you would like us to obtain food and shelter for you, we would be happy to do so. Would you like us to make the arrangements?"

Fruitful pulled himself to his feet. Clovis Buckworth backed off. Fruitful always smelled worse when he moved.

"I can do jes fine on my own," Fruitful hissed through what passed for clenched teeth. Having come face to face with the concept of conflicting rights, Fruitful Willis tried to do the logical thing. "Mebbe my lawyer be more int'rested."

Clovis Buckworth suppressed a smile. "Perhaps he would, Mr. Willis. Why don't you get in touch with him? Here . . ." Clovis began writing on a piece of scrap paper, "this is his address and telephone number. His name, in case you have forgotten, is Herbert Whiffet. That is an excellent idea, Mr. Willis. Consult your attorney."

Cornelia Pembroke had decided to atone by doing a follow-up story on the Fruitful Willis affair. Although she was convinced that such a follow-up would make terrific tele-vison, others might not share that view—Michael P. Iserson,

News Director, for one. Iserson pathologically shied away from news-about-news stories, and even though this one had great human interest, it would have to be done so as to avoid any hint of culpability by WRCT.

She planned her presentation carefully and went to see her boss the moment she arrived the following morning.

Iserson waved her into his office. It was a glass-walled cubicle in the newsroom, fitted with venetian blinds that were only drawn when someone was being fired. The news director was positively ebullient, the sure sign of a hot story, and the shooting of Lawanda de Bourbon was as hot as they come.

"Glad you're in early, Corney," he trumpeted. Iserson rarely spoke below a bellow and had a nasal delivery that would have sounded sarcastic even if he had been addressing Mother Teresa. "We're really going to hit on this de Bourbon thing and I want to get everything straight before you go out."

Cornelia had expected this. It would not be easy to turn Iserson's attention.

"Mike," she began, trying to generate some infectious excitement of her own, "I've got an idea I want to run by you."

"Shoot." Iserson leaned back in his chair and clasped his hands behind his head, waiting to hear how Cornelia was going to use the death of Lawanda de Bourbon to enhance WRCT's already envied ratings.

Now that the moment had arrived to present her idea, Cornelia was struck by what a hare-brained scheme it was. Had she really expected Iserson to pull her off the de Bourbon case to cover a retired deli owner in a condo in Florida? Cornelia decided to alter her well-rehearsed pitch.

"It's not really about Lawanda de Bourbon," she ventured tentatively.

Iserson brought his hands down, which swung his large body forward like a wrecking-ball. "No?"

Cornelia shook her head. "No. It's about something I would like to do in conjunction with the de Bourbon story." Cornelia had substituted 'in conjunction with' for 'instead of.'

"Yeah?"

Cornelia cleared her throat. Mike did not like to be distracted from his focus and already viewed this conversation as wasting his time.

"I want to do a follow-up on Willis and the deli owner. I found out some things that I think would make a great piece."

Iserson's eyes narrowed. "Yeah? Like what?"

Cornelia filled Mike in on the upshot of the first story. She embellished the account as much as possible, trying to create the appropriate image. Throughout the presentation, Iserson sat still and did not change expression.

"Is that it?" he asked when she had finished. His tone was not a good omen.

Cornelia nodded and waited.

"Corney," began Iserson very softly, the tone generally reserved for the drawn venetian blinds, "let me get this straight. You want to take some of your time away from a case that promises to be the biggest bombshell of the year, where the facts are as yet unknown and the implications are explosive, where the reporter who sorts it all out could easily win an Emmy, all to fly to Boca Raton to interview a deli owner who has retired to play with his grandchildren, interview a cashier in Queens and track down a bum, demonstrating that WRCT shares the responsibility for running an old man out of business? Is that what you are proposing? Please correct me if I misunderstood you."

Cornelia crossed her arms in front of her chest. "I think it's an important story. It shows how television can be manipulated by media-wise hustlers." Damn, I shouldn't have said that.

"Oh, I'm sorry, Corney," Iserson replied in mock apology. "I didn't realize the full extent of what you had in mind." He shook his head and gazed heavenward. "This station is not in business to extend *mea culpas* to its audience. We report the *news*. If, on occasion, the journalistic process is successfully co-opted by an opportunist, that, my dear, is the price of a free press. A free press presupposes free access.

"Now," continued the news director, "as to your idea. The answer, as you might suspect, is no. You are to devote your full time and energy to the de Bourbon story. To that end, I suggest you contact your friend, Herbert Whiffet. He, as you know, is the attorney for the de Bourbon family. He has let it be known that he has evidence in his possession that would contradict the official police version of the events."

"But there is no official police version yet," replied Cornelia, tactically dropping Fruitful Willis and Murray Plotkin.

Iserson grinned, glad to get his reporter back. "True, but Whiffet considers the story that the Rodriguez kid apparently told to IAD to be the official police version. He's already charging cover-up and he hasn't even held his first news conference yet."

"What's his evidence? Any clues?"

"Not a whisper. But Herbie's really crowing this time. And, Corney, I think he finds you irresistible. That news conference is scheduled for three o'clock. Why don't you see if he'll talk to you first?"

Cornelia agreed. A visit with Herbert would serve both purposes.

Herbert Whiffet sat in his office on 125th Street and thought about the tape in his safe-deposit box. He was sure he was under surveillance and dared not retrieve it to get another look. Although the quality was poor (the excitable Mr. Rios apparently unable to hold the video recorder steady in the face of an all-nighter at the social club and the sight of Lawanda de Bourbon's *tietas*), Herbert had absolutely not seen a gun in Lawanda's hand when he had viewed the tape on the morning of the shooting. Of course no one was talking about a gun at that point.

What he had seen was a policeman calmly (or so it seemed) pump one shot into Lawanda de Bourbon sending her over the low wall on the roof to tumble to her death. He was sure he would have noticed if she had a gun.

Not that it made a difference at this stage of the proceedings. The cop's posture was clear enough and anyone viewing the tape would assume that he had executed an informant. That in itself was sufficient to support the accusations he was prepared to make at the news conference. This one would not be any one-station affair either. Every local station and representatives from every national bureau would be present. On the platform with him would be the grieving parents, the leader of the black caucus in the State Assembly, one or two respected clergymen and the head of the Marcus Garvey Coalition, sure to be a mayoral candidate in the coming election. It was an impressive crew, the most impressive of Herbert's career, and he intended to make the most of his opportunity.

As he was going over his notes, his private line rang.
"Oh, Cornelia," Herbert stammered when he realized who it was, "how did you get this number?"
"You gave it to me, Herbert," replied the reporter, disarming even on the telephone.
"I did?" Herbert never gave his private number to members of the press although he had always thought of Cornelia as special.
"Yes, Herbert," Cornelia replied playfully, immediately moving the mood from professional to personal.
"Okay," he shrugged, "perhaps I did. Well, Cornelia, now that you've got me, what can I do for you?"
"I'd like to see you. This morning."
"I'm sorry, my dear," Herbert replied sternly. "That isn't possible. I'm not granting any exclusives. No private audiences until after the news conference." Herbert felt a rush of sexual energy from the wielding of power over Cornelia Pembroke, the cream of white-shoe womanhood.
"Come on, Herbert," persisted the reporter, "just fifteen minutes. Besides I want to talk to you about something else too. Something we did together."
Despite the transparency of Cornelia's ploy, Herbert took the next step.
"What thing that we did together?"
"Fifteen minutes, Herbert. I'll come to your office."
"I can't do it, Cornelia. The others will see you come in. I just can't be giving exclusives." He realized that he didn't sound very firm but the reason was solid enough.
"No one has to know," whispered his self-appointed coconspirator. "I'll come in through the back entrance."
"What back entrance?"
"The one that comes through the apartment of the brownstone on 126th Street."
"How did you know about that?" asked the stunned attorney. Had he told her about that as well?
"I'm sorry, my love," giggled Cornelia. "I have to protect my sources." She went for the closer. "So how about it, Herbert? Fifteen minutes. I promise not to break anything before you go public."
Herbert knew he should continue to refuse but, what the hell, what harm could it do?
"All right, Cornelia, fifteen minutes. Be here in an hour."

Why did it have to be a cop?

Phil Gagliardi crushed out another cigarette that was no longer his last. No sense pretending he was going to quit with this case driving him crazy. The worst part was that all the beautiful complexities were the very things that got his detective's nostrils flaring. This one was a beauty, the kind that lends itself to the slow, painstaking sniffing of every fragment, every new trail, the closing off of gate after gate until the truth begins to emerge, a logical form slowly revealed in the half-light of a murder case.

But this was not just a murder case. It was a goddamn IAD investigation. Ten minutes after he finished the interviews the inspector was all over him. Well, what did he think? Did the kid do it on purpose? Was he working for someone? Was he implicated in something? Was it stupidity? An accident? What about the gun? Were D'Angelo and his people involved? Were they popping the dead chick? How soon would his report be ready?

It was all Phil could do to get seventy-two hours to try and put the pieces together. *Seventy-two hours.* Shit, this was the kind of case that could take seventy-two *days*. The first conclusion the detective had drawn was that he would not make it home to Amityville for the duration, and when he did finally straggle in, Vicki would be all over him about only two more years before he can retire on full pension. Who the hell wants to retire at forty-seven?

Under this kind of time pressure, Phil knew that ordering the investigation was the most important thing. The first question, of course, was the kid's motive, for if the rookie had really shot in self-defense, or even what he thought was self-defense, the rest of the shit didn't matter. It didn't mean a thing, who was boffing who, if Lawanda had really aimed a piece at young Jimmy's heart. Since there was no way to get inside the rookie's head, and Phil didn't trust polygraphs (not because of the usual fear of the false negative, but because of the even more damaging false positive), the question of the gun was *numero uno*.

Of course, if Patrolman Rodriguez had had the presence of mind to follow the progress of the gun and not the victim, this entire affair might already be buttoned up and Phil might this very evening sit over a gin and tonic with Vicki having headed off the retirement sermon. As it was, Phil Gagliardi had seventy-two hours to either confirm an implausible alibi or come up with some explanation for the disappearance of the gun before tossing the kid off the same roof.

Okay, if the rookie was telling the truth, what happened to the gun?

Detective First Grade Gagliardi was not going to find the answer to that question in his makeshift office so he hauled himself out of his seat and out of the station, heading for 107th Street. Phil walked instead of taking a car. It was a clear, warm day and a good detective always thinks better on the move. During the ten minutes it took to cover the distance to the scene Phil formed pictures in his mind covering a number of different scenarios.

When he reached the building, Phil flashed his badge at the officer who was guarding the premises. There were barricades around the entire area festooned with placards proclaiming "Do Not Cross—Crime Scene. NYPD." A small walkway had been left so that the occupants of the buildings could come and go. There would be similar barricades on the roof and the officer Phil had acknowledged was a member of but one of the three shifts keeping a twenty-four hour vigil to maintain the purity of the evidence.

Time pressure or not, Phil was determined to keep some method in the investigation so he headed up the stairs to the roof to begin at the beginning. He again flashed his shield to the assigned sentry and walked to the scene of the shooting. The entire area was covered with chalk marks depicting key events and where all the participants stood (and one fell) the morning before.

Phil Gagliardi positioned himself about five feet from the spot and reconstructed the shooting as the rookie had described it. With weapons drawn, Rodriguez and Blakemore had rushed around the corner of the water tank housing, which was a fifteen-foot square, seven-foot high brick structure. They had stopped there—Phil looked at two sets of marks—and encountered Lawanda de Bourbon there—he looked at a third set about six feet away from the others. She had a piece aimed at them and Rodriguez fired once, the impact knocking the girl backwards against the retaining wall there—another set of marks on top of the thirty-inch high barrier—and she fell over. Phil walked to the edge of the wall and peered down to the unobstructed view of the row of chalk-marked garbage cans below.

Uh-huh, he said to himself, turning to examine the water tank housing. The homicide crew had already been over the scene, of course, but a new set of eyes never hurt. Phil examined a spot about three feet up the north face of the structure, highlighted with yet another set of chalk marks. Two bricks had been pulled loose, evidently having been false-fronted as a hiding place.

For a gun? The location would check. Easy to get to for someone on the move. Lawanda de Bourbon would have turned the corner out of sight of her pursuers with enough time to grab the weapon. Phil made a note to ask the coroner if any fragments of brick were found under Lawanda's fingernails.

Phil then looked heavenward. Strange that the helicopter crew had not spotted the chase on the roof. You'd think that the sight of Lawanda tear-assing half-naked might have attracted some attention. Phil made another note.

Back to the actual shooting.

Phil checked the path of Lawanda's fall once again. There was nothing protruding close enough on either the left or the right to impede her progress. Just a straight four stories down. The homicide crew had checked the spot where Lawanda had fallen and most certainly would have spotted a stray piece. Phil would check again, of course, but was not likely to score. No fire escapes either, not in the front, so even if the gun flew out of Lawanda's hand there was nothing to keep it from reaching the ground except the window ledges.

Phil leaned over the edge trying to make a picture. Was it possible that the gun had landed on a window ledge? Where the hell else? They stuck out around nine inches and had little grates around them. Most of the occupants had placed flower pots in the space between the grates and the windows.

The residents of each of the apartments that faced the street had been questioned of course, but no gun had turned up. That was no surprise in this neighborhood, but it meant Rodriguez' alibi had absolutely no corroboration. (Blakemore's word was totally useless—no one believed one cop vouching for another cop, not even other cops.) Of course, he may have thought he saw a gun, but what else could

Lawanda have been holding that looked like a piece? It certainly wasn't a stray article of clothing and nothing was found at the scene to support that theory either.

Shit, Phil breathed, his hopes for a quick solution gone. Okay, what if the kid was lying?

Cornelia Pembroke always felt a thrill when she went to Harlem or Bed-Stuy or any other tough black or Spanish neighborhood. There was this Wild West feeling about it. She never went alone, of course. She was always accompanied by at least two of the biggest, toughest, meanest technicians WRCT had to offer and only ventured on to the street at the site of an event, where the police or other news crews were usually present. But even driving through the ghetto to get to her destination, Cornelia felt at the center of the action, part of the racing pulse of the city.

This visit blended intrigue into the mix. Cornelia was on her way to keep a clandestine rendezvous behind enemy lines, the enemy in this case including her fellow reporters as well as the indigenous population. To minimize the chance of being spotted, she rode in a beat-up Toyota belonging to a member of the crew, unidentified as being affiliated with the station and lacking the tell-tale 'NYP' license plates.

Cornelia and her companions, both black technicians, had taken a circuitous route to the tenement on 126th Street that served as Herbert's private entrance, overshooting the target and approaching from the northwest. Cornelia was slumped down in the back seat, so any set of prying eyes merely saw two beefy guys driving through the neighborhood. Just to be sure, they drove past the entrance of the tenement, checking that no members of the competition were lurking about. Then once around the block and back to the entrance and Cornelia was ready to go.

Before leaving the car, Cornelia and her escorts checked the street once more. It looked like any other street in Harlem, rows of tenements, loitering youth and women with shopping carts making sure to get their marketing done before dark. It seemed as if none of the other crews that were most certainly perched on Herbert's doorstep on 125th Street had thought to stake out 126th.

The man on the passenger side, Willie Moss, a cameraman, turned around.

"Ready?"

Cornelia nodded. "Let's go."

With military precision, both doors flew open and Cornelia and Willie shot across the tiny courtyard and ducked into the vestibule. They were on the street not five seconds. They pushed the buzzer for apartment 3B.

"Who is it?" crackled an electronically garbled voice through the intercom. Cornelia decided this was probably one of ten working intercoms in the entire neighborhood.

"It's Cornelia," she replied loudly.

There was a pause while whoever was on the other end checked her out. After about ten seconds the buzzer rang and Cornelia and Willie headed for the stairs and apartment 3B. The staircase was clean and the walls unmarked by graffiti. When they arrived they pushed the doorbell, also in fine working order. Cornelia saw a speck of light at the peephole as the occupant surveyed the visitors.

Suddenly the door swung open and an angry looking young black woman with straightened hair stood just inside.

"Okay," she barked, "you . . . ," indicating Cornelia, "come in. You stay there."

Willie glared at the sentinel.

"Bullll-shit," he growled. "I ain't hanging out in no hallway for fifteen minutes, sister."

"I ain't your sister," snarled the woman, "and you'll do what I say or the meeting is off."

Ordinarily Cornelia would have prevailed upon her companion to accede to the request, but she understood Willie's reluctance to wait unattended in a hallway on 126th Street, however clean and neat it might be.

She levelled her own glare at the woman. "You tell Herbert," she said evenly, "that Willie waits in the apartment. That is a non-negotiable request."

The black woman started. Who was this white bitch to be making demands? She was lucky enough to have a chance to talk to Mr. Whiffet in the first place.

"You both wait here," she barked again, but the steam was out of it. The woman shut the door and Cornelia and Willie could hear the sound of footsteps. In a moment the woman returned and opened the door once more.

"Okay," she said coldly, "Mr. Whiffet said he can wait in here. But he can't go into the office."

"That's a deal," Cornelia replied. So that's it, she thought. Herbert doesn't want any witnesses, especially a technician who could be wired. Isn't he worried that I'm wired?

In fact, Herbert Whiffet was not the least bit concerned whether Cornelia Pembroke was wired or not. Nor did he care whether Willie Moss was wired. He did not intend to say anything revealing. He simply enjoyed imposing conditions on members of the press who bid for his time. It was one of the trappings of his position.

So, in keeping with the mood, Herbert did not get up when Cornelia strode into his private office through the door that had been fashioned to connect the two buildings. Cornelia noted the lack of chivalry and easily flopped into the over-stuffed leather chair opposite Herbert's desk. She casually crossed her legs making sure that the hem of her dress settled just above her knee.

"Nice of you to see me, Herbert," she said softly but seriously. Brains and legs—how could Herbert resist?

Herbert smiled in return, looking every inch the man in control, but Cornelia knew he was struggling to maintain his even gaze and not let his eyes drift southward.

"Before we talk about the de Bourbon case," she began, reverting to disarming, "I'd like to ask you about something else."

Herbert started to say 'We're not going to talk about the de Bourbon case,' but bit it off. "Is this that 'something else we worked on together?' "

Herbert held a pen in his hands, just below his face, and rolled it alternately forward and back between his fingers. It gave him the look of a deep thinker as well as cutting off his line of sight from the temptation of Cornelia's crossed legs.

Cornelia smiled, wondering if Herbert had learned the pen trick watching 'Perry Mason' re-runs.

"Yes, Herbert, I'd like to ask you about Fruitful Willis. He was the homeless . . ."

"I remember who he was," Herbert snapped, then immediately wondered why he had taken a harsh tone. Annie Holdsworth's perfect face popped into his head, then out again.

Cornelia never blinked. "Do you have any idea what happened to him?"

Herbert rolled the pen again. What was this about? Cornelia could not possibly have pressed so hard for a private meeting to discuss a dead-end story like Fruitful Willis and the old Jew. Herbert lifted the pen another inch, signifying the raising of his guard, and then played along.

"Yes, Cornelia, as a matter of fact I do. He had a run-in with a couple of Korean grocers—the deli closed, you know—and filed another complaint with the Mobilization for the Homeless." Although to Herbert, Fruitful Willis was now just another disgusting bum, an example of the very lowest level of black manhood, the Champion trod softly.

"Do you know what happened?" asked Cornelia, leaning forward, the stretch of her body moving the dress a bit more up her thigh.

Herbert brought his hands down and shifted sideways in his chair. The movement allowed him a quick glance at the lower half of Cornelia's body. Damn, he thought, angry at his weakness, sure she had noticed.

"Clovis Buckworth sent Mr. Willis to me. Unfortunately, this case lacked the *prima facie* rights violation of the first and I was forced to so advise Mr. Willis."

Actually, Herbert had refused to see the bum and had placed an angry call to Clovis Buckworth to complain about the prank, a call that had pleased its recipient to no end.

Cornelia looked disappointed. "So you don't have any idea where he went?"

"No, Cornelia," replied the lawyer with mock patience, "no idea at all."

Herbert changed position again, this time forcing himself to glance away from the reporter. She knows exactly what she's doing, he thought. The bitch. Letting her dress ride up like that.

"Cornelia," he asked, speaking as if the question demonstrated penetrating insight, "why do you care about Fruitful Willis? You couldn't possibly have come here for that."

Cornelia demurely pulled down the hem of her dress so that it regained its original deployment just above her knee. Herbert reflexively followed the motion of her hand.

"No, of course not, Herbert," she replied. "I came about the de Bourbon story. But I'm also thinking of doing a follow-up on Willis. Tracing the plight of one homeless man, his wanderings, his life, that kind of thing."

Herbert Whiffet shook his head. "Doesn't sound like much of a story to me, Cornelia." Herbert leaned back in his chair, the smug look of the man with the winning cards crossing his face. "So I guess you wasted your time on two counts, since I'm not going to talk about the de Bourbon case."

"That's too bad, Herbert. I was hoping you'd comment since we already have a lead on the eyewitness."

Herbert Whiffet didn't move, he didn't blink, he didn't change expression nor break a sweat. But some are born poker players and some are not, and Herbert Whiffet was not. His indecision as to Cornelia's real level of knowledge fairly leapt across the table and Cornelia Pembroke, who *was* a born poker player, knew she had scored.

"You're fishing, Cornelia," smiled Herbert. "You know as well as I that there were no reports of an eyewitness."

"True enough, Herbert. And I take it you are unwilling to discuss the matter further in advance of your news conference."

"That is correct. 3 PM at the New Canaan Baptist Church on St. Nicholas Avenue. I think you'll find it interesting."

"I'm sure I will, Herbert."

Herbert made a show of looking at his watch. "And as much as I love to talk to you, Cornelia, I'm afraid your fifteen minutes are up."

Cornelia rose fluidly, her dress making the slightest *whoosh* against her nylons. Herbert Whiffet felt a distinct twinge in his stomach when he heard the sound. The twinge was followed by the beginnings of a knot, as if he had just finished making a fool of himself. Nonsense. I've got them just where I want them.

There was one more thing.

"Cornelia," he asked, giving in once again, "how did you know about the back door?"

The reporter turned and winked. "The same way I knew about the eyewitness." Then she was through the door and gone.

Herbert's placid demeanor vanished with Cornelia Pembroke. Could she possibly know? She never mentioned a tape. Had Fernando talked? Or sold out? Had one of his people tipped her off? How else could she know about the back door? Maybe she was bluffing about the eyewitness. Maybe she got it from the cops. He picked up the telephone and quickly dialed a familiar number. "Renee Lieberman-Smith, please," he said in his perfect, unethnicized diction when a strange voice answered. "Tell her it's her cousin."

# CHAPTER NINE

The New Canaan Baptist Church had long been a major repository of Harlem's political power. It had achieved notoriety in the sixties as the home base of Lemuel Matthews, its activist pastor, who had gone on to four terms in the state assembly and two in the United States House of Representatives before fleeing the country for Ghana, taking with him approximately five million dollars that the Justice Department was about to accuse him of stealing from the federal government.

The church had kept a low profile throughout the seventies, although Matthews had remained a folk hero. (Stealing five million dollars from the United States Treasury was hardly considered a crime in Harlem.) In the early nineteen-eighties the church appointed Leotis Chestnut as pastor, and the Reverend Mr. Chestnut had strived, with great success, to return the church to its glory days as the center of political activity in the black community.

When Herbert Whiffet was beginning his career as an activist lawyer, he had made contact with the activist pastor and an immediate bond was forged. It was one of those friendships where each of the participants thinks he is hearing his own words as they are spoken by the other. The New Canaan Baptist Church was always available to Herbert Whiffet and Herbert would pick up the cudgels for any unfortunate whom the Rev. Chestnut referred.

Unlike the slight, soft-spoken, light-skinned Herbert Whiffet, Leotis Chestnut stood six-foot-four, was dark-chocolate brown and was blessed with a booming baritone to go with an imperious manner. The Rev. Mr. Chestnut would have sounded impressive while reading the recipe for Chocolate Whizzies off the back of a candy box.

As they both struggled through the mid-nineteen-eighties

to make that leap into public awareness, to be quoted somewhere other than in the *Amsterdam News*, each man took great pains to accommodate the other. Recently, however, success had reared its ugly head and, as the big moment approached, Herbert Whiffet hoped that Leotis Chestnut would not try to horn in on his glory.

This is my case, thought the lawyer, what I've been working for. I don't mind spreading some credit around, but I have a right to get most of the air time. Every time Leotis sees a television camera he sticks his face in front of it and acts like the second coming of Paul Robeson.

The news conference was scheduled to begin in fifteen minutes and Herbert was as nervous as a young actor in his first performance of 'Hamlet.' His shirt was soaked and he prayed that he would remember everything he intended to say. Fully aware that the white reporters would love him to slip up and look foolish, Herbert had spent the last two hours rehearsing his statement in his head.

Through all the internal turmoil, Herbert Whiffet sat with outward calm on the temporary platform erected for this momentous occasion in the church's 'community room,' a large auditorium in the basement. Herbert surveyed the bustle of activity as the television crews set up their lights like so many lab technicians preparing to examine some mysterious new microbe.

The best indication of the importance of the event was the number of requests from leaders of the community for seats on the platform, most of which Herbert had been forced to deny. It was also an indication to Herbert of his growing power—he alone had decided who would receive the coveted invitations to stand behind him as he spoke, members of a chorus of sobriety and outrage.

In his silent prayers for success, Herbert included Booker T. and Mahalia de Bourbon—God should not let them destroy everything that had taken so long to build. Although a couple of Leotis' trusted minions had been assigned to babysit the couple, their behavior at the news conference was an unwelcome wild card. Booker T. had been drinking since noon, claiming to be unable to see the matter through without a taste, and Mahalia was alternately morose and raving. It was no mystery to Herbert that Lawanda had been prompted to leave home at such a tender age. Perhaps the suit and the frock purchased by the church to add respectability to their appearance would have a serendipitous effect. They had certainly been made aware of what was at stake and coached on how to handle the media.

As the high-intensity lights began to burst to life to allow the crews to take readings, the room began to crackle with energy as if it were the electrical equipment and not the people that gave the event its legitimacy. Leotis Chestnut appeared on the platform as though beatifically transported, shaking hands and greeting the faithful, his *sotto voce* remarks carrying to the far reaches of the hall. Herbert frowned as his partner turned up his intensity to match the television lights, and was forced to leave his seat and go through the same charade lest members of the media think that this was a Leotis Chestnut production.

Mercifully for Herbert, who despite his public posture was a rather shy man, there was little time for small talk. Three o'clock was soon upon them and it was time to begin.

Herbert strode to the microphone as the sober and outraged chorus closed ranks behind him. The Rev. Mr. Chestnut managed to secure a place just to the right of the podium, virtually obscuring Alvin Wilkes, the head of the Marcus Garvey Coalition. No man with mayoral aspirations can afford to be upstaged so perfunctorily and a well-placed jab in the small of the Reverend's back cleared an opening through which Mr. Wilkes' sober and outraged face could be plainly visible to all.

Herbert waited until the reporters took seats in the folding chairs set up in six rows facing the podium. Herbert noticed Cornelia sitting in the third row, wearing the same dress, with only a blink of eye contact to remind him of their earlier meeting.

Clearing his throat, about to begin the most important speech of his life, Herbert Whiffet cursed his fortune not to have been blessed with Leotis' commanding baritone and inspirational delivery. Herbert need not have worried. Just hanging around Leotis Chestnut all these years had dropped his voice an octave.

Pausing just a moment to let the tension hang in the air, Herbert placed his hands on either side of the podium, now filled with a dozen microphones.

"Ladies and gentlemen, I would like to begin with a prepared statement after which I will take your questions." Herbert was pleased with himself. The first line had come out serious and tough, no sign of nerves. Buoyed by the victory, Herbert plunged in.

"I have asked members of the press here today to witness the birth of a great coalition, a coalition formed by these men behind me . . ." Herbert extended his arm, open handed, palm up, to indicate the august band bunched at his shoulder. "A coalition forged from injustice, from blatant racism, and from the *execution* of a young and beautiful black woman by the police of this city."

Herbert paused to let the initial salvo register. That was some opening, he decided. Leotis could not have done it better.

"The *official* police version, the *cover-up* version, the *lying* version of the shooting of Lawanda de Bourbon, is that her executioner claimed that this young woman, roused from sleep at 6 AM, dressed only in her night clothes, and a *gun.* Well, ladies and gentlemen, Lawanda de Bourbon had no gun, and we in the community have documentary proof that Lawanda de Bourbon had no gun. Furthermore, we have proof the executioner calmly walked up to her and pulled the trigger, shooting an unarmed eighteen-year-old girl in the chest, causing her to fall four stories to her death."

There was a soft wail from the chorus. Herbert paused to allow Mahalia de Bourbon's grief to punctuate his remarks. Please, he prayed, that's perfect. Please don't scream. But the de Bourbons were playing their parts well and the wail subsided.

"And why, you ask, would the police execute an unarmed teen-ager on the roof of an apartment building, why would they shoot this young girl down in *cold blood*?"

Another wail, just a bit louder this time. "Because, ladies and gentlemen, she was one of their own, on the police payroll. Lawanda de Bourbon knew things about police corruption, about the involvement of the detectives of Manhattan North in narcotics trafficking and she was *shot down* to ensure her silence."

Mahalia de Bourbon's escalating wail was drowned out by every reporter suddenly screaming the same question at Herbert Whiffet.

"What evidence do you have to support the allegation of police involvement in narcotics?"

Herbert raised his hands to quiet the crowd. "There will be

time for questions." He heard a rumble emitted from the chorus and in that moment Herbert Whiffet saw his dream fulfilled. It was just a matter of time.

"Even now, as we sit here, the police department, abetted by the *DISTRICT ATTORNEY OF NEW YORK COUNTY*, is falling all over itself to *white*wash this execution, this *cold-blooded murder*." Another wail, this time accompanied by "Lawdy, mah little girl." Herbert decided to finish up and get to the questions before Mahalia de Bourbon lost it altogether.

"So we," indicating the chorus, "the citizens of this community DEMAND, not request, DEMAND, that the mayor or the governor or even the president take appropriate action to bring to trial and convict the murderers of Lawanda de Bourbon."

The lawyer paused once more. The room was still. Even Mahalia de Bourbon.

"Now." Herbert Whiffet placed his hands flat on the podium. "Questions."

Each reporter screamed the same question once again.

Herbert nodded in response. "Yes, we have proof. We of the African-American community have evidence to support our charges. The police department and the *DISTRICT ATTORNEY* are systematically engaged in a cover-up to hide the involvement of the police in narcotics trafficking."

"Will you turn this evidence over to the proper authorities?" asked a reporter.

Herbert Whiffet looked at the man as though addressing a mental defective. "Are you serious? Give over our evidence to the very people who are trying to cover their crimes? We may be African-American, sir, but we are not stupid."

Another rumble from the chorus.

"What about the FBI?" asked another reporter. "Will you turn over your evidence to them?"

Herbert shook his head. "Until we of the community are satisfied of the commitment of the Justice Department to *JUSTICE*, we do not intend to let any evidence out of our possession."

Cornelia Pembroke raised her hand and, reflexively, Herbert acknowledged her. Before she spoke there was again that microsecond of eye contact that told Herbert that Cornelia thought he was either bluffing or just plain lying. Herbert felt his stomach tighten as she asked her question.

"What form does this evidence take? Of the shooting, I mean. You used the term documentary evidence. That would imply an eyewitness."

Herbert stared at Cornelia as Annie Holdsworth once again flashed in his head. "I am not prepared to discuss specifics at this time. We have no intention of facilitating the tasks of those who wish to cover up this crime."

The slight drop-off in his partner's energy all he needed, the Reverend Mr. Chestnut moved to Herbert's side.

"We are all here," he boomed, "to serve notice on *allll* members of the power structure, that a *newww* day has dawned and from now forward, *noo* black man—or woman—need *fearrr* the police, for the Day Of Judgment has *ARRIVED*."

A cheer arose from those on the platform with some *Amen's* sprinkled in to boot.

He did it, Herbert growled to himself. He waited for the very end and then he did it. There was no doubt in his mind that every feed of the event would include Leotis Chestnut's sermonette—and the impression the two co-activists had held a joint news conference. Then, his father's lessons springing forth, Herbert felt ashamed and remonstrated himself for the sin of vanity. Certainly there was enough renown to share. After all, Leotis had provided the facilities and the staff, and had paid his dues with years of working for the same things as had he. This was a crusade of conviction, not personality, and Leotis Chestnut was an invaluable resource in the struggle.

Still, Herbert felt himself cringe just slightly when Leotis put his arm around him, a gesture of solidarity duly recorded by the media.

As expected, the charges raised at the news conference were the lead story on every local news broadcast and even received prominent play on the network shows. The addition of charges of police corruption was a brilliant stroke, adding national significance to an otherwise lurid but limited case of questionable police conduct. With the war on drugs among the country's top priorities, complicity in drug dealing by the New York City Police Department was a front page story.

In the face of such charges, the response by the mayor and the police commissioner that an internal investigation was proceeding and that all charges would be investigated and any guilty party punished sounded hollow indeed. After all, who trusts a fox to investigate crimes in the hen house? Howls of 'fix' and 'cover-up' began to rise from every corner of the city. Lawanda de Bourbon's posthumous bandwagon—those who shared the outrage at the shameful violation of the young woman's rights—grew by the hour.

Phil Gagliardi took in the news in the squad room of the 24th, watching on an ancient black and white set.

The detective heaved a sigh. Just what I need, he grunted, although the news conference did not come at all as a surprise. No activist worth a damn would let this one go by.

Not that Phil believed Herbert Whiffet's version of the events for a second. Unlike most of the viewing audience, Phil had the benefit of the facts and eighteen years experience and he was sure this was no conspiracy.

First of all, the coroner had confirmed the presence of traces of brick and mortar under Lawanda de Bourbon's fingernails as well as fragments of fingernail on the wall where Lawanda had apparently pulled the bricks out during her flight. That didn't prove a thing, of course, but since nothing had been stashed, it meant something had been removed, reinforcing the gun theory.

Second, the helicopter had not spotted the chase because there was a report, unfounded as it turned out, that there was a sniper on the roof of a building on 109th Street. The report had been filed by a civilian, so it was safe to assume that it was not a contrivance to divert attention from a hit. The chopper crew had turned its attention to the events on 107th just in time to catch Lawanda's swan dive on to the garbage cans.

Third, and most important, although Phil did not know what, if anything, was going on in Manhattan North, the chances of D'Angelo or anyone else in the command using Jimmy Rodriguez to ice a dangerous informant were absolutely zero. Rodriguez and Blakemore had been assigned to the roof only fifteen minutes before the raid by the Feds, who insisted, as always, on running the show. Rodriguez, from everything Phil had dug up, was the Puerto Rican Mr. Clean—an associate's degree in criminal justice, no drugs, no alcohol, engaged to a nurse (wasting the lady killer theory), lived frugally, totally within his means, and helped support his mother and sister. Unless this kid had a Swiss bank account somewhere, Whiffet was just blowing smoke—there was no evidence of drug involvement.

Phil sighed again for, unfortunately, in a case like this the facts didn't really matter. In a case like this the department—and any of its members unlucky enough to stumble into the public spotlight—were guilty unless incontrovertible evidence could be produced to the contrary. The right of due process simply didn't exist for an accused cop. Oh, he might get off in the courts, but never in the minds of the public, or even with the brass. An accused cop might as well retire and go into another line of work, unless he had a lifelong ambition to be assigned to the mounted division, cleaning the stables.

Phil reviewed the reports of the interviews with the tenants of the building where Lawanda took the plunge. As expected, no one knew shit about any gun. What gun? Was there a gun? You mean the girl had a gun? There were six apartments that had ledges where the gun might have come to rest, although Phil still could not figure out what kind of fucked up trajectory the weapon must have taken to land in some lady's flower pot. Of the six apartments, three of them contained tenants who, in the detective's opinion, might avoid reporting finding a piece. Those residents could be watched, of course, but nothing was likely to turn up in the forty-eight hours he had left.

Without a recovered weapon, Phil could not even propose the theory. An official police version that claimed a gun existed but was missing because the department believed it had fallen on a nine-inch window ledge was unlikely to silence the howlers. Phil made a note to visit the building again and chat with the tenants. That was the best he could do.

The one thing in the news conference that had interested the detective was when that hot chick from WRCT had asked about an eyewitness. The same theory had occurred to Phil, but a canvass of those who lived on the block had turned up zilch. Perhaps it might be a good idea to plant a plainclothes guy to spend some time in the local bars to see if anyone was talking.

Phil laughed to himself and opened the reports again. Wouldn't it be a kick if an eyewitness did turn up? God knows, I'd love to shut Whiffet's big mouth.

While Phil Gagliardi was fantasizing about an eyewitness, Fernando Rios was sitting in La Cantina polishing off a beer. Pepe had the television on, but instead of the usual sports or Spanish-language programming, Pepe, in a first for La Cantina, had turned to the local news broadcast. After all, the shooting of the *negrita* was a big story in the neighborhood and speculation as to the facts of the case had become a more popular pastime than trying to decide if the Iron Sheik would polish off Hulk Hogan. Not that the denizens of La Cantina, or anyone else in the neighborhood for that matter, had any doubts that the shooting was a police hit.

While the others watched with interest, Fernando sat tight-lipped, feeling certain he was being ripped off by his lawyer and agent. The sloughing off of the question about an eyewitness was particularly galling. *He* was the eyewitness. *He* should be up there on that platform. *He* should be on television answering questions from the press.

True to his word, Fernando had not spoken to anyone about his adventure in film-making but now, thirty-six hours later, his trust in his agent had eroded and Fernando's deductive mind was active once again. What could he do if Whiffet was screwing him? He no longer had his evidence. Fernando was suddenly furious with himself for letting the precious tape out of his possession, a fury that could not be slaked by just another beer. Fernando ordered a shot of whiskey to note the significance of the problem and continued to deduce.

As he felt the pleasant burn of the whiskey on his throat, the solution, simple and obvious, popped into Fernando's fertile brain.

"*Conejo*," he muttered, ordering another shot. Fernando laughed out loud as Pepe poured. Fernando was known to be a bit *loco* so Pepe suppressed his curiosity as to the source of his customer's mirth.

Fernando polished off the second shot as quickly as the first and fleshed out his plan. So what if he gave up the tape? He had *made* the tape. He was the eyewitness! If Whiffet tried to screw him, Fernando would go to the news people himself. Ha! Let Whiffet stick that one up his ass.

So taken was Fernando with his latest stratagem that it was all he could do not to call up some television station right then, the one with the little *chiquita* that had asked about the eyewitness, about him.

But no. That would not be smart. No need for that yet. The first thing to do was to have another meet with his agent. Fernando decided to go the next morning. It was only a short walk to 125th Street.

Renee Lieberman-Smith was also upset with Herbert Whiffet and for much the same reason as was Fernando Rios. As she watched his performance, on WRCT of course, Renee wondered for the first time whether she was being used. Even as the thought popped into her mind, she was ashamed of herself.

Can't be, Renee decided. This is just the way he has to handle it. Surely he was right about being careful. If she was seen with him, especially in some conspiratorial setting, she would probably be fired and Herbert's credibility would be shot. Still, it would be nice to get a little recognition, or at least be allowed some type of participation. After all, she mused, it's me who's running the risks.

Just hours before, she had taken a call from Herbert at the office. Not that there had been a risk of the secretary recognizing Herbert's voice, but who knew when the DA might bug a couple of telephones? Leaks were always a problem and the district attorney had every right to record calls to and from his offices.

But Renee, as she always had, ignored the personal danger and had given Herbert the information he wanted. Even though she was not involved in the de Bourbon case, it was a hot item and word of any progress was sure to make its way around the place. As far as she knew, the police had not turned up an eyewitness and so she passed that information along. Herbert had seemed relieved, a curious reaction for a man trying to obtain justice. Renee would have thought an eyewitness invaluable in a case where the police were sure to concoct a story to obscure their culpability.

Without giving the matter too much thought, Renee concluded that Herbert must have his reasons. She imagined him deep in counsel with others engaged in the struggle and wished she could be there with them. One of these days, she decided, she would resign from the DA's office and do some real legal work. Then she could be out on the front lines where she belonged.

Imagining herself the Rosa Luxemburg of the equal rights movement, Renee poured herself the evening's first scotch and tried to decide if she should order dinner from the local Chinese restaurant or make herself a tuna sandwich.

Clovis Buckworth also watched WRCT that night, something he had not done since the Fruitful Willis business, perhaps on the theory of out of sight, out of guilt. But Cornelia Pembroke herself had called that very day and asked for an appointment and Clovis was all too happy to renew his viewership with the station.

As he watched Herbert Whiffet sail through his litany of charges, Clovis chuckled and shook his head. Old Herbert had sure come a long way. In the early days, the struggling young activist lawyer had to scramble around to find candidates for his services, to scrounge for those whose rights he could protect. In those days, when no one gave a damn about Herbert Whiffet, he was often forced to pay for tips, in effect buying his cases. Not that Clovis had ever accepted any money, "referral fees," Herbert had called it, "just like doctors or any other professionals," but many others had.

Well, one thing was clear. Herbert Whiffet had paid his last referral fee. After the dust clears from this one, Herbert might end in public office somewhere. Clovis shook his head again. Mayor Whiffet. Whew! On the day Herbert gets elected mayor, I go back to Newport.

When the camera switched to Cornelia Pembroke asking her eyewitness question, Clovis leaned forward. God, she was so pretty. He doubted if she would look as good in person; they never did.

The shooting of Lawanda de Bourbon was right up there with the World Series in its ability to arouse public interest and debate. In fact, the point of view taken by a member of the body politic in regard to such an event reveals a great deal about that person's social philosophy, background and perspective on supply side economics. In the suburbs, for example, an overwhelming majority of the white, upper-middle-class residents common to such communities were of the view that the police have a dirty job to do and generally do it honestly and fairly, and that if Lawanda de Bourbon was shot on a rooftop during a narcotics raid, she most certainly had done something to deserve it. Members of inner-city ghettos, on the other hand, take for granted that cops are universally dishonest and racist and would think nothing of murdering a young black woman and then lying to conceal the crime.

In one particular group, however, neither of those rather simplistic alternatives represented the prevailing view. This group was more sophisticated in these matters than any random group of citizens, more than the mayor, the governor or the president, more than Herbert Whiffet, Cornelia Pembroke, or Irwin Pzytriek. In fact, lacking the investigative tools available to Phil Gagliardi, this group had reached similar conclusions as had the detective, both in terms of the facts of the case and its eventual outcome.

In the day room at Rikers Island, the assembled inmates, who express their opinions of the day's events with gusto, roared as they watched Herbert Whiffet recite his charges on the communal television. The local news was a must for the prisoners since crime always gets top billing. Although they would never admit it for attribution, the former ghetto-dwellers at Rikers had much the same take on the de Bourbon shooting as the white suburbanites. No way some dirty narcs would put up a rookie to pull the trigger. No way. Either Lawanda had a piece or the kid thought she did.

"I'd a been shook up too," crowed Termite Jackson, doing two-to-five for breaking and entering, "lookin' at them bouncin' titties. The cop's gun musta gone off when his dick twitched."

Almost every member of this ultimate captive audience heartily agreed.

Sitting at the rear of this astute group of social observers, feet up on another chair, hands clasped behind his head, a position of relaxation that neither the guards nor the inmates dared disturb, was one of the few who did not appreciate Termite's humor. Ali Abdul Akbar, Triple A or Trips to his friends or members of the media, Mr. Akbar to everyone else, found the entire affair immensely irritating and Ali Abdul's interest in the Lawanda de Bourbon shooting was not simply academic. Ali Abdul had decided that Lawanda de Bourbon had been lucky—one bullet, quick death. After hearing the revelations of Lawanda's relationship to the local police, Ali Abdul Akbar had imagined many slower, exquisitely more painful ways for Lawanda to die. Even from prison Triple A could have seen to it. For although bail had been denied, Ali Abdul Akbar still ran the Ghosts with Tsarist autocracy and Lawanda de Bourbon, whom he had granted the appellation of 'Diana,' had provided him with any number of memorable evenings. It had occurred to him more than once in the past twenty-four hours that his very presence in Rikers, with its concomitant forced association with low-lifes and morons, may have been a direct result of Diana's big mouth.

One does not rise above his fellows in Akbarian fashion without the ability to recognize opportunity, and to Ali Abdul, Diana's dive to the garbage where she belonged fairly reeked of opportunity. Since hearing of the event from a sympathetic (and well paid) guard only ninety minutes after it happened, Ali Abdul Akbar had been trying to find a way to make the shooting work for him. Triple A was no fool, and facing twenty to life as an accessory to second-degree murder, he knew he needed something to turn the tide his way.

Despite the distaste with which he watched Diana's story, the lawyer's speech gave him an idea. As the idea flowered, a big smile flowered along with it and Ali Abdul's gold incisor gleamed.

Mr. Akbar slowly pulled his way to his feet and sauntered to the public telephone in the corner of the room. The telephone was the most precious item in the entire prison, and although every call was routinely recorded, inmates waited on line for hours in order to gain some small, precious contact with the outside world.

Mr. Akbar, however, had not struggled to reach a position of prestige and authority to stand on telephone lines in the Rikers day room. Mr. Akbar walked to the front of the line and made a quick motion with his thumb across his throat. The Puerto Rican car thief dared not even an expression of disapproval, but immediately terminated his conversation and left the instrument to Mr. Akbar. Ali Abdul nodded perfunctorily in thanks and placed a call to a trusted associate.

After some coded small talk which told Triple A that the Ghosts were still in a tizzy over Diana, he issued a simple directive.

"I want to see that lawyer—Whiffet. Get him here tomorrow."

# CHAPTER TEN

As fascinating as the intricacies of the Lawanda de Bourbon shooting may have been, not everyone considered the case the focus of their existence. For some, the exigencies of their daily lives outweighed the scandal.

In the weeks since Murray Plotkin had abandoned New York for the life of a professional grandparent in Boca Raton, Clarissa Taylor had sought a way to maintain the standard of living that her now-defunct employment had provided.

Clarissa had been judicious in spending her severance pay, restricting the family to bare necessities until such time as some continuity could be established. Even so, the requirements of a family of four in Forest Hills were such that the actual savings that Clarissa was able to realize were minimal. Rent and utilities were substantially fixed and what little could be saved on food and luxuries (like dry cleaning) were eaten up by the costs of seeking another job.

Since she was well known to the other merchants in the old neighborhood, particularly those who had frequented Murray's, she began her quest there. Although she received universal sympathy for her plight, none of the shopkeepers had any work to offer, particularly at anything close to what Clarissa had earned at Murray's. The only tangible result of the visit was a referral from Dr. Armenakis, the optometrist. His brother-in-law ran a restaurant in Brooklyn and had constant difficulty in securing honest help. The doctor had called his brother-in-law and given Clarissa a rave recommendation. The brother-in-law expressed immediate interest and an appointment was made for the following day.

"Now Clarissa," warned the optometrist, "my brother-in-law can't pay you what Murray paid you, but he isn't a cheapskate and he knows you're a friend of mine." He wrote down the address on a piece of paper. "Do you know where this is?"

Clarissa looked at the address and shook her head.

Dr. Armenakis laughed. "I'm not surprised. It's in Mill Basin. It might be a bit of a trip."

'A bit of a trip' turned out to be a two-hour-and-fifteen-minute serpentine journey through the New York City Transit System. Three trains, a bus and a four-block walk later, Clarissa Taylor found herself on the doorstep of a one-story sprawling building surrounded by a parking lot. A large neon sign displaying the name of the establishment, 'Mill Basin American Restaurant,' flashed overhead. Clarissa, a prudent woman, had left herself more than enough time for the trip, almost two hours, but still found herself twenty-five minutes late.

As she had walked from the bus stop, Clarissa had been aware of strange, sidelong glances from the few pedestrians she passed. Clarissa had nodded pleasantly and said hello but was either ignored or greeted with twisted, tight-lipped smiles. Everyone she had encountered had been white.

Clarissa took a deep breath and entered the restaurant. The Mill Basin American Restaurant was a glorified diner, the type of place that features a ten-page menu with every variety of ethnic food to be found in New York. Being near the water, the document proclaimed, 'Fresh Fish Our Specialty,' and featured a large, smiling piscine creature that a patron was to believe simply could not wait to grace his plate.

As it was between breakfast and lunch, only a few diners occupied the tables and booths. What little conversation there was ceased when Clarissa walked inside. Instead, she was subjected to the same scrutiny as on the street. Clarissa headed for the cashier as tentative chatter started up once again.

"I'm looking for Mr. Kaye," she said politely. "My name is Clarissa Taylor."

The cashier, a rail thin white woman of indeterminate age whose teased, dyed blond hair seemed to be a vestige of the Kennedy administration, looked Clarissa up and down.

"You got an appointment? Mr. Kaye is a busy man."

"Yes, I do," replied Clarissa, hoping against hope that Mr. Kaye would be a pleasant surprise.

"Chester!" the woman called out suddenly. "Someone to see you."

Chester Kaye (nee Kakotonis) emerged from the back, every bit the man who would own the Mill Basin American Restaurant. About forty-five, Chester stood five and one-half feet tall and would have been bald if not for the strands of hair just above the back of his neck that he combed forward, giving him the effect of wearing a hat. He wore checked polyester slacks and a sport shirt with a huge, flaring collar, another remnant of an era gone by. Clarissa felt as if she were caught in a time warp.

Chester Kaye strode to the front of the store as purposefully as could a man of his appearance. He seemed affable enough and looked at Clarissa straight on, a welcoming smile on his face.

"Hello," he said, extending his hand, "you must be Clarissa." The cashier sat on her stool watching them as if observing some disagreeable ritual of a primitive tribe.

Clarissa ignored the woman and focused on the friendly face. "Yes, Mr. Kaye. It's very nice to meet you."

Chester Kaye looked at his watch, a huge Rolex strapped around a chubby wrist. "Took you a while to get here, huh?" he said without a hint of accusation. "Probably had trouble finding the place."

"Oh, no," Clarissa replied quickly, not wanting to appear to be unable to follow directions, "I found it easily enough. I just didn't realize how long I would have to wait for the bus."

"The bus?" Chester's eyes seemed to open wider. "You mean you came here by bus? Subway too? Don't you have a car?"

No, my Cadillac is in the shop, thought Clarissa, never changing expression. Who the hell has a car in New York?

"No, I'm afraid I don't," she replied sweetly.

Chester Kaye shook his head as if Clarissa had just informed him that she had contracted a rare disease. "No car, huh? Ronnie never told me."

"Is that a problem?" she asked, knowing it was.

Chester's expression had deteriorated to funereal. He seemed like a decent man, but Mill Basin had little in common with the rest of New York. It was as if Clarissa Taylor was applying for a job in a suburb of Johannesburg.

"Well, Clarissa, here's the story. As you have seen, the buses don't run too often and they're even worse on the weekends. I don't even want to think about the subways. The job I have open requires both Saturday and Sunday. Weekend pays more, of course, but if you have to take the subway and the bus . . ."

Clarissa was suddenly exhausted, facing another two hours plus trip to get home. This was a wasted day, wasted at a time when every day was precious, when every day had to be put to maximum use, when every day without pay put her family one step closer to poverty.

"I'm sure I could make do on the subways, Mr. Kaye," she said, more out of reflex than conviction.

Chester shook his head sadly. Clarissa glanced to her left and detected a hint of a smile in the corners of the cashier's mouth.

"I'm sorry, Clarissa," the little man said, pronouncing sentence, "I just don't think it would work out. There would be too many days that you just couldn't get here."

So there it was, the end of a four-minute job interview. That worked out to over an hour of travel for every minute of Chester Kaye's precious time.

After her misadventure in Mill Basin, Clarissa tried more obvious avenues of approach in a search for suitable employment. She canvassed the merchants in her neighborhood, registered with employment agencies, read and followed up the want ads and signed up for unemployment insurance, the last as much for the twenty-six week stipend provided by the state as for the actual prospect of obtaining work.

It was an exhausting labor, much harder than actually working, and wherever she went the story was the same. Clarissa Taylor could not expect to earn what she had earned previously and, what's more, her prospects for finding work at all were not good. She lacked education, training and marketable skills and there was an enormous pool of unskilled labor that competed for what little work there was, a pool consisting of younger people without three children and an apartment in Forest Hills to support.

Clarissa found that her address and previous salary worked against her. Many of those with whom she was now forced to deal, especially her fellow blacks, seemed pleased that an upitty nigger had been brought down. At her labor department interview, the woman with whom she spoke was so incredulous at her income from Murray's that she requested verification from the tax department.

Through these first weeks of struggle, the kids saved Clarissa's sanity.

"Don't worry, Mom," Matthew had said, the man of the house, "we'll get by. We'll all work and chip in and you'll get a good job. Somebody out there will know a good thing when they see it."

Unfortunately, Matthew was not sufficiently schooled in economics to understand how precarious was the family's fate. In order to support the treasured apartment in Forest Hills, Clarissa had to bring in a certain amount of money. If she accepted a job for less, she was effectively removing herself from the market, thus guaranteeing a less than subsistence level income. If she refused low-paying work in the hope of finding something better, she depleted the family's ever more finite resources.

It wasn't long before Clarissa realized that one job would not do the trick. If she worked two jobs and the children took care of the housework, and each other, they might just make out. But Clarissa was having scant success finding one job, let alone two.

One day, at the labor department of all places, Clarissa's fortunes seemed to change. There was an opening for a cashier at a discount shoe store in Jamaica. The neighborhood was terrible and the pay not much better, but at least it was work. Clarissa took the referral card and headed immediately for the appointment.

In another stroke of good fortune, the shoe store was not too far from her apartment and easily accessible by bus. If she was lucky enough to land this one, she would still be close enough to home to spend some time with the kids as well as to look for supplementary work. Clarissa's spirits were high when she arrived at the bus stop. Maybe things might work out after all.

Even devastated, post-apocalyptic Jamaica Avenue was not enough to dull her enthusiasm. Although it had been years since Clarissa Taylor had been forced to brave the broken-bottle, litter and derelict-strewn streets of the ghetto, she was a veteran urban warrior and street skills, once acquired, are never completely lost. She picked her way through the carnage, maintaining the right balance between non-aggression and 'don't fuck with me.'

Clarissa turned on to 164th Street and immediately encountered her destination. Hot Feet was typical of Jamaica's retail establishments: cheap merchandise, security guards at the entrance to discourage light fingers, top-of-the-line iron gates to be pulled shut and locked as soon as the store was closed. The store stocked hundreds of styles and seemed particularly popular with teen-age girls, about ten of whom were trying on the hottest new styles that Hot Feet had to offer, accompanied by the usual giggling and pubescent sexual banter.

Clarissa told one of the guards that she was there about a job.

"That's cool, Mama," the man replied, looking Clarissa up and down. "We could use some new blood around here. You got to see Russell. He be in the back."

Clarissa nodded, ignoring the stare. Being called 'Mama' like that reminded her of Freeman. She wondered for a moment what had become of him, whether or not he was even still alive. By the time she reached the back of the store and knocked on the locked office door, Freeman had once again receded into pre-history.

The door swung open and revealed an immense black man. He was at least six-foot-six with a girth that seemed as large.

"Yes?" he asked in a high-pitch voice that made Clarissa start.

"I'm here about the cashier's job. From the labor department . . ."

The giant smiled. "Good, good. We need someone right away. What's your name, honey?"

Although it was difficult to guess the giant's age, he was definitely younger than Clarissa, which didn't make the 'honey' any more appealing.

"Clarissa Taylor."

The giant extended a paw. "Hi, Clarissa, I'm Russell. Russell McKey. Pleased to meet you."

Clarissa watched her hand disappear in Russell's, although she was surprised at the gentleness of his grip. They spent the next five minutes discussing her experience and the particulars of the job. Clarissa decided to avoid difficulty and lied about how much she had made at Murray's, cutting the figure by half.

"Well, Clarissa," laughed Russell the giant, "we can't pay that much here."

"That's okay, Mr. McKey, I just want the work."

"Honey," laughed the giant once more, "you want it, you got it. And don't call me Mr. McKey. Make me feel old and fat."

For the first time since she got off the bus, traces of a smile appeared at the corners of Clarissa's mouth. There was something 'down home' about Russell McKey and, despite the 'honey,' something ingenuous as well. Clarissa generally had good instincts about people and she trusted this huge man with the incongruous voice.

"Thank you, Russell," she replied. "I'll take it."

"Great!" exulted the giant. Russell proceeded to outline the particulars; five-day week, ten to six, then alternating Saturdays and Sundays.

"Now one last thing," said the giant, dropping his voice half an octave to denote seriousness, "this isn't Park Avenue like you're used to. This here is Jamaica. You best keep yo' eyes open, 'specially when yo' going home from work. And you got to watch yo'self in the store. We been held up, you know. If you see anyone looks suspicious, just give the high sign to Rudy or whoever's at the door. They'll know what to do. But whatever happens, honey, you just be cool, you dig?"

Clarissa smiled and nodded. "Don't worry Russell. I'm no lamb."

"Okay then," replied the giant, his voice returning to normal, "see you in the morning."

There is an exultation in getting work that goes beyond the specifics of the job. Obtaining work satisfies a fundamental need, just above food and shelter on the primal scale. It demonstrates usefulness, belonging, and function. It gives hope for the future. It has been argued that the most insidious aspect of public welfare is that, by replacing work, it robs the recipient of more than it provides. Although Clarissa Taylor lacked a degree in social psychology, her sense of fundamental truths was sufficiently acute to understand that her new position at Hot Feet was cause for celebration.

When the children arrived home from school on that warm May afternoon, they discovered that their Mom had packed a picnic and, after a quick change of clothes, they set off for an outing in Forest Park. As Clarissa watched Matthew, Veronica and Jeanette run and laugh, their futures now so tenuous, she vowed to continue to push ahead, to do whatever was necessary to ensure that her children would never have to face the job market with no education, no training or no skills.

So forward thinking was Clarissa Taylor that when she got the telephone call from the woman at the television station asking for an interview, she had no idea what it was about.

For Fruitful Willis the downspiral continued. Although he was, in fact, no worse off than before his score at Plotkin's of Flatbush, the drop in his recent fortunes only emphasized how sweet life had been for those blissful weeks in front of the deli. After his failed effort to see his lawyer, Fruitful had given up on Lexington Avenue and realized that his survival skills would once again be put to the test. The man with rights realized to his chagrin that someone must guarantee those rights in order that they have any meaning, and no guarantor was currently available for Fruitful Willis.

As Fruitful walked the streets in search of a suitable location to ply his trade, he noted again how the ranks of his fellows had swelled. He was also struck by two other changes in the competition. First, most of those seeking public supplication as homeless were *young*, little more than kids. How could they have become homeless in such a short time? It had taken Fruitful almost ten years to become a bum. Second, these new, young homeless were . . . educated . . . well spoken. Most of these guys didn't seem disadvantaged at all. Yet there they were, taking the best corners, armed with the obligatory beat-up paper coffee cup to receive their alms, plying their raps on passersby and, when no one was looking, rousting Fruitful Willis worse than the cops ever did. (One of the guys actually asked people for change to pay the mortgage on his condominium. What happened to just asking to 'git somethin' to eat?')

Whatever the reason for the logarithmic increase in street people, Fruitful Willis did not have the resources to fight this new wave for uptown territory. They were younger and stronger and had the same rights to use the public thoroughfares as had Fruitful. So, like a top, Fruitful was spun rudely and steadily downtown, headed inexorably for the human landfill of the Bowery. As only those who had experienced its terrors can understand, the Bowery is an awful place, the spot where every category of vermin, human and otherwise, congregate to feed on the weakest and the most helpless.

When Fruitful was evicted from Union Square by yet another young and well-educated member of the homeless, panic began to set in. Fruitful feared and hated the Bowery. As he moved farther and farther downtown, he began to look quickly from side to side to spot predators. His eyes bugged. He walked bent over in an attempt to be inconspicuous. For a few moments he even considered going to a city shelter.

The irony, which eluded Fruitful Willis, a man with a limited sense of such things, was that he would have been much better off if he had never been granted rights at all; if he had remained a bum. The moment society changed Fruitful's designation and granted him rights, thus removing the traditional stigma that was attached to his profession, society also made that profession more attractive to hordes of others. And, with the laws of nature remaining unaffected by the laws of man, the 'fittest' in this new, destigmatized sub-culture dominated the others. Thus the charity that was intended by this change in status was greedily gobbled up by those for whom it was never intended in the first place.

So the man with rights but no guarantor headed for the land of disease and vomit, of outsized rats who thought nothing of chewing on a sleeping man's foot, of passing teens who might set a man on fire, of men who protected nonexistent possessions with old razor blades and pieces of broken glass. Hope had never been a luxurious commodity for Fruitful Willis, but what little he may have had was evaporating as the malignant magnet of the Bowery pulled him in.

# CHAPTER ELEVEN

The following day, Lawanda plus two, Cornelia Pembroke began at the Mobilization for the Homeless. She had decided to follow up the Plotkin/Willis affair on her own and, if Iserson still refused to air the piece, she would shop it as a print article, as Karen Pzytriek if necessary.

She arrived at the large, neo-Gothic Upper West Side church at 7:30 AM. This Buckworth fellow said he got to work early and Karen had to get this over with before Cornelia was expected on the de Bourbon case. Even at that delicate hour, the section of the church that had been cordoned off to provide space for the Mobilization was crowded with people, mostly families it seemed, and surprisingly young. Was it possible that this group of relatively well-dressed men, women and children were typical of the organization's clientele? Karen had expected to see a parade of Fruitful Willises moaning and raving in the hallways.

The families eyed her as she walked down the hall. The women particularly stared at her clothing, the men seemed ashamed, the children curious. All bore the alert, suspicious look of creatures in the wild where constant vigilance is required for survival.

Karen was equally surprised when she knocked on the open door to Buckworth's office and looked inside. Clovis Buckworth, except for the rings of perspiration under his arms that stained his open-necked, button-down blue oxford shirt, seemed rather studious and benign. He appeared to be of average height, average weight and average age—in fact, just plain average. He sat behind an institutional-gray desk in a beat-up wooden chair that looked like a board of education discard, speaking in Spanish with a young woman sitting across from him.

Buckworth looked up when she appeared. He reached for

his glasses then stopped. His face began to turn a soft but deepening pink.

"Excuse me," he said, his eyes flicking her way then back to the woman, "I'll be done in a second."

"No, please," Karen replied, "whenever you have a chance." Although she was in a hurry, she suddenly did not want to be put ahead of the families in the hall.

Clovis Buckworth smiled. "Really," he said, "it'll only be a minute."

Karen took a step back into the hall as the conversation resumed in Spanish. She turned to take a closer look at the other families waiting to see Clovis Buckworth, forced inquisitiveness overcoming the otherwise powerful instinct to avoid looking, as though indigence were a deformity.

Except for one or two of the families where either the mother or father evidenced the ravages of drugs or alcohol, Karen was astounded at how *normal* they looked. As she glanced from family to family, she realized that the women and a few of the men had begun to glare at her. She wished she was dressed in blue jeans instead of Cornelia's 'sexy yet professional' Calvin Klein ensemble earmarked for tonight's on-air shots.

Karen felt her professional dissociation erode as she became the focus of the anger and shame of this mournful congregation. To her immense relief, Buckworth escorted the Spanish-speaking woman out of his office and bade her to enter.

Karen stuck out her hand, reflexively reverting to business mode, then immediately wished she hadn't.

"Hello, I'm Ka . . . Cornelia Pembroke."

Buckworth hesitated a moment, apparently surprised that the reporter had trouble pronouncing her own name. "Clovis Buckworth," he replied. "What can I do for you?"

"Mr. Buckworth, I want to do a follow-up story on Fruitful Willis. Do you remember him?"

Buckworth flinched at the mention of the homeless man's name. "Yes," he answered softly, "I remember Fruitful Willis."

"You don't happen to know where I might find him?"

Clovis Buckworth shook his head. "I've no idea whatever."

If Karen wasn't going to get any answers, maybe Cornelia would be more successful. "Mr. Buckworth," she asked, shifting into disarming, "I don't understand. Weren't you the one who originally brought the case into the public eye?"

Clovis Buckworth leaned back in his chair and crossed his arms, reminded that he was talking to a reporter. "Yes, when I first heard Mr. Willis' story I thought it appropriate to pass along the particulars."

"To Herbert Whiffet?"

"Yes, to Herbert Whiffet."

"From your reaction, might I assume that you regret having done so?"

Buckworth cleared his throat. "Perhaps," he replied.

Disarming only exacerbating the distrust, Cornelia returned to Karen. It had been her first choice anyway. "Well, Mr. Buckworth, I wouldn't be surprised if you did. I certainly regret doing the story."

Buckworth blinked despite making an obvious effort not to. "Oh?"

Karen smiled. "Yes, I regret it. I think I was taken in, although I'm not sure by whom. I'd like to find out how it happened. I think that might make a better story than the first one. Care to help?"

Buckworth uncrossed his arms and placed his hands flat on the desk. Karen noticed that he was not wearing a wedding band.

"Maybe," he replied. "How do you intend to go about it?"

"By doing what I should have done in the first place—some research. It would help a lot if you would tell me why you referred the case to Whiffet in the first place. What was it that you hoped to gain by the publicity the story would attract?"

Buckworth stared at her for a moment. His eyes were very blue behind the hornrims.

"You see those people out there?" he began. "I noticed how surprised you were. Didn't expect families, did you? Expected a bunch of winos, drug addicts and slobbering lunatics. That's what most people expect when they think about the homeless. Well, what's happening in this country, in this city, the financial capital of the world, is that we no longer choose to provide housing for all our citizens. And it's getting worse. Ten years from now New York City may resemble Calcutta. So, when a Fruitful Willis comes in here and gives me the ability to publicize society's treatment of *those* people, I jump at the chance. And Herbert Whiffet may be a self-aggrandizing media hound but he knows how to make the most of this kind of thing."

Clovis Buckworth leaned forward.

"Now why, you might ask, must I resort to using a Fruitful Willis and a Herbert Whiffet instead of one of those families you see out in the hall? Surely their need is more acute. Surely their plight is closer to the public consciousness. The answer to that, Miss Pembroke, is that you of the news media don't want to do stories that focus on ordinary people who have no place to live. That's old news you say. We've done that story you say. Give us a story with *meat* in it you say. If the owner of a welfare hotel rapes a pregnant homeless woman, every station will be there like a shot. Unfortunately, the problem is more banal, more day-to-day."

Buckworth sighed. "Fruitful Willis had something. He was a natural for television, as you saw. I tried to use him for a worthwhile end. It was a mistake."

Karen sat up straighter. Who was this guy to lecture her? "Well, Mr. Buckworth," Cornelia said smoothly, "you certainly answer a question. One thing though—I thought Herbert Whiffet was your friend."

Buckworth grinned and Karen immediately returned.

"Herbert Whiffet is everyone's friend," he said. "Everyone who can help him, that is. Now that he seems to have scored with this de Bourbon case, I doubt that I'll ever hear from him again."

Karen looked at her watch and realized that Cornelia was late. Damn.

"Speaking of the de Bourbon case, Mr. Buckworth, I have to be getting downtown." She hesitated a moment. "But maybe we could continue this discussion sometime."

Clovis Buckworth nodded. "That would be nice." He looked past her into the hall.

"What about tonight?"

"Tonight?" Unprepared for fantasy to become reality, Buckworth placed his hands in his lap and leaned back.

"Yes, if you're not busy . . ."

"I'm not busy . . ."

"I know a great hamburger place . . ."

"Terrific . . ."

"Oh, yes," she said, standing to leave. "One more thing. Call me Karen."

Herbert Whiffet had an early morning appointment of his own.

Ordinarily, the rules at Rikers Island forbid meetings between prisoners and their attorneys outside of visiting hours unless it is before a scheduled court appearance. However, a consultation involving two such eminent personages as Ali Abdul Akbar and Herbert Whiffet demands concessions from the authorities and those concessions were readily granted. At 8:30 AM, Herbert sat in a private room, without his briefcase, thoroughly searched and metal detected, awaiting the appearance of Triple A Akbar.

He had received the request for his presence at Rikers late the previous evening from one of Triple A's underlings (a request delivered with a distinct undertone). After only a moment's consideration, he had accepted, uncontrollably curious to meet one of the city's pre-eminent black entrepreneurs, a man who had risen from just another street victim to a position of power and respect. In a better world, this was the type of man who might have run a major corporation or become a United States senator.

The door opened and a white guard led in the senator, then retired to allow the two black men to speak in private. Herbert stood up, more out of reflex than courtesy; Triple A could certainly fill a room. Herbert was surprised when he realized that Akbar was no taller than he and only slightly stockier. Somehow he had expected a much larger man.

"Nice of you to come, Mr. Whiffet," said the senator, extending his hand, his tone conveying the impression that he was merely being polite since Mr. Whiffet did not really have any choice in the matter.

"My pleasure, Mr. Akbar," replied the lawyer, accepting the handshake. Triple A's grip was firm without the crush common to more insecure men.

Triple A sat down and Herbert took a seat on the opposite side of the table.

"I'm sure you are wondering why I asked to meet with you," Akbar began, speaking with a smooth and easy deep voice that Herbert immediately envied. Without waiting for an answer Triple A continued.

"I was impressed with the way you handled yesterday's news conference." Although aware that he was being addressed by a drug dealer, Herbert Whiffet was flattered, an emotion for which he was immediately embarrassed.

"I knew Lawanda de Bourbon, as you know, although I was unaware that she was on intimate terms with the police." Triple A smiled at his little play on words, his gold incisor reflecting the fluorescent overhead lights.

Triple A then modulated his voice in a manner that expertly combined respect and menace. "I was so impressed, Mr. Whiffet, that I want you to represent me."

Herbert had prepared himself to hear those very words—and had been equally prepared to decline. But now in the presence of the man, Herbert realized that one doesn't summarily refuse Ali Abdul Akbar. Instead, Herbert smiled, trying to seem complimented, stalling while he tried to find a way to turn down the drug dealer without giving offense.

Triple A flashed his gold tooth again. "I see that my solicitation of your services displeases you."

"Not at all . . ." Herbert protested.

Triple A cut him off. "Don't I have the same right to a defense as anyone else?"

"Of course . . ." Herbert agreed.

"I can certainly afford your fee," continued the senator. Herbert realized that Ali Abdul Akbar was enjoying himself; it gave him pleasure to toy with frightened adversaries.

"Well, it's like this, Mr. Akbar," replied Herbert in his firmest tones. "My law practice is predicated on accomplishing certain goals, not merely taking random cases. As I'm sure you are aware, I'm trying to force the criminal justice system to respond to the needs of black people. Your . . . business, is simply not conducive to the furthering of those goals."

Triple A's gold tooth stopped flashing as his face hardened. Herbert clenched his fist under the table.

"And what business is that?" countered the senator. "Do you know that I, me, Ali Abdul Akbar, fund five, *five* different day-care centers in this city and that *I* pay the rent for almost *one hundred* people every month? Are you also aware that without me, a lot of kids would go hungry and others wouldn't have no clothes on their backs? So spare me the pious bullshit, counsellor. I do more for the black community in one month than you done in your whole motherfuckin' life."

Then the eruption ceased and Triple A smiled at Herbert

once more. "We all do our part, counsellor. I didn't have no Daddy to get *me* into Tulane."

Herbert started. The last thing he had expected from Triple A Akbar was copious research. It gave the meeting a malevolent intimacy.

He smiled softly at the senator and leaned back casually in his chair. "That's very good, Mr. Akbar, but I didn't come here to debate the entrance requirements at major universities. Tell me . . . all of this money that you so generously dispense to the black community. Where does it all come from?"

Trips flashed his incisor once more. "I'm an entrepreneur, counsellor. My many enterprises allow me to engage in charitable works."

Herbert leaned forward, knowing he must take the offensive. "If you expect me to represent you, our discussions should be on a somewhat higher plane. So, Mr. Akbar, why don't we cut the bullshit?"

The senator laughed. It was deep, full and infectious. "Fair enough, counsellor. Let us assume that you have an idea where the money comes from."

"Fine," replied Herbert. "And what is its original source?"

"What do you mean?" asked Ali Abdul, for the first time unprepared for a turn in the discussion. His brows furrowed, giving him a decidedly satanic air.

"I mean, Mr. Akbar, does it come from white industrialists? Does it come from the federal government? Or does it come from poor black people, dependent black people, people who must often rob and commit violence on other black people to secure the necessary funds to do business with your representatives?"

Triple A did not respond, merely continuing to glower. But Herbert's momentum was up and he had no intention of stopping.

"So Mr. Akbar, it seems that you are not a Robin Hood, robbing from the rich and giving to the poor, but rather you rob from the poor and dispense some small portion of your wealth back to its source, all of which expands your image and your influence in the community."

Ali Abdul Akbar's face suddenly softened and he laughed once more. Herbert was taken by surprise.

"Well, counsellor, you make a good case. Triple A is certainly a bad fellow." The bad fellow became serious once again. "But I ain't been convicted of nothin' and here I sit in Rikers on some trumped up murder-two bullshit charge. Like it or not, counsellor, *I am an economic leader of the black community*. What about my right to due process, or a fair trial, or against unjust imprisonment? Or do you restrict yourself to protecting the rights of bums and police informants?"

Herbert Whiffet was confused. The man across the table from him was a drug baron, one of the most vicious, despicable men in the entire City of New York. Yet, in Triple A Akbar, Herbert had found an intelligence, an energy and a grasp of political and economic reality—and a charisma—that was in desperately short supply among traditional black leaders. As much as Herbert's training and powers of reason told him to say no, he couldn't cut himself off from this man. Not just yet.

"Give me a day to think about it," he said.

The senator nodded. "It's a deal."

Herbert forced himself to ask the big question. "What if I say no? What then?"

Triple A Akbar flashed his incisor one last time. "If you turn me down . . . I go back to Jew lawyers and you go back to bums."

"That's it?" asked the lawyer.

"What else?" shrugged the senator.

Herbert Whiffet changed his shirt as soon as he got to his office. With the laundry up to two dollars per, he had already sweated through a clean one before his first official appointment. What was worse, facing a full schedule, mostly reporters and others involved with the de Bourbon case, he had encountered Fernando Rios in his waiting room as he arrived. Fortunately, Rios had the room to himself. There was no question as to the advisability of getting Rios in and out before anyone else showed up.

Herbert sighed, poured himself a cup of coffee and buzzed his secretary to admit his client.

"Mr. Rios," he exclaimed as Fernando sidled in, "it's good to see you. Would you like a cup of coffee?"

Fernando Rios accepted his agent's hand without enthusiasm or trust. "No coffee," he said sullenly. "Got a beer?"

Herbert shrugged and shook his head, then moved behind his desk.

"Well, Mr. Rios, to what do I owe the pleasure of this visit?"

Fernando sat in the chair facing his agent, his powers of deduction at full acuity. Although he wasn't aware of the word in either English or Spanish, Fernando Rios knew he was being patronized. "I saw jou on TV."

Herbert nodded and smiled. "I hope you enjoyed it. You're a big part of this, you know."

"Oh yeah?" replied the film-maker. "I didn' see me up there."

Herbert smiled again. "Of course not. A good lawyer never reveals the identity of his star witness in the opening statements. I think things are going rather well."

The lawyer began to smell worse and worse to Fernando, although in this case the olfactory stimulus was figurative. He was getting screwed, pure and simple. This guy thought he was dumb.

"Maybe things goin' well for jou, man. Jou on the TV. I don' see shit for me so far."

Herbert raised his hands palms up and tried to look innocent and trustworthy. He wondered a moment if he was overacting but then decided his audience required a certain broadness of approach. In this, Herbert underestimated his adversary and his deductive powers.

"But, Mr. Rios," he intoned, "I thought we agreed that the maximum profit is to be obtained if we first build the demand. Then every station will bid to get exclusive rights to the tape—and, I might add, to your personal observations."

"Jou agreed," replied Fernando. "When jou figger all this good shit gonna happen?"

"I'm not sure," said Herbert. "Next few days, maybe even a week or two."

"Wha'jou figger I do till then? I gotta live."

So that was what this was all about, thought the lawyer, underestimating Fernando once more. "Well, Mr. Rios, I'm sure I could see my way to granting you a small loan—against royalties, of course. How much do you think you would need?"

Fernando narrowed his eyes. "How much jou got?"

Herbert smiled but was churning inside. He hated the

memory of the need to buy cases and paying off Rios smacked of those early days of humiliation and struggle.

"I think I could see my way clear to loan you two hundred."

Fernando grunted. "Okay, I'll take it." Two hundred stinking dollars, he thought. That's a long way from five thousand.

When Herbert had removed the money from the box he kept in his drawer and the transaction was completed, the lawyer again assured his client that all was going according to plan and that Fernando would soon be wealthy and the star of the Six O'Clock News.

Within minutes, Fernando had been ushered out, leaving with two hundred in his pocket and his lawyer's bullshit rattling around in his deductive brain. As Fernando trudged downtown for La Cantina, shifting a ten-dollar bill into another pocket (no need to let his *amigos* in the bar know about the windfall) Fernando pored over his options. A natural strategist, Fernando settled on an ancient but effective strategy employed by the weaker in fighting the stronger—the pre-emptive strike.

Cornelia had met her crew and was en route to the site of Lawanda de Bourbon's demise when the call came through. Iserson was on the other end.

"Hi, Corney," he bellowed. Cornelia wondered why he bothered using the telephone. "On anything hot?"

"Nothing that can't hold."

"Good." Iserson was exultant. "Get back here right away."

"What's up?" asked Cornelia, feeling her pulse quicken.

"We got a call. Anonymous. He would only speak to you. Said he's going to call back in an hour. Sounds like a PR. Said he was an eyewitness to the de Bourbon shooting."

# CHAPTER TWELVE

Herbert Whiffet yawned. Here it was not yet noon and he was having trouble staying awake. People don't understand, he thought wearily. They are under the mistaken impression that handling a big case is an exciting and pulsating job. Little do they realize that most of the time is spent in meetings and other unpleasant administrative activities, tedious drudgery.

Since his dismissal of Fernando Rios, the attorney had been forced to deal with a steady stream of community leaders, activists and minor politicians, each with his own idea of how the de Bourbon affair should be handled. By coincidence, each and every individual ushered through his door had proposed a strategy that maximized his or her own involvement or that of the group they represented. Herbert was growing testy as he heard the same rap repeated throughout the morning. Let them go and get their own case.

Also, Herbert, after the impact of his first two meetings, was finding it difficult to focus on this procession of hustlers. Triple A Akbar had entered his consciousness and was now a presence not easily dismissed or controlled. Fernando Rios, on the other hand, might have been dismissed easily but could prove equally difficult to control. After Fernando had departed, it occurred to Herbert that if his client demanded money from him, what would prevent him from doing the same thing elsewhere? And if Rios did open his mouth, what would he say? Herbert realized that he had to view the tape again to satisfy himself once and for all that Lawanda de Bourbon did not, in fact, have a weapon.

That was it, he decided. He must retrieve the tape and check again, and in private. He listened idly as his current supplicant completed his pitch. It was a young man, representing the Harlem Freedom Fighters, who was seeking Herbert's permission to establish the Lawanda de Bourbon Brigade, a group of elite young men who would execute one white policeman for every black person killed unjustly while in police custody. Herbert declined to participate in this particular incarnation of the revolutionary struggle and showed the young man out, after which he instructed his secretary to cancel all his appointments for the next two hours.

Then, his palms already moist at the prospect of the coming intrigue, Herbert knocked and opened the door that adjoined the apartment on 126th Street. Verna Poole, the woman with the straightened hair, presented herself immediately, ready to do the Champion's bidding.

"Verna," he said softly, "I need a car right away. Someone reliable."

"For how long?" inquired the woman.

"A couple of hours."

Verna went immediately to the telephone and made a call. She spoke quickly to the party on the other end. No time was to be wasted if Mr. Whiffet needed his car right away.

Herbert watched Verna arranging his transportation. He admired the woman, her commitment, her dedication and her seething rage for justice. Verna's husband had been convicted on what the woman was sure was a manufactured armed robbery charge (although he had no alibi and had been identified by seven eyewitnesses, all of them black), and her battle to get his conviction overturned dovetailed perfectly with the needs of the broader movement. It was people like Verna Poole that ensured that Herbert Whiffet's own dedication never flagged.

Verna hung up. "Five minutes, Mr. Whiffet. Downstairs." She paused for a moment. "I take it this trip is on the sly."

Herbert nodded. Verna went to a closet and emerged with a raincoat and a baseball hat. "Here, Mr. Whiffet. Wear these until you're in the car."

Herbert did as Verna suggested although he felt distinctly foolish. (Why don't I wear a false beard while I'm at it?) Nonetheless, the cloak-and-dagger disguise added to the front-lines thrill that administrators rarely experience but always envy, a giddy fear that is somehow so close to sex. The stakes were high and Herbert Whiffet had become a man of action. He knew that the police would kill—literally—to get their hands on the tape.

When the five minutes had elapsed, he left to meet his

ride, Verna's kiss on the cheek proof of the danger that rode with him on his mission.

Before darting out into the street, Herbert checked as best he could for signs of surveillance. His untrained eye detected nothing but the double parked, beat-up Chevy that would spirit him out of the neighborhood. Realizing that he was not savvy enough to detect a watcher, Herbert held his breath and made for the car, head down and preoccupied, walking briskly but casually, a man late for an appointment with the dentist.

He ducked into the Chevy and greeted his driver, a young man who seemed barely out of his teens. The youth gunned the motor immediately and they were off. The sight of someone so young exacerbated Herbert's nerves. Had Verna gotten him a high school dropout?

The young man grinned as soon as they had turned the corner. He headed uptown, the initial ploy in determining if anyone would follow. He turned to his passenger, obviously amused. Herbert realized he was still wearing the raincoat and the hat and quickly removed the undignified camouflage.

"I'm twenty-three," he said.

"Oh . . . that's good," Herbert stammered, wondering how the kid had read his mind.

"My name's Bruce," the twenty-three year old continued, "Bruce White. Verna's my aunt. Where are we headed, Mr. Whiffet?"

Herbert flinched at the mention of his name. Revealing his identity violated the first rule of espionage. He glanced again at his driver, who had made another turn and then another, all the time watching the rear-view mirror for pursuers. Bruce White seemed totally relaxed, unappreciative of the danger.

Herbert cleared his throat. "I'd like to end up on 92nd and Fifth. I'll walk from there but I'd like you to wait. After that there's another stop."

"You got it, Mr. Whiffet," replied Bruce, having a fine time wending his circuitous route through the neighborhood. "By the way," the young man smiled, "it's an honor to be able to help."

"Why, thank you," Herbert said, grinning crookedly. "We all just serve the people."

Bruce White nodded. "I know. I'm attending law school in

the evenings. I hope to use my degree to continue the work you have started."

Herbert wished the young man luck, but the satisfaction of riding with an admirer was soon dissipated by increasing proximity to the destination.

"Are you sure we weren't followed?" Herbert was now taking pains with his tone, loath to give the wrong impression to one who would follow in his footsteps. Champions must always be cool and in control.

"Positive, Mr. Whiffet."

The Chevy pulled to the curb on the appointed block, the only illegal parking spot still available on the street. Herbert noted the unticketed vehicles, evidence of the Police Department's tolerance of petty violations of law in well-to-do white neighborhoods. He told Bruce to wait, then headed down 91st Street to Madison Avenue.

For security reasons, Herbert Whiffet had obtained a safe deposit box in a bank frequented by his enemies. While he tried to pretend to irony, in fact Herbert Whiffet enjoyed his occasional forays into the bank, where he was treated with the same deference as any other well-dressed customer.

Herbert walked down the stairs to the subterranean vault and presented his key to the guard. It was always the same man. Herbert admired the consistency and continuity of white institutions, recognizing the feeling of security that accompanied them; another example of the rule of perpetuation. His own people had never been permitted to reach that stage of development; constant shifting of personnel and rules preventing the social anchoring that was a precursor to economic growth.

In a few seconds, Herbert was alone in the vault, just him and the small iron box that held his most precious possessions. He lifted the cover and looked for a moment at the tape casette, the most precious possession of them all, the spark that could ignite the dried, rotting foundation upon which the white political machine rested. Or would the tape corroborate the cop's alibi and be just one more dead end in the quest for equal rights? It was a possibility that Herbert had acknowledged only when paranoia reached its peak, when the prospect of one more injustice played on his soul. He slipped the casette into his coat and returned the safe deposit box to its sleeve.

Soon Herbert was back in the Chevy, giving directions to his apartment building. He felt a short rush of embarrassment. The high rise on Lenox Avenue housed a goodly portion of the economic and social aristocracy of Harlem, a rather elite accommodation for a man of the people. But Herbert believed in leading by example, and who would wish to emulate a lawyer who still lived in a hovel?

While Bruce White waited in the car once more, Herbert took the elevator to the tenth floor. The fear that had thus far lived only in an untraveled corner of Herbert's mind had turned cancerous, ingesting his confidence, stoked by his attempts to dispel it.

It couldn't be, he thought, I'd have noticed a gun. Yet even when he had viewed the tape for the first time, before there had been any talk of a self-defense plea or Lawanda's shifting loyalties, he had wondered why a rookie cop would gun down Lawanda de Bourbon. It must have been something, he had told himself. Maybe the girl said something that the cop took as a slur on his manhood—all Spanish men were sensitive to that kind of thing—and the cop simply fired out of anger.

Herbert darted into the bedroom where, in the fashion of those who spent their nights alone, he kept his television and VCR. Even as the tape began to roll, Herbert felt his dream of DA Whiffet receding. From the first frame it was apparent that his priceless videotape, his documentary evidence, his ultimate instant replay might be inconclusive. That damned Rios had used an old tape; it must have been run fifty times. The quality was poor and the drunken Puerto Rican had jiggled the camera more than he had remembered.

Wait. There . . . there was Rodriguez, next to the abutment, *his* gun clearly visible in his right hand, and there was Lawanda no more than six feet away, her hands too low to see if anything was in them. God, Herbert breathed, the images returning, no wonder Rios couldn't hold the camera steady. Lawanda de Bourbon had the most fabulous . . . breasts. Herbert blushed at the thought, even though he was alone in his bedroom. He knew in that moment that he would accept Triple A Akbar as his client.

Then the shot. Herbert could barely make out the puff of smoke through the interference on the tape. Had the quality been as bad the first time? It must have been, yet Herbert remembered it being much clearer. The entire incident had occurred with total clarity in the first viewing.

Then Lawanda jolts backward, hits the wall, her hands fly up . . . Her hands, check her hands . . . Herbert hit the freeze button, and looked closer. My God, I can't see her hands. They're above the top of the frame. Rios had zoomed in on the woman's torso. And worse, as her left hand had come up it was blocked by her body . . . Herbert realized his clothes were soaked and his body fluids had desiccated.

*I can't prove she was unarmed.*

Herbert took a deep breath and tried to calm down as Lawanda de Bourbon teetered on the abutment, balanced for one suspended moment on her left hip, and then began her descent. Her hands were now clearly visible—and empty.

All right, Herbert. Think clearly. How could Lawanda de Bourbon have had a gun? She didn't drop it on the roof—the cops would have recovered it. It didn't fall on the street—they searched there too. It didn't go over with her, at least not in frame. But what if when the force of the bullet knocked her backwards the gun flew out of her hand and landed . . . where?

Suddenly Herbert relaxed, the cancer self-consumed. This is crazy. There was no gun. The cop lied. That's all there is to it. The only difference is now I need Rios in addition to his tape—an unpleasant prospect but nothing I can't live with.

So what if I can't prove she was unarmed? They can't prove she wasn't.

This is still my case, Herbert Whiffet resolved as he packed up the tape for the return trip to the bank. A slight change of strategy is nothing I can't handle. It's going to happen all the time when I get to be DA.

Deductive minds think alike and Fernando Rios was, at that very moment, initiating a change in strategy of his own.

"Hey lady, what jou mean jou don't pay no money?" Fernando's dream of thousands was floating away.

"Just what I said, Mr. Rios," replied Cornelia Pembroke. "It is not the policy of WRCT to pay for stories. I think you will find that no other reputable station will pay you either."

Fernando sucked up his beer. That fuckin' lawyer, he was full of shit. Wait a minute, Fernando postulated, maybe this broad was just playin' hard to get. He decided to feel her out.

"Lady, jou full of shit. I heard plenty of times people get paid for stories."

Cornelia took a sip of her beer and tried to decide how to handle Fernando Rios. She glanced around the darkened saloon where Fernando had insisted on meeting, trying to think of a way to get what there was in the shortest possible time. At least she had talked him out of meeting at that bar in his neighborhood.

"Not by us, Mr. Rios. After all, we don't even have any proof that you actually saw the shooting."

"Oh I seen it awright. Don' jou worry 'bout that. The cop, he just shot the bitch right in the . . ." Fernando gestured idly with his hands but looked straight at Cornelia's chest to ensure that she understood. The white chick didn't have such bad *tietas* herself, he decided.

"Yes, Mr. Rios," replied the reporter, seemingly oblivious to the direction of the little man's stare, "everyone who watches television knows that. But how can you prove you saw the shooting? What can you tell us?"

Fernando ordered another beer and sized up the situation. He had hoped to avoid mention of the videotape at this preliminary stage of the negotiations. It would do him no good if the broad tipped the cops and they grabbed his golden nugget before any money could be gotten for it. That was no better than leaving it with that fuckin' lawyer.

"Wha'jou mean, what can I tell? I tol' jou I *saw* it."

The reporter took another sip. Shit, look at the way she drinks the damn beer, thought Fernando. This broad need to get laid.

"Why don't you tell me what happened? Then maybe we can figure out what to do." This was ordinarily the moment that Cornelia would shift into disarming but that simply wasn't feasible with Fernando Rios, eyewitness extraordinaire, staring fixedly at her breasts. It was all she could do to pretend to be helpful.

For his part, Fernando had deep misgivings about telling anyone anything until he had received assurances that his information would be rewarded. But, deducing furiously, he was forced to admit that he had to give out something in order to provide some incentive for continuation of the negotiations. So the eyewitness reluctantly related his version of the events on the roof, regaling the reporter with graphic details. She want proof, she get proof.

To his disappointment, the white broad who needed to get laid didn't favor him by cringing or showing any adverse reaction to his tale but simply nodded at the points where Fernando's recitation coincided with her knowledge of the events.

"So, lady, wha'jou tink? I seen it awright. You gonna put me on TV now?"

Cornelia sipped her beer again, an excuse to look away from the little man and decide what to do. Fernando Rios was certainly not the world's most convincing witness, but he was all there was at the moment. Suddenly, Murray Plotkin flashed in her head.

"Mr. Rios, your story sounds excellent. I'd like to check it out and then if everything fits we'd be happy to put you on TV." The little man grimaced. He didn't seem thrilled at the prospect of being 'checked out.' "By the way," the reporter continued, "did you see a gun in the woman's hand?"

Although Lawanda de Bourbon's hands were the last features of her anatomy that had occupied Fernando's attention, he was well aware that the question was a set-up. No answer, no TV appearance. But which answer did they want? An easy decision.

"No, lady. No gun. The bitch . . . the girl wasn't holding nothin'."

"Are you sure, Mr. Rios?" pressed the reporter. "Maybe in the heat of the moment you missed it."

Fernando became agitated at this slur on his powers of observation. "Wha'jou crazy, lady? I tol' jou. I saw the whole ting. There wasn't no fuckin' gun."

"All right, Mr. Rios," nodded the white broad who needed to get laid as she slid her beer across the bar, ending the conversation. "I'm going to check your story and if everything works, we'll put you on the show. You might even rate a bulletin."

Bulletin shit, thought Fernando, a member of the immediate gratification generation. This broad fuckin' with me just like that fuckin' lawyer. Shit, he deduced, I ain't got no choice.

"Hey lady," he mumbled, "what if there was somethin' else? Somethin' to prove what I said."

Cornelia leaned forward, braving the space between herself and Fernando Rios. This was it—she knew it. "Like what, Mr. Rios?"

The little man fumbled with his beer, his reluctance firing Cornelia's anticipation.

"Like a . . . picture."

Iserson couldn't sit down. He paced around his cubicle, covering every inch of unoccupied space, like a tiger in a cage just before feeding time. But instead of raw meat, his mind focussed on ratings, which perhaps for him served the same function.

Although Cornelia had become inured to her boss's chain reactions of energy, this display was setting records on the Richter scale and the mood was infectious. Cornelia felt an urge to bite her fingernails, a habit she had broken when she had gone into television. She chewed on a small piece of skin on the inside of her cheek instead, an alternate favored by fashion models, actresses and other women for whom unchewed fingernails are essential to their image. It demands a deft touch to avoid drawing blood, but Cornelia had a good deal of experience.

"So," the news director crowed, "your buddy Herbert has the tape. Waiting to spring it on the DA at the propitious moment, no doubt."

Iserson nodded in the direction of Fernando Rios, waiting in the newsroom, amusing himself by watching technology at work. "You believe him?"

"I didn't," replied Cornelia, "until he told me the part about Herbert and the tape. It's just like Herbert. He always thinks he's smarter than everyone and he gets patronizing. I didn't think Fernando there had any other occasion to know about that." Cornelia looked longingly at her left thumb and the morsel that had grown on the end, undisturbed. "Yes," she said, her voice conveying conviction that she did not feel, "I believe him."

"Me too," agreed Iserson. "Call Whiffet. Give him a chance to comment. If he refuses, run Rios. If he wants to comment, get a crew up there." The news director paused for a moment. "But Corney . . . don't be too forthcoming with him. Allude to what we've got but be as vague as you can. I'd much rather run this story without Herbie's face in it. He'll have plenty of opportunity to comment on tomorrow's follow-up story."

Cornelia agreed but that damned Plotkin thing popped into her head again. Shit, she thought, I can't worry about that every time I do a story. This one isn't like the Fruitful Willis fiasco. Rios is an eyewitness to a major crime, and we've checked his story as much as we can. What am I supposed to do? Suppress the news? Being prudent is fine, but I'm still a *reporter*. I *report*.

Cornelia picked up the phone in Iserson's office and placed her call to Herbert Whiffet.

# CHAPTER THIRTEEN

One place Cornelia Pembroke would have heard a different version of the events on the roof was the records room in the 24th Precinct, for that was where Patrolman James Rodriguez had been assigned pending disposition of the IAD investigation.

James Rodriguez was not a Champion. James Rodriguez was just a young kid who wanted to be a cop. Although deeper meanings are often attached when members of minority groups take that non-traditional path, in this case the surface explanation was the correct one. The fourth of eight children of a second generation family from the Dominican Republic, James had been bitten with the police bug when only five years old, watching an episode of 'The Untouchables.' Unlike other boys smitten with the same affliction, the disease never went into remission and James, immediately upon receiving his associates' degree, took and passed the test for the police academy. Upon graduation he had been posted to the Two-Four so that the department might avail itself of his proficiency in Spanish.

Now, only eleven months after achieving his dream, Patrolman Rodriguez spent his tour filling and filing, processing the endless minutia required by the department's tapeworm bureaucracy, a typewriter substituted for his service revolver. Loss of the gun was the worst part, an emasculation the department performed on those under review.

His current duties gave Patrolman Rodriguez a good deal of time to reflect and at the moment he was reflecting on his bad luck in being granted superior foot speed to Patrolman Blakemore. For had his partner been the quicker one, James would at this moment be touring the neighborhood in a squad car, doing the things he had signed on to do instead of filling out forms while most of the criminal justice apparatus of the City of New York sought to prove him a liar.

Although discussing the case was forbidden to all personnel, there is more gossip, innuendo, rumor and sub rosa information passed around a police precinct than at a meeting of the Jewish Grandmothers Society. Unfortunately for Patrolman Rodriguez, he was all too aware that no evidence had been uncovered to support his case. As he completed the precinct's stationery requisition for the coming month, James Rodriguez was forced to admit that without the recovery of Lawanda's gun, his story sounded so improbable that he was no longer sure *he* believed it. After all, distinctive metallic objects do not evaporate or disappear into some 107th Street version of the Bermuda Triangle.

And it gave Patrolman Rodriguez scant consolation to realize that the evidence was equally insufficient to get him convicted of a criminal charge. His career would be over all the same. The Lawanda de Bourbon shooting fell into one of the gray areas of law enforcement, a case without definitive resolution. Such cases leave a bad taste in everyone's mouth, like a tie in the Rose Bowl, and it is much more pleasant for the department if those implicated in such an affair simply disappear—like Lawanda de Bourbon's gun.

To make matters worse, everyone was being so damn sympathetic and supportive that James Rodriguez felt like a death row inmate for whom all appeals had been exhausted. Other cops were invariably patting him on the back, assuring him that everything would turn out all right but he could almost hear the clucking in the locker room where he was certain no one was taking bets on his survival.

Notably absent from his booster section was the guy from internal affairs who was investigating the shooting. It was particularly difficult for the patrolman to watch Gagliardi come and go, always looking like he was making funeral arrangements. The young patrolman, who knew nothing of any plainclothes involvement in neighborhood commerce, had little doubt as to whose funeral was being arranged.

In fact, as a result of his recent discoveries, Phil Gagliardi was fitting himself out for the shroud. The application could be literal if D'Angelo's boys were on the take and got wind of the investigation, but at least figurative if he was forced to expose any corruption at Manhattan North. Phil had a cop's sense of irony and he hardly failed to note that he was now in the same boat as Rodriguez, the presupposed subject of the inquiry. Departmental scandals were dirty affairs and the messenger was often banished with the guilty, another reason internal affairs work was less than popular.

All this, of course, was lost on James Rodriguez who, in any event, could not focus on any predicament other than his own. It was the helplessness that was so frustrating—being unable to lift a finger in his own defense, required by regulations to allow the department to impartially gather the evidence and then hang him. Maybe if he had been a twenty-year man and Irish, or had a fourth-generation legacy, he might have some hope. But minority officers never really crack the brotherhood and all Patrolman Rodriguez had to look forward to was another 'cheer Jimmy up' dinner with Maria.

Social actualization varies with the person and, for Maria Torres, working as a nurse, married to a New York City policeman, and living in a neighborhood where eight-year-olds didn't get held up for their lunch money was every bit as impressive as coming out at the debutante ball and wintering in Palm Beach. The pact she had made with James to save money and pursue their dream had thus far survived any attack the *barrio* could muster.

But now Maria Torres was worried. She, of course, had no doubt whatever as to her fiancé's innocence, and did not even agree with James about his being the scapegoat. She was sure that the truth would come out in the investigation and that he would be cleared. Surely, all they had worked for was not to be destroyed because James had done his duty during an action to rid a community of drug pushers. After all, didn't James have the same rights as any other citizen, to be considered innocent unless proven guilty, and there was certainly no evidence to support the ravings of that black lawyer, that Whiffet or whatever his name was.

No, what worried Maria Torres was James himself. He had always been optimistic and upbeat. During tough times it was always James and his hopes for the future that had pulled them through. He believed that hard work and honest effort could overcome poverty and accident of birth and then had gone out and proved it. Maria had become so used to that perspective that its disappearance was unnerving.

Since the shooting James Rodriguez seemed to lose everything that had made him successful. For the first time since she met him, James wondered what he might do for a living if he wasn't a cop. His spirit seemed to have dropped off the roof along with Lawanda de Bourbon. He kept insisting that Maria prepare herself for the worst, that Lawanda's gun would not be found, and that his public humiliation or worse would be the convenient solution for city government in its stand-off with the activists.

But what frightened Maria the most was that last night at dinner, for the first time since she had known him, her fiancé had gotten drunk.

Cornelia was disappointed that she had been forced to cancel her interview with Clarissa Taylor but the Fernando Rios story clearly took precedence. (Karen, however, would be able to keep her dinner date with Clovis Buckworth.)

Following Iserson's instructions, Cornelia had been vague when she solicited Herbert Whiffet's reaction to the possible presence of an eyewitness. With no specific mention of Fernando's identity and certainly none regarding the existence of a videotape, Herbert had simply repeated his unwillingness to disclose any details of the documentary evidence he claimed to have in his possession.

"Cornelia, why are you asking me about this again? I thought I made my position clear at the news conference."

"You did, Herbert," replied the reporter. "But obviously an eyewitness would substantially alter the complexion of the case and we want to give you every opportunity to comment."

The bell finally went off in Herbert's ear. "Are you saying that you have come up with an eyewitness?" This was bad. Herbert couldn't be sure whether or not she was bluffing, and if not, was their eyewitness Rios or someone else, and if it was someone else had they seen a gun in Lawanda's hand?

"You'll have to watch the show to find that out, Herbert. So, for the record, you have no further comment on any potential eyewitnesses in the de Bourbon shooting, nor will you comment on the documentary evidence you claim to have in your possession?"

Cornelia heard the Champion cough on the other end of the line. After a long pause, he answered the question, speaking softly and tentatively. "That is correct."

"Thank you, Herbert," said Cornelia brightly. "You've been a great help."

Now, sitting in the editing room (they dared not put Fernando on live), Cornelia pondered the possible slants to the story. Was it to be tampering with evidence by the lawyer or the possibility of a cover-up by the police? Neither case was clear-cut and Cornelia was not particularly well disposed to either of the parties. Unable to chose, she decided to just this once violate the cardinal rule of television journalism that required a story to have but a single subject and a simple focus and opt for the 'nest of vipers' approach, demonstrating how each side sought to pervert justice for its own ends.

In another break with precedent, Cornelia's account was to be rendered from the studio instead of the streets, the reporter seated next to Roger Harte, the anchorman. This was unquestionably the biggest moment of her career, objective proof of that fact supplied by Iserson, who had spent the past hour walking around congratulating himself for his foresight in grooming the young woman for the stardom she was about to attain.

She read her copy for the fourteenth time. It was big stuff all right, but more importantly, it was good journalism—fair, even-handed, asking questions without presuming answers. Even her father would approve—if it was possible to ever get him to approve of anything.

As six o'clock drew closer, the moment that Cornelia's headline story would be announced to four and one half million people, she found herself as nervous as at her first television appearance, then a student reporter for the college station at Yale. At the thirty-second call her throat became so dry that she was sure no sound could pass through her unlubricated larynx. She frantically signalled for the water that she had forgotten to place under the desk. A helpful tech fetched a full cup, but immediately after drinking she felt the dryness return. Cornelia fought back the urge to signal to Iserson to get her off, to allow Roger Harte to read the copy.

At ten seconds, the tiniest moisture began to work its way into her throat. I'm going to do it. I'm going to do it. Even if I just croak like a frog, I'm going to do it. At five seconds, Cornelia let out a yell, a common ploy of performers just before air.

Then the urgent, powerful theme music began and they were on.

"Tonight," Roger Harte intoned after the intro in his urgent, powerful baritone, "an exclusive on the Lawanda de Bourbon story . . . An eyewitness account of the shooting that has all of New York in an uproar."

Cornelia braced herself as Roger read the remainder of the promo for the show. Her stage fright had vanished and she was ready.

"And now, from the studio, Cornelia Pembroke . . ."

The red light went on on camera two and Cornelia heard the director's voice in her earpiece.

"Go!"

"A huge break in the shooting of Lawanda de Bourbon came today when WRCT obtained the exclusive statement of Fernando Rios, a resident of 42 West 107th Street, directly across the street from the building where Lawanda de Bourbon met her death . . ."

Cornelia paused, although only for effect. Her voice was fine, every bit as urgent and powerful as Roger Harte's.

"In an exclusive videotaped statement, Mr. Rios gave the details of what he saw on the morning of May 18. Although shocking in terms of the shooting, his revelations have a much deeper significance with respect to the manner in which the case is being pursued by the police and touted by members of the black community."

The red light on camera two went out and Cornelia turned her attention to the monitor where excerpts of the interview were being run.

The now-familiar face of Fernando Rios filled the screen. It was ludicrous to refer to the little man as 'Mr. Rios,' but one doesn't diminish the credibility of one's own witness.

" . . . so I heard all the noise an' stuff (he had said 'noise an' shit' on the first take) an' I went to the window. I seen this cop and this black lady ('bitch' the first time) onna roof. She 'bout six foot away from th'cop. Then, all of a sudden, 'boom' he shoot her, right in the . . . chest. She kinda hang for a minute an' then she fall over."

Fernando paused and Cornelia's voice overlaid the picture. "How can you prove this is what happened, Mr. Rios?"

(On the first take, Fernando had once again taken umbrage at the question. "Wha'the fuck jou mean, lady? I already tol' jou." Once they had explained to him that the question was solely for the benefit of the cameras, Fernando had calmed down.)

"When I seen th'whole ting happen I went an' got my camera, jou know for tapes an' . . . stuff." Fernando smiled for the benefit of four and one half million people. "I got th'whole ting on tape."

Another voiceover. "And what did you do then, Mr. Rios?"

"I bring the tape to that lawyer, Whiffet. He tell me to keep my mouth shut, he gonna take care of everythin'." The station had edited some choice words regarding Mr. Whiffet that had followed.

"And as far as you know, Mr. Whiffet still has the tape."

"Jes. As far as I know."

"One more thing, Mr. Rios. When you witnessed the incident, did you happen to notice if Lawanda de Bourbon was armed?"

"Nah. She didn' have no gun. The cop just shot her."

Then the light was on again on camera two, and Cornelia added the coda. "So it seems that the tragic shooting of Lawanda de Bourbon has attracted a number of political opportunists much the way a freshly dead animal attracts vultures. This report ends with questions. In view of previous rumors of corruption at Manhattan North, are the police concealing evidence of one of their number committing a cold-blooded murder? Has Lawyer Whiffet decided to use this case as a springboard to political office without regard for justice or due process? What exactly is on the tape that Fernando Rios claims he gave to Mr. Whiffet for safekeeping?

"WRCT and this reporter will try to find the answers."

Roger Harte, looking suitably impressed, as if he had just heard the story for the first time, thanked Cornelia for a fine piece of reporting. Mike Iserson, watching the feed in his office, leaped out of his chair and punched the air. He couldn't be happier. Everyone would be squirming at this one.

Phil Gagliardi, who had been tipped to watch the show, took in Fernando's performance in the squad room. Even as Cornelia Pembroke was promising to find the answers, his chief had telephoned the precinct ordering Phil to find the answers. The only difference in the two quests was that the reporter was given the time to conduct a proper investigation.

"Phil," the chief said, "I want everything you've got on my desk first thing in the morning."

The chief had left no room for negotiation but a detective's instincts are powerful and with a finality of their own.

"Sure, Chief," replied Phil, "but what you're going to get is an abortion. I'm sure the Rodriguez kid is telling the truth." (Even as he said it, Phil was angry at himself for going that little distance out on a limb. From such perches are early retirements born.) "If we conclude the investigation now, we're just throwing the kid into the shit house."

The chief's voice turned colder, a man trapped in an abhorrent predicament and not appreciative of being reminded of it. "And what do you suggest we do, Phil? Conduct a six-month-long investigation and allow the assholes to crucify the department? They're already accusing us of dragging our feet and covering up. If there's no gun, there's no gun."

What the chief meant but would never say was that if the Rodriguez kid was tossed into the maw of the political storm, perhaps the beast would be satiated and the department might be left to handle any corruption within its ranks.

But Phil Gagliardi was not about to allow this prostitution of his profession to pass unprotested. "Damn it, Chief, you know we can't turn a gun in that neighborhood in forty-eight hours. 107th Street is not exactly the good citizenship capital of the world. At least let me talk to Rios. He looks like some prince of a witness."

The chief paused and Phil could feel his anger recede. "Well," he began, "the local command should interview Rios . . ." Phil realized how distasteful all of this was for his boss. "But I see no reason why you shouldn't talk to him too." The chief paused again. "Okay, Phil, here's what we're going to do. Talk to Rios—if you can find him. I have a feeling he won't be home. I still want a report on my desk in the morning, but I see no reason why your investigation has to stop there." Phil smiled for the first time in two days. At least he was going to have a chance to be a detective. "But be careful, Phil. Anything you do after tomorrow morning is going to look like a corruption inquiry. Everyone is going to be out for your ass."

What else is new? thought Phil. "Thanks, Chief," he replied. "My ass has been there before."

"This is no joke, Phil. If D'Angelo is involved in something, I don't want to be digging a bullet from a .38-Special out of your back."

Phil took in the chief's words of wisdom and hung up. Then he headed out the door to find Fernando Rios.

Leotis Chestnut shook his head dejectedly but Herbert sensed that he was somehow pleased.

"Well, Herbert," intoned the reverend, confirming Herbert's suspicions, "I told you we couldn't trust Rios."

There was no point in arguing with the obvious so Herbert merely nodded. As he often did in crisis, after receiving Cornelia's telephone call, the Champion had sought the counsel of his long-time collaborator. And, as was invariably the case, once in the reverend's company, Herbert wondered why he had subjected himself to Leotis' sanctimonious criticisms of his handling of the affair.

"The question, Leotis," Herbert growled, trying to demonstrate displeasure at his comrade's remark, "is what to do next. We cannot allow this case to be turned back on us. It would be a disaster for the movement." To say nothing of Herbert's incipient campaign for district attorney.

Leotis Chestnut smiled. Herbert was a talented young man, but the important decisions must be made by someone with greater maturity—and intelligence.

"Herbert, my colleague," he began patiently, "the answer to that question is quite simple. Your reporter friend . . ." (Herbert flinched at the attribution), "has provided the perfect solution."

Leotis stopped there. Herbert knew what the pompous ass wanted, and hated giving it to him. But Leotis would not be moved and Herbert was forced to capitulate.

"And what is that, Leotis?"

Leotis dipped his head in one giant nod, as if answering a rhetorical question about sin in one of his sermons.

"We go on the offensive, my dear Herbert." Leotis' voice was going down register as he warmed to his plan. "*Of courrrse,* we withheld the tape. *Of courrrse,* we kept Rios under wraps. After all, we are dealing with a *corrrrupt* police department and a *corrrrupt* district attorney." Leotis smiled at that one. "How can *annnyone* expect us to give our evidence to the *verrry* people who have committed these *CRIMES*?"

As much as he resented the source, Herbert began to see the light. He had to admit it—Leotis could really come up with them.

"So, my friend," the Reverend Mr. Chestnut continued, "tomorrow we call a news conference and *demannnd* that the governor himself appoint a special prosecutor—a black special prosecutor—and until he does we will not hand over *annny* evidence so that these corrupt and racist forces of our society can further hide their crimes against our people."

That sounded pretty good to Herbert except for one small problem with the facts.

"Fine, Leotis, but what happens if the governor actually does appoint a special prosecutor and we are forced to hand over the tape? I told you—it's hardly conclusive."

The Rev. Mr. Chestnut stared at his comrade and wondered what Herbert would do without his advice.

"So what? First of all, Rios has stated publicly that there was no gun. Second, you told me there is no evidence of a gun in the frames in which Lawanda is falling off the roof. And third, and most important by the way, is that by the time the tape is actually seen, public opinion will be with us regarding the outrageous abuses of justice by the white racist criminal justice system. And that, my dear Herbert, is the point, isn't it?"

Herbert could not suppress a frown as Leotis was correct again. The reverend seemed to misinterpret his friend's reaction.

"Herbert, I don't think you should view all of this as a moral transgression. If you don't believe in the overall justice of our cause and the righteousness of our struggle, perhaps you should give your participation second thoughts."

Although moral qualms were not the source of the Champion's discomfort, he was certainly not about to reveal that to Leotis. As much as he respected the reverend, there was no doubting his shark-like qualities, and one moment of indecision could cede control of the case.

"I think those remarks are unnecessary, Leotis. I believe I have demonstrated a level of commitment every bit as deep as yours."

"Of course, of course," replied the reverend with a wave of

his hand. "I was speaking rhetorically." (Like hell you were, thought Herbert.) "It is only important that we stick to our strategy, that we use this shooting to further our cause. God grants each of us few opportunities for greatness, and we must not squander ours."

Herbert was afraid Leotis was going to begin quoting the scriptures, as he often did to emphasize a point. Somehow God's word was not appropriate at this moment and Herbert pre-empted the sermon.

"You're quite right, Leotis. I'll call a news conference for first thing tomorrow morning."

In his cell at Rikers Island, that astute observer of the social and political scene, Ali Abdul Akbar, lay on his bunk with his hands cradled behind his head. Things were going so well that he had even begun to stop thinking bad thoughts about Lawanda de Bourbon.

Diana had certainly done him a favor, getting offed like that. A mere two days ago Triple A was scrambling to find a defense that could get him out of the murder-two and then, with beautiful dramatic irony, Diana provided him with the means to escape that which she had gotten him into and accomplished that most difficult task by stopping a cop's bullet. So perfect was the touch, so fitting for his plans, that Triple A wondered if he had willed the incident from behind the walls of the prison.

All that was left was to persuade that pussy little lawyer to take the case. And that, if Ali Abdul was any judge of character at all, had already been achieved.

Patrolman James Rodriguez, whose tour had ended at 4 PM took in the news at Maria's apartment while awaiting her return from the hospital.

James was surprised at his reaction, or rather the lack of it, as he watched Fernando Rios push him further down the path of professional disgrace and humiliation and even, for the first time, criminal indictment. He did not rant at the screen, hurl epithets at WRCT, vow to clear his name or even to persevere through this nightmare. He merely sighed deeply and went into the kitchen to pour himself another drink.

# CHAPTER FOURTEEN

Clarissa Taylor was relieved that the woman from the television station had cancelled her appointment. Her first day at Hot Feet had left her with sore feet—and a sore back that went perfectly with the splitting headache. At Murray's, she had performed her duties seated in a high counter chair but Hot Feet provided no such luxury. As a result of its clientele, the decibel level in the store constantly flirted with the point that causes fainting, although the kids, the guards, the salespeople and Russell McKey seemed oblivious to the throbbing din.

Despite the first day ailments, Clarissa was elated. She was working. Her pride had returned and she could again face her children as a head of the household who was discharging her responsibilities. As soon as she arrived home, the change in mood in the apartment was evident. The kids had prepared dinner of course, but it was the smiles and the energy that marked the change, not merely the Taylor children pitching in with the family chores.

In the midst of all this good cheer, Clarissa momentarily forgot her vow to get a second job and that her salary at 'Hot Feet' was less than break-even.

After a perfectly serviceable dinner of roast chicken, mashed potatoes and string beans, Clarissa retired to the living room and did something that she had feared to do since Murray had left for Florida—take stock of the family's finances. In this, she did not focus on day-to-day living expenses, but on the capital budget—the money that had been set aside to send Matthew to private school.

She had feared to allow the cache to enter her consciousness before, lest it be considered part of the family's assets. And it was not part of the family's assets, at least not in a way that blurred it with money set aside for food and shelter. The school money was the future, their hope. And Clarissa, who had been exposed to more human weakness than most, realized all too well that once the dam was breached, the savings touched just once, there would be no end to it.

But, thanks to Russell McKey and Hot Feet, that eventuality receded into the part of Clarissa's being that was reserved for nightmares. Sitting in her comfortable living room in her middle-class apartment in Forest Hills, a nutritious, balanced meal slowly metabolizing in her belly, Clarissa felt secure in parking those nightmares for just a bit longer.

Dinner was a different type affair for Karen Pzytriek. She had chosen Amazing Gray's, a new addition in the city's latest craze of 'down-scale' bistros, as having the right mix of youthful energy and non-evident opulence. Even so, dinner for two, just free-range chicken and a couple of glasses of white wine, promised to run upwards of fifty dollars. Karen wondered whether she should pick up the check.

"So tell me," she began, playing with her wine glass, "how exactly did you come to the Mobilization for the Homeless?"

Clovis Buckworth picked at a plate of *pomme frites*. "I started it, actually," he said, glancing off toward the bar.

"Really," she replied. Cornelia was so completely at ease with this kind of background questioning that it was a struggle for Karen to keep her away from the table. But without her, Karen could not think of what to say next.

Clovis lifted the wine bottle out of the ice bucket at the side of the table, held it in the towel and refilled Karen's glass. He replaced the bottle and sat for a moment looking at her. Karen looked down into her glass.

"I don't quite know why I started working with the homeless," he said suddenly. "Maybe because I thought it was the most worthwhile thing I could do. One day, walking down Madison Avenue trying to decide what to do with an MBA in marketing, I looked into an alley that ran behind one of the apartment buildings. There was a woman in there, scrounging through the trash. Before I could look away, she pulled out a piece of discarded food and fed it to a small child who was hidden between the garbage cans.

"So I walked into the alley and talked to the woman. And

to my absolute surprise, she was a completely lucid and intelligent person who had been burned out of her apartment by an arsonist hired by her landlord. She and her daughter had fallen through the cracks of city agencies and she ended up on the street."

"What did you do?"

"I got her and her daughter something to eat then took them to the Department of Social Services myself—the cab driver was none too pleased with his passengers, I remember. We waited about two hours—and that was with me there. Who knows how long she would have waited if she'd been there alone. We then proceeded to get the runaround. All they offered was a shelter in the Bronx. So I took them to my apartment."

"Your apartment? You mean you trusted . . ." Karen broke off her question.

"Trusted them not to rob me, you mean? The possibility crossed my mind. But they didn't. Then the next day we went shopping for some new clothes and when mother and daughter were properly spruced up, I used my good offices to get them a small apartment of their own and even managed to secure the woman employment.

"The whole episode made me feel rather good actually and I realized what it was that I wanted to market. I went back for a degree in social work."

"What happened to the mother and daughter?" asked Karen.

Clovis Buckworth smiled. "She lives in Brooklyn, still working. Her daughter is in school, doing quite well." His expression sombered. "One of but a few success stories, I'm afraid."

"That's . . . lovely," Karen said softly.

He shrugged. "Maybe. Anyway, after my experience with the city, I founded the Mobilization to provide some alternative to the city bureaucracy."

"But where do you get your money? Government grants?"

Clovis shook his head and laughed. "No. No government money. I don't want to take orders from federal bureaucrats either. We work on private donations."

"Foundations, you mean?"

Clovis leaned back in his chair. "I endowed it."

"You? You have that kind of money?"

"Not any more," he said. "I used my trust fund. Much to the horror of my family, I might add. I think they were considering having me declared incompetent."

Karen stared across the table, trying to determine if he was serious.

"But I refuse to discuss the Buckworth clan. Suffice to say that there is no shame in being the black sheep of that particular family. How did you get into journalism?"

Karen hesitated. "Am I in journalism?" she asked, sipping her wine.

"What's the matter?" asked Clovis. "Don't you believe your own stories?"

Karen looked up to check for signs of sarcasm. She detected none and decided she was just overly sensitive.

"It's not that . . . I guess now that I realize the power I have, I'm almost afraid to put on *any* story. Take tonight . . . if Rios is lying, I could be responsible for another miscarriage of justice, the same thing that happened to the deli owner. But if I don't put him on I might well be abetting the very kind of official misconduct that the press is in business to expose."

Clovis nodded. "Did you check him out?" he asked.

"Of course," sighed Karen. "As best we could anyway. The problem with any uncorroborated eyewitness story is that it can rarely be verified one hundred percent. A good journalist has to trust her instincts, and right now I don't."

Clovis shrugged. "I don't see the problem. If you've checked out your story as best you can, and it's legitimate news, you *have* to run it. Or else find yourself another line of work. If you have doubts, follow them up. If you think Rios might be lying, stay on the story. It's hardly dead, you know." Clovis chuckled. "I'm sure old reliable Herbert Whiffet will keep things hopping."

"Maybe," Karen replied, shifting in her seat. "How did someone like you ever get involved with Herbert Whiffet?"

"Herbert lives in a world of shifting expediency. When he was just getting started, the homeless were a convenient cause—in the public eye and needing all the help they could get—and Herbert hitched up for a while. But given the current state of his campaign, I don't think Herbert will be giving any emotional speeches espousing the rights of the homeless for a while."

For the first time that evening, Cornelia, who knew a telling phrase when she heard one, joined in. "What do you mean, Herbert's campaign? What is he campaigning for?"

Clovis hesitated. If the only result of the dinner was some inside information for Cornelia Pembroke, the summer might turn out to be very dismal indeed.

"I'll be happy to answer that if Karen is asking," he said. "But for the purposes of this discussion I'd prefer not to be speaking to Cornelia."

Karen shook her head. "I'll tell you what. I won't use anything you say, with or without attribution, unless I get your specific permission. But in the spirit of your earlier remarks—I can't very well follow up the story without some cooperation from the public."

She had him there. Actually, she had him everywhere. "Fair enough. Herbert Whiffet nurtures a rather thinly disguised ambition to be district attorney. Mayor eventually, but Manhattan DA first. Thus it is in his interest to do all he can to discredit the current occupant of that office, who, of course, happens to be white."

"Well," she said, "until yesterday I'd have thought it laughable, but now, who knows? Maybe Herbert can ride this case into the DA's chair. He wouldn't be the first."

"He's certainly laid the groundwork. Two years ago, he bragged that he had a high-level contact inside the DA's office—someone who fed him sensitive information."

Cornelia thanked Clovis and Karen smiled at him. For a moment she was tempted to ask him back to her place, but then decided against it. She didn't want to risk burning this one out in one night.

Night was the worst time on the Bowery. The terrors sprung from childhood imagination pale before the very real terrors of those unlit streets and infested alleyways. Every sound, every trace of movement can be the precursor of pain or death.

Fruitful Willis no longer had rights. It didn't matter what anyone said. The lawyers, the public servants, the reporters and the politicians had just teased him with rights, enticed him into the public eye so they could use him to prove that the homeless were still bums, vagrants and crazies. No one cared. No one had ever cared.

But Fruitful had fallen for the con. He had acted like a

man with rights, a citizen like everyone else, exposing himself to the fatal sin of rising expectations. As a result, in some grotesque perversion of justice, a triumph for those who had laughed at Fruitful's rights, he now lay huddled in his rags between two desolated buildings in the pit, moving not a muscle, a desperate attempt to blend in with his surroundings so that he might rest undisturbed for just one more night. For when you are a bum on the Bowery, the days pass like a flick in time while the nights are forever.

Fruitful heard a sound a short distance away. He turned his eyes as far as he could without moving his head. He could see no form large enough to be human, but that was no guarantee since survival in this jungle demanded camouflage skills that the most seasoned guerrilla would envy. Fruitful held his breath and hoped it was a rat. Not that he had any love for carnivorous vermin, simply that rats took only small bites. A much more terrifying possibility was that even here, in a dank alleyway, filled with broken bottles, rotting garbage and emulsifying human waste, even here, Fruitful might have intruded on the resting place, the turf, of one of his fellows.

If that was true, the consequences might be a pitched battle, the weapons being anything that was available, a sliver of glass, a nail, an errant razor blade or a brick. Territoriality was more acute down here than in wars of nationalism, and a confrontation in this theatre held no possibility of mediation or truce.

Fruitful heard the little squeal again and drew a small breath. It was most certainly a rat, foraging among the discards that all residents of the Bowery must share. Fruitful congratulated himself on his disguise, so effective that even the rodent was unaware of his presence. Satisfied that he had survived the crisis, Fruitful Willis closed his eyes, hoping to get some sleep, or what passed for sleep in a place where predators might fall on you at any moment.

In a few minutes, Fruitful began to drift off, visions of his days on Lexington Avenue working their way into his head. But Fruitful had grown soft on Lexington Avenue, his skills had eroded. As he reminisced about his television appearance, he drifted off just a bit too much. Just enough that he did not notice a large form emerging from the pile of trash where he had thought he heard the rat . . .

# CHAPTER FIFTEEN

Perhaps justice did exist. After years of working in obscurity in her job and behind the scenes in the struggle for the rights of the oppressed, Renee Lieberman-Smith had been rewarded. She had gotten her case and, in a fitting note, it was the same case that promised to vault her Champion into prominence. So, she would be working, albeit circuitously, with Herbert after all.

To be fair, the prosecution of James Rodriguez was not really *her* case. It was far too important politically to be entrusted to an assistant. The DA intended to handle the public aspects of this case personally. But all the legwork, the grand jury presentation, and the eventual indictment was to be handled by Assistant District Attorney Renee Lieberman-Smith.

As Renee walked into work that morning, three days after the murder of Lawanda de Bourbon, she had expected that the newscast the night before would send her boss scurrying about to save his political face—and hide. (That damn Pembroke woman. Renee knew full well how she enticed people into making statements.) But she certainly did not expect to be the beneficiary of her hated rival's exclusive. Although she detested the feeling, Renee was pleased to be a secret compatriot of the reporter as much as it pleased her to be a secret compatriot of her Champion. Perhaps it was desirability by association.

The DA had called her in first thing to give her responsibility for building a case against Patrolman James Rodriguez. She was overjoyed to be handed such a plum but could not help but wonder why she had been chosen for such a gratuity when others in the office had more seniority and, frankly, were considered stronger lawyers.

The reason was quite simple. The shooting of Lawanda de

Bourbon was as much a political case as a legal one. The requirement of zealous, single-minded pursuit of a conviction was as important as zealous, single-minded pursuit of the truth. If James Rodriguez was convicted on flimsy evidence the political fallout would be far less severe than if he were acquitted on the same evidence. The case, under the best of circumstances, would be weak and if the prosecution was unsuccessful someone must be available to be fitted for the coat with the bull's-eye on the back.

Renee Lieberman-Smith was perfect on all counts. Her political views were well known, she had served the office loyally long enough to be granted a major case, she was a tireless and fastidious worker without outside commitments to compete for her time, her sex made the DA appear to be an equal-opportunity employer by appointing her, and, if she was unsuccessful, her loss would not be missed.

Sitting across from the venerable and respected District Attorney of New York County in his private, wood-panelled office, occupying the same chair as had other assistants before her who had ridden the crest of a prosecutorial wave to fame and respect, Renee Lieberman-Smith was reminded of her entrance interview years before. How many times had she cursed that interviewer for entrapping her in this glorified civil-service position? But now even the interviewer was granted a commutation for, however unwittingly, his promise had been fulfilled. The district attorney's office was being dragged into the struggle for the rights of the oppressed and Renee Lieberman-Smith was right there to see that it would not be the last time.

As soon as the DA had finished his briefing, ("This is *top* priority, Renee. You are to drop everything else and handle this case exclusively, and I want *results*.") Renee ran to the conference room to review the confidential files. One of the first things she noticed was that although the transcriptions of the initial interrogations were there, the official police report of the incident was missing. Evidently internal affairs had not yet had the time to concoct a suitable *apologia* for the shooting. Renee made a note to demand the report immediately. The longer it took, the greater the likelihood that the department would find a way to cover the crime.

Renee reviewed the statements of neighborhood residents, members of the raiding party, the helicopter crew and even the murderer himself. There was little there that she didn't know or could not have deduced. Then she came upon something a good deal more interesting. It was a classified police department memo summarizing the results, or lack thereof, of the undercover team that was keeping Herbert Whiffet under surveillance.

Most of the memo detailed Herbert's comings and goings such that any private citizen could obtain if they had any interest. Herbert's political associates were well known so all of this seemed like a waste of the taxpayer's money. There were two items however, one an omission, the other an inclusion, that aroused Renee's most intense interest. The omission, which gave Renee enormous relief, was any mention of Herbert's clandestine meetings with one Assistant District Attorney Lieberman-Smith. How she had escaped detection she did not know, but it must have been fate. One thing was sure—she would have to be a good deal more careful in the future. Herbert had been right after all in refusing to see her 'privately.' Renee was immediately contrite. She had judged Herbert Whiffet harshly and unfairly.

As Renee read a bit further, her contrition vanished, replaced by hell-caliber fury. The report discussed information supplied by an informant, identified only as 'V,' who indicated that Herbert, on the morning of his news conference, had held a private, secret meeting with . . . *Cornelia Pembroke*! So that's how that bitch had found out about Fernando Rios and the videotape. It was Herbert's way of leaking the information to the public and he had used *Cornelia Pembroke*, obviously his 'good friend.'

Renee slammed the file shut and sat shaking, her hands turning white in a death grip on the conference table. That bastard! He had been two-timing her all along. No wonder he always had an excuse for avoiding her. He was sleeping with *Cornelia Fucking Pembroke*.

Renee's first instinct was to get even by blowing the case, by making sure that whatever alibi the police divined for Rodriguez, it held up. Fortunately for Renee's career, that suicidal impulse was short-lived, the ephemeral reaction of a woman whose fantasy life had just been turned into a cruel joke. There was a much better way. She would pursue this case with as much energy as before, maybe more, but in the process would see to it that base manipulations of the legal system for personal political gain were exposed and punished. And what's more, she would achieve that latter objective under the nose of the manipulator and he would never know.

The manipulator began his day unaware that he had lost his Champion status with his contact in the DA's office, or even of his good fortune in having Renee handed the Rodriguez case. He only knew that the DA would be forced to move on Rios' accusation and that he was lucky to have a pipeline to the action.

Herbert's day was to be dominated by two major events, the news conference at which he would take the initiative in the battle for justice, and his acceptance, at least on a contingency basis, of Ali Abdul Akbar as a client. The Champion had attempted to create a suitable rationale and justification for the latter but conceded to himself that his inability to tell even Leotis Chestnut of his decision was as significant as the act itself.

But Triple A would have to wait to consult with the newest member of his legal team. The lawyer's first order of business was locating his current client, the now-elusive Fernando Rios. Ever since his starring role on WRCT, Fernando had gone underground, unavailable to either the police investigators, who were most eager to speak with him, or to his counsel and agent. Even the staff of WRCT, hoping to keep their star witness on ice a bit longer, were unable to determine what had become of New York's newest media celebrity after he had left the studio. They would not have even let him go except for his protests of pressing family business and his promise to remain available upon request. When he did leave, Willie Moss was asked to follow him but Fernando Rios had evaporated in a crowded subway car and had become officially at-large.

Had Fernando, he of the deductive mind, decided to milk his celebrity status through selective availability? Was there indeed family business to attend to? In fact, Fernando's disappearance was not in the least bit strategic, not in any way a ploy to increase his cachet in the hearts and minds of New York's media watchers. Fernando had simply decided that his appearance on television was cause for celebration and, with the remainder of Herbert's two hundred dollars scorching his pockets, had repaired to the famed Rosalita's for an uninterrupted evening of R&R.

Had Herbert been able to wait until mid-morning he would have located his client at the Rios apartment on 107th Street. Unfortunately for the lawyer, the combination of his pressing schedule and the size of Fernando's bankroll caused the two ships to miss each other in the morning smog.

Although it was dangerous to attack the district attorney and the police department without prior consultation with the eyewitness, Herbert and Leotis decided that since they had the tape and the gist of Fernando's testimony had been preserved in the public record they should press ahead. In the battle for media advantage, striking the first blow was essential. In that way, the public consciousness could be conditioned to the attackers' point of view and any subsequent statements by their opponents would be viewed with a jaundiced eye. It was the rare adversary who could successfully counterpunch and turn public sympathy his way.

So, with Booker T. and Mahalia de Bourbon in tow, abetted by an only slightly smaller chorus, Herbert Whiffet and Leotis Chestnut headed for 155 Leonard Street and the offices of the District Attorney of New York County to hold their open-air 10 AM news conference. Thanks to the Reverend Mr. Chestnut's cadre of volunteers, despite the short notice, every news organization had been informed of the momentous event—every news organization except WRCT, whom the activists had decided to boycott due to their scurrilous report of the night before.

That was not to say that WRCT would not be represented. That station was sure to respond to the summons from the most newsworthy Herbert Whiffet along with the rest of the fourth estate. In issuing invitations to the other television stations, Leotis' volunteers were careful to mention the boycott of WRCT, thus ensuring that as an act of professional courtesy the invitees would inform their excluded colleagues of the event. Having a media antagonist present merely enhanced the potential impact and neither Herbert nor Leotis were taking any chances that WRCT might boycott *them*.

It had been all Herbert could do to maintain his status as chief spokesman in the face of Leotis' claims that his voice carried better outdoors. By making the obvious point that the presence of microphones made a booming baritone unnecessary, Herbert succeeded in beating back his colleague's transparent attempt at claim jumping and at 10 AM prepared to press his case with the people.

This time there was no pre-speech socializing and Herbert went right for it. The case, now established in importance, an echo of 'Amens' accompanied his every phrase.

"Ladies and gentlemen, we have come here to bear witness." Herbert paused to survey the crowd of witnesses to his witnessing. "To bear witness against an *eevil*, against an *innjustice*, against a *violaaation* of our children's *RIGHTS*." Herbert paused again to let the 'Amens' and Mahalia de Bourbon's omnipresent wail punctuate his opening remarks. He decided he was getting pretty good at this.

"Last night, you *allll* saw a report on a television station that I will not dignify by stating its name, a report by a *racist* woman whose opposition to the rights of those of African descent is *wellll* known, a report that made *scannndalous* accusations as to the motives of those who have dedicated their lives to the struggle for equal rights. That report implied that certain evidence in the *cold-blooded murder* of Lawanda de Bourbon (moooan) was being suppressed by the African-American community for self-serving purposes. Well, ladies and gentlemen, that report was a *LIE*.

"We of the African-American community have declined to entrust our documentary evidence of this *murder* to those who *would* suppress it, in order to promote truth and justice—justice for Lawanda de Bourbon, who was paid for her cooperation with the police by a bullet in the chest."

Herbert let the MOOOAAAN subside. He had come to appreciate Mahalia de Bourbon's ability to do it just right and no longer feared that Lawanda's grieving mama would slip over the line and become an embarrassment.

"So, we of African-*Amerrrican* descent *demannnnd* justice and we will not rest until the murderer of Lawanda de Bourbon *payyys* for his heinous deed. We will *not* turn over our evidence to the *raaacist* district attorney. We will *not* turn over our evidence to the *raaacist po*-lice. We *DEMAND* that the governor himself appoint a *BLACK MAN* as a special prosecutor so that finally, for black Americans, the prosecution fits the crime."

Phil Gagliardi did not attend Herbert Whiffet's news conference and was therefore available when the detective staking out Fernando Rios' apartment called the precinct to say that the eyewitness had returned. Phil was out like a shot, pleased to be able to keep occupied before his interview with D'Angelo at noon. D'Angelo had successfully dodged him yesterday, (as had Fernando), prolonging the intestinal malaise that Phil had contracted at the prospect of nailing his old boss. And there was no hope of a reprieve. The narcotics connection would be pursued regardless, independent of the results of the de Bourbon investigation (which was now incidental, since he had filed his report first thing in the morning).

When Phil got to Rios' place, Burke, the surveillor, confirmed that Fernando was still inside. Phil tossed away his only half-finished cigarette and, accompanied by Detective Burke for corroboration, hiked upstairs. He had always hated ghetto work—the smell of urine and garbage lingered in his nostrils and his clothing all day. Fernando lived on the fourth floor so Phil and Burke were required to negotiate that many flights of stairs—dodging the crack vials, broken glass and mouse shit—to reach Fernando's apartment. The doorbell didn't work and Phil had to knock three times before he heard rustling inside. Fortunately the fire escape was staked out so he didn't have to worry about Rios lamming out.

"Jes? Who th'fuck's there?" asked a drugged out voice on the other side of the door. Fernando was either recently roused from a deep sleep or stoned.

"Police," growled Phil in his no-nonsense, don't fuck with me voice. "Like to ask you some questions."

For a moment there was no answer from the other side, as if a deductive mind was considering alternative strategies. Then finally, "Jou got a warrant?"

Phil rolled his eyes heavenward. "I don't need a warrant. We're not here to search. I just want to ask you some questions."

He heard the sound of grumbling on the other side of the door. Fernando was talking to himself. Phil knew enough gutter Spanish to make out 'fuckin' cops' and a few other complimentary phrases. After the completion of the soliloquy the door slowly swung open and the diminutive eyewitness stood before the team of detectives.

"Can we come in," Phil asked, "or do we have to talk in the hall?"

Fernando knew that letting the cops inside was always dangerous, but the flush of stardom was still within him and after all, he deduced, it makes him look guilty of something to deny them entry.

"Sure," replied Fernando magnanimously, "come on in." As the detectives entered, Fernando broke out his broadest grin. "Jou guys want a beer?"

"No, thanks," Phil declined politely. "Ten in the morning is a little early for me." Burke merely shook his head.

"Suit jourself," shrugged Fernando, who went to the refrigerator and grabbed a cold one.

After Fernando had helped himself to that first long swig, Phil began. "Mr. Rios, I saw you on television last night. That was a very impressive statement."

The detective was doing his best to be charming but his efforts were limited by two days of minimal sleep, the general state of affairs in this fucked-up case and the fact that this little beer-guzzling piece of shit across from him was more than likely going to send a good young cop, and one of his own, to the pen. That's why the damn PR's never made anything of themselves, he thought. They'd sell their brother for a quarter.

For his part, Fernando knew full well when he was being bullshitted. No matter what they said or how friendly they might act, these cops were here for one thing—to trip him up. But they too underestimated the powers of Fernando's deductive mind. He would play along with them, matching cordiality with cordiality, but would stick to his story. They could shove that right up their Irish asses.

"Thanks, officer," Fernando grinned, helping himself to another swig. He had only recently gotten to sleep so this little session was like an extension of the night. "What can I do for jou?"

"Well, Mr. Rios," said Phil casually, trying to keep the little man's attention off Burke and the copious notes he had begun to take, "we're trying to fill in some of the pieces. We only saw excerpts on the news. Perhaps you would be good enough to give us the full account of what happened on the morning of the shooting."

Fernando agreed with a smile and a wave of the hand and proceeded to spin his yarn. He left out the part about being at the social club all night, preferring to let the detectives believe he had been roused by the commotion.

Phil smiled when Fernando had completed his account. "That was very clever, Mr. Rios. Deciding to record the event, I mean. You must have realized that a tape of a narcotics raid might be a valuable piece of property. Even without the shooting the news people would have been interested."

Fernando was not sure how to take that. He had not thought of selling the property when he had first recorded the raid. Was the detective just flattering him or trying to trap him? After a night at Rosalita's, deduction was not what it should be.

"Uh, thanks, Officer. But I jes wanna have th'whole ting on tape. I didn' tink nothin' more until I seen th'cop mess up that black chick's *tietas*."

"Yeah," Phil mused, "she sure had big tits. I guess you couldn't take your eyes off them, huh?"

Oh no, thought Fernando. I'm not fallin' for that shit. "Well," he leered for effect, "they was great, man . . ." He rolled his eyes in memory of the departed *tietas*. "But I tell jou, Officer, I seen the whole ting anyway."

"Did you see the pistol in the woman's hand?" Phil realized that he was not handling the interrogation well. Subtlety and entrapment seemed to have vanished with his sleep. Well, perhaps he could get by with Rios. It wasn't as if he was talking to Sherlock Holmes, for chrissake.

Fernando shook his head vehemently. "No gun, man. The chick didn' have no gun."

"Are you sure?" the detective asked, in a manner that implied that Fernando had just contradicted other evidence.

"Jeah, I'm sure," the little man insisted, thrusting his bestubbled chin forward for emphasis. Rosalita's or no, there was one thing Fernando Rios knew with certainty. This cop was bluffing. Nobody seen nothin' except him. If the cops had another witness they wouldn' be so nice to him.

The detective nodded wearily. "Okay, tell me about the tape . . ."

Fernando told the officer the whole unexpurgated story of the videotape and of the connivance of his fuckin' lawyer in trying to ace him out of the profits. The detective listened sympathetically.

"Do you still have the camera?" asked Phil, lighting a cigarette to emphasize the off-handedness of the question.

"Sure . . ." blurted Fernando, and then stopped himself. He had blundered but quickly decided that there was nothing to do but run a bluff as well.

"Can I take a look?" asked the detective absentmindedly.

"Uh, sure," replied the film-maker. He slowly got up to fetch the machine, cursing himself for his slip. Maybe the cop wouldn't notice. Fernando got the machine out of his bedroom closet and flirted briefly with the idea of ducking down the fire escape. Can't do it, he realized. It would blow everything, and besides, they probably had someone watching.

So, adopting a casual air of his own Fernando brought the camera into the living room and handed it to the detective.

"This is a nice piece of gear," said Phil admiringly. Then he looked up, his face as innocent as a nun's. "Even a zoom lens. Where'd you get it?"

"Uh, I bought it from some guy inna bar."

"No kidding," Phil smiled. "Did you get a deal?"

"Jeah, pretty good."

"I guess you wouldn't buy an expensive piece of equipment like this from someone you didn't know."

Fernando was caught. He either admitted to being stupid or risked admitting to something worse.

"Is funny, man, but I didn' know him. Just some guy inna bar."

The detective smiled again and handed the camera to his partner who dutifully copied the serial number on to his pad.

"We'll have to keep this for a while, Mr. Rios. It's evidence in a murder case. Detective Burke here will give you a receipt."

"Uh, sure," replied Fernando, rushing to get another beer. "Anyting jou need, man."

James Rodriguez was not used to starting the day with a headache, but then he was also unused to ending the previous night with a drink. His recent adoption of alcohol as the anesthesia of choice had one advantage: James now walked around with the feeling that he was watching a movie, that the events he observed were not part of his existence, that perhaps he had died and was watching a replay of his own life. Thus when the watch commander informed Patrolman Rodriguez that as a result of the eyewitness account of the shooting of Lawanda de Bourbon he was to be suspended indefinitely pending disposition of criminal and departmental charges, the young man merely shrugged and handed in his badge. When he was told to obtain the services of an attorney, now-temporary-civilian Rodriguez laughed. He laughed in a way that made the watch commander think about the department psychologist.

"What the fuck do I need a lawyer for?" James smirked. "Everyone knows I'm guilty. I've been guilty ever since that fucking lawyer went on television and I'll stay guilty until he stops."

The watch commander wanted very badly to soothe the patrolman's feelings, to tell him that the department was not about to cave in to political pressure, that they would use all their resources to find the truth and expose loudmouth opportunists like Whiffet who sought to use the police to further private ambitions, that James should keep the faith and ride this out . . .

But the watch commander didn't say any of those things. He didn't want to make the suspended rookie feel worse by lying to him, especially with such transparencies. Instead the watch commander quietly accepted the patrolman's shield and suggested he speak to the PBA representative about the attorney. James Rodriguez laughed again and, shaking his head, left the station house.

# CHAPTER SIXTEEN

Herbert Whiffet now understood why so many members of the general public were fascinated with gangsters. As he hurried from the just-completed news conference, Herbert had satisfied his search for justification to take on Ali Abdul Akbar as a client. His upbringing demanded some rationale to make the immoral moral, to turn a surrender to base impulse into an intellectual act.

Herbert had settled on the 'expansion of knowledge' approach—the need to understand why such an obviously talented man chose to be a drug lord rather than a corporate leader or a doctor. This approach would be pre-empted by the explanation that Triple A, for all his brains and talent, was simply a violent, sociopathic hood, so Herbert was forced to hypothesize that Ali Abdul Akbar was himself a victim—a victim of racism, injustice and the failure to grant him equal rights. In the face of such a determined effort to keep him down, Triple A Akbar had turned to the only avenue open to him.

Herbert decided that made perfect sense. He remembered how Triple A had bragged about his community service. It must be true that a man like that was just waiting for someone he respected to entice him to the other side of the fence, the side where he might be a superior ally in the battle for equal rights. Certainly better than a windbag like Leotis. And, if Herbert could send Triple A down the righteous path, it wouldn't hurt his chances at DA either.

Armed with this convenient and self-contained set of logical conclusions, Herbert fairly bounded through the visitor's entrance at Rikers to inform his new client that he had taken the case.

To the Champion's disappointment, Triple A did not react with pleased surprise at his new lawyer's proclamation of acceptance. If anything, this most recent leader-designate in the battle for racial justice was rather blasé, as if there had never been a question in his mind that any offer he deigned to make might be refused. Herbert swallowed the let-down. After all, a convert with the power of Ali Abdul Akbar doesn't change his behavior at first inducement.

"Okay, counsellor," said Triple A, "let's get to business." Although Ali Abdul was making an effort to be as cordial as before, there was no mistaking the slight alteration in tone, the manner of addressing an employee, an underling. With those very first words a feeling flashed through Herbert Whiffet, a feeling that he strove mightily to ignore or dispel, a feeling of menace, a feeling that he had just jumped out of his league.

"What was it you had in mind, Mr. Akbar? You are obviously well represented in your current case."

Triple A had retained the services of Melville Seltzer, perhaps the top criminal defense lawyer in New York, a legal scholar as famous for his writing on the rights of the accused as for his courtroom histrionics. If there had been a defense lawyer hall of fame, Mel Seltzer might be its Babe Ruth.

"Well represented?" Triple A mocked, flashing his gold incisor at his new attorney. The tooth was rather more fearsome than it had appeared yesterday. Maybe it was the light. "Shit, man, if I was well represented I wouldn't be here, beating my meat in Rikers, would I?"

"Perhaps and perhaps not," Herbert countered. Herbert knew it was desperately important not to be bowled over at this meeting. If he was there would be no opportunity to recover.

"Even Mel Seltzer cannot succeed in getting bail approved for a suspect in a capital crime who is considered as likely to flee as you are—and who also happens to be the number one target of the entire criminal justice machine in the City of New York. If the DA can succeed in obtaining your conviction, he won't have to prosecute another case for the next two years. That's about his average anyway."

Ali Abdul grinned once more and it seemed that the gold incisor had again turned benign. "That is all true, counsellor. Mel Seltzer cannot persuade the powers that be to grant me bail. But you can."

"And just how can I do that?" Herbert asked, although he

was reasonably sure where Triple A was headed. It seemed that he was not the only one to think of the drug lord as society's victim.

"By showing the public what a sack of shit this indictment is. The cops took the word of some junkie who they provided with stuff *on top* of letting him out of a string of B&E's and robbery ones. Tell me, counsellor, how often in your experience has the DA taken the uncorroborated word of such a pillar of society against a man with a verifiable alibi?"

"Not too often," Herbert smiled. "Although I'm sure your 'alibi' is not given great credence, particularly as it was supplied by an associate."

"Associates, counsellor, associates. Nonetheless, your point is well taken."

Herbert was fascinated at the manner in which Triple A could switch from street talk to perfect corporate English and back again without sounding the least bit odd.

"As to the primary witness," Herbert continued, "while it is true that ordinarily the word of such a man would be discounted in the pre-trial process, and if not there, most certainly by a jury, in a case where a, shall we say, leader in his field is involved, no reasonable offer of evidence will be refused."

Triple A again flashed his incisor benignly, as if in humble acknowledgement of his lofty position in the body politic.

"But all this is premature," said Herbert. "Why don't you fill me in on the facts of the case? All I know is what I read in the papers." Herbert realized with some disquiet that he was eager to mount a defense for Triple A Akbar. He wanted to show his new client that he was every bit as smart and powerful in his arena as Trips was in his.

Needing little encouragement, Ali Abdul proceeded to tell the tale of entrapment and deceit that had landed him in this predicament. It seems that an interloper, a corporate raider in the street economy, had begun to make small but significant inroads on the fringes of Ali Abdul's territory. (At no time was the purpose of the 'territory' mentioned specifically. Rather, Triple A preferred corporate euphemisms, such as 'high mark-up item,' 'market penetration,' and 'unfriendly takeover bid.')

After initial negotiations aimed at an amicable resolution failed, Triple A was forced to consider more serious action.

After all, in the world of corporate raiding, any perception of weakness within the target company merely encourages further incursions. ("I got to swim with the sharks," was how Ali Abdul phrased it.)

As positions on both sides hardened, the public, as is often the case in these affairs, was an unfortunate recipient of the fallout. In the street economy, however, coin of the realm is not shares of stock but lives, and as Triple A and Marvin (Psycho) Bates plied their strategies, four civilians were left dead on the streets in the wake of shoot-outs. The last of these was a four-year-old boy, and while the trigger men were caught almost immediately (given up by Ali Abdul who knew the folly of protecting child killers), the outcry was sufficient to send the police brass scurrying in an attempt to end the violence.

The police did not delude themselves into thinking that they could end the drug trade in the area, merely the territorial dispute and the associated random gunplay. In that, they had no favorites. The first of the warring leaders to slip would go down and leave the turf to the other.

A man sensitive to his surroundings, Ali Abdul Akbar was aware that haphazard violence at this delicate time would only decrease his chances for victory, so he was forced to consider a more surgical approach. (At this point the story got a bit vague, since Triple A was taking the position that the ensuing events were coincidence.) It seems that Psycho's brother was persuaded to leave his home in Roosevelt, Long Island, by four unidentified men. Three days later, his beaten, quite dead body was dumped on Psycho's doorstep with a note pinned to his chest. The note read, "You mama's next." It was a threat that could not be reciprocated since Triple A Akbar had no living relatives.

The coincidental death of brother Bates had the desired effect. The dispute was, for the time, resolved in Triple A's favor. But no one was kidding themselves. The tensions continued to simmer and it was all too clear that Psycho would exact his revenge when the shock wore off.

About this time, one Trevor House, the aforementioned junkie and one-time Ghost, swore on a pack of Bibles that he had overheard Ali Abdul Akbar plot the abduction of brother Bates. House's word was immediately accepted, a grand jury speedily impanelled, and an indictment handed down.

"So here I sit," concluded Triple A, "my thumb up my ass, no bail and Psycho out there ready to shoot up the streets if he gets a whiff that I might be convicted. And make no mistake, counsellor," warned Triple A, to lend the air of community service to Herbert's task, "Psycho Bates *is* a psycho. They don't call him that 'cause he looks like fuckin' Tony Perkins. There'll be a lot more dead kids if I don't get out of here to cool things down."

"Well, then," said Herbert, "it seems that the indictment itself poses no threat to you, only the enforced absence from the streets while they prepare their case."

"You got it," nodded Triple A.

Ali Abdul didn't feel it appropriate at this juncture to mention that the trial might indeed be a threat to his survival if Diana, who unlike Trevor House, *had* been present when he had ordered Bates' brother offed, had offered some premortem evidence to her friends at Manhattan North. There had been no indication that the cops had obtained such information, but the CEO of the Ghosts could not be too careful.

Herbert digested his assignment with some disappointment. "So you are not hiring me to replace Mel Seltzer, merely to supplant his efforts at securing your speedy release on bail."

Triple A flashed his incisor sympathetically. "Now, counsellor, while I value your association and, frankly, the brotherhood of blackness that we share, Mel Seltzer is the best defense lawyer in town and there's no harm in using the hymies for what they're good at. But you, my friend, have a power over the politicians that Mel Seltzer could never hope to have . . ." (Herbert once again fought the feeling of gratitude at the flattery), "and can do something that is beyond his capabilities. And besides, it fits in with your agenda, showing how the honky establishment twists the law for itself, using it to keep black folks down."

Herbert sniffed. "You're not exactly black folks, Mr. Akbar."

Triple A glowered once again and the smirk was whipped right off Herbert's face. "Don' you forget, counsellor," growled Trips, "I ain't never been convicted o' nothin'. Not since I was sixteen. This case against me is bullshit. They know they's gonna lose, but if they can keep me in here long enough that maniac Bates'll do their dirty work for them. So, Mr. Herbert Whiffet, the next kid gets gunned down on the street, it be yo' doing as much as mine."

"YOU DID WHAT?" Leotis' voice boomed even though Herbert was right next to him. Life-long sinners would have been frightened into repentance.

"I'm representing Ali Abdul Akbar in his bail appeal," Herbert replied, drawing himself up to his full height to repel the assault of the huge reverend. "His being held without bail is a political act, not a legal one. I make no judgment as to the man himself, only his right to bail under our legal system."

"Herbert," said Leotis, shaking his head, "you done fucked up. Triple A Akbar is the lowest. Herbert, he sells drugs to *children*."

Herbert started. In the excitement, he had almost forgotten what his new client did for a living. Still, he was in it now, and since there was no turning back (one didn't turn back on Ali Abdul Akbar), he felt compelled to persuade Leotis that he had made the correct decision.

"Leotis, every citizen has a right to a legal defense. Don't you see? If they deprive a powerful and influential man like Akbar of *his* rights, they can do it to any of us. Believe me, Leotis, I have no intention of promoting Akbar's profession, only his right to due process. Why should only white lawyers defend our people because we make judgments on the quality of their right to a defense? Mel Seltzer hasn't exhibited any of these sensibilities, why should I?"

"Because Mel Seltzer," Leotis replied patiently, "is not running for DA and because Mel Seltzer doesn't give one god damn what happens in the black community."

Herbert decided to ignore the second reason and focus on the first. "I don't think defending a man's right to bail will hurt my chances of becoming DA."

Leotis rolled his eyes heavenward, asking the Lord's help in enlightening his addle-brained colleague. "Herbert, my friend," the reverend said slowly, "I don't think it will help."

So, with Leotis' words ringing in his ears (this time from content as well as volume), Herbert Whiffet trudged back to his office, refuting the reverend's portents of doom with carefully constructed syllogisms demonstrating precisely how defending Akbar would serve both the movement and his chances at political office.

At the top of the stack of messages that greeted Herbert as he walked in the door was a sign that perhaps God had not deserted him after all. The little pink piece of paper fairly screamed out the solution. It read "Assistant DA Lieberman-Smith called. She's in charge of the de Bourbon case and wants to make an appointment."

Renee! In charge of the de Bourbon case. Renee Lieberman-Smith. Herbert skipped into his office like a leprechaun. Renee. His Renee. Camp follower Renee. Sexually available Renee. Politically committed Renee. The district attorney, his arch enemy, the object of his most intense scorn had assigned Herbert's lover to handle the Lawanda de Bourbon case.

Herbert grabbed for the phone and quickly dialed Renee's number. This time he identified himself accurately and was immediately put through.

"Ms. Lieberman-Smith," he said cordially but officially, "thank you for calling. I also believe that a meeting between us is appropriate in ensuring that justice is done in this case."

"Excellent, Mr. Whiffet," answered a woman's voice, almost unrecognizable in its efficiency. "Would you care to come to our offices? I believe you know where they are."

Herbert was not prepared for the official Renee, but he quickly decided she was merely being prudent.

"Uh, yes, I would be happy to. When would be convenient?"

"Two o'clock?" said the voice.

"Today?"

"Of course. This is an important case to all New Yorkers and I think we should know each other's positions as early as possible."

"Uh, okay." This Renee did not seem to be a pushover. "I'll be there at two."

Phil Gagliardi decided against using the interrogation

room in the precinct for his chat with Vince D'Angelo. In the first place, he owed the captain that much and in the second, an off-premises meeting could prove more illuminating. Open air might encourage open conversation so Phil and Vince strolled the block and a half to Central Park.

Captain D'Angelo was no virgin. A twenty-seven-year veteran, he had stopped two bullets and earned a fistful of citations as a patrolman, and during his rise through the ranks had been given every dirty job that a department famous for dirty jobs could think of. Vince D'Angelo was a 'street cop,' which meant a record that was far from spotless, but certainly indicated a dedication to duty, justice, and the department, although not necessarily in that order.

Vince had no doubts as to the purpose of the chat but his awareness had no effect on his affability. As they both knew, that made Phil's job all the more difficult.

"Captain," Phil began, "we have to talk."

D'Angelo laughed. His laugh always made his beer barrel torso shake. The effect might have projected softness or flabbiness to the unwary. "That's some opening, Phil. I didn't assume we were going to study the flowers."

Damn, Phil thought with a scowl to match Vince's smile. They looked like a pair of drama masks. "Captain, this isn't a joke. I got big problems."

"I know, Phil, I know," replied the captain, turning sober, although Phil was unsure if the change was simply another ploy. "You got problems with my command. You think we're dirty."

"Are you?"

Vince smiled softly and led Phil over to the concrete bleachers by the baseball fields, the site of weekend *fiestas* during the summer when the Latin semi-pro teams take over the north end of the park. Vince sat down on the slab that was the second row and beckoned Phil to sit next to him. They both looked out toward the field as if taking in some spectral game.

"Phil," the captain began, dropping the bravado. "I'm in charge of narcotics. *Narcotics.* It is without question the dirtiest, most tempting, most corrupt, most violent and most risky job that there is anywhere in this department or in any other department. No case is made without informants or undercover, the bribes offered to lay off the big boys are beyond anything you've ever seen, and the bad guys will resort to anything to protect their business. Anything."

The captain turned to his former subordinate and grabbed his wrist. "Phil, I was offered *one half of one million dollars*, five hundred grand, to look the other way. How many people you know gonna turn down half a mil?"

Phil Gagliardi tried not to be staggered by the amount. He had to maintain objectivity. This was a corruption investigation and he was about to hear about corruption.

"So what are you telling me, Captain? You turned down half a mil but accepted a thou? That the big money means that every narcotics operation has got to be a little dirty?"

Captain D'Angelo looked hard at Gagliardi, the glare still possessing some of the intimidation bred of the past relationship.

"I never took a dime. Not one dime. Directly or indirectly. I don't have a second home in the Bahamas, I don't have a secret bank account, I drive a three year-old Chevy and I do a filthy piece-of-shit job the best I can."

Phil felt as if the captain's wrecking ball fist had landed square in his solar plexus. "Sorry, Captain," he mumbled, his initiative lost. "I had to ask."

Vince nodded and his face softened, although his pose of affability was not rekindled. "I know you gotta ask, Phil, but you don't gotta accuse."

Phil nodded, trying to regroup. They both knew the subject was not closed. But D'Angelo wasn't finished.

"To answer the second part of your question, I don't think it's possible to conduct a narcotics operation with squeaky clean cops. They won't get nowhere. Shit, Phil, you know as well as anybody . . . an informant has to be *cultivated*. It's like growin' tomatas in the backyard. If you don't get some dirt under your fingernails you get shitty tomatas."

"So what are you telling me, Captain?" Phil was pleased that he had gotten the sentence out.

"I'm telling you, Phil, that I don't ask my men to turn their pockets inside out at the end of every shift and make 'em account for every fuckin' nickel. I'm telling you I know the difference between a clean cop and a dirty cop and that's what I make my judgments on. And I'll tell you somethin' else, Phil. On the day the department doesn't trust me to make that judgment, on that day I'll turn in my papers."

"And go grow tomatas?" Phil felt better with all the shit out in the open. At least now they were talking cop to cop.

"Yeah, maybe." D'Angelo was smiling again.

"Tell me about Lawanda de Bourbon, Captain."

"Sure, Phil," grinned the captain and for the first time Phil Gagliardi knew he was on probation. If he stopped with the de Bourbon affair, his life would go on as before. If he decided to open up a more detailed investigation, his life might not go on at all.

D'Angelo interrupted Phil's musings on his life expectancy. "Lawanda was a strange one. She came to us. Totally unsolicited. One day one of the boys . . ."

D'Angelo stopped and looked curiously at Gagliardi. "Phil, I hope you don't mind, but if I'm going to tell this to you straight I gotta pat you down first."

"You think I'd wear a wire on you, Captain?" asked the detective, hating the IAD job and all that came with it.

D'Angelo shrugged and proceeded to expertly frisk his fellow cop. In five seconds the captain had satisfied himself that the only place that Gagliardi could have hidden a wire was up his ass and that would muffle the sound anyway.

"Like I was saying," D'Angelo continued as if nothing had happened, "one morning around 2 AM, one of my guys was doing some routine shit when this de Bourbon broad hits him up. Says she got inside dope on Psycho Bates."

"Bates?" Phil asked, surprised. "I thought she was banging Akbar."

"Lawanda de Bourbon," D'Angelo said solemnly, "was banging *everyone*."

Phil whistled, remembering that magnificent body. Just his luck to be in IAD.

"Anyhow," the captain continued, "my guy tries to feel out Lawanda . . . you know, to find out if she's full o' shit or it's a set-up or what. So Lawanda shows her good faith by giving my guy a tip on a shipment and further shows her good faith by screwing his brains out right in the back of his car. That, my dear Phillip, was the beginning of an all-too-short but extremely rewarding relationship between Lawanda de Bourbon and Manhattan North."

"Did she ever give you anything on Akbar? Since he was her main squeeze, maybe she was working for him with Psycho then passing the stuff along to you."

"Nope," replied the captain, shaking his head, "not possible. She gave us great stuff on Ali Abdul. Who do you think turned Trevor House?"

"No shit. You mean House is telling the truth?"

D'Angelo grinned, a failed attempt to appear sheepish. "I wouldn't go that far. He *says* he's telling the truth. When someone is willing to finger Triple A Akbar in a capital crime, we tend to give him a lot of latitude."

Phil shook his head. "If House is fulla shit, Mel Seltzer will eat him alive at the trial."

D'Angelo shrugged again. "Could be. But by then Psycho will have taken over Ghost heaven and the street war will be done with. Besides, we have some good feeds into Psycho's operation. He'll be easier to control than Triple A. Akbar is just too fuckin' smart. Lawanda was the only crack we ever had."

This was the crossroads for Phil Gagliardi. Does he probe deeper? Ask the identity of the detective who first turned Lawanda? Ask about pay-offs? Ask about anything?

Phil realized it wasn't the implied threat that was making him sweat, but his identity as a cop. He was as convinced that the department could not do better than Vince D'Angelo as he was that Jimmy Rodriguez had not offed Lawanda as part of a plot. If he went further, D'Angelo would go down, he'd end up on a slab, and the narcotics division would lose another round to the Akbars.

"Okay, Captain," he said pushing himself to his feet, "that about does it."

D'Angelo stood as well but still eyed Gagliardi. "You sure, Phil?"

Gagliardi screwed up his face and nodded perfunctorily. "Yeah, I'm sure."

# CHAPTER SEVENTEEN

Every time he entered the offices of the District Attorney of New York County, Herbert Whiffet felt a chill. He chalked it up to 'one day this will all be mine,' but was too self-appraising to discount a different possibility—the institution scared him. This was, or at least always had been, white man's country, a place where no black man could feel he had a friend. Although he had every intention of changing all that, the present was still the present.

This visit was especially awkward. For the first time he would meet with Renee Lieberman-Smith in her official capacity at her official residence. Despite his complete confidence that she was firmly in his camp, Herbert had a vague feeling of disquiet. Maybe it was her voice on the telephone, maybe his fear that her new power would go to her head but somehow this was not the same available, acquiescent Renee that he had been able to bounce around at the end of a string.

Herbert stopped in the hall to catch his breath. This is ridiculous, he thought. Renee is still Renee. Everything is as it was. It's just that the stakes are higher. Herbert realized that these feelings of risk and doom had begun to dog him everywhere—with the tape, with Triple A Akbar and now with that most malleable of women, Renee Lieberman-Smith. Okay, this is enough. Go in there and do it.

Armed with his adopted purposefulness, Herbert strode through the door with the same rights as any other citizen. Almost immediately he realized how foolish he had been. ADA Lieberman-Smith walked over to greet him, shaking his hand with a little squeeze and telling him with just a hint of extra emphasis how glad she was that he could make it.

"Thank you, Ms. Lieberman-Smith," he replied, reciprocating her eye contact. "I look forward to working *closely* with the district attorney's office to obtain justice in this case."

"That is our interest too, Mr. Whiffet. It would be more comfortable if we spoke in the conference room. There are one or two others working on the case who I would like to have sit in, but perhaps you and I might have a brief word first."

"Of course, Ms. Lieberman-Smith."

As Renee led him across the floor in the direction of the conference room, Herbert Whiffet felt like cheering. This was perfect. Renee was understated and professional, all the while communicating her intention to do the right thing. He almost found her attractive again.

Once they were inside the room and Renee had closed the door, she grabbed Herbert's wrist and spoke softly and quickly.

"Herbert, I want you to know that despite anything I do on the outside, any difficulty I may seem to pose for you, I intend to pursue this case in the way we both want. So, please," she squeezed his wrist and looked him in the eye with the adoration that the maiden reserves for the rescuing knight, "meet strength with strength. This will work out. Trust me."

The Champion could only nod, so perfectly had things fallen into place. There is nothing like an air of conspiracy to make the unlikely believable. Renee smiled in return, then opened the door and summoned two of her colleagues to begin the official meeting.

As they entered the conference room, Herbert greeted a young waspy-looking man, Gregory Bock, and a squat black woman, Willa Ward. He took an instant dislike to both, especially Willa,who combined a pugnacious anti-sexuality with a pose of intellectual superiority. Little did she realize that she was sitting in the company of her future boss.

Renee got right to business and, as she had indicated, took the hard line. "Mr. Whiffet, as you know, the district attorney's office has decided to seek an indictment against Officer James Rodriguez in the shooting death of Lawanda de Bourbon. As a result of eyewitness accounts, of which we understand you had been aware since the day of the incident, we will present the evidence to the grand jury with the object of trying Officer Rodriguez for murder in the second degree."

Herbert nodded his approval. Negotiations are fun when

you know they will be resolved in your favor. "I'm pleased to hear that, Ms. Lieberman-Smith, although we in the African-American community continue to maintain that prosecution of one member of a racist criminal justice system cannot be entrusted to another member of the same system."

Willa Ward carefully placed her pencil on the notepad in front of her. "And just what 'African-American community' do you claim to represent, Mr. Whiffet? How many votes did *you* get in the last election?"

Herbert turned on the stumpy Ms. Ward who would soon be looking for other employment. "The fact that black people do not get justice within this system has too long a history and is too obvious a fact for me to go into here. And you, of all people, Ms. Ward, should be all too well aware that by keeping the black community politically fragmented, the white racist power structure denies us a say in our destiny and condemns us to be pawns in their self-perpetuating control. So don't get upset if the black community begins to assert itself and seeks redress outside a system that has been its enemy in the past."

Renee put up her hand. "Much of what you say may have merit, Mr. Whiffet, but this meeting is not to debate history. It is to find the best possible way in which to vigorously pursue a conviction in the murder of Lawanda de Bourbon, and to that end we at the district attorney's office are prepared to do everything we can to ensure a conviction."

"I have no doubt of your personal sincerity, Ms. Lieberman-Smith," replied the Champion. "We simply doubt the commitment and the will of the district attorney to prosecute a member of the police department for a capital crime. We feel that only a special prosecutor, and, in this case, a *black* special prosecutor, can serve the needs of the community."

Renee nodded again, carefully reflecting on the lawyer's words. "I'm sorry, Mr. Whiffet. We are forced to disagree. We think that entrusting the prosecution of this case to our office will well serve the needs of the entire community. And to that end, we must ask you to turn over to us all materials that may be in your possession that have pertinence to this case."

Herbert folded his hands on the table and looked across at his adversary/conspirator. She was playing it just as she said. Had they not spoken privately, Herbert might well have taken a cautious approach here, utilized a delaying tactic, something to allow him time to size up the situation. But there was no need—he had already been told what the situation was.

"I'm sorry, Ms. Lieberman-Smith," he said with finality and conviction, "I cannot turn over any materials to your office until such time as a black special prosecutor is appointed to pursue this case."

Renee sighed and shrugged. "Very well, Mr. Whiffet. If that is your position, I've no choice but to present you with this." Renee slid a folded document across to her Champion. "That is a subpoena, instructing you to turn over any and all materials in your possession, including but not limited to a videotape of the event, to the office of the District Attorney for the County of New York within seventy-two hours. Failure to comply with this subpoena will result in a request by this office that you be held in contempt."

Herbert fingered the subpoena as Renee spoke. Even as she droned out the conditions, her eyes were saying 'trust me,' and even as Herbert assured himself that she must know what she was doing, that feeling of doom returned.

The meeting ended with Herbert announcing he would defy the subpoena and Willa Ward smirking at the potential consequences. As the Champion was cordially shown to the door, Renee stood and watched, still the very picture of thoughtfulness and consideration.

*Cornelia Fucking Pembroke*, she thought.

"It's quite simple, Herbert," said Leotis, booming out his opinion as if it were a commandment, "you must ignore the subpoena and dare that honky DA to put you in jail."

"That's easy for you to say, Leotis," grumbled the man being volunteered for incarceration. "You don't have to go."

With a scowl, Leotis launched a volley of fire and brimstone at his colleague. "Sonny, I been in jail more times than you done had a woman. I been sittin' in an' ridin' in an' marchin' an' gettin' spit on and pissed on an' beat up since before you decided that yo' people needed yo' legal skills. So don't you go whinin' to me about a couple days in the can to make a point."

Leotis had him and Herbert knew it. Martyrs to justice are not easily refuted, especially when they lapse so convincingly into the vernacular. He needed to find a way out without appearing squeamish. Squeamishness was decidedly un-Championlike behavior.

"I don't know what point I'm going to make by sitting in a cell," Herbert offered. "My absence will merely allow the DA to make his case with one of the chief antagonists on ice." Herbert was fairly pleased. That sounded quite believable.

But Leotis did not seem to share Herbert's opinion of his gambit. "Herbert, you just don't get it. You been doin' this for some years now, and sometimes I swear I don't know how your mind works."

Herbert clenched his teeth but did not reply. He hated when Leotis played 'Daddy.'

"Herbert, the whole idea is to use this case, but it could have been any case, to *express* the conditions we oppose. The case, the facts . . . they don't matter so much. What matters is that we get the opportunity to *demonstrate* that the system is racist and the cards are stacked against black people. The idea is to create *outrage* in the black community, *outrage* that will eventually find its way to the ballot box and the appropriations committees.

"What could possibly serve us better, could better arouse the black community, than the honky DA puttin' you in jail for holdin' to your principles? For insisting that the man give up prosecution of his spiritual bedmate so that a fair trial can be ensured?"

"That's all fine, Leotis," countered Herbert. "But what happens when people actually *see* the tape? It's going to look like a big hoax."

"Like hell it will. Just remember, Herbert, no gun is visible in the girl's hand at any time. You will take the position that *because* there are some unimportant frames where the girl's hand is not seen, *because* of that, you wanted to make sure that whoever prosecuted the case, they didn't allow the murderer cop to elude justice by pretending there was a gun. Don't forget, my friend, the police *have* an eyewitness."

"Some witness," muttered Herbert. "A first-year law student could take him apart."

"Maybe so, but he'll do just fine for our purposes. Herbert, you must ignore the subpoena and you must do it publicly."

"Maybe you're right, Leotis," sighed the Champion, facing the unpleasant prospect of taking his crusade to jail.

Herbert Whiffet suddenly felt like the horse he had been

riding into town to save the day was now riding him. And, in retrospect, he realized that he had walked out of the DA's office having allowed Renee Lieberman-Smith to set the rules without making a peep in protest. Whatever grand plan Renee was hatching, it had better be good to justify all of this.

Herbert decided that perhaps he should make an effort to find out.

Cornelia Pembroke finally found out what had happened to Fruitful Willis.

As a service to news-hungry New York, the city coroner prepares a daily listing of all unnatural deaths that have occurred within the previous twenty-four hours. Reporters regularly scan this list in search of notables, once-notables or never-notables who may have some connection with a past story. Cornelia happened on WRCT's copy of what had been christened 'The Stiff List,' and browsed the alphabetically ordered release, pondering, as she sometimes did, what histories these otherwise anonymous travellers may have had to end up in the coroner's Who's Who.

As she reached the end, there it was, next to last, a name to whom she could fit a face.

"Willis, Fruitful, male negro, Age 34, body discovered by Officer Franklin Yee during routine patrol in an alley, Stanton Street, between Bowery and Christie. Current address: None. Occupation: Vagrant. Cause of death: Brain hemorrhage, brought on by blow or blows to the head. Possible cause: Striking with blunt instrument or severe fall. Ruling: Accident. Follow up: None. Identification: Fingerprints, NYPD. Willis had a record of thirty-two misdemeanor arrests, including two outstanding warrants from 1980 at which time he had dropped from sight."

So that was it, the Fruitful Willis story. Cornelia remembered she had forgotten to reschedule her interview with Clarissa Taylor and made a note to do so. For a moment she was tempted to do a little checking into the man's background, to find out what tortured path had led a man only thirty-four years old to die an old man's death on skid row.

The idea quickly faded. Human interest pieces on someone's fall to vagrancy were old and stale. Fruitful Willis would have to be satisfied with what little notoriety went with a paragraph on the Stiff List.

# PART II

# CHAPTER EIGHTEEN

For the next weeks, while the district attorney threatened and Herbert Whiffet stone-walled and Leotis Chestnut blustered and Cornelia Pembroke reported, Clarissa Taylor went back and forth to her job at Hot Feet. While most of New York was held enrapt by the posturing and theatrics surrounding the Lawanda de Bourbon case, Clarissa was focussed on more fundamental issues.

It had become clear that working two jobs was a pipe dream. As it was, she could hardly stand when she arrived home at 6:45. A cashier at Hot Feet didn't simply wait behind the cash register for orderly patrons to bring their intended purchases forward. A cashier at Hot Feet needed abilities most often found in jailers and zoo-keepers. In addition to the constant attempts to liberate Russell McKey's wares, the youth of Jamaica played with the stock, brought open soft drinks or hot dogs into the store, some of which invariably found their way on to the merchandise, and generally dared the establishment's authority figures, including the cashier lady, to stop them from turning the store into a dance hall.

What was worse, for all of this exhausting work, Clarissa's take-home pay was only a fraction of what it had been at Murray's, and there was no longer the occasional extra 'for the kids.' For the first time Clarissa realized how much higher the cost of living was in Forest Hills as opposed to, say, Jamaica. Clarissa took to buying groceries after work at a local supermarket and toting them home on the bus rather than pay the higher prices at the store only a block from her building.

Although Clarissa tried to maintain her optimism, the kids sensed the change as well. Matthew got a job after school delivering groceries from the very store where Clarissa could no longer afford to shop. The girls, too young to work, picked up any slack with the housework. Still, as each day passed, the Taylor family grew ever so slightly poorer.

As July steamed in, Clarissa was forced to consider the potential savings if the family scaled down what was by far their biggest expenditure—rent. It wasn't as if they had to move to the South Bronx; there were any number of neighborhoods where working class black people could live comfortably while paying moderate rents. Clarissa began to realize all the things she had always disliked about Forest Hills; the snootiness, the undercurrent of racism, the lack of a real 'community' spirit. Perhaps she was doing the children a disservice by making them live in a place where their racial identity was forcibly submerged.

Clarissa's musings were invariably extinguished as soon as she got off the bus in Jamaica, where the trash, both human and material, reminded her of what most neighborhoods reserved for blacks were like. As a result of years of living and working in areas where sights and sounds were modulated, or as modulated as things get in New York, her senses had grown more open, less able to perform the selective editing process necessary for day-to-day existence in the ghetto. Making her way from the bus stop to Hot Feet, it seemed as if that bum who had driven Murray out of business had been replicated a thousandfold. Picking her way along the sidewalk, Clarissa noticed every crack vial, every discarded beer bottle, as only someone who feared to fall into society's sub-basement would.

While her sensory apparatus let in any variety of unwanted images, it failed to detect others. Life in the Jamaicas of the world demands more than simple editing; it demands redirection. While the ability to tune out the majority of everyday stimuli allows the ghetto dweller to avoid the madness of overload, the ability to discern which of those stimuli are life-threatening is necessary for survival. Clarissa Taylor, despite constant self-reminders to be vigilant, no longer possessed that fine tuning that some call a 'sixth sense.'

'Broad daylight' has a strange and primal connotation, as if crimes committed while the sun shines brightly are more heinous than those committed in the dark. 'Broad daylight' is that time when the helpless and the enfeebled are allowed to walk the streets in peace while nightfall signals the time when even the strong venture out at their own peril. When the public reads of those victimized by muggers or rapists at 3 AM, they subconsciously ask, "What were they doing out at such an hour?" as if somehow that fact alone had made them an accomplice in the crime. Neighborhoods in which a large number of crimes are committed in 'broad daylight' are invariably marked as society's worst.

In Jamaica, Queens, of course, 'broad daylight' was no inhibition to those who would rob, rape or murder. In fact, simply *because* a greater number of easy targets ventured out on to the streets, 'broad daylight' was a quite popular time to commit mayhem.

In the Northern Hemisphere, July is a time when 'broad daylight' lasts the longest, and thus presents a rare opportunity for those who must be indoors after dark to stretch their day. Since night did not invade Jamaica until after 8 PM, Clarissa Taylor had the freedom to shop at leisure after leaving work and still have plenty of time to catch the bus. This evening's venture to the local fruit stand had been particularly successful. Fresh fruit and vegetables abound in July, and even the ghetto green grocer had an ample stock of just-ripe peaches and unwilted broccoli. Clarissa had come to be friendly with Mr. Paik who often saved some of his more choice stock for her.

Heading home with her prize, Clarissa failed to notice the three teen-age boys whose destination seemed to parallel hers. It wasn't that they were creeping silently behind her as much as there didn't seem to be anything that separated them from the dozens of other teen-age boys she encountered daily.

But these boys were different. They were, in fact, not boys at all. The trio, whose street age, elongated by crack and the desperation of poverty, far outdistanced what a calendar would measure, was an organized, disciplined wolf-pack, urban predators whose survival, defined as the ability to procure drugs, was directly related to the ability to attain a steady and rather hefty cash flow. It was to this end that the three adopted all the mannerisms of carefree teen-agers, an effective disguise in an area where youth was the dominant force of street life.

Walking with her packages, Clarissa finally became suspicious when she turned a corner of a side street, the last leg of her journey to the bus stop. She hesitated a moment before the turn, some instinct telling her to take the long way. But Clarissa was already late and the packages were heavy. Besides, this was broad daylight and she couldn't spend her life afraid of shadows.

So Clarissa Taylor headed down the short block that separated her from the busy avenue and safety, the short block that would be a watershed in her life and the lives of her children. For, before she had taken five more steps, the three boys who were not really teen-agers burst upon her with such speed that Clarissa did not even have time to turn her head, and before another image had a chance to fix itself in her mind, her packages were scattered, her purse was gone and she was lying on the ground, the tops of the buildings spinning against the backdrop of the sky.

Although she did not have an especially large sum of money in her purse, any money was precious and her instinct was to chase and apprehend whoever had perpetrated such an invasive act. So without waiting to gather her wits, Clarissa jumped to her feet and began to scream at the figures fading up the street. As she tried to stand and before she could complete her intended sentence of "Stop, Thief," Clarissa was on the ground again. Her senses were returning and she became aware of a warm liquid flowing down her face and into her eye. She reached to wipe her face and as she pulled her hand away realized the liquid was blood, undoubtedly hers although she couldn't tell from where.

Clarissa tried to sit up again but could not. She became aware of a pulsing, not painful really, in the vicinity of her left temple. Maybe that was where the blood was coming from. Clarissa reached her hand up again, but suddenly the sky got very spotty, like bad television reception, and it was hard to breathe. Then the sky was gone.

"Mrs. Taylor . . . ?"

Was someone calling her name?

"Mrs. Taylor . . . ?"

Woman's voice. Young. Friendly. Jeanette? Veronica?

"No, Mrs. Taylor. I'm a nurse. This is Jamaica Hospital. You've had an accident."

An accident? Where? In a car? The sky . . .

"Can you hear me, Mrs. Taylor?"

Uh-huh. Can I? Time to wake up and go to work.

"Can you open your eyes? Or tell me your name?"
Cla . . .
Clarissa forced her eyes open to end the dream. Can't sleep the day away. But she was not in her bedroom. It was a bright room . . . there was a girl in a white dress. Not Jeanette. Not Veronica. What had she said? Jamaica Hospital? Was she dying?
Although speech was still an order of awareness away, Clarissa communicated her disorientation and terror with wide, darting eyes.
"You're okay, Mrs. Taylor," said the girl in the white dress. Her voice was soothing and kind. Clarissa pulled back from her panic and took in the room. It was large, with three beds like hers and . . . that's right. Jamaica Hospital. She was a patient, but she was okay. The girl just said so.
Clarissa heard a strange voice ask, "What happened?" then realized that the voice was hers.
The girl in the white dress smiled. "That's very good, Mrs. Taylor. Do you remember what happened?"
Remember? The spotted sky against the buildings . . . blood on her hand . . . "A little," said the strange voice that was hers. "There were . . . boys, three boys."
Then, despite the soothing girl in white, Clarissa was gripped by panic again, although this time the source was different. "My purse! My money! I was robbed!" By reflex, Clarissa tried to sit up and then was thrown back by a hot knife that ripped into her left eye and traveled through to the top of her head. The girl in the white dress held her softly.
"Lie still, Mrs. Taylor. It's good that you remember. You must have hit your head when you fell, or one of the muggers did it. You've suffered a concussion. The police recovered your purse, but all the money was gone."
Clarissa felt a wave of relief. Her purse was somehow her identity, almost as a photograph was to members of primitive tribes in New Guinea, and the idea of it being in the possession of her attackers would stretch the terrible incident indefinitely. But the money was lost.
"Did the police catch them?" asked the voice, more recognizable. As long as she did not try to sit up, Clarissa felt much better. She had a clear idea where she was and the robbery was now fixed in her memory.
"No," replied the nurse, a young white woman. "I'm afraid

they didn't. One of the local detectives would like to speak to you when you're up to it."

Clarissa nodded. "I can do it now."

"Are you sure? He would be happy to come back later."

"No," said Clarissa, "now." The sooner she spoke to the police the better the chance her attackers may be caught. "Oh, nurse," she said, her senses fully returned, "has anyone spoken to my children? They'll be worried that I'm not home yet."

The nurse smiled and took Clarissa's arm. "Don't worry, Mrs. Taylor. The police contacted your children and told them that you were all right. They wanted to come to the hospital but the police told them to stay home. The boy, Matthew, he said he would wait to hear from you. Perhaps before you speak to the detective, you can call them."

"Yes, thank you. Could you dial the number and hand me the telephone?"

Clarissa gave the nurse the number and held the telephone against her ear as the young girl dialed. Someone answered on the first ring.

"Hello?" asked a young male voice. Clarissa could feel Matthew's fear.

"Hello, son," she replied, making her best effort to sound just like Mama.

"Mama!" cried her oldest. "Are you okay?"

"I'm fine, son. Just a little shook up, that's all. But they're takin' real good care of me."

"Oh, Mama, we were really worried. When the detective told us you had been in an accident, hit your head an' all . . ."

"Well I'm just fine. Your Mama's got a pretty hard head."

Matthew laughed, relief mixing with the fear. "The girls want to talk."

"Okay, but just for a minute."

Veronica and Jeanette must have grabbed the receiver at the same time because both voices, one over the other, came through at once. "Mommy." "Mommy." "How are you?" "When can we see you?" "Are you okay?" "Can we come to the hospital?" "When are you coming home?" "When are you coming home?"

"Whoa," replied Mommy, her head beginning to ache again. "Slow down. I'm fine and you can come to see me as soon as the doctors say it's okay. I love you both. Now put Matthew back on."

The man of the house took the receiver once more.

"Now, son. Take care of everything. You find out who my doctor is and you and the girls can come to see me if he says it's okay. Is everything all right at home?"

"It is now, Mama."

"Good. Now throw Mama a kiss good night and go take care of the girls. I love you, Matthew."

"I love you too, Mama."

As the nurse hung up the telephone, Clarissa looked up and saw an overweight black man in jeans and a plaid shirt that looked like it had not been changed in days.

"Hello, Mrs. Taylor," the man smiled. Harried though it was, the smile had a twinkle to it that made Clarissa feel safe. "I'm Detective Hoopes."

Clarissa felt herself smile in return at the outsized detective. There was something about his bulk and world-weary appearance that was reassuring.

"Hope you're feeling better, Ma'am." It was funny to be addressed as Ma'am by a man who was at least her age. Did she look that old?

Detective Hoopes pulled a chair up to her bed and lowered his bulk into it as if he had just completed a trek across the Himalayas. With some effort, he pulled a notebook and ballpoint pen out of his pocket.

"Let's start with what you remember straight out. Describe what happened as best you can. Don't worry if it's spotty. We'll fill the rest in later."

Detective Hoopes also had a very soothing voice which took the pressure off the pain in her head that seemed to grow larger with each hammer blow.

"Well, there were three of them. Boys, about eighteen maybe. They must have followed me from the vegetable man on 167th . . . I didn't think much of it . . . just three teenagers. But when I turned down the block to head for the bus stop, I heard them turn too and I got scared but before I could do anything they were on me."

"That's very good, Mrs. Taylor," said the detective, scribbling as they spoke. "Was there anything you remember about any of them? Anything at all. Looks, voice, clothing . . . anything."

Clarissa shook her head and the pain made the detective go fuzzy. She shut her eyes.

"You okay, Mrs. Taylor?"

"Yes." Clarissa ventured a smile. "I've got to remember not to move my head. But I'm sorry, Detective Hoopes. I don't remember anything. They came at me from behind and it happened so quickly . . ."

The detective shifted in his chair, the movement creating a ripple effect down his body. "You know, Mrs. Taylor," he said easily, "it's amazing how much we see without realizing it. For example . . . you said that you knew three boys were following you. Well, how do you know it was three? How do you know they were boys?"

"Well . . ." Clarissa was confused and she was afraid it would make her head hurt again. "I must have glanced at them sometime. But I don't remember."

Detective Hoopes, whose poundage was proportional to his skill as an interrogator, knew that he only had another minute or two before he lost his witness to pain and fatigue.

"I'll tell you what, Mrs. Taylor. Close your eyes again. Just relax. Don't try hard. Just let the picture you had of the boys come into your head. Then take kind of a photograph with your mind and, when you're ready, tell me what you see."

Clarissa did as the detective asked. It was a blessing to shut her eyes anyway. But he was wrong; there was no picture. Just three shapeless forms. Then . . . there was one thing. The boy in the middle was taller than the other two. How could she know that? She *must* have seen them. A glint. What was it? A gold chain, a thick gold chain on the one with the painter's hat on sideways . . .

Clarissa opened her eyes and smiled at the detective. "You were right. It's coming."

Hoopes made a motion for Clarissa to close her eyes again. "That's fine. There's no rush. Just take your time and tell me when you're ready."

Back in the screening room of her memory, Clarissa saw the three boys who were not teen-agers. In fact, she remembered being struck with how serious they looked. Walking with the swagger. Red sneakers. The tall one had red sneakers. What about the one on the right? His head was shaved.

Clarissa opened her eyes and told Detective Hoopes all she had seen. Before she had finished, he began to nod and ask questions of his own. "Did one of them do anything unusual with his hands?" Yes, she remembered. He swung his right hand like he was twirling something.

After another question or two, the detective stopped. "Thank you, Mrs. Taylor, you've been very helpful. The three boys who attacked you fit the description of three who have committed a number of robberies in the neighborhood. All women and the elderly, of course. If it makes you feel better, we have a line on them and before you know it, you may get the chance to help send them to prison."

A couple of pleasantries later, Detective Hoopes was gone. The pain in Clarissa's head seemed to have been removed some distance away and was now more like an echo. Things began to drift and run together and Clarissa tried to imagine what home-lives those boys must have had to be now robbing other boys' mothers. But her imagination was too overburdened to find an answer to such a complex riddle and she escaped into sleep.

The arm of coincidence is long and often are the innocent accused and even convicted on coincidence's whim. In court it is called circumstantial evidence and the rights of the accused demand that such problematic indications be overwhelming in order to establish guilt.

Once again, coincidence seemed to be claiming an innocent victim. The rash of violence and war for turf in Manhattan Valley that post-dated by only a matter of days the release of Ali Abdul Akbar on bail from Rikers Island was laid by cynics directly at that noted community leader's door.

Some of those same cynics sought out the newest member of the Akbar defense team, Herbert Whiffet, to demand an explanation for the activist lawyer's actions. Whiffet had been instrumental in obtaining the release of the feared patriarch of the Ghosts, who, their leader returned, were once again asserting themselves in their neighborhood at the expense of the followers of Psycho Bates as well as the public at large.

"I don't know what all the fuss is about," Herbert Whiffet said to the reporters gathered to question him about his new client. "If Ali Abdul Akbar is convicted in a *court of law* for dealing in narcotics, I will be the *fffirst* to *demannnd* that he be sent to prison. If probable cause is established to suggest that Mr. Akbar may be guilty of a crime, I will be the *fffirst* to *demannnd* that he be brought to trial. But Mr. Akbar is *still* a citizen, although his being *BLACK* usually obscures that fact, and has a *right* to bail and has a *right* to be free of contrived charges by a *desperate po*-lice and a *desperate* dis-trict attorney. And I say to the *desperate* dis-trict attorney, 'If Mr. Akbar is *guillllty*, convict him. Don't cover your *own* failures by manufacturing evidence.'"

Although the cynics continued to sniff at the lawyer's explanation, those on the ramparts in the battle for equal rights applauded such courageous action. Imagine Herbert Whiffet, at the risk of his reputation and in the face of what was sure to be gleeful vilification by a hostile, racist press, taking on a case of such controversy, such underlying significance, purely as a matter of principle.

No one was more surprised at the support the Champion received than his long-time friend and colleague, the Reverend Leotis Chestnut. So impressed was the reverend at the astute judgment of Attorney Whiffet in his choice of clients that he paid him the highest of compliments. He insisted on appearing with Herbert at the news conference where the lawyer issued his stinging challenge to the incumbent DA. A modest man, the reverend allowed his colleague to spearhead the assault. After all, Herbert should be allowed some reward for such a brilliant tactical ploy.

During the media hullabaloo, the subject of the raging controversy remained above the fray. Having obtained his release through an adroit use of his rights, Triple A Akbar was now faced with too sizable an agenda to concern himself with petty questions of justice and the rights of the accused.

Nor did he particularly care who was district attorney. Ali Abdul was a man whose political instincts rivaled his street sense, and if there was one sure thing to bet on in the next election, it was that the district attorney, the chief prosecutor in Manhattan, the guardian of white business and white property and white bodies in the center of white financial, political, artistic, and social life of perhaps the entire planet, would most surely be white. Herbert Whiffet's chance of usurping that post was about the same as Ali Abdul's being named the DEA's Man of the Year.

Dismissing the broader social issues, Triple A set himself to his task from the moment he was released from Rikers. After the initial inconvenience posed by the horde of reporters at the prison gates, where Ali Abdul was forced to give some asinine statement reaffirming everyone's right to due process and that he was merely a local businessman caught up in a web of police corruption and racism, he ducked into a Ghost van and immediately dropped from sight.

Then, forty-eight hours later, in the beginning of the aforementioned coincidence, two of Psycho Bates' street captains were found on West 106th Street, piano wire around their slit throats, handcuffed to each other around a sapling planted by hopeful neighborhood residents. A little sign, "Please Keep Your Dogs Away—Manhattan Valley Civic Association," was covered with the two men's blood.

Later that day, in broad daylight, an unidentified van sped up 105th Street, and, passing a building known to be a Ghost stronghold, sprayed the entire courtyard with automatic weapons fire. In an incredible display of good marksmanship or just another coincidence, the three people who were killed were all members of the Ghosts, one a fourteen-year-old, 'Spiderman' Jiggers, whom Triple A was grooming for greatness.

Akbar himself was riding out the storm in Yonkers, secreted in a building which he owned under one of his many corporate aliases. When the news of the escalating violence reached him, Triple A smiled. Losing Spiderman was a blow, but it meant the overall plan was working. Ali Abdul Akbar knew that good things happened when events moved fast and only the quickest thinkers survived. And he intended that things move at lightning speed. Then, when everyone was caught in the dizzying eddy, he could focus undisturbed on his number one priority—finding where the cops had stashed Trevor House.

# CHAPTER NINETEEN

True to their word, the doctors at Jamaica Hospital released Clarissa Taylor after forty-eight hours of observation. Although there seemed to be no permanent damage as a result of the concussion, she was told to stay off her feet and rest for the next two to three weeks. Failure to follow these instructions could result in a relapse, the next occurrence being more severe and carrying a greater risk of complications.

That was easy for them to say, thought Clarissa on her first day home. They don't have to worry about *their* jobs.

And worry about her job she did. She had called Russell McKey from the hospital the morning after the incident. The police had already informed her employer of the robbery and Russell was filled with concern. But when he asked how long she thought she would be absent from work, there was just a hint in his tone that the wrong answer would result in the stay being permanent.

"Don't worry, Russell," she laughed, as casual as she could manage. "A couple of days. I've got a pretty hard head."

Russell laughed as well, but his high-pitched squeak was modulated by suspicion. "I don' know, Mama. A concussion . . . You sure the doctors tol' you that you could come back to work right away?"

"Sure, Russell. It's fine, really. I know how much you need someone on the register."

"Yeah, that's true all right," he replied. "But Mama, if somethin' happens to you on the job, I'm responsible. So you make sure you be all right befo' you come back."

"Thanks, Russell," Clarissa said, relieved at dodging the crisis. "I'll be careful. See you in a couple of days."

She had hung up, upset with herself for lying, but what else could she do? Even though Medicaid paid most of the bills, there was a piece of the hospital charge that she had to foot herself, to say nothing of the lost wages and stolen money. Maybe big executives could afford to be sick, but not a woman in her mid-thirties with three kids competing in a tiny job market against girls half her age.

So now, her first day home from the hospital, she decided to try and go to work tomorrow. The thought of walking the same streets where a mere three days ago she had been set upon and robbed reignited the flame in her left temple. The doctors had warned her that tension could aggravate her symptoms, leaving her dizzy and headached, but they had scant understanding of the tension that was created lying at home while her job passed to a younger, healthier woman.

The kids came home right after school to tend to their mother but, despite their good intentions, the fussing and fawning by Matthew, Veronica and Jeanette was not exactly the most restful environment. Clarissa tried to stay calm, to rest with her eyes shut, saving the strength that she knew she'd need for the trip to Hot Feet in the morning.

Clarissa also needed a night of sound sleep but her dreams did not oblige. Rather than the nightmares of the mugging she might have expected, her unconscious dredged up memories of Freeman, filthy and alcohol-breathed, beating and virtually raping her in a vermin-infested bedroom. Morning came as a relief.

She maintained a casual air until the children left for school—no need to have them worry about her safety on top of everything else. In the fifteen minutes between their departure and hers, Clarissa sat with a cold washcloth over her eyes, trying to quell the pain that had started even before she could leave the house.

Finally, she pushed out the door and on to the bus stop to begin her run of a gauntlet of noise, flashing lights and fear. The thirty-minute bus ride, usually an opportunity to think quietly and relax, was hardly that as Clarissa, unable to find a seat, was forced to hang on to a hand-hold as if it were a line securing her to a lifeboat in a raging sea.

Soon a young man offered her a seat. His features seemed vague but from the look on his face Clarissa could see that he knew that there was something wrong—and the something must be with her.

Once she was seated a strange sensation began to take

hold. It was an other-worldliness, a distance, where nothing that is happening relates to you or can hurt you, and even though Clarissa knew that her head still hurt, somehow it was someone else's head. The closest thing she could remember was the way she felt when she snorted some heroin behind the high school when she was sixteen.

But this was not high school. With an effort, Clarissa remembered that she was headed to a job she desperately needed and concentrated on the passing streets so that she would not miss her stop. Finally, the bus arrived at her destination and Clarissa forced herself to her feet and got off. She had become accustomed to the bouncing bus and solid ground was disorienting. Clarissa stood for a moment, leaning against the one wall of the bus-stop shelter that had not been broken out by vandalizing youths and then set out for Hot Feet.

Had she been in better health, retracing the steps that had led her to be robbed might have been a daunting experience. Under the influence of her concussion-induced narcosis, however, the streets themselves, dipping and swaying, occupied her entire concentration.

Without exactly realizing how she had done it, Clarissa Taylor arrived at Hot Feet.

She nodded hello to Pookie, the security guard, who returned the greeting with a look that was either suspicion or concern. Clarissa realized that she must straighten up before she saw Russell or he would send her home.

When she got to the office, Russell came out and looked her up and down with the same expression as Pookie.

"Mama, you okay? You look a little twilight zone." Russell's voice seemed higher than usual.

"Yes, Russell. I'm fine, thank you. I just want to get to work." Clarissa heard her voice with a slight but distinct echo.

Russell shrugged. "If you say so, Mama."

After Clarissa got to her post, Russell gestured for Pookie to come to the back where the security guard and the giant engaged in some brief conversation, Russell talking and Pookie nodding.

Fortunately for Clarissa, the morning hours at Hot Feet were the least crowded, the teen-age clientele preferring other activities to shoe buying. But at 10:30 the store did receive an unusual visitor.

"Hello, Mrs. Taylor. Remember me?"

Clarissa looked up from her daze. "Of course. How are you, Detective Hoopes?"

To her surprise, the detective had the same expression on his face as had Pookie and Russell. Why did everyone have to look at her like that? Clarissa felt like an exhibit somewhere.

"Mrs. Taylor, should you be at work? Didn't the doctors tell you to take a few weeks off?"

"If I took a few weeks off, Detective, I'd be taking off for good."

Detective Hoopes scowled and nodded. At least someone understood. "Is your boss giving you any trouble, Mrs. Taylor? I could have a talk with him."

Clarissa shook her head, anxiety causing her to forget the effect it had. She winced. "No, please don't bother yourself, Detective Hoopes. Russell has been very nice. That's just the way things are."

The detective nodded once more. Raised in the ghetto himself, he knew the way things were. "I looked for you at home, Mrs. Taylor. When you weren't there, I came here." The detective, who she realized could have been the 'after' to Russell's 'before,' smiled softly. "We got 'em. All three of them."

Clarissa just stared back at him.

"We arrested the three guys who robbed you. Got 'em on fifteen counts each. I came to ask you if you could come to the precinct and try to identify them."

Suddenly, Clarissa was desperately afraid. She wanted them caught, of course. But now the anonymity of her attackers, her way of allowing the event to recede out of short-term and into long-term memory, was being taken from her.

"Don't be frightened, Mrs. Taylor. These boys are going up for a long time. We already have four positive ID's. We would just like yours too, if you could manage it."

Clarissa struggled to cope with this new invasion. "Well, Detective Hoopes, I can't really leave work and since you already have four others . . ." Why did she so fear to see those boys?

The detective leaned closer to her. "Look, Mrs. Taylor. You can never have too many ID's. It's a way of showing the judge the quality of individual he's dealing with. You do want these guys put away, don't you?"

"Of course," she protested. The store was starting to take on the complexion of the buildings against the sky.

When the detective saw Clarissa's eyes begin to roll, he pulled back, then smiled, the same benevolent smile as in the hospital. "That's okay, Mrs. Taylor. Why don't you forget it for now? If you change your mind, you can reach me at the station."

Clarissa nodded, decreased proximity to the detective allowing her to regain her bearings. As he turned to leave, Clarissa asked, "Who were they?"

Hoopes turned. "Who? The three guys? Just kids. Each of 'em has a long record going back to juveniles. They used to be in a drug gang but they got hooked and were tossed out."

Unaware of the severe discipline enforced by their leaders, Clarissa watched the detective leave, wondering why three members of a drug gang were banished for becoming users. She assumed they all were.

Soon after Detective Hoopes' departure, the regular Hot Feet clientele began to drift in. Even at the beginning the noise was deafening. It seemed like every boy had a boombox turned up to stratospheric and every girl had a piercing laugh that would shatter plate glass. Clarissa found herself forced to hang on to the counter once or twice. How could a person breathe in such noise?

It was a sunny day which turned all of Jamaica out on the streets. It was one of the rare occasions when the neighborhood's honest membership took over and, by sheer force of numbers, made those streets safe to walk. For Clarissa Taylor, whose poor timing had caused her to walk the streets three days earlier, the festive atmosphere only intensified the assault on her battered senses. She had to focus on the cash register keys to make sure she hit the right ones and even then made a number of mistakes.

Her effort to concentrate was so total that she didn't see Pookie drift to the rear of the store to talk with Russell McKey. Then suddenly there was a tap on her shoulder and Clarissa looked up to see a man that looked just like her boss standing by the register.

"Okay, Mama," said a voice that sounded just like her boss, "the game's up."

"What?" This man seemed to be trying to tell her something.

"You just can't work, Clarissa. You got to go home to bed."

"No. I can work. Really. I can."

But the man shook his head sadly. "No. You can't."

He pressed something in her hand and she looked down to see a piece of paper. It looked like money.

"Here's ten bucks, Clarissa," said the man softly. "I'm gonna put you in a taxi. Now you go home and rest. When you feel better, you come on back to work."

"Really? Can I? As soon as I feel better?"

"Sho', Mama. As soon as you feel better."

"Okay." As soon as she agreed to the man's idea, Clarissa relaxed. "I just need to lie down a little while."

"You can lie down at home. Here, let me get you the cab."

The man then ushered her out the door and before Clarissa could force anything out of her mouth she was inside a gypsy cab. There didn't seem to be anything to do then but give the driver her address and sit back and close her eyes.

When Clarissa 'felt better,' two weeks later, she did indeed call Russell McKey. Russell was very sorry, of course, but there had been no way of telling how long Clarissa would be gone, or if she'd come back at all, and, well, he needed someone on the register, and he'd hired someone, just temporary at the beginning, but she was working out and she had two kids too, and Russell was very sorry but . . .

Clarissa Taylor was again out of work.

Renee Lieberman-Smith, on the other hand, had never worked so hard in her life. The de Bourbon case was her chance to escape the doldrums of being 'just another assistant DA' and she was well aware that she might not get another.

The shooting itself presented minimal difficulties. It was a rather standard case of a questionable plea of self-defense where the evidence showed no threat of bodily injury to the defendant. In such circumstances an indictment was easy to obtain and the trial was merely a case of prosecution and defense vying for credibility. When the defendant was a policeman who had committed the crime in the line of duty, the political climate at the time of the trial was often a greater determinant of the verdict than the evidence.

But in the Lawanda de Bourbon affair, the shooting itself

was only one facet of a more complex scenario. Renee realized if she took the narrow construction of her boss's mandate and focused only on the Rodriguez prosecution, she was doing both herself and the community a disservice. There were the broader questions of police corruption in Manhattan North, the complicity of the police in the shooting, and the manipulation of evidence by both the police and onetime Champion, now lying, self-serving sneak, Herbert Whiffet.

As she had expected, Herbert had refused to hand over the videotape, and as promised she had obtained a contempt citation. She had allowed Herbert to stall by means of a number of 'show cause' orders and negotiations for the eventual surrender of the evidence. It was immaterial to her whether he actually went to jail or not. She knew Herbert, and to him the threat of incarceration was every bit as frightening as the actual occurrence. Watching Herbert tap-dance his way through the legal system in an attempt to stay out of jail was quite an enjoyable first act.

And Herbert had not even caught on yet. He still thought the whole procedure was part of some grand plan to discredit the DA's office and sweep him into contention for the job.

At first, Renee had been surprised when Herbert surfaced as Triple A Akbar's attorney, but then decided it was simply further proof of her gross error in judgment in ever investing him with Champion status in the first place. The movement would be well rid of Herbert Whiffet.

Due to the sensitivity of the case, no files were permitted out of the office and thus Renee was forced to spend long hours at Leonard Street reviewing transcripts and taking notes. One file that particularly aroused her rancor was the whitewash that the internal affairs investigator, that Gagliardi fellow, had done on the whole rotten situation at Manhattan North. A conclusion of 'no evidence to support charges of widespread corruption or involvement in local narcotics activities' was absolutely ludicrous. There wasn't a narcotics operation anywhere in the world that didn't involve the local law enforcement personnel. And to make matters worse, the police brass and even her boss, the DA, had accepted the conclusions of the report and ordered that the case focus only on the shooting and the conduct of the activists.

What gutless bastards! How did they ever expect to make an impact on the narcotics trade if they were afraid to attack the corruption problem? And to restrict the investigation to the shooting left some key questions unanswered. For example, if Lawanda de Bourbon was indeed a police informant, why did she go for a gun at the sight of a policeman? That should have been the last thing she feared. Gagliardi hadn't even mentioned that one in his 'report.'

Renee jumped as the night phone rang and shocked her out of her reverie of injustice and corruption.

"Lieberman-Smith," she answered, now proud to be in the office at 9:30 at night.

"Ms. Lieberman-Smith," a familiar but unplaced woman's voice replied, "I'm glad to find you. I tried your apartment all evening then decided you might still be at work."

"Who is this?" asked Renee, although the voice was pleasant and seemed to pose no threat.

"I'm Cornelia Pembroke, Ms. Lieberman-Smith. I work for WRCT. I was wondering if we could meet somewhere and talk."

Phil Gagliardi had not ignored the questions that had proved a cover-up to Renee Lieberman-Smith. Why had Lawanda de Bourbon gone for a gun?

Once his report on Manhattan North had been filed, Phil had decided to do a little checking on his own. He didn't mind stretching the truth for the sake of the department, but he didn't want to be conned by Vince D'Angelo either. With the onus of an official investigation passed, Phil knew he'd have better luck in uncovering some answers.

But for even the best of detectives, some mysteries must remain mysteries with only degrees of probability separating one hypothesis from another. Lawanda de Bourbon's actions in the moments just before her death seemed destined to remain filed with a question mark. As Vince had said, Lawanda de Bourbon was, in fact, screwing everyone. Even at eighteen, she had discovered that a good body is one of the few stocks-in-trade that allow a ghetto girl to make a quantum leap of fortune and she had apparently hedged her bets by using sex to ingratiate herself with every power center in the neighborhood. The down side of such an indiscriminate dispensation of affection is a constant fear that one side will consider her something of a bad risk.

That led Phil to three possibilities to explain Lawanda's policephobia. First, that one of the cops she was banging had it in for her, either because she had betrayed him to Trips or Psycho or even because she was trying to squeeze him herself. Second, that one of the drug lords had gotten wind of her double agent status and fingered her to a cop that owed him a favor. Third, and in Phil's mind the most likely, was that Lawanda de Bourbon, ever in the middle, *always* feared death from *any* source. Her shifting allegiances overlaid the shifting loyalties in the drug war leaving her unsure which ally may have become an enemy.

The questions surrounding Lawanda's motivation underscored the real problem in Manhattan Valley; that allegiances *were* constantly shifting and the police department was merely another player in the game, at best, on occasion, the referee, but never in control. That is why, as Vince D'Angelo pointed out, it was not possible to conduct a narcotics operation without police who would be considered, in other contexts, dirty. And now, with the release of Triple A Akbar, a full scale war was brewing, and D'Angelo's command was no more immune to its effects than were the Ghosts or the Psychos.

Phil packed a box in what was now his former office at Manhattan North. He was going home to Amityville and Vicki to take a few days comp time and fix the automatic door in the garage that had busted. He was leaving Manhattan Valley to Vince D'Angelo and Triple A Akbar and Psycho Bates and the ghost of Lawanda de Bourbon and what was sure to be the professional ghost of Jimmy Rodriguez. This case had turned out to be every bit as shitty as he first figured. His only small victory, the only thing that he could feel the least bit good about, was that he had protected the department by not throwing an able captain to the wolves. Not that he was sure that he had done Vince a favor.

Phil tagged his box and told the desk sergeant to forward it downtown. Then Phil Gagliardi walked out of Manhattan North and got in his car to head home, reminding himself to file his transfer papers when he returned to work.

# CHAPTER TWENTY

Karen Pzytriek felt like a journalist again, not just a face that showed up at the scene of an incident to mouth the standard interchangeable phrases that were the fodder of Cornelia's profession. Ever since her first dinner with Clovis, she had been working on something that both intrigued her and would be an important impact story. The morning after that dinner she had gone to Iserson and asked permission to follow up on what Clovis had told her about Herbert Whiffet, his ambition to be district attorney, his possible use of the de Bourbon case to further that end, and, most important, his mysterious contact inside the DA's office.

"Great idea," crowed Iserson. "See, I don't mind follow-up when it's a good story."

As any professional biographer knows, digging into someone's past to explain their present creates an intimacy with the subject that may even outstrip that of a spouse or a close friend. The danger is that the biographer, like the friend or spouse, remakes the subject in her own image, resulting in a half-truth picture that can be worse than a lie.

Although Karen was aware of the danger and guarded against it, no one can achieve complete objectivity, particularly when one's emotions are already involved. Theoretic physicists have proved that the presence of an observer always affects the result of an experiment, and in this case the observer had also been part of the experiment.

So, by making every effort to be fair to Herbert Whiffet by doing a copious background study (not making the Murray Plotkin mistake again), Karen allowed a simple reading of the facts to damn him. His admission to Tulane was judged to have been as a result of paternal arm-twisting without understanding that the Herbert Whiffets could not gain admission to such schools without it. The same could be said for law school and his brief, educational stay at Gray, Steinford & Hodge.

Thus the picture that emerged was of an upwardly-mobile hustler, willing and even anxious to use the redress of racial injustice as a substitute for genuine achievement. It followed that Herbert's current ambition was merely an extension of his past successes and that his commitment to equal rights was as flimsy as had been his commitment to the homeless.

Yet, after weeks of work, the project still lacked that one hook, that one piece of hard evidence on which a public who liked its packages simple and neat could focus. Since Karen had not seen Fernando's tape, she had no way of knowing it contained anything more (or less) than corroboration of his interview statement. Herbert's acceptance of Triple A Akbar as a client might be debated on quality of judgment but could certainly be construed as principle over personal interest. (After all, why else would a man who aspired to the district attorney's chair do something so dumb?) All that was left was Herbert's possible malfeasance as a result of his mysterious contact, the legal version of insider trading.

With nothing solid to go on, the problem became one of analysis and deduction, not generally part of Karen's day. Since public employees are public record, obtaining a list of all those employed in or by the Manhattan DA's office was rather simple. Then, she ran all the names through a computer program called SEARCH which had compiled and cross-referenced virtually every American according to background, affiliation with clubs and professional organizations, convictions, if any, credit rating, any public statement or mention in any newspaper and anything else about a person that wasn't strictly 'private.' Subscriptions allowing access to the SEARCH program were carefully controlled, not available to the general public, but had often proved invaluable to news organizations. SEARCH could be asked questions along any number of criteria, so it was not difficult to narrow the field of those who might be sympathetic to Herbert Whiffet because of race, political leanings, personal history, common affiliations or any other trait where the program might find a match.

Karen was pleased that the match list consisted of only forty names. There were so many ways to match, she was certain the entire department would have made it one way or another. Of course, there was no way of telling that Herbert's contact was actually on the list. It could be someone with whom no apparent link existed or someone to whom a link existed outside of the available data. But certainly these forty names were a good starting point.

When Karen sat down with the list to prioritize the names in a tentative order of probability, among the ten or twelve where a distinct alignment of views existed, one name popped off the paper. Renee Lieberman-Smith, the assistant DA who had just been put in charge of the de Bourbon case, was right up there with the radicals and malcontents. Her entire background showed an unmistakable favor for left-wing causes, from feminism to Nicaragua to nuclear power, and she was on the mailing list of any number of civil rights organizations. Was it possible that Herbert's contact was now posing as his adversary?

No, couldn't be, she decided. If this Renee Lieberman-Smith was Herbert's contact, why would she be pressing him on a contempt charge for refusing to turn over Fernando's tape? And pressing she was. Although she currently seemed content to bounce Mr. Whiffet on the end of a string, she had received high marks among conservatives for taking the aggressive approach in repelling the activist's charges. It seemed to be working, too. Many in the press community had voiced surprise that Herbert Whiffet had not been more vitriolic in attacking his new enemy in the DA's office. Hard to believe Renee Lieberman-Smith was the same person who had risked her career, and possibly her freedom, by feeding Herbert information.

Still, it was out of character for someone of her background and political views to be so determined in the pursuit of a man who was merely espousing a point of view to which she herself subscribed. Karen made it a point to try and talk to Renee Lieberman-Smith.

There was another name on the list which also might prove interesting, although the prospect was less likely. Willa Ward, a junior assistant who was working with Renee Lieberman-Smith on the de Bourbon case, appeared much lower down on the probability curve, in fact seemed to be present only because she was black. Willa's interests seemed to be more in career and personal achievement than social activism. She had been raised in Harlem but had attended parochial school, City College and Fordham Law School, famed as a springboard to the FBI or Secret Service. Willa Ward seemed less drawn to her blackness than trying to escape it, which, if true, meant that a huckster like Herbert Whiffet would pose more of an embarrassment than anything else. Still, 'roots' and all that . . .

Even narrowing the list down to ten or so probables, the task was by no means easy. Trying to deduce from circumstantial evidence which of the ten it might be was hard enough. And even if she succeeded, she had to prove it, or at least demonstrate the possibility with sufficient urgency to justify the station taking the risk and airing the piece.

Karen sighed and locked the file in her desk. This was a problem that required the correct approach in order to have any chance of a favorable resolution. It was time to meet Clovis anyway. He would certainly have some helpful suggestions on how she should proceed. He always did.

There was one last thing to do before she left. She tried Renee Lieberman-Smith at home again. No answer. Could she be working this late? Karen picked up the phone again and this time dialed the private night line at the DA's office.

Counting the receipts in a high-volume cash business is an event which imparts a unique sense of power to anyone who happens to be present, even those in whose pockets not one dollar of those receipts will eventually lodge. Bank tellers and casino dealers regularly experience such delusions of importance and position as do betting clerks at racetracks and workers at the United States Mint. But in the new, plasticized society, most of those who now handle large sums of cash do so as a result of transactions that do not appear in anyone's annual report: bookmakers, loansharks, and, most of all, dealers in illegal drugs.

As anyone who has ever supervised such an operation will tell you, the handling of cash demands seriousness, order and organization. Even the lowest street thug develops a respect, even a reverence, for the coin of the realm and handles money with the same serious professionalism as a Wall Street trader.

The Ghosts, under the direction of Triple A Akbar, kept its books with a level of detail and scrupulousness that a Big Eight accounting firm would envy. After each day's business (which for a nocturnal enterprise like drug dealing was early the following morning, seven days a week, no holidays or vacations), the receipts, generated by street sales, coordinated by captains, collated by colonels and, finally, approved by the general himself, were counted and proceeds allocated in a sealed, guarded room chosen by Triple A and moved regularly to discourage incursion. Triple A was generally present and if not, a trusted underboss was in charge. (Ali Abdul's absences were random and never announced in advance, and oftentimes he would pop in at odd moments to spot check.)

Despite the Yonkers sleeping arrangements, Triple A had made it a point to be a visible leader since his release on bail. These were delicate times and strength of character was more in need now than at any time since the organization was founded. One look at the day's numbers made it clear why Ali Abdul could not simply ride out the storm in Westchester, treating the exile as a well-earned vacation.

Only $85,000. That was off thirty percent. *Thirty percent.* Between Psycho Bates and the cops, Ali Abdul Akbar was being bled dry. Eighty-five thousand might seem like a lot of money for one day, but no one realized his expenses. His payroll was enormous and, between legal fees, 'good-will' payments to local officials and the money he kicked back to the neighborhood, eighty-five was not much better than break-even.

Nothing prompts action like a little economic downturn, and, even though Ali Abdul's plan was working, financial necessity was about to turn up the heat. Only after Trevor was disposed of and the threat of that perjurious bastard getting him convicted on a murder-two was eliminated could he deal with the main business at hand—the disposal of the very real threat posed by Psycho Bates.

Ali Abdul Akbar had never read Clauswitz, but for some the classic strategies were a matter of instinct. Triple A knew just what to do.

After the disastrous count was complete and the allocation of the money determined, Ali Abdul Akbar called a policy meeting, just himself and his top three aides. Triple A had chosen well. All three were totally loyal, perfect number two's. Each was ruthless, tough and sufficiently intelligent to be aware that he did not possess the business acumen of the leader and thus each considered himself fortunate to have attained such high rank in a prestigious organization like the Ghosts. In this *noblesse de robe,* each felt his fortune completely tied up with that of the boss and each would do anything, almost without question, that was asked of him.

Triple A called the meeting to order with a frown. 'Sheik' Salaam elbowed 'Wrath of God' Watts to put down his orange juice and listen.

"Well, boys," began Triple A, every bit as somber as the CEO of an American electronics firm in the seventies, "we come down to some serious shit."

Three heads nodded in agreement. Eighty-five a day was indeed serious shit.

Triple A played with his fingers. For what he had in mind, a good deal of discomfort and remorse was necessary, even with this crew. "I don' gotta tell y'all what's gonna happen if we let Psycho keep cuttin' us out o' our territory. They gonna find all o' us in pieces somewheres."

Three heads nodded once again.

Triple A looked up from his fingers. His eyes burned and his tooth looked about to shoot flame. "We gotta take the heat off us and stick it right up Psycho's ass."

"Dat de fuckin' truth," agreed Wrath.

Triple A smiled at his not-so-Greek chorus. "An' here's how we gonna do it."

Three heads leaned forward.

"We gonna do somethin' so fucked up and so ugly that everybody in this city gonna be so pissed off that the cops are gonna have the heat up their ass . . ."

Three faces registered confusion.

"Then we gonna blame it on Psycho!"

Three faces broke into broad grins and three laughs filled the room. "Dats tits, boss," chuckled Wrath. The Sheik heartily agreed as did 'Uzi' Jones, the most violent, least stable of the crew. Uzi, named for his preference in armaments, got all the really ugly jobs, anything that required a complete lack of social conscience.

"How we gonna do it, boss?" asked Uzi, conveniently providing Triple A with his opportunity.

"What we gonna do," replied Ali Abdul, once again donning his mask of regret, "is get ourselves a Psycho van . . . actually we just gonna steal a van an' paint it like a Psycho van, then we gonna drive up 108th Street an' shoot some folks."

"But dems our folks," said Wrath, puzzled.

"Of course they's our folks," countered Trips.

Uzi took over from there. "Dat way nobody gonna lay it on us." He turned to the leader. "Right boss?"

"Right."

Three heads shook in wonderment at the strategic brilliance of their leader. Sheeeiitt.

Ali Abdul laid out the details of his plan to his three eager associates, each of whom itched to get such a plum assignment. The issue, however, was never really in doubt.

"Who gonna do dis, boss?" asked Wrath, pulling himself up in his chair to demonstrate desire and suitability.

"I think we'll give this one to . . ." Triple A grinned at the three contestants. Shit, he thought, this is like the fuckin' 'Dating Game.' "Uzi."

Uzi laughed and clapped his hands as Wrath and the Sheik looked downcast.

"Now look, Uzi," Trips cautioned, "this ain't no ordinary whack out. This here's *public relations*, you dig? Dat means you gotta get just the right folks. We don' want drunks or no customers . . ." Triple A's gold tooth flashed sardonically. "We want *innocents*. Women . . . a kid or two. It gotta look like Psycho was goin' for one of our dealers but the crazy fuck whacked out some kids. This way the cops'll be ready to do anything to get that maniac off the streets."

"You can trus' me, boss," said Uzi gravely. In a task of this nature, Triple A certainly could.

Mel Seltzer loved this kind of case. An unpopular defendant charged in a criminal offense that was as much a political indictment as a legal one. These cases were invariably headline grabbers, projecting an aura of the entire criminal justice system levelling its sixteen-inch guns at one target of its outrage. And, as everyone knew, such a defendant had virtually no chance to survive the resulting barrage. Thus, any defense attorney who managed to secure an acquittal in one of these three-ring judicial productions was conferred by society with its Perry Mason/Matt Dillon legal gun-slinger award. And *no one* had a better record in these cases than Melville Seltzer.

The irony, which Mel Seltzer never failed to appreciate *in extremis*, was that this very type of case was the absolute, number one, top of the mountain easiest to win. No question. Patrick Ewing misses more dunk shots than a decent lawyer loses a political case disguised as a criminal charge. And, the more serious the charge, the easier the acquittal.

The hardest part was not the trial. The hardest part was getting the case in the first place.

So, when the case he was currently preparing had come up for grabs, Mel Seltzer was first on line, and, with his record for bending juries to his point of view, his offer was immediately accepted.

This one was textbook, all right. One of society's prejudged guilty charged with murder in the second degree, the prosecution's case entirely circumstantial except for the testimony of one unreliable witness whose credibility was, to say the least, easily impeached. In twenty-eight years of practicing law, Mel had never seen a star witness with less appeal to a jury. To make things even easier, the defendant had a countervailing witness, at least of equal quality with that of the prosecution. And this defendant could take the stand in his own defense. He was someone who would undoubtedly impress a jury.

Yeah, this was a good one. This case could end up in the book he was planning detailing the top ten cases of his career. It would be a fitting companion to the three volumes he had already produced, commentaries on the judicial system, the last of which had made the best seller list.

Who'd a thought it thirty years ago at NYU Law School, when young Melville Seltzer bristled under the sobriquets of 'Alka' or 'Bromo' or 'Two-cents Plain?' He'd shut them up then and he was still doing it three decades later.

Mel Seltzer stopped daydreaming and returned to the file. He shook his head again. How can the DA even press such a piece of crap? Jesus, a well versed chimp could get this guy off. Of course, Mel was also well aware that the defendant's troubles would not end with the acquittal. But at least he wouldn't have to go to the can.

Shit, thought Mel Seltzer, I can't wait for this one to start.

It didn't even matter to the lawyer that he had accepted the case at only a fraction of his usual fee. Mel Seltzer was already rich. It gave him the luxury of looking a defendant in the eye and saying that a case was a matter of principle. And to this defendant, principle was very important.

Mel Seltzer was going to enjoy defending James Rodriguez.

# CHAPTER TWENTY-ONE

New York is a dangerous place to cross the street. Crazed third-world immigrant cabbies, sadistic truckers and misanthropic bus drivers pose a constant risk to life and limb. One of the first things any New York child learns upon being granted leave to stray from the confines of his own block is that you never daydream while crossing the street and you don't think that just because the law grants right of way that you are safe from attack.

But in most neighborhoods in New York, residents are safe from vehicular homicide when sitting on a stoop or lounging in a doorway. Those who live in Riverdale or Forest Hills need not fear passing traffic when they are situated ten or more feet from the curb. This rule, however, does not hold true for those who live in the drug-ravaged, gang-controlled sections of the city where passing vehicles, especially smoke-windowed vans, can shoot death from any distance. Ghetto dwellers must learn to recognize any suspicious conveyance and head indoors as soon as one is spotted.

Unfortunately, all the vigilance in the world may not be sufficient to protect the slower or more vulnerable from a speeding van with automatic weapon-armed thugs inside whose express purpose is the elimination of an enemy without regard to how many innocent bystanders are taken down with their quarry.

So, in the late morning of August 1, when a black van with smoked windows turned from Amsterdam Avenue down 108th Street, tires squealing, those idling on the block quickly made for cover.

Most were successful but five were not.

In less than ten seconds, two adults and three children lay in the street, blood streaming or spurting from their wounds. And less than one minute after that, three of those victims were dead. They included Slick Sims, a low level drug dealer and member of the Ghosts who had the misfortune of trying the Dodge City approach and firing back at the van, a twenty year-old woman and a fourteen year-old girl. One of the wounded children survived almost until the EMS truck arrived and the fifth actually made it to St. Luke's in critical condition.

In a city like New York, where violent crime is as commonplace as a trip to the market, rarely does a shooting sufficiently excite the public consciousness to propel it to front page status. But some crimes are so heinous, so wanton, so capricious, so indicative of the anonymous danger that awaits all of the city's residents, that they become the focus of public attention and the target of New York's massive bureaucracy. It then becomes crucial to run the perpetrators to ground and heap the public's vengeance upon them as much because apprehending murderous felons is such an uncommon occurrence as for any question of justice.

And so it was with what the tabloids dubbed the "August First Massacre." The shooting was almost immediately followed by outraged pronouncements from the mayor, the police commissioner, the district attorney, the Manhattan Borough President, the president of the Manhattan Valley Civic Association and even the man on the street, all decrying the violence, the brutality and the atmosphere of drug dealing which made such events a part of the community's daily life. Local television stations sent in representatives to do background stories on the drug gangs and the poverty that creates them and the networks sent in their top reporters to give dispassionate, intelligent editorials on the inevitability of violence where the industrial-sized profits of drugs are involved. Even the Vice-President of the United States gave a speech on the corner of 108th and Amsterdam re-emphasizing the nation's commitment to stamp out this plague forever.

And through all of this breast-beating, the unhappy recipient of the responsibility for actually solving the crime, the end of the line in the shit-rolls-downhill syndrome, was New York City Police Captain Vincent D'Angelo.

Despite all the pledges of assistance from state and federal law enforcement authorities, it was clear from the start that only cops familiar with the neighborhood, those with a scorecard of the players, with hooks into stoolies and an ear for a break were going to solve this one. So, while the FBI and state police investigators looked over his shoulder, a constant reminder that if he did not bring this case to a speedy resolution and get it out of the damn headlines it was his ass, Vince D'Angelo broke his balls to squeeze the shooters out of the community.

There was no question that the shooting was part of the Akbar/Bates war, although Vince, unlike most of those looking over his shoulder, was not convinced that Psycho had done the deed. Psycho Bates was nuts, true, but he wasn't stupid. No general with half a brain was going to risk a drive-by shooting to get Slick Sims. Slick Sims could have been had any night at all. And there didn't seem to be any other reason for the van to spray automatic weapons fire on 108th Street.

No, Vince decided. It was all too convenient. Psycho commits a terrible crime, the public outcry pushes the cops to get Psycho, Psycho goes away and Ali Abdul Akbar is left with the neighborhood all to himself, just like the old days.

But the FBI and the state police investigators and the police commissioner didn't see it that way. Did Captain D'Angelo have any proof of his theory? No, he did not. Was the van recovered? No, it was not. Were there any rumblings in the neighborhood that Triple A had set this up? No, there were not. Okay then, the captain was told, let's have less theorizing and more action.

A captain in the narcotics division becomes inured to the realities of dealing in street justice, outside the strict boundaries of the criminal code. What holds him together is the knowledge that he is protecting society from those who use the rights that are provided them to circumvent the law and corrupt and addict society's youth. A narcotics cop knows more than anyone that what goes on in the streets is less a police process than a war. And no one talks about the rights of the accused in wartime. It is the right of the citizenry to survive that is the only question.

With their personal morality hanging by a thread, the narcotics cops must not be too severely criticized for taking the expedient route when the hypocrisy of the streets is transferred to the mayor, the DA and the commissioner.

Thus, on August 8th, one week after the 'massacre,' Ali

Abdul Akbar got a message in his Yonkers hide-away that Captain D'Angelo wanted a meet.

Triple A laughed out loud when he got the news. Even his gold tooth seemed to share the glee. "See," he grinned at Wrath, who had presented the missive, "what'd I tell ya?"

The meet was set up for that night along the strip under the Henry Hudson Parkway viaduct which houses the last of the uptown meat wholesalers. There was a spot at the north end which could be accessed in a way that would ensure both safety and privacy.

At 11 PM, the captain's unmarked Dodge cruised to a halt beside the innocuous looking Chevy (Triple A having eschewed the Mercedes for anonymity's sake). Although there were no other vehicles in sight, D'Angelo was sure that Trips had provided ample security so that they would not be disturbed.

As the Dodge stopped, the rear door of the Chevy opened and a short, stocky figure in a raincoat and pull-down hat slid quickly across the six feet separating the vehicles, into the passenger seat of D'Angelo's Dodge. (No way was the captain going to have this conversation in Triple A's car and have his picture taken or his voice recorded.) Then, as arranged, the Dodge cruised fifty feet to the pilings at the edge of the river.

The captain turned to his passenger. "I gotta pat you down, Trips."

Ali Abdul smiled. "O' course, Captain." His voice was an octave higher and his tooth radiated innocence and sincerity.

The formality was completed in fifteen seconds. (There was no need for Ali Abdul to take similar precautions. His presence at the meeting could not cause personal or professional embarrassment. Besides, he had no intention of saying anything incriminating.)

D'Angelo began the negotiations. "Well, Trips, how's Uzi?" Vince might be forced by circumstance to make a pact with the Devil but had no intention of allowing the Devil to think he didn't know it.

"Uzi?" inquired the ever-innocent Ali Abdul. "He's fine. Why do you ask?"

Vince looked across the front seat and smiled although his eyes did not participate in the gesture. "No reason. He hasn't been around these past few days. We all miss his happy face."

Trips nodded and returned the captain's grin. "Yeah. Well, he's been studying for his final exam in advanced economics. You know how much time that takes."

"Of course," nodded Vince.

Now that they both understood each other, D'Angelo got to it. "We seem to have a situation on our hands."

"We sure do, Cap'n." Ali Abdul was being extremely considerate. After all, *his* problem was about to be resolved.

"I'm sure that it's making things hot for everyone."

"Times been better," Triple A admitted.

"Well, you know what's been goin' on at our end," D'Angelo continued. "That Psycho Bates must be one crazy motherfucker, doin' a drive-by like that."

"He be that," agreed Triple A.

"Well, we gotta get the shooters." D'Angelo stared at Triple A. If he had had a gold tooth, it would have been glowering. "And we gotta end the war."

"So why you comin' to me, Cap'n? Hows come you ain't goin' to Psycho?"

"Well, wasn't it Psycho that done the shootin'?"

"Sho'nuff, Cap'n."

"Then it looks like we took sides in the war, doesn't it?"

Ali Abdul Akbar played with one of the gold rings that festooned his fingers. "You tellin' me that ol' Triple A ain't so bad after all? You tellin' me that the DA an' everyone else gonna stop dummyin' up evidence from lyin' pieces o' shit like Trevor House just to get me inside so's to leave that maniac runnin' around by hisself?"

D'Angelo nodded although he stared straight out the window with twenty-eight years worth of hatred for the stinking deal he was about to cut.

"Well, then," Ali Abdul grunted. "I think you an' me can do business. Figurin' o' course that you guys gonna do somethin' to show your good faith. After all, I ain't got no reason to trust y'all."

"Yeah," growled D'Angelo. "Wha'ja have in mind?"

Ali Abdul Akbar looked up and shrugged. "Shit, Cap'n. I don' know. What you figurin' on doin'?"

Vince D'Angelo continued to stare out the window. All he had to do was pull out his service revolver and one shot later the city would be rid of one of its lowest. He placed his hands on his knees. From there it was just a short move to the holster in his belt.

"You know, Captain," said Triple A, suddenly deep voiced, "if I don't leave here, you don't either."

Vince turned idly to the man in the passenger seat. It was true, of course.

Akbar continued. "And all you'd do is leave the territory to Uzi Jones or the Sheik or even Psycho Bates. That worth dying for?"

Vince D'Angelo knew it wasn't. That was the worst part. He wasn't really a cop. He was just a guy who had some say in which asshole ran the neighborhood.

Triple A went for the closer. "So why don't we just do this right? You pull that lying junkie off me and I'll make sure no more civilians get hurt." Ali Abdul smiled. "An' besides, Cap'n, I can git you the shooters. You know, those bloodthirsty maniacs dat Psycho got to shoot up 108th."

The captain sighed. That was, after all, why he was here. "I can't pull House off you. We're not holding him."

"Who is, Cap'n?"

"The DA. He's got him stashed upstate. I'm not sure you can get to him even if I tell you where he's at."

Ali Abdul shrugged. "Why don' you leave dat to me, Cap'n. Don't affect the deal none. I keep my side once I know where House at." Triple A saw D'Angelo slump a bit in his seat. "C'mon, Cap'n. Don' take it so hard. You know no Trevor House never heard shit about anythin' I was doin'. The whole thing is bullshit."

Suddenly, D'Angelo sat up straight and turned to Triple A. With hands as fast as a professional boxer's he reached over and grabbed a bunch of Triple A's collar in one huge fist.

"Listen to me, you low ass piece of shit," he hissed. "Don't pull that innocent shit with me. I know who you are and who you whacked and that you couldn't give two shits about killin' kids in your own fuckin' neighborhood. So don't push your fuckin' luck or I might decide that it *is* worth it to die just to whack you out."

Ali Abdul Akbar never flinched. He sat with the captain's hand next to his throat and met the enemy eyeball to eyeball. For a moment, the position was frozen, a duel of the very toughest. Then D'Angelo relaxed his grip.

"He's in the Dutchess County Jail. In the infirmary. Under the name of James Brown."

Ali Abdul straightened his collar. "Thank you, Captain. We got ourselves a deal."

Within forty-eight hours, two key events in the lives of the citizens of Manhattan Valley occurred. Trevor House was found stabbed to death in his isolation cell in the infirmary of the Dutchess County Jail. The three men who constituted the twenty-four hour guard on his room were all questioned but each claimed that no one had been allowed to enter without authorization and only then in the company of the guard. All three stuck to that tale throughout the most vigorous interrogation although, on advice of counsel, citing the right to avoid self-incrimination, each declined to submit to a polygraph.

Later that day a van was found containing the bodies of three members of the Psychos, apparently killed in a gun battle with unknown enemies. The van was positively identified as belonging to the gang and the weapons found inside were matched through ballistics tests with those used in the drive-by shooting on 108th Street.

And within forty-eight hours of those two events, there were two additional occurrences of equal significance. Melville Seltzer filed a motion in State Supreme Court that the indictment for murder in the second degree against Thomas Jefferson Smith, aka Ali Abdul Akbar, be dismissed for lack of evidence. After a half-hearted protest by the district attorney's office, the motion was approved. In a less public forum, the territory won by Psycho Bates in his war of attrition with said Akbar began to revert to the original owner and Psycho's star was seen to be most clearly in descent.

Then, in mid-month, a final incident took place that guaranteed the restoration of peace to the troubled neighborhood. (Peace being defined in this case as merely the usual complement of shootings, muggings, rapes, beatings, screaming, fights, and intimidation of the weak, elderly, and infirm that was standard in Manhattan Valley.) On August 16th, the detective division at Manhattan North received word that a body was to be found in a trash can in the

Frederick Douglass Houses, a low-income project that occupied an eight-square-block chunk of the community.

The tip turned out to be not entirely accurate. In fact, pieces of a body were discovered in six separate trash cans, neatly divided by limbs, torso and head. A cursory examination in the coroner's office revealed the human jigsaw to be none other than Marvin Bates, affectionately known as Psycho.

Although the homicide bureau waved at solving the murder, they knew that this one would remain open forever. Not that they or anyone else had the slightest doubt as to the identity of the killers or the circumstances of the crime. In fact, from the next day forward, most of the residents of the community treated Ali Abdul Akbar like a returning conqueror, a beloved vassal, even a protector. Ali Abdul responded by dispensing three times the usual patronage to the adoring multitudes. In those August days, no resident of Manhattan Valley went without a meal or was left short of funds to pay the rent. The day care center received a year's worth of funding and the free lunch program in the local elementary school was similarly endowed. After the long months of siege, Manhattan Valley had its patriarch back.

And, with the pressures of the war removed, the dealing of crack and heroin again picked up, even exceeding pre-war levels. In the heat of summer it seemed that the urban anesthetic was particularly popular among those in their early teens. So heavy was the demand that the Ghosts were forced to initiate some twenty new members.

# CHAPTER TWENTY-TWO

No one likes being fired. For Herbert Whiffet, receiving word from Mel Seltzer's secretary that his services were no longer required in any of the legal entanglements of Ali Abdul Akbar was just one more disaster in what had been a pretty terrible month. Renee's strategy was no more clear now than when he had first heard it, the threat of the contempt citation loomed larger all the time, Leotis was all over him about losing momentum in the de Bourbon case, and, worst of all, the press was no longer treating him like a serious spokesman for the struggle for equal rights. Rather, many commentators had begun to take shots at the man who they accused of railing at the district attorney to convict a killer cop while withholding a key piece of evidence which he claimed would ensure that conviction.

But it was not any of these things that brought him to Leotis' office on that morning in August. It was something that promised to outstrip all of Herbert's recent problems, something that could present an impediment to his plans every bit as serious as if *he* had been caught sleeping with Lawanda de Bourbon.

Herbert Whiffet had just received word that WRCT, specifically Cornelia Pembroke, was preparing an investigative report on him that promised to be little more than journalistic assassination. As with Akbar, the identity of the antagonist was every bit as painful as the sting of the attack.

"Darn it, Leotis," said Herbert, trying to keep his voice from breaking into a whine, "it's not that I ever thought she was my friend. It's just that I never thought she hated me."

"That don' matter, Herbert. It's your own damn fault for buddyin' up to white reporters." Leotis paused than waved off the personal invective. "But forget it. Only the movement matters. What's she got? What'd you do that she mighta got hold of?"

Herbert threw his hands in the air and paced back and forth in front of the trophy case that contained the Rev. Mr. Chestnut's many civic awards. "I don't know, Leotis. Really. I've never done anything dishonest. But, damn it . . ." Herbert paused for a second, shocked at his language, "Leotis, you know that if the press wants to manipulate the facts to make someone look bad, they can most surely do it. And for what we have in mind . . ." (first person plural was important here), "the appearance of impropriety can be every bit as destructive as genuine guilt."

The tarnished Champion stopped at the window and stared out at the dirty streets and broken tenements that he had hoped to improve single-handedly. "Leotis, you know as well as I do . . . when you deal with the press, you lose all your rights."

The reverend laughed, although it came out as more of a sniff. "Do I." Leotis walked over to the window to join his comrade. "Herbert, bein' a man of God, I always try to tell the truth." Leotis chuckled. "At least to myself." He put his arm around the shorter Champion and felt his colleague flinch.

"Let's be straight with each other. We been manipulatin' the facts for years. That's what it's all about, isn't it? Makin' the facts come out the way you wan' em. Makin' people see the truth by showin' them another side of things. Up 'til now, the white man's always done it better. It's his game, you dig? I ain't no revolutionary, Herbert, but like the man said, 'You don' make no omelets without breakin' no eggs.'"

"So what do we do?"

"Well, Herbert, I think for starters you gotta sit down with this Pembroke woman. Find out what she's up to. Like you said, she owes you one for the exclusive you gave her before the first press conference. If that don' work, we gotta fight fire with fire. We gotta fin' out if Cornelia Pembroke can stand up to the same treatment she be givin' you."

Herbert moved away from the window to escape Leotis' fatherly grasp. "I don't know, Leotis . . . going to see Cornelia might just let her think that she's really got something."

The Reverend Mr. Chestnut shrugged. "Well you got a better idea? You gotta do somethin'."

Herbert spun around. "How come it's always me that's 'gotta do somethin'?' How come it's never you?"

Leotis reacted to his partner's outburst with a soft smile, as if speaking to a man who could not see God. "Because you, counsellor, have claimed this case for your own. Because you want to be DA. Because you thought you could charm the lily white pants off o' that Pembroke woman. Because you . . ." Leotis paused. He loved drama. "You slept with an assistant DA to get information."

"How did you know about that?" asked Herbert, although his voice had suddenly gone raspy.

Leotis grinned again. "Just you make sure Corn-e-lia Pembroke don' know it."

Corn-e-lia Pem-broke was not, at that point, aware of Herbert's link to Renee Lieberman-Smith, but she had an appointment to interview the assistant district attorney that very day.

For Renee Lieberman-Smith, a confrontation with her tormentor, her hated competitor, the woman who slept with Herbert Whiffet to get information (as opposed to herself, who slept with him in order to give it) was every bit as daunting as giving her first opening argument to a jury. This was her one chance to see what made Cornelia Pembroke tick—and to best her. Renee stood before her bathroom mirror that morning, taking stock. She was dressed in her best, most professional blue suit, a string of pearls around her neck instead of the usual bow-tie, wispy hair pinned flatteringly in place and wearing just a touch of make-up and lipstick. Not bad, she decided.

Yes, this was her chance, all right.

The interview was scheduled for 9:30 at a coffee shop near Canal Street, just north of the complex of buildings that housed the city court system and its adjuncts. The diner itself attracted a mixture that was pure New York: lawyers, artists from SoHo, construction workers, punkers from the Lower East Side, and old Jewish street philosophers who had been frequenting the place for years. When Renee arrived, she immediately spotted Cornelia Pembroke at a table near the back, a location that would allow for a certain amount of freedom of speech among the other noisy diners.

Despite the pains she had taken with her appearance, at

the sight of Cornelia Pembroke, Renee immediately felt dowdy and plain. There was the reporter, dressed in jeans and a blouse, hair pulled back and tied with a ribbon, wearing little or no make up, yet still looking sleek and beautiful. If anything, her beauty was enhanced by the simplicity of her appearance. Why am I always either overdressed or underdressed? wondered Renee.

"Good morning, Ms. Lieberman-Smith," said the reporter, rising to greet her. Renee found the voice pleasant, even soothing. But she was not about to be soothed.

"And good morning to you, Miss Pembroke," Renee replied. "I have been looking forward to meeting you. I've seen you often on television." Renee was pleased—the greeting had come out quite naturally. The interview would have been torture had she revealed her feelings in the first skirmish.

"Would you like some coffee?" asked Cornelia graciously. "Or breakfast, perhaps?"

"Just coffee thanks. I usually don't eat breakfast." Denying her eating habits at once made Renee feel fat.

But Cornelia seemed not to notice and merely went to the counter to place the order. Renee watched her adversary move across the floor. She was one of those people who made a room look more classy just by being in it.

"Well, Ms. Lieberman-Smith," Cornelia Pembroke began with a smile once she had returned with the coffee, "the district attorney must think quite a lot of you to give you responsibility for such a pivotal case."

Renee stifled her instinct to match Cornelia's affability. After all, the woman was a *reporter*. It occurred to Renee that in accepting Cornelia Pembroke's request for an interview, she had failed to inquire as to its subject. Or clear it with the boss.

Renee took a sip of her coffee. "I'm quite flattered, of course, Miss Pembroke," she replied in her best professional tones, "but I regret that I cannot discuss the details of an ongoing investigation."

"Of course, of course," smiled the reporter, with a wave of the hand, dismissing any hint of impropriety. "By the way, call me Cornelia . . ."

"And I'm Renee." What's next, she thought, a chummy discussion of brands of eye shadow? "What did you want to see me about . . . Cornelia?"

"Frankly . . ." Cornelia smiled once again, 'just us girls,' "I'm interested in the effect that all the outside hoopla has on your ability to conduct an effective investigation."

Renee shook her head. Cornelia Pembroke was not about to make a fool of *her*. "I told you, Cornelia . . . I cannot discuss . . ."

"I assure you, I'm not interested in any of the details of the prosecution of James Rodriguez, Renee. I'm not here to compromise anyone."

Renee looked into the innocent face across the table from her. No wonder she gets so many exclusives.

Cornelia continued. "I'm interested in this new breed of political case. We seem to have more and more instances where the judicial details become secondary to the political and social implications of the case. I suspect that puts increased pressure on the prosecution."

"Yes, that's true," Renee admitted.

"And," continued Cornelia, her toe just inside the door, "it seems to me that the rules of evidence might sometimes be tortured by the necessity to satisfy the public as well as a jury."

Renee nodded and began to reach for a cigarette but changed direction and took a sip of coffee instead. "To whatever extent that's true," she replied, "it is, I believe, you in the media who are responsible." Listening to her own voice, Renee Lieberman-Smith was quite satisfied. She was being every bit as professional and reasoned as she had hoped while giving the reporter nothing that could cause embarrassment later.

"It is the reporters, if I may say so," she continued, "who fan the flames of public anger, even in those cases where the prosecution is pursuing indictments and convictions as vigorously as the evidence allows."

Cornelia nodded reasonably. "I'm sure there is a degree of truth in that."

Renee pressed on. Cornelia Pembroke was quite clearly impressed. "You are eager to air the most sensationalist points of view while ignoring the simple, non-newsworthy truth."

The reporter nodded in agreement once more. "You mean, like Herbert Whiffet?"

"Uh, yes." Suddenly, Renee was heading in a direction that was unanticipated and dangerous. "I think it is a matter of public record that Herbert Whiffet has attempted to put pressure on the district attorney's office with respect to the prosecution of Officer Rodriguez. I don't think even Mr. Whiffet would deny that."

Cornelia laughed. "On the contrary. I think he'd brag about it."

You'd know, thought Renee, but she forced herself to smile.

"I must say, Renee," the reporter continued, shaking her head in a gesture of respect, "you have certainly reacted to that pressure well. Many of my colleagues were rather surprised that you went right back at him with the threat of a contempt citation. To be honest, the DA has generally been viewed as willing to give in to pressure to avoid political embarrassment. Have you had any problems over the way you've been handling things?"

"Oh no," Renee answered too quickly, "none at all."

"Well," Cornelia said with a grin, "I'll bet Herbert was pretty surprised. He's not used to such treatment."

Herbert now, is it? "I suppose he was."

"Yes indeed," added the reporter. "I'm sure the last thing Herbert Whiffet expected was to be pressured by the district attorney. He's come to expect far more conciliatory treatment." Cornelia took a sip of her coffee. "As a matter of fact, Herbert used to brag that he was wired inside the DA's office—that he had a contact who would pass along sensitive information on cases that were still pending."

Renee looked at Cornelia with surprise. "You're kidding." Then she shook her head. "I'm sure it was just idle boasting. Herbert's been known to do that, you know . . . would it bother you if I smoked?"

"Not at all." Cornelia smiled again but showed concern as well. "But you should try to quit. It really is bad for you."

"I know," admitted Renee, suddenly desperate to have this over with. "I've tried."

"I'm lucky," said Cornelia. "I never started . . . where were we?"

"We were discussing the political questions surrounding the Rodriguez case," ADA Lieberman-Smith replied quickly. "To sum up, I'd just like to say that despite any pressures that may be exerted from the outside, the district attorney intends to pursue this case like any other, and to prosecute the crime with the same vigor as any other. And, I might add, no one is 'wired into our office,' as I believe the facts amply demonstrate."

"Of course. Well, Renee, thank you for your time. I appreciate this interview. I hope we can talk again sometime . . ."

"That would be fine," Renee replied flatly. With that the reporter rose, shook the assistant district attorney's hand, and, with a last smile, glided out of the diner. Renee stood for a moment, watching. For some reason, she felt like crying. Then she picked up her briefcase and hurried out the door.

Herbert Whiffet was surprised that Cornelia greeted his request for an audience with such enthusiasm. As Herbert hustled off to the fountain at Lincoln Center, the place where they had agreed to chat, Herbert decided that perhaps Leotis had been correct once again.

As it happened, Karen Pzytriek, having excused Cornelia in order to think, had been considering calling Herbert when his call came in. The interview in the coffee shop had exceeded her expectations. That Renee Lieberman-Smith was some strange woman; she had clearly come to the meeting with the intention of saying nothing, then, with only the slightest prodding, was willing to speak at length in a manner that was . . . what? It was friendly, yet somehow . . . competitive. She had done her hair and make-up and dressed fastidiously. The background report indicated that Renee Lieberman-Smith was kind of a slob. But why was Renee Lieberman-Smith competing with her? And then, when she fell for the bait and referred to Herbert Whiffet as 'Herbert' in a familiar tone after previously referring to him with disdain . . .

Yes indeed, Karen decided, there was certainly something there between Herbert and Renee Lieberman-Smith. But why had she consented to an unauthorized interview with a reporter if she had something to hide? And then walk into it like she was trying out for the cover of *Working Woman*?

As she approached the fountain, Karen donned her very best Cornelia face.

"Cornelia," Herbert beamed, walking over to greet his old friend, "it was nice of you to come."

"Don't be silly, Herbert," Cornelia replied, flashing a smile and taking his hand in both of hers. "I always have time for you."

"I'm pleased to hear that, Cornelia. We hadn't talked in a while. I thought you might be angry with me."

"Angry with you, Herbert? Of course not. Where would you get such an idea?"

They stood facing each other, two counter-punchers waiting for the other to lead, each wondering at the source of the strained cordiality of the other.

Cornelia, as the invitee, had the slight advantage, so she took the initiative. "Well, Herbert. Why did you want to see me?"

"Yes . . . well . . . it wasn't really anything specific, Cornelia. It's just that, as you know, matters are coming to a head in the DA's cover-up of the murder of Lawanda de Bourbon and, well, to be frank, WRCT seemed strangely silent on the story."

Karen realized that she had the upper hand. Not only did Herbert want something from her—he didn't know that she wanted something from him.

"I don't agree," she replied, taking a seat on the ledge surrounding the fountain. "I think the station has followed the story quite scrupulously. And as to a cover up . . . I don't think there has been any evidence to support such a theory. In fact, it appears that the DA is pursuing a conviction in the shooting rather zealously."

Herbert sniffed and moved closer to Cornelia to make his point. "That's just to distract attention from the bigger issue. Of course there's no evidence of a cover-up. Look who's doing the investigating. It's like . . . assigning the Grand Dragon of the Klan to investigate racism."

"Be that as it may, Herbert. Do *you* have any evidence of a cover-up?"

Herbert put on his 'I know what I'm talking about' face. "Believe me, Cornelia, it's there. Do you really believe that the police investigation found *no trace* of police involvement in the narcotics business up there? *No trace*? You know as well as I that wherever there are illegal drugs there is *some* police involvement."

"You would know, Herbert. You defended Akbar."

Herbert leaned even closer to Cornelia but she refused to

draw back. "I did not defend Akbar! I merely asserted his right to bail. When that was done I resigned from his defense."

Karen stood up to escape Herbert's facial assault. "Resigned? I heard that you were dismissed. That Akbar only retained you to use your public posture to get him released so that he could protect his territory from Marvin Bates—which, by the way, he seemed to do quite effectively."

"That's a lie," Herbert hissed. "Akbar did not fire me, although it is true that we agreed that I would only work on the bail issue." Herbert's eyes burned at Cornelia. "But that agreement was mutual! I was not fired!"

"Okay, Herbert," shrugged the reporter. "Anything you say."

"That's the trouble with this case," Herbert continued. "The press seems more interested in getting something on me than it does in investigating a district attorney and a police department that systematically denies black people their rights."

"Oh, Herbert," Cornelia grinned. "We're alone here. Can't we do without that bullshit?"

"It's not bullshit!" Herbert fumed. "Can you deny that I am the subject of an inquiry? Can you deny that the press seeks to discredit me in order to inhibit the movement? That the only investigation currently under way at your station is into my personal life and not the broader and much more important questions of the way that justice is dispensed in our city?"

So that was it. "It is true, Herbert, that WRCT is preparing a report on your career. Can you blame us? You're news. I'm sorry, Herbert, but once you injected yourself into the political process, the people had a right to know your background."

"Right to know," Herbert sniffed again. "You just use that to justify doing sensationalist stories to get ratings."

To put Herbert strategically out of control was one thing, to incite open warfare was another. Cornelia stopped herself short. It was time for diplomacy. She took Herbert's hand and sat him down. "I really don't know why you're so upset," she said, at once ingenuous, sincere and conciliatory. "You've become an important person in this city. And once you run for public office your life story comes out anyway. So why not now?"

"Who said I'm running for public office?"

"Come now, Herbert. You don't exactly make a secret of your desire to be district attorney. Nor should you. You've got a legitimate point of view and it is the right of any citizen to try to make that point of view the prevailing one through the ballot box."

Despite his suspicions of the high-flown civic tone, Herbert was forced to agree. "That's true, Cornelia, but why didn't you tell me you were doing the piece? I'd have been happy to cooperate."

Cornelia shook her head. "That wouldn't do, Herbert. It does not look particularly objective to do an investigative report when the subject of the investigation provides the input. The piece is being done according to standard procedure. You'll have your chance to comment at length before the piece is aired. That I promise you."

Herbert stared at the reporter, trying to decide if she was telling the truth. Was it possible this story could work in his favor? "So you're saying you're not out to get me."

"Out to get you? That's not how we work. As a matter of fact, since I started this I've uncovered some rather impressive stuff." Cornelia shook her head and chuckled to herself. "Imagine getting a pipeline to the DA's office by . . ." She laughed out loud. "If he only knew."

Herbert crossed his arms and squinted to cover the quick involuntary flicker of the eyelids. "Only knew what?"

"Well, Herbert," Cornelia continued, chuckling conspiratorially, "in view of the assignment in the de Bourbon case. I think it's rather funny. Don't you?"

"I'm sure I don't know what you mean, Cornelia." Herbert looked at his watch. "I'm sorry, but I've got an appointment in fifteen minutes. I've got to get back uptown."

When Renee Lieberman-Smith read the surveillance report on Herbert Whiffet's meeting with Cornelia Pembroke, she was livid. Not two hours after she herself had talked to the reporter, there she was, giving the details to Herbert. Damn, what possessed me to agree to speak to her in the first place?

Maybe she couldn't get to Cornelia Pembroke but she could certainly put the screws to Herbert.

# CHAPTER TWENTY-THREE

South Ozone Park wouldn't be so bad.

Clarissa Taylor watched the moving truck stow the boxes in which the family's possessions were packed and looked around. A few curious white faces on the street were observing the moving ritual, perhaps wondering where this black woman and her three children were going, but most ignored the scene as those who live in New York ignore almost anything. Clarissa noticed that no one said anything and that none of her neighbors wished her luck. No, she decided, I'm not going to miss Forest Hills.

When the landlord had originally offered her the deal she had reflexively turned it down. To Clarissa, in a kind of autoracism, any move back to a black neighborhood was a step down. But when the landlord had explained the details, it had sounded better, and, in the family's current condition, might even prove to be a Godsend.

Realizing that Clarissa was unemployed and could not expose herself to the rigors of a job, perhaps for some time, the landlord had offered to buy her out of her lease. After all, he said, it's better than facing eventual eviction. He had then offered to return her security deposit and give her one month's rent in cash in return for relinquishing the lease on her apartment. In addition, a friend of his owned some buildings in South Ozone Park, two story, four family frame houses, each with its own little court and backyard. He would guarantee Clarissa another place to live, more space at half the rent, and even foot the moving costs himself. It sounded like a con, of course, but Clarissa realized that a few more months in their current apartment and the rent would begin to suck her family dry.

So South Ozone Park it would be. She had looked at a top

floor left apartment that the landlord's friend had available and had been surprised at the bright, rather cheery accommodations that were available at such a low price.

Of course, Clarissa Taylor had checked the building out in the daytime. During the day, the underside of South Ozone Park slept. Some of those cheery, attractive frame houses had, in fact, been converted into crack dens, used by addicts purchasing and smoking the lethal substance before making their way back to the street to further infect the neighborhood.

But fortunately for Clarissa Taylor, her house was not a crack den. On the bottom floor lived a transit worker and his family and a retired school janitor, and on the other half of the top floor was a woman, husbandless like herself, living with two small children.

Moving into a new home is generally an exciting experience and so it was for Clarissa and the children. The girls would share a bedroom, Matthew had his own little room and even Clarissa had a room of her own. The living room was tiny but the kitchen was ample, with enough space for a table and chairs. The backyard was a bit overgrown, but perhaps Clarissa could organize the residents and clean it up. As the family unpacked, Clarissa Taylor, her immediate financial burden eased, once again had a little hope for the future.

The next days were spent arranging furniture, checking out the surrounding areas, picking a local market and chatting with neighbors, standard activities for new members of a community. In almost every way, things were better than Clarissa had expected. It was noisy at night, unlike Forest Hills, but the bedrooms faced the back and besides, what was wrong with a little street life?

The initial euphoria faded in the first weeks as economic reality once again asserted its pre-eminence in the Taylor household. Clarissa was still unemployed and likely to remain so, at least in the immediate future. She was precluded by her infirmity from holding most jobs, and the things she was currently capable of doing—baby-sitting and light cleaning—were not jobs that often went begging in South Ozone Park. Even the few dollars Matthew had brought home from delivering groceries were no longer available. Both mother and son found that a neighborhood with unemployment problems of its own was unlikely to throw work at new arrivals—too many with seniority were already waiting.

While Clarissa tried to decide how to deal with the shortfall, the children did what children will do in the summer months. They found playmates their own age and expended a seemingly endless supply of energy in cramming as much playtime as possible into every day.

Matthew in particular seemed to enjoy the new surroundings. When it became clear that he would be unable to secure a job, he took advantage of living in a neighborhood of his own people for the first time since he was five. In South Ozone Park he was no longer the only black kid among scores of whites; he no longer felt the tacit separation from even his closest friends; he was no longer an oddity. Here, Matthew Taylor was just one more kid, a little weird and bookish perhaps, but funny, amiable and energetic.

Far more aware than her son of the perils that lurked in such a place, Clarissa monitored her son's new friends as best she could. She was relieved to find that he seemed to have fallen in with a group that went to school and had some ambition. There were changes, of course. Rap replaced punk, basketball replaced baseball, and Matthew was soon dressing in the flashy, life-urgent style of his new black friends. Nevertheless, his group seemed to reinforce one another in their desire to finish school and become successful in some of the loftier areas of human endeavor.

But Matthew and his friends were not the only examples of neighborhood youth. One afternoon Matthew came home earlier than expected. Although he headed straight for his room, a mother's instinct caused Clarissa to call after him, asking if anything was wrong.

"No, Mama," he replied from the bedroom, "everything's fine."

From the tone of her son's voice, however, it was quite clear to Clarissa that everything was not fine. "Could you come in here a minute, Matthew?"

"I'm busy, Mama."

"Matthew!"

"All right, Mama. I'm coming."

As soon as her son walked into the living room, Clarissa could see quite easily what was wrong. Matthew had been in a fight. His lip had been bloodied and his left eye was swollen. Clarissa was not too alarmed. A twelve-year-old boy getting into a scrap was not exactly unheard of.

"What happened son?" she asked sympathetically, but not overly so. She didn't want to make him feel like Mama was overbearing or in any way stifling his coming manhood.

Matthew sat down heavily and looked at the floor. He didn't seem hurt as much as embarrassed. "A couple o' big kids tried to get Earl to give up his allowance money."

"So how come *you* got in the fight?"

"Well, you know Earl. He's kinda little. So when these guys kept hasslin' him I told 'em to cool it." Matthew glared at the floor from the shame of it all. "Then one of them punched me out."

"And he was bigger than you?"

"Yeah, Mama. He be much bigger. He musta been sixteen . . . at least."

Clarissa nodded in sympathy at the one-sided odds. Actually, she was just as concerned at the deterioration in Matthew's speech since the move as in her son's experiencing the first rites of the teen-age male. "Well, son," she said firmly, "it seems to me that you should be very proud of yourself. Coming to the aid of your friend like that."

Matthew still didn't look up. "But Mama . . . they got my allowance money, too."

So that was it. "Matthew, come here." Clarissa sat across from her son, who would not raise his face. At his mother's beckoning, Matthew merely shook his head quickly as if any other movement would bring forth the tears that hung suspended just inside his eyelids.

Clarissa rose and walked to her son. She sat on the edge of the chair and put her arm around him. "Matthew, there are those in this world who pick on others who cannot fight back. They are cowards and bullies. None of us can fight off everybody. Even the very toughest person will sooner or later find someone tougher." She took Matthew under the chin and raised his face in order to look at him. "Matthew, *we do the best we can.* And I think you should be proud of yourself for having the courage to try and help your friend. I know I'm proud of you."

"But, Mama, the money . . . I know how much we need it."

Clarissa laughed. "Matthew, with all the money that's been

flyin' out of this house, your allowance be just a drop, just a drop." Hell, Clarissa thought, I'm starting to talk like him.

Matthew's face turned hopeful, the tears receding. "You mean it, Mama? Really?"

"Really. Now, you want to do something for your Mama?"

"Sure, Mama. Anything."

"Matthew, I don't want you talking like a street nigger. One of the things you learn in school is how to speak properly. Good speech is one of those things that will make a big difference later on. I want you to speak properly."

"But Mama," Matthew protested, the crisis past, "when I speak properly the other boys call me 'faggot' and 'pussy.' Even Earl."

Clarissa smiled. The age old problem. Being called 'faggot' by your friends. "Matthew, I don't care what they call you. You are educated and I expect you to sound it. Don't you remember hearing Michael Jordan speak? Do you think his friends call him faggot?"

"Michael Jordan? Never, Mama."

"All right, then. Promise me."

Matthew promised and for a while it appeared is if he had taken the promise seriously. But the pull of peer pressure can be intense, eroding even the best intentions of a twelve-year-old boy. Although Matthew made the effort at home, enough street jargon found its way into his conversation to let Clarissa know that outside her influence he was aiming for acceptance, not superiority. She hoped it was just a stage.

It was not that Matthew Taylor meant to disobey his mother, it was just that, well, she didn't understand. She didn't know what it was like to be different in a place like South Ozone Park. And for Matthew, a boy who had been looked upon as different from the moment the family had moved to Forest Hills, the opportunity to fit in, to be one of the guys, to avoid the odd looks and behind-the-back whispers was simply too desirable a prospect to be ruined by a silly little thing like manner of speech.

What Matthew did not see, although Clarissa saw it all too clearly, was that the pull of street life was not limited to speech, and the desire to fit in, to be accepted, once acknowledged and catered to, could become the dominant force in a boy's life. And the risks associated with street life were particularly acute for a boy raised in a section of town where some of the more unpleasant by-products of that life were things seen only on the news.

For some, the trials of boyhood are replaced by the much more straitened trials of manhood. And occasionally the trials of the spirit are manifested by the trials of the courtroom. For James Rodriguez, his coming trial for murder in the second degree represented only the first step of a process certain to test his mettle in every way.

It had been difficult for James to work up the energy to appropriately participate in his own defense. When you're playing against a stacked deck, he decided, you can at least deny your enemies the satisfaction of watching you involved in the process leading to your pre-ordained destruction. Although his lawyer, and a very good one at that, had urged him to wage a vigorous battle against the malicious, politically-motivated campaign against him, James Rodriguez had come to look at all of them as members of the same conspiracy.

James Rodriguez' attitude presented a problem for Melville Seltzer. About the only thing that could sink this case was a self-destructive defendant. As the first phases of the trial neared, Mel Seltzer spent more and more time playing cheerleader to his client.

"Look, James," the lawyer exhorted for the twentieth time, "there's no case here. It's total bullshit. The only risk you have in this trial is death by self-pity."

James Rodriguez looked around the lawyer's office, where this latest in a never-ending series of meetings was being held. Photographs on every square foot of wall space attested to Melville Seltzer as a man with access to any stratum or nook of society. The man who defended Ali Abdul Akbar could be seen smiling or shaking hands with eight senators, one president, the cardinal of the local archdiocese, the Israeli foreign minister, the mayor, and a gaggle of show-business notables. If the man in these pictures said the case was bullshit, it probably was.

James Rodriguez nodded to his attorney to acknowledge his acceptance of the bullshit concept.

Mel Seltzer leaned forward across his huge rosewood desk. "So if you know it's bullshit, James, what's the problem?"

Must they go through this again? "Come on, Mr. Seltzer. Does it really matter if I beat the murder-two? I'm the pigeon and everyone in New York knows it. Even you know it."

The lawyer decided to try a new tactic. "You're right, James," he said softly. "You are the pigeon."

Rodriguez looked up. What was this? Truth?

"Yeah," Mel Seltzer continued, "there's no getting around it. The department is on the spot and they need an out. And right now, you're it."

"Thanks for that, anyway," mumbled the suspended patrolman.

"Even if you beat the criminal charge, they'll certainly have the departmental guns set up and waiting for you . . ."

Seltzer paused.

"But," he went on, shifting into summation voice, "if you don't beat the criminal charge because you're up to your asshole in feeling sorry for yourself, all that 'why me?' crap, then you do their dirty work for them. James, I don't know if you can beat the departmental case or not, but I do know this. If this criminal trial turns out to be the travesty I think it will be, you can walk into that departmental hearing with some guns of your own."

"Yeah," Rodriguez grunted, "but does it really matter?" The young officer was trying to maintain his disinterest, but Melville Seltzer knew when he had someone hooked.

"I don't know, James. How do you want to go out? You know, one of the reasons I took this case was that I heard that you were a tough kid, someone worth fighting for. I'm taking a big loss on this case. Shit, the private detective alone costs more than the fee the PBA has authorized. To be honest, I'm not thrilled with the idea of you making me look like a *schmuck*."

Mel Seltzer wondered why he hadn't tried this approach sooner. Honorable men like Rodriguez were always susceptible to the 'you're making me look bad' move.

"Okay, Mr. Seltzer, let's say you're right. What the hell can I do?"

That's more like it, thought the lawyer. "First of all, cut out the drinking—especially in public. You are supposed to be the honest, clean-living young minority patrolman, set up by circumstance and a bunch of self-serving politicos and jerk-offs like Herbert Whiffet as part of a greater political struggle. That image is hard to sell if you turn into a drunk before you even go on trial."

James Rodriguez looked to the floor than up again. "That's fair."

"Second, actually 1-A, is, start conducting yourself like the man we are selling in the trial. That shouldn't be too hard. You actually were that person before you fell into this."

Rodriguez smiled ruefully. "Yeah, I guess I could do that."

Melville Seltzer put steel in his voice, going for the closer. "I don't think you fully understand, James. The one way for you to get out of all of this is to make it politically unfeasible for the department and the DA and anyone else who needs an out to make it you."

Rodriguez nodded once again, but this time with a look in his eye that Mel Seltzer had not seen before but had hoped for since he took the case.

"Mr. Seltzer?" asked the cop. "Tell me one thing . . . no bullshit. Do you think I can beat this? The whole thing I mean."

Mel Seltzer sat for a moment, as if weighing some great issue of law and sociology. "Yes, James, I think you can."

Well, thought the attorney for the defense, I can be forgiven for one small lie.

The appeals had run out and the negotiations were over. Herbert Whiffet had twenty-four hours to turn over Fernando Rios' home movies or be placed in jail.

"Well, we agreed, Herbert," intoned the Rev. Mr. Chestnut, "you cannot give in and turn over that tape."

"I can't understand it," replied the Champion, shaking his head. "She promised. Something must have gone wrong. It must be her boss or something."

"The only thing gone wrong, Herbert, is your powers of thought. You really believed some white DA bitch gonna blow the biggest chance she ever figure to get to help *you*? You think you got that kind of effect on women?"

Herbert did not respond; things were moving too fast. What possible cause could Renee have to betray him? Herbert began to leave the reverend's study.

"Where you goin'?" asked Leotis, suspicious of any action taken without his approval.

"I'm going to find out what's going on," Herbert replied, closing the door behind him.

Herbert Whiffet decided to find out what was going on

right at the source. He called the DA's office and asked for an immediate meeting with Assistant District Attorney Lieberman-Smith. Ms. Lieberman-Smith would be happy to see you, he was told and within forty minutes, Champion-Under-a-Cloud Whiffet was waiting in the conference room for his appointment.

Herbert was relieved when Renee entered alone. Although he had asked for a one-on-one, there was always the possibility that Renee would have thought it necessary to bring along a colleague.

"Hello, Renee," he said glumly as she entered the room.

"Hi, Herbert." Renee was as perky as the Champion was not.

"Uh, Renee," continued Herbert, getting right to business, "I got the order today."

Renee nodded, still smiling. How could she be so sanguine about all of this? wondered the Champion. Maybe she doesn't know.

"The order from Judge Broom giving me twenty-four hours to produce the tape."

Renee nodded once again. She leaned back and lit a cigarette, waiting for Herbert to continue.

"Did you know about this?" demanded the activist attorney of his presumed co-conspirator.

"Of course," replied Renee, as wide-eyed and innocent as he had ever seen her.

"What do you mean?" he asked, trying to keep his voice from going shrill. "Renee, they're going to send me to jail."

"Unless you turn over the tape."

"Is that what you want?" asked Herbert, now completely confused.

"Of course not, Herbert," replied Renee, leaning closer to her Champion, some of the cigarette smoke getting in Herbert's nose and eyes. "Quite the opposite." She was almost winking at him. "I know you won't give in to that kind of pressure. After all, it's a matter of principle, isn't it?"

"You expect me to go to jail?"

"Of course." Renee was exultant. "What could possibly serve the movement better? A man of your caliber willing to go to jail rather than give in to the racist power structure in their attempts to compromise this case. Isn't it perfect?"

Assistant District Attorney Lieberman-Smith sat back and admired her handiwork.

Herbert Whiffet was trying to gather his wits but his mouth was working too fast. "You mean this was the plan you talked to me about? This was what you meant when you told me that everything would work out fine?"

"Sure," chirped Renee. Then she turned concerned. "But Herbert . . . you seem upset. Don't you think that this is exactly what you needed—the kind of outrage that will rally the community behind the movement?"

"Uh, well, yes, Renee . . . I see your point . . ." Was she serious? Did she really think that sending him to jail was best for the movement? She certainly seemed serious. "But you don't understand, Renee. If I'm in jail, there's no one to run things. No one to prepare the case."

Renee waved off the objection. "Oh Herbert. Don't be silly. They'll never keep you in jail. The people will rise up in protest."

Finally, Herbert Whiffet got it. Renee Lieberman-Smith actually believed all of the rhetoric thrown around within the movement. She really believed that the 'people,' whoever the hell they were, would abandon their own personal interests to demand justice for an imprisoned lawyer. Who did Renee think he was, Nelson Mandela?

"Renee, I think you've got it wrong here. I don't think my being in jail on a contempt citation will cause a popular uprising. The only thing that will happen is that I'll have to stay in jail until the trial and the appeals are exhausted . . . unless, of course, I turn over the tape."

Renee's expression dropped. "Do you really think so?" she asked. "Do you think it was a mistake?"

"I'm afraid so. Now I have to figure out what to do. It would be a disaster for . . . the movement if I were put in jail."

Renee Lieberman-Smith was contrite. "Oh Herbert, I'm so sorry." She looked into her lap. "You must hate me."

Damn, thought Herbert, there she goes with that whipped dog look again.

"No, Renee, I don't hate you. We all make mistakes." (Although not like this one.) "I'll work it out."

Renee looked up, her eyes full of apology. "Thank you,

Herbert. You're being terrific about this."

The Champion shrugged and smiled.

Two hours later, the videotape of the shooting of Lawanda de Bourbon was turned over to the office of the district attorney.

# CHAPTER TWENTY-FOUR

Matthew was late. He was very responsible so Clarissa was worried when he was still not home at 3:45, three quarters of an hour after he was due. Her own experience in Jamaica was still fresh in her mind, as it always would be, and the mother could not help but worry for the son.

Clarissa tried to keep herself busy in order to suppress the urge to go to the school yard and look for him. It was not a good thing for a twelve-year-old to have his mother show up just because he was a little late getting home. Once a 'Mama's boy' tag gets hung on, it doesn't come off easily and Matthew's speech and good manners had already put him on thin ice with his friends. Still, thought Clarissa, how can a mother who lives in a city neighborhood not go out after her child?

But about four o'clock, in walked Matthew, quite obviously not the victim of foul play. In fact, Matthew wore the biggest grin she had ever seen on him.

"Guess what, Mama?"

He was so pleased about something that Clarissa forgot the hour's tardiness and smiled back. "What Matthew?"

He puffed out his chest and looked every inch the budding man.

"Mama, I got a job!"

"Matthew, that's wonderful." Clarissa was pleased for the income, of course, although the few dollars that Matthew might hope to make was hardly likely to save the family from financial ruin. What pleased her more was the pride her son had taken in helping his mother and sisters out, a willingness to give up the rest of his summer to bring in some money.

"What kind of job did you get, Matthew?" she asked, allowing her son to luxuriate in his triumph.

"I'm a messenger, Mama. I work for 'Speedy Service' on

Atlantic Avenue. Five days. It only pays minimum wage, but I get tips too."

"I'm very proud of you, Matthew. How did you get the job?"

"This dude . . . boy in the school yard. He say . . . said that Speedy was looking for people. So I told him I wanted it and he sent me over."

"And they hired you just like that?" After the first burst of exultation, Clarissa began to wonder about a business that up and hired twelve-year-olds. "Aren't you under-age?"

Matthew was too excited to stop and consider petty matters of age. "I guess, but Ralph, he run the place, don' care. He say he just want kids who want to work, to make a little extra."

"That's fine, son. Tell me about Ralph."

"Oh, he cool, Mama. Ralph got a whole string of messenger places. It's big business." Matthew nodded wide-eyed at this little-known economic fact. "Ralph got this bad Cadillac and he dress really fine."

"And he hires twelve-year-old boys who want to make a little extra?"

"Yeah, Mama. Ralph say that when he was a kid somebody give him a break and he want to return the favor for other kids in the neighborhood."

"That's very civic minded of Ralph," grunted Clarissa. "And you say the name is 'Speedy Service' and it's on Atlantic Avenue?"

"Uh-huh."

"Well, Matthew, I think your new job is terrific. Congratulations." There was no need to stifle the boy's enthusiasm until she had gotten some answers about Ralph and his business. Clarissa wasn't sure, but it seemed as if Matthew had just signed on as a numbers runner.

The job also provoked some thought on a different but related subject. Clarissa still got almost daily headaches and was frequently dizzy when forced to be on her feet for any period of time. She fatigued quickly. So Clarissa Taylor must now do what she had sworn never to do. She sighed deeply and decided that she would go to the welfare department tomorrow. Right after she took a little side trip to Atlantic Avenue.

The next morning, Clarissa ate a big breakfast. Although not from recent personal experience, she knew what a draining experience the day-long application process at the welfare department promised to be. To make matters worse, the nearest office was located only four blocks from Russell McKey, Hot Feet and the scene of the robbery. Any thought of Jamaica brought back vivid memories of that terrible evening as well as the shame that came with the knowledge that she had never gone to the police station nor testified at the trial of her assailants. It was scant comfort to learn that the three, although under-age, had been convicted as adults, and had each received two-to-five.

But before the trauma of Jamaica came the perusal of Speedy Service. She had looked up the address in the telephone directory and went to the location at Atlantic Avenue and 185th Street. She hoped that Matthew would be out on a run when she arrived; it would not do to seem to be checking up on him.

When she arrived on the bus, she quickly located the building, a rather seedy two-story commercial structure. On the second floor, a couple of adjacent windows held the legend, Speedy Service—Reliable Deliveries Anywhere in the Five Boroughs. Clarissa hoped that Matthew was not being sent to Manhattan or the Bronx. He was too young to be riding the subways by himself.

The messenger service at least seemed to be a legitimate business and Clarissa slowly climbed the stairs to the second floor. She paused on the landing before going in. When she had caught her breath, she entered the office. It certainly looked like a messenger service. There were two old desks, one with a thirty-ish man seated behind it going through some files. On every inch of bare wall were maps of New York City: street maps, subway maps, bus routes and a couple that Clarissa didn't recognize. Each of the maps was decorated with stick-pins of various colors. The only thing missing were the messengers. The man behind the desk was the only one in the room.

After a moment, the harried looking man glanced up. "Yes, Ma'am. Can I help you?" His voice was soft and he smiled easily.

The man was dressed in expensive clothes, a silk shirt and

slacks, a large gold chain around his neck and three different style gold rings on his fingers. It was an odd contrast with the down-scale office, but his politeness put her at ease.

"Yes," she replied. "Is Ralph here?"

The man's eyes narrowed. "Why you want to see Ralph?"

"My name is Clarissa Taylor. My son Matthew started work here . . ."

"Oh sure. Matthew Taylor's mama," replied the man, his face brightening once again. "Matthew's some nice boy. Well mannered, intelligent . . ."

"Why, thank you," said Clarissa, flattered despite her suspicions. "I just wanted to speak to Ralph about Matthew's employment. By the way, where are the messengers?"

"They're all out. Can't make any money with messengers in the office. And I'm sorry, Mrs. Taylor," shrugged the well-dressed man, "Ralph's at one of the other locations. My name is John Gault. Maybe I can help you."

"Perhaps you can, Mr. Gault . . ."

"John."

"John. I was just wondering why Ralph would hire someone as young as Matthew. Hiring under-age youngsters can be a risk for the employer if anything happens . . . you know what I mean."

John Gault leaned back and smiled, even more broadly this time. "I must say, Mrs. Taylor, that I wish I had someone to look out for me like that when I was a kid. There are risks in hiring youngsters, it's true. But Ralph remembers when he was young and needed a job to help support *his* family, and couldn't find anything. No one would give him a chance. So now, when an eager young man like Matthew walks in here and says that his mama's had an accident and can't work, well, Ralph can't help himself."

"Matthew told him that?" asked Clarissa, suddenly embarrassed.

John Gault nodded sympathetically. "But don't worry about it, Mrs. Taylor. Things can happen to anyone; especially in these kinds of neighborhoods. Ralph is all too happy to help out."

Clarissa shook her head. She was beginning to feel ashamed of herself as well. "Well, Mr. Gault, I must say I'm surprised. I was afraid . . ."

"Sure, Mrs. Taylor. It's understandable."

"This Ralph certainly sounds like quite a fellow. I'd like to meet him one day. What's his last name?"

"Jones. Nothing fancy. Just Jones."

After a few more pleasantries, Clarissa Taylor left Speedy Service, heading for her next destination feeling a good deal better than she thought she would.

After she left, John Gault stared after her. Shit, he thought, I hope the boss knows what he's doing. Hiring these kids as couriers when they don't know what it is they're toting just might bite them all in the ass one day. Oh well, it was the boss's funeral. Old 'Nothing Fancy Jones.' John Gault had neglected to mention that Ralph Jones was generally referred to by a nickname that was a little fancier—Uzi.

For Clarissa, the other stop did not provide the pleasant surprise that the messenger service did. The Department of Social Services, Jamaica Office, was every bit as stifling, dehumanizing, fatiguing, and infuriating as she had expected.

Most of those in the large common waiting room where the process began seemed like seasoned veterans of the drill. They sat, bored and vacant, waiting for their numbers to be called, simply to be interviewed and sent to another line. Clarissa had at first tried to strike up a conversation with her neighbors. After all, the time might pass more quickly with a little chat. But none of the other women waiting to begin the day's journey through the labyrinth were the least bit interested in lightening the day. They seemed to take the position that affecting disinterest was the best approach. After a couple of rebuffs, Clarissa stopped trying.

Although Clarissa Taylor waited at the welfare office for a total of five and one half hours, the actual time that she spent with a caseworker was only twenty minutes. (An additional eight minutes was spent with five different clerks, each of whom told her that she was waiting for the wrong person and to wait somewhere else instead.)

When she finally got to the caseworker, she discovered to her surprise that it was a pleasant and earnest young black woman, someone who seemed immediately sympathetic to her plight.

"Please come in, Mrs. Taylor. Have a seat." The young woman indicated a cafeteria-style plastic and metal chair across the desk in the cubicle. Before Clarissa could do as instructed, the woman stuck out her hand. "I'm Valerie Frazier. How do you do. Please, Mrs. Taylor, sit down."

This time Clarissa was allowed to do so without countermanding orders. "Thank you, Miss Frazier. I've waited a long time to see you."

"Yes, I know," replied the social worker. "I'm terribly sorry for the delay, but this is your first time and sometimes this kind of thing happens. Oh, and please call me *Ms.* Frazier."

'Ms.' Frazier then shuffled through the stack of papers that held Clarissa Taylor's future. Periodically she smiled at the subject, occasionally she made a note in the margin, and, when she was done, she carefully ordered the official documents and tapped them lightly on her desk so that they would be perfectly aligned.

"Well, Mrs. Taylor," she said, smiling once more but this time with her mouth tightly stretched across her face. Clarissa knew there was something wrong.

"Am I in the wrong place again?"

"No, no, Mrs. Taylor. This time you are in the right place."

"What is it then?" Being in the right place was somehow more frightening than being asked to move on.

"Mrs. Taylor," Ms. Frazier began, cheeriness more strained, "while public assistance is a right available to all our citizens, we are forced to maintain strict guidelines in order to weed out those who would abuse that right."

Ms. Frazier paused and seemed to wait for a reply although Clarissa had no idea what she was supposed to say.

When the subject showed no comprehension, Ms. Frazier continued. "And those guidelines preclude the granting of public assistance to those whose resources are sufficient so that they can make do without it."

Ms. Frazier again paused and Clarissa was again confused.

"Well then," Ms. Frazier continued, an edge now in her voice, "you, Mrs. Taylor, are one of those people."

"One of which people?"

"Mrs. Taylor," she replied, now in clipped, official tones, "I see here that you have at your disposal a rather large sum of money, sufficient to support your family for some months."

"Where? You mean . . . ?" Clarissa stopped. She must explain herself clearly so that this woman would understand. "Ms. Frazier, that money has been set aside for my son's schooling . . . I've been saving that money for twelve years. No matter what has ever happened, we never touched it . . . Don't you see, Ms. Frazier . . . ? Without that money the family has no future."

Seeing not the least change of expression on the social worker's face, Clarissa began to panic. "Ms. Frazier, I'll tell you what. I'll sign a promise never to use that money for anything else than Matthew's education. Someone else can even hold it . . ."

Ms. Frazier finally held up her hand, cutting off the rambling woman in front of her. Ms. Frazier was quite calm, clearly experienced in dealing with this type of problem.

"I'm sorry, Mrs. Taylor. It won't do. The guidelines, as I have said, are quite clear. These guidelines exist to safeguard everyone's rights. They are there for your protection."

"My protection?"

"Of course. If we gave anybody who walked in here the right to claim public assistance, pretty soon no one would have any rights left."

"You don't understand," pleaded Clarissa, realizing that even welfare, the bottom of the barrel, might not be available to her, "without the school money everything we've tried to do will be for nothing. Just because a bum drove my boss out of business and I got mugged by three drug addicts. Don't I have any rights, Ms. Frazier?"

"Of course you do," snapped the social worker. "You're here aren't you?"

"I'm sorry," said Clarissa softly. She wasn't, but antagonism wouldn't get her anywhere. "Isn't there anything I can do?"

"I'm sorry," apologized Ms. Frazier, meaning it not one whit more than did Clarissa. "We don't subsidize education."

"But without education, what hope do we have?"

Ms. Frazier was rapidly losing patience. To her, Clarissa Taylor was just another in a continuous parade of spongers. "It isn't my job to make those judgments, Mrs. Taylor. I just follow the rules."

"What if you didn't know? Didn't put it down, I mean. The money . . ." Clarissa could not believe she had asked such a thing.

"Mrs. Taylor!" Ms. Frazier had sat up a little straighter. "What you are suggesting is a crime, a felony. You are lucky that I don't report your suggestion. As it is I will merely notate your file so that any attempt by you to circumvent the rules and guidelines will be immediately spotted."

Clarissa's shoulders sagged. "But what about my family?"

"You should have thought of that earlier. You said you can't work, Mrs. Taylor. Maybe you should try disability." With that, Ms. Frazier closed the file, ending the interview. She wore the self-satisfied look of one who had just saved the taxpayers from the leeching of a parasite.

Murray Plotkin had always assumed that he would miss the noise and the urgency of New York City; that the quiet and tranquility of the country would drive him crazy. How wrong a man can be. Settled into his condo in Boca Raton, seeing his family regularly, making new friends, playing gin rummy, and even registering in an 'Aerobics for Seniors' class, Murray was astounded at how quickly he fell into his new routine. If I hadn't been such a hard-headed *schmuck*, he decided, I could have done this years earlier.

Murray was sunning himself on the patio, reading the *Miami Herald*, when Glenn, his son's nine-year-old, skipped out to get him.

"Grandpa, it's the phone. For you."

"Is it Feivel?" Murray asked. He had a gin rummy game scheduled for later in the day.

"No, Grandpa. It's a woman."

"A voman?" Murray immediately went to take the call. Could it be Mrs. Mandelbaum? She was the best looking widow in the development, and only sixty-one.

"Hello?" Murray asked, keeping the eagerness out of his voice.

"Hello, Mr. Plotkin. It's Clarissa."

Murray was stunned. New York City was now as far away as Warsaw. "Clarissa?"

"Yes, Mr. Plotkin. Clarissa Taylor. Don't you remember?"

"Of course, I remember," replied Murray, digging into ancient history. "How are you, Clarissa?" He realized his voice was stiff.

"Not so good, Mr. Plotkin," continued the woman on the other end, ignoring the cool reception. Clarissa proceeded to detail her succession of misfortunes. Murray Plotkin did not interrupt.

When she had finished, Murray realized that he must say something. "So vhat is it you vant from me, Clarissa?"

The woman on the other end paused. The question seemed unexpected. "Uh, well, Mr. Plotkin, I was just wondering . . ." Murray Plotkin remained silent. "Maybe you know someone here, someone you could call to give me a job. I want to work, Mr. Plotkin. I really do."

The woman was selling, Murray decided. Murray Plotkin knew a touch when he heard one. "I'm sorry, Clarissa. I'd help if I could. But I'm retired now."

There was a pause as the voice from New York realized that Murray did not intend to say anything further. "Okay. Well, thanks anyway, Mr. Plotkin. I'll say hello to the children for you."

"Thank you, Clarissa. Please do." Murray Plotkin hung up the telephone. He walked back to the patio shaking his head.

No matter how much you do for some people, he thought, they always want more.

When Matthew got home, his mother was waiting. In his first full day as a messenger, he had earned $40.

# CHAPTER TWENTY-FIVE

Things were coming together for Karen. She had been surprised when the Reverend Mr. Chestnut had agreed to her request for an audience, and even more surprised when his only condition was that his input remain confidential, a condition to which she was happy to accede.

He had welcomed her into his study with booming baritone and ingratiating down-home conversation. When Cornelia had attempted to remain evasive as to the subject of her report, the Reverend Mr. Chestnut had only laughed.

"Why Miss Pembroke," he intoned, "there's no need to beat around the bush with me. I know that you are doing a report on Herbert. Let's just have things out front, shall we?"

It was not the words as much as the open, reasonable manner that prompted Karen to admit her motives and go from there. It was quite disarming.

"Very well, Reverend Chestnut. I am, in fact, in the final stages of researching a report on Herbert Whiffet. He has become quite a public figure and some details of his background, methods and ambitions is long overdue. I was hoping you might fill in some of the missing pieces."

Leotis Chestnut laughed. It was deep and infectious. "I'll just bet you were, Miss Pembroke."

Karen found herself laughing as well. "Am I insulting your intelligence, Reverend?"

"Not really," replied the clergyman, "since both of us know exactly what you mean."

"Perhaps," replied Karen. "But what do *you* mean, Reverend Chestnut?"

"Me?"

Karen laughed again. "Innocence does not become you."

"What a pity," sighed Leotis. "I thought I did it quite well."

Karen shrugged and shook her head.

"Now I'm insulting your intelligence, Miss Pembroke."
"I don't think you would do that, Reverend."
"No," admitted Leotis, "perhaps not."
"So, Reverend, back to my question. Why did you agree to see me, knowing what I was working on, and then only on the condition that the interview remain confidential?"
"Before I answer that question, Miss Pembroke, let me ask you one. What are your intentions in preparing this report?"
"I told you . . ."
"Miss Pembroke, I thought we had come to an agreement not to insult each other's intelligence. I believe this discussion will work in both of our best interests—if we are mutually honest."
Cornelia crossed her legs, but Leotis Chestnut merely glanced at the exposed knees in a manner that was both casual and sexual. Cornelia pulled down the hem of her dress.
"Mutual honesty may well prove mutually valuable," she said. "But for the moment, I am being asked to give you information with only the promise of reciprocation."
Reverend Chestnut smiled once more. "That's fair, Miss Pembroke. Let me start by telling you this. What matters to me is the movement. *Only the movement.* I have spent my life working for my people. Being white, Miss Pembroke, and obviously the product of a privileged upbringing, I don't think you can imagine what life is like for most black people in this country. It's not even the obvious discrimination—substandard housing, lousy jobs, unfair application of the laws. The worst part, Miss Pembroke, is *attitude.* The *attitude* that most whites convey, either openly or subtly, that blacks are somehow *inferior, lower* on evolution's ladder. Black children, Miss Pembroke, must first prove to *themselves* that they are equal before they can even begin to compete with whites. And black children cannot avoid the issue simply by changing their names . . . Miss Pzytriek."
Karen tried to smile casually but realized the flush she felt in her face was betraying her. "Touché, Reverend. You have obviously done your homework."
Leotis continued, now conciliatory. "Don't get me wrong, Miss Pembroke," he said with open-handed sincerity, "I don't fault you in the least. I would venture to guess that many black people would immediately adopt a new skin color to get

a better job—if it could be done as easily as changing a name. Particularly if the original identity could be easily readopted when it suited. Like to impress an otherwise cynical beau."

"All right, Reverend," Karen replied, all traces of her smile vanished. "I believe you have made your point."

"I hope so, Miss Pembroke." Then the Reverend Mr. Chestnut laughed once again. "But I did not wish to cause you any discomfort, merely to impress upon you the depth of my commitment to this movement. Because if you did not understand that, you might well misinterpret the remainder of this discussion."

"And what is the remainder of this discussion to be about?"

"Why Herbert Whiffet, of course. Isn't that why you came here?"

Jury selection is often the key to ultimate success in a trial. All the testimony, the exhibits, the objections, judicial bearing and adversarial by-play can be irrelevant to the outcome if a lawyer is stuck with an unfavorable jury. Thus, that stage of a trial will be the scene of intense wrangling and politicking as the People and the defense attempt to rack up points before the first argument is made.

Mel Seltzer was approaching the jury selection in the James Rodriguez case with an attitude that was uncharacteristically sanguine. On that first morning, he sat at the assigned table with the defendant and his associate, a member of his firm picked specifically for the occasion. As the first group of jurors was led in, Seltzer, as he always did, adopted his 'star' pose, slightly bent forward, examining notes before him, the very picture of coiled judicial power. Mel Seltzer knew that his books had made him something of a celebrity and these prospective jurors, most of them working people, anointed him with a similar status as they would, say, Lee Iacocca.

Judge Broom called the room to order and the process began. Awaiting his turn at this first cross-section of the cross-section capital of the world, Mel Seltzer glanced to his left. Rodriguez had certainly done his bit. He sat next to his attorney, straight and proud, every inch the man any prospective juror would want as the guardian of his welfare. Rodriguez wore a flattering dark blue suit, fashionable, conservative, and obviously not too expensive. (Mel had intentionally worn one of his Armanis for contrast.) He looked past his client to his associate. What a coup. Smart, tough, female, black, and beautiful. The perfect contrast to Lawanda de Bourbon. This is what a black woman *should* be. This one case made all the money it had cost him to lure Annie Holdsworth away from Gray, Steinford & Hodge worth it.

Annie would handle most of the preliminary questioning. She was totally competent and would be more likely to elicit honest responses. No telling when one of the panelists might lie to impress a celebrity. It had the additional benefit of allowing Mel Seltzer to observe each of those queried from a slightly removed angle—a much more illuminating vantage point.

The selection process went quickly. At times, the assistant DA who was handling jury selection for the prosecution seemed surprised at the ease with which some jurors sailed through, men and women she would certainly have challenged if she were defending Rodriguez. That, thought Mel Seltzer, is why I have Annie Holdsworth and the People have Renee Lieberman-Smith.

By afternoon, ten of the twelve were seated and all that remained was to select the remaining two and the alternates. Judge Broom, a man who despised loquacious attorneys and artificially extended proceedings, flashed a few half-smiles in the direction of the defense table. Mel Seltzer pretended not to notice, although he was sure Broom knew he did. Judge Broom had been an able prosecutor in his day and must know what the score was on this one.

At three o'clock, the judge adjourned for the day, the jury still short one-sixth of its complement. No matter. That would be dispensed with quickly the following morning, and things could get under way.

As they left the courtroom, Mel Seltzer took his client by the arm. "Well, James, what do you think?"

"About what?"

"About the jury," replied Seltzer. "What do you think of the ten?"

"I'm not sure," replied the accused. "I like the construction worker and the guy who owns the dry-cleaners, but that black advertising guy . . . he seems a little like a cop hater to me."

Mel Seltzer chuckled. "He is, James, he is."

Karen Pzytriek missed the first day of the trial, a story she would ordinarily cover. Rather, she was with a crew at Herbert Whiffet's Harlem office, allowing the subject of her piece the opportunity to comment on any charges that might be in the story, as well as to present a general picture of himself (subject to editing, of course) that he wished to convey to the viewing public.

"Well, Herbert? Do you wish to deny it or not?"

Herbert Whiffet, a man with many hours of on-the-job media training, knew that whatever fear, discomfort or indecision he was feeling must not show up on the tape. He leaned back in his chair and smiled comfortably, hoping that the camera did not pick up the glisten of perspiration between his nose and upper lip.

"This," he said evenly and calmly, "is merely another set of scurrilous charges raised by a racist system to discredit any black man who has the temerity to challenge it."

"So you deny engaging in a sexual relationship with a member of the district attorney's staff, a relationship that resulted in your being given certain confidential information regarding a number of cases whose outcomes were still pending?"

That was it. Herbert knew he had no choice but to answer directly. Anything less, according to the laws of television, would be construed by most viewers as an admission of guilt. "Of course I deny it," he replied, shaking his head at the absolute ludicrousness of the thought. "The entire concept is ridiculous."

The next step was merely to tough out the rest of the interview and hope that Cornelia was fishing or acting on information that was not sufficient to broadcast the claim. But Herbert simply had to know.

"Cornelia," he asked pleasantly, "may I have a word with you in private?"

Karen debated with herself a moment whether or not to grant the concession. Then she asked the crew to leave the room and took a seat on the visitor's side of Herbert's desk.

"Yes," she said coldly. With the crew gone and the cameras off, Karen did not feel obliged to maintain her 'impartial journalist' pose.

"Cornelia," Herbert began, his on-camera face vanished as well, "who is accusing me? Why are you trying to undercut my work? Especially now, with a pivotal case coming to trial."

"Yes," nodded the reporter, "a pivotal case indeed. So pivotal, in fact, that no one seems concerned about whether or not the guy who actually has to face the consequences gets anything even resembling a fair trial. The rights of the defendant, which you, Herbert, so passionately espouse, have become something of a joke in the case. Or at least certain people would make them so."

"That is untrue," protested the besieged Champion. "Since when are you in the press the guardians of morality? I've spent my entire career advancing the cause of people for whom the legal system is a sworn enemy. In this case, I simply don't agree with you that Rodriguez is a victim. And for that you are willing to air the most vicious lies about me without even allowing me to face my accuser? My congratulations, Cornelia. This is certainly a shining example of fairness in journalism."

Had Karen Pzytriek not studied the career of Herbert Whiffet so carefully, she might well have been swayed by the logic of his argument. Instead, she knew to dismiss anything Herbert might say as just another attempt to intimidate the press.

"Come on, Herbert," she sighed. "Your interest in this case has very little to do with the guilt or innocence of the defendant."

Herbert knew he had broken the first rule: Never get drawn into an acrimonious discussion with a reporter . . . on or off the record. But he was fed up with Cornelia Pembroke and the gutter journalism that she so infuriatingly mixed with the implication of moral superiority.

"What does that have to do with it? My interest in this case as an example of the injustice that the legal system regularly inflicts on black people is no less legitimate than your interest in it as ratings material."

Karen took a breath. "That's fair, Herbert, I'm sorry to say. Journalistic standards are not what they might be. But I'm not here to discuss the philosophic constructs underlying television news. I'm here to give you a chance to respond to material that will go on the air Monday regarding the manner in which you have conducted your professional affairs and aspects of your personal life that may bear on that material. And let me assure you, Herbert, I intend to present this report as fairly as I can . . ."

"Fairly," Herbert sniffed. "How can you even suggest fairness when I don't get the right to face my accuser?"

"I'm sorry, Herbert. I am not willing to reveal sources to whom I promised confidentiality."

"What if you're wrong, Cornelia? What if whoever it was that started such a ridiculous rumor has lied to you?" In his furious calculations, it never occurred to Herbert Whiffet that his original accuser was, in fact, himself. But his conversation with Clovis Buckworth those many months ago was now the farthest thing from his mind.

"We believe our sources to be accurate, Herbert," replied Karen, proud of herself for not allowing Herbert Whiffet to once again manipulate the press, "but if you feel that you have been unfairly wronged, your alternatives are quite clear. You are, after all, an attorney."

"So, in the end, you're just like the rest, Cornelia. You use your access to people's homes to get what you want, no matter whether it's true or not."

Karen laughed. "Tell that to Jimmy Rodriguez."

Herbert had to force himself not to respond. What was the point? She had taken him in and now was going to do her best to make sure the uppity nigger didn't give her friends any more trouble. He looked at her, smug and almost sneering. Well, he wasn't finished yet.

The crew was called back and the interview completed with Herbert sticking to his denials. He did admit, however, that he was considering a run at the district attorney's chair. "How else are black people supposed to get justice?" he shrugged.

Karen left the office feeling rather good about herself. She was indeed going to use her access to the airways, but to promote something worthwhile, something she believed in. It dampened her spirits only slightly to realize that Herbert Whiffet must often feel the same way.

Jury selection in the Rodriguez case was completed the following day, Friday, and the long-awaited duel between Mel Seltzer and the district attorney was scheduled to begin with opening arguments on Monday morning. The final panel was comprised of seven women, three of them black, two Hispanic, one black man (the advertising executive) and one Oriental. Courtroom observers could not remember a jury for an important trial on which so few whites were seated.

This was widely seen as a victory for the prosecution, but when questioned, Melville Seltzer merely smiled and said that he was completely satisfied with the make-up of the jury.

The defendant, who had watched for two days as his legal team failed to challenge any number of representatives from groups usually considered anti-cop, did not share his attorney's enthusiasm. Although he certainly respected Mel Seltzer for his record in the courtroom, it seemed to him that the lawyer had left himself with a particularly hard sell. When he raised the point, Seltzer simply grinned and told him not to worry.

"We're going to win this one, James. Just trust me."

That wasn't easy. James Rodriguez was not exactly filled with trust for his fellow man these days. Instead, he tried to figure out why his lawyer would allow an unfavorable jury to be impanelled when there seemed to be other alternatives available.

James went to dinner at Maria's determined not to let his suspicions get the better of him, but that was an effort doomed to failure.

"You're wrong, *cariño,*" said Maria, taking her fiancé's hand. "Mr. Seltzer is one of the best lawyers anywhere. He didn't get that way by *losing* cases. He must know what he's doing."

James sniffed. "I'm sure *he* knows what he's doing, Maria. I'm just not sure *we* know what he's doing. You should have seen them, my jurors, the way they looked at me. The cop who shot an eighteen-year-old girl down in cold blood."

Maria shook her head and withdrew her hand. Not this again. "James, under the circumstances, isn't it possible you're not reading them right? But if you want, I'll come and watch for myself."

"No," he snapped. "I told you . . . stay away from the courtroom. The reporters are all over. They're like animals. I don't want you to go through that."

"But I don't mind. And Mr. Seltzer thinks it would be a good idea."

"No. That's it, *cariña*. No argument."

"Okay, James. If that's what you want." Although the feeling shamed her, Maria found herself rather sick of James' self-pity. Certainly he had every right to be depressed with the strain he was under. Still, it occurred to Maria Torres that this may no longer be the man with whom she had fallen in love.

Rodriguez picked at his food, a nice top round with a baked potato. One thing about being a defendant . . . he was eating well.

"Don't you see, Maria?" he said after a long pause. "The more we show them we care what happens, the more fun they can have torturing us."

"Who is 'they,' James?"

"Them. All of them. The DA, the press, the department, even my own lawyer. They."

Shit, she thought, I rush home from work to make this dinner and all I get is that 'everyone's out to get me' crap.

"Damn it, James, I thought we were over this. You gave your word to Mr. Seltzer, and to me. You were going to see this through like a man."

James stared at her. His body seemed to be quivering. For the first time since she met him, Maria feared James Rodriguez. Maybe he was capable of shooting that girl after all.

"Mr. Seltzer," he hissed. "Mr. Seltzer. Well, *Mr.* Seltzer got me a cop-hating jury. I'm telling you, Maria. There's something up. Maybe between Seltzer and the PBA. Maybe they *want* me to be convicted so they can make some big political stink out of it just like that creep Whiffet wants to make something out of it if I get acquitted."

Maria sighed and nodded wearily. "Well, James, if you're so sure that you're going to get screwed, why wait? Drink yourself into oblivion or blow your brains out or something. Finish it now."

"Don't think I haven't thought of it," he grunted, but most of his anger had dissipated in the air over Maria's kitchen table. But anger is a communicable disease, and Maria Torres had caught the full dose.

"Well?" she said, her voice hard-edged. "What stopped you? All you're doing this way is driving everyone crazy."

Rodriguez looked over at his fiancee, and was suddenly embarrassed.

"I'm sorry, Maria. You're right. But tell me one thing. Don't *you* think this is all a set-up? Tell me the truth."

Maria sighed. "The truth is, James, that I don't have the

slightest idea. There's no question that the DA wants a conviction to show everyone how fair he is and the department wants to be rid of you so that no one will look any further than the killer cop. But more than that? We'll only know at the end of the trial. But James, don't you see? There's nothing we can do about it anyway. We might as well trust Mr. Seltzer. We don't have any other choice."

"Yeah," he nodded sadly. "I suppose you're right."

Look at that face, she thought. Like a puppy's. Maria suddenly remembered why she had fallen in love with James. She again put her hand on top of his across the table.

"The only thing you have that you know no one can take from you is your honor," she said softly. "And you, James Rodriguez, are an honorable man."

James smiled weakly. "I hope you still think that if I end up as a security guard in a supermarket."

Herbert found himself in Leotis Chestnut's study once again. The reverend was in a foul temper. "Damn, Herbert, it don' matter who told her if she's got the goods on you. Why is it so important to find out how she got it? The only question, seems to me, is *if* she got it."

"Leotis," rejoined Herbert, "how come these philosophical questions are always so easy for you? Could it be that it is because you're never the one under the gun?"

Leotis waved him off. "We been through all that, Herbert. The only question is where to go from here, and it seems to me that you should start keeping your head down a little so's that it don' get bit off. You don' do yourself or us no good if you're disbarred."

You'd like that, wouldn't you? thought Herbert. "No chance, Leotis. Once I back off, I'm done. I'm going after them."

Leotis jumped out of his seat, an uncharacteristic move that caused Herbert to flinch. "You crazy, boy? You goin' to parade yo'self in front of the cameras screamin' denials to a charge you know is *true*?"

"Is it true, Leotis?" Herbert smiled. "And where do you get your information? Do you have pictures? Tapes? No, I didn't think so. Well, neither does anyone else. And I'll be *damned* if I let my actions demonstrate the guilt that the station has no way of proving without me." Herbert was shocked at how his language had begun to deteriorate. He was definitely spending too much time with Leotis.

"Well, Herbert," Leotis snapped, booming baritone replacing even, carefully enunciated syllables, "if you insist on taking action to protect yourself at the expense of the movement, you do so on your own."

Herbert Whiffet leaned back and laughed at the Reverend Mr. Chestnut. "That's very funny, Leotis. As if I haven't been on my own through this entire affair. I beg to remind you that this was *my* case. Rios came to *me*. Now that things are reaching a conclusion, wouldn't you just love to step in and make it *your* case? Well, Leotis, that is simply not going to happen."

# CHAPTER TWENTY-SIX

Mel Seltzer, who considered himself something of an expert in jury relations, was less than impressed with his opponent's opening statement. He found the delivery flat and the entire speech rather lackluster, not a performance worthy of a man elected six times to be New York's number one crime stopper.

That's what happens when you only appear in court once a term, thought Mel.

Now it was the defense's turn. Mel Seltzer sat for a moment slightly hunched over the papers on his desk. He knew that the jury was waiting for their first taste of the celebrity lawyer, and the world-weary pose would pave the way for his remarks.

Finally, Mel Seltzer pushed back his chair and stood up. He walked slowly across the open space to the jury box, punctuating his steps with little shakes of his head. When he arrived he leaned on the rail, next to the advertising man, the foreman.

Seltzer took a deep breath. "Ladies and gentlemen, I just don't know what to say about this case. I don't know what I'm doing here." He sighed again. "That is because, ladies and gentlemen, I am defending a man who never should have been brought to trial. The district attorney has implied that Officer Rodriguez had other motives for pulling the trigger than of acting in what he considered self-defense. He *implied* other motivation because he cannot *demonstrate* other motivation. And he cannot *demonstrate* other motivation, because there *wasn't* other motivation.

"James Rodriguez, who had fulfilled a life-long dream and become a police officer, surviving, by the way, the pressures and temptations of growing up in a poor neighborhood, pressures and temptations with which some of you are familiar, found himself on a roof top during an action against some of the most vicious and dangerous criminals to be found anywhere in this country. He found himself face-to-face with someone he believed to be armed and a danger to himself and his partner. In that one-tenth of a second, that blink where a life-or-death decision must be made, Officer Rodriguez chose self-defense.

"After you have seen and heard what passes for evidence in this case, I think you will agree that any reasonable person would have made the same choice."

With another sigh at the injustice of it all, Mel Seltzer turned slowly and returned to his seat. As he passed the prosecution table, he glanced unobtrusively at his adversary. The district attorney was shifting his weight in his seat, uncomfortable with the veiled attack on *his* motivation. Mel Seltzer, back to the jury, allowed himself a little smile. The DA's discomfort was sure to be noted by the twelve men and women who were charged with determining whose motivation rang the most true.

Although the American legal system postulates that the burden of proof rests on the prosecution, in most criminal trials a presumption of the guilt of the defendant exists in the minds of the jurors. After all, if the accused mugger or rapist or car thief *didn't* do it, how did he end up in court in the first place? The standard defenses of mistaken identity, mitigating circumstances, or police misconduct rarely have an impact on this subliminal inversion of the innocent-until-proven-guilty precept.

Now, with one shift of his body, the district attorney had restored a cornerstone of the judicial process. As the prosecution prepared to question its first witness, Mel Seltzer was confident that the jury would view the People's case with a jaundiced eye until such time as an overwhelming case was established. And that time, Mel Seltzer was confident, would never come.

The first group of witnesses were the parade of technicians establishing the time and place of the crime, the nature of the wounds, and the cause of death. Seltzer referred to this as the Boris Karloff phase, the prosecution attempting to use the ghoulish imagery of the forensics testimony to paint a lurid picture in the minds of the jurors. Unless there is some question of circumstance, it is usually good practice for the defense to dispense with these witnesses as quickly as possible.

In this case, however, Mel Seltzer decided to make an exception. The district attorney, already strained at actually having to be in a courtroom, allowed his chief assistant on the case, Renee Lieberman-Smith, to handle the Karloff phase. While a competent questioner, Seltzer found ADA Lieberman-Smith rather plodding and just a bit too eager to have the jury check the police photographs and hear the description of the effect of the fall on Lawanda de Bourbon's lithe young body.

Let her talk, he decided. Nothing advances the notion of a frame-up more than a DA who tries too hard. For his part, Seltzer told Annie Holdsworth to question each Karloffian crisply and professionally, thus emphasizing the contrast between prosecution and defense. By the time they recessed for lunch, the uncommon thoroughness of the defense in cross-examining pro-forma technical witnesses and the attempts at persuasion through luridness on the part of the prosecution had made it clear that the Karloff phase would last through the day. Thus all New York was forced to wait an additional twenty-four hours to hear what promised to be the high point of the event—the testimony, complete with visual aids, of Fernando Rios.

New Yorkers were not yet aware that first Tuesday in September that they were about to be treated to a week of late summer news diversion to rival even the most fiercely contested pennant race, a week in which one Page One story followed another. As it was, the beginning of testimony in the trial of Patrolman James Rodriguez barely squeaked in as the lead story. WRCT had the Whiffet piece and its chief rival, WDEF, was countering with an exclusive interview with Herbert Whiffet, (granted, of course, in the aftermath of Cornelia's most recent visit to Herbert's office.)

At 11 PM, each station was in the unusual position of being forced to include references to the other, but the early news created two distinctly different impressions of the activist lawyer. Those who watched WRCT saw a picture of a man who, although probably with good intentions, sought to pervert and manipulate a system that fairly begged for such treatment. Those who watched WDEF saw a crusading altruist, trying to overcome the odds stacked by a corrupt, venal power structure to obtain simple rights for the oppressed. And while the Champion did not specifically deny that he had obtained confidential information from inside the district attorney's office, he most certainly implied that any such information that might have been obtained had been offered to him freely, without solicitation, by outraged members of the district attorney's staff and that certainly he, Herbert Whiffet, had done nothing wrong in obtaining it.

The two opposing Herbert Whiffet reports combined with the catalytic opening of the Rodriguez trial to create the volatile atmosphere in which the press thrives. As soon as the pieces first aired at six, speculation began to fly about (in the form of carefully worded, judiciously delivered journalistic queries), as to whom Cornelia Pembroke might have been referring. One commentator even suggested the ironic possibility of the assistant DA currently working on the Rodriguez trial, Renee Lieberman-Smith. (For her part, Renee was particularly incensed at the 'freely given, unsolicited part' in the WDEF piece which she viewed at eleven, only a telephone call from an associate tearing her away from a reviewing of Cornelia Pembroke.)

The district attorney was forced to call an evening press conference to deny WRCT's charges and state categorically that such irresponsible journalism would have no effect on the prosecution of James Rodriguez and that he retained complete confidence in the professionalism and honesty of Assistant District Attorney Lieberman-Smith. (Privately, he called in his chief investigator and instructed him to find out "what the fuck is going on around here.") The district attorney scoffed at the possibility that his opponent, Melville Seltzer, would ask for a mistrial based on these charges. First, he pointed out, using his best official voice, honed from two decades of like press conferences, there were no specific accusations brought by a specific accuser, and second, there was not the slightest indication that what hazy and unspecified charges had been levelled had any relation to the current case.

"I generally do not find myself on the same side of a question as Herbert Whiffet," he intoned, "but in this case I believe WRCT's report is a clear violation of his rights. I would not be the least surprised to see Mr. Whiffet file suit as a result."

Mel Seltzer chuckled when he watched the DA squirm at the news conference. A mistrial? With the DA knocked back on his heels? Not a chance. There was always the danger

Judge Broom might declare a mistrial, but, with the jury sequestered and Broom's penchant for getting it done, that was unlikely. Mel Seltzer wondered if his client appreciated the timing that had just added another straw to the DA's back.

James Rodriguez did not. He merely wondered, with everyone tossing rights back and forth at each other, what had become of his?

The following morning, the Rodriguez case reconvened with all the expectation of an updated Christians vs. Lions. The courtroom howled silently as Judge Broom strode in to begin the proceedings. It was immediately clear that he had no intention of letting things get out of hand; his normally sober countenance was turned up to glowering and his eyes shot thunderbolts in the direction of both the attorneys and the gallery. The moment he took his seat on the bench, he turned and addressed the jury.

In the deep tones that God must have used when instructing Noah to build the Ark, Judge Broom informed the jury that anything they may have heard or read regarding peripheral aspects of the case before them must not create preconceptions and must have absolutely no bearing on the deliberations that would eventually follow.

"You are charged," he commanded, "with determining the future course of a young man's life, to determine whether or not he has committed the most serious crime in our system of law—the unjust taking of the life of another. If any of you feel that you are now unable to discharge that responsibility with a fair and open mind, unswayed by outside influence, now is the time to speak. There is no penalty for such an admission. In fact, the court demands that no juror be forced to sit in judgment without a mind and a conscience that is clear."

Judge Broom then polled the jurors, requiring each of them to stand and confirm that no outside influence would prevent them from rendering a fair and impartial verdict in the case before them.

Behind his expressionless mask, Melville Seltzer was grinning ear-to-ear. What juror was going to disqualify him or herself from the hottest case of the year, just because of some news report? The chance to see a best-selling author up against the DA himself. And as to outside influence . . . until they invented human beings whose brains ran like computer circuits, 'outside influence,' be it a news report or simply which attorney the jury liked more, would always play a silent but often pivotal role in the dispensation of justice.

After Judge Broom had satisfied himself as to the continued impartiality of those charged with determining guilt or innocence, the People were instructed to proceed. Heads turned and whispers buzzed as the district attorney summoned Fernando Rios to take the stand.

The little man walked down the aisle, only vaguely resembling the Fernando Rios who had sleepily shot the now-famous videotape. This new, improved Fernando Rios was clean-shaven and well groomed, wearing a sport jacket, slacks, and a tie that had mysteriously materialized in his wardrobe just days before. He walked with the self-confidence of a man who knew that truth, (and the district attorney), was on his side. That same district attorney, who rose to question his star witness after the swearing-in, knew better than to press his luck. Both Fernando and his visual aid were shaky and, as even minds not nearly as acute and deductive as Fernando's could surmise, the cross examination would be a delicate business.

The district attorney ventured a quick glance at his opponent before beginning his questioning. Although he was sitting casually, looking almost bored, the DA felt sure he could detect an expression in the defense lawyer's eye akin to that of a crocodile getting ready to eat.

The district attorney smiled at the witness, perhaps to convey confidence, then began.

"Mr. Rios," he began prosecutorially, although years of politicking had left his voice with a perpetual campaign speech air, "would you please tell the jury where you were on the morning of May 18th of this year."

Heads leaned forward all through the courtroom and the artists scribbled furiously, all to catch the opening of Fernando's testimony.

"I was in my 'partment. Asleep 'til this noise woke me up."

"What noise was that, Mr. Rios?" The 'Mr. Rios' repeated as many times as possible was an absolute necessity. Anything to lend the witness credibility.

"It was the co . . . the police. They was raidin' some buildings 'cross the street . . ."

The district attorney then led Fernando carefully through the events that led up to his deciding to film the event. The questions were simple and required a similar style answer. The district attorney obviously did not fully appreciate a deductive mind.

"Then, Mr. Rios, after you decided that the raid was interesting enough to record on videotape, what did you do?"

"I put in a casette, jou know, the film thing, and I went to the window. Then I see this sh .. stuff happenin' onna roof, so I swing the camera up an' see some cop got this . . . lady up there."

"What cop . . . police officer, and what lady?"

"Jou know, Rodriguez . . . over there."

Judge Broom broke in. "Let the record show the witness indicated the defendant."

Fernando Rios shot a look of irritation at the judge for interrupting him. "An' the lady was Lawanna de Bourbon, the girl that got shot."

The District Attorney smiled benevolently. "We're getting ahead of ourselves, Mr. Rios. Just describe what you saw next."

"Oh yeah. So I seen this cop, jou know, Rodriguez, wit' his gun out and then 'boom' he just shoot this girl."

"From your vantage point, Mr. Rios," the district attorney continued softly, hoping Fernando remembered what 'vantage point' meant, "could you tell why Officer Rodriguez shot Miss de Bourbon?"

The district attorney half-turned to the defense table, expecting an objection. But Mel Seltzer was merely examining some offending ort under one of his fingernails. Even Judge Broom seemed surprised at Seltzer's non-action.

Fernando Rios shook his head. "No reason I could see. He jes' shoot her, right in the . . . chest." Fernando smiled, pleased that he had referred to the area of the wound in such a dignified manner.

If Seltzer was so unconcerned, thought the district attorney, maybe I should go for all of it. "Did you see a gun in the possession of Miss de Bourbon?"

There was not a sound from Mel Seltzer.

"No," replied Fernando Rios with a firm shake of the head. "No gun."

"Can you positively state, Mr. Rios, that from your *unob-*

*structed* vantage point, Miss de Bourbon was not holding a gun or in any way threatening Officer Rodriguez?"

"Jes."

"And you recorded all of this on videotape."

"Jes."

The district attorney addressed the bench. "Your honor, if the court please, the People wish to play this videotape and introduce the original into evidence."

Mel Seltzer looked up as if unhappy at being forced to turn his attention from his fingernail. "No objection, your honor."

Judge Broom nodded. The lights were lowered, a VCR wired to a large screen was quickly produced and in short order the home movie that Herbert Whiffet had attempted to hold for ransom from the City of New York was played for all in the courtroom to see.

As the district attorney had hoped, despite the tape's poor quality, the picture of a young, scantily clad, seemingly defenseless woman being shot and toppling over the edge of the roof had an immediate and powerful impact on the jury. Even James Rodriguez, seated next to Annie Holdsworth, was shocked at the apparent brutality of his act.

There was a rustle through the courtroom which caused Judge Broom to pound his gavel. "This is not a movie theatre in Times Square," he rumbled. "Talking to the screen is not permitted. Anyone who cannot sit quietly will be tossed out of here."

No one wanted to miss the next act and silence was quickly restored. The lights came up but the VCR and screen remained where they were.

"Mr. Rios," said the district attorney, "is the tape we have just seen the tape you made on the morning of May 18?"

"Jes," nodded Fernando, "thas it awright."

The district attorney breathed an inaudible sigh, grateful that Fernando Rios had at least survived direct examination. He turned to the still-fastidious Melville Seltzer. "Your witness."

Mel Seltzer nodded perfunctorily at his adversary and raised himself slowly, as if with effort, from his chair. He smiled graciously at the witness, who, despite returning the gesture, had long since deduced that this second interrogator was not on his side. In fact, in the long hours of pre-trial interviews, the district attorney and his assistant, that white broad at the table, had spent more time warning him about Seltzer than on his actual rendition of the events.

"Mr. Rios," he began, still smiling, "the people of New York are fortunate that you had the presence of mind at such an early hour to think to record this event for posterity."

Although he didn't know what 'posterity' meant, Fernando had no doubt that he had just been insulted.

"Jeah, well, it was a big deal . . . jou know, a cop shooting some girl onna roof."

"Yes, it was certainly a big deal," Mel Seltzer agreed. "Tell me, Mr. Rios, how long was it between the time you woke up and when you realized that you wanted to make a tape of the events?"

"Wha'jou mean?"

"Well, many of us would be a little fuzzy-headed at six in the morning, being awakened out of a sound sleep by noise in the street. It might take some people a little time to get their bearings. How long did it take you?"

The district attorney shifted in his seat.

"I don' know wha'jou mean. I was kinda 'wake anyway."

Mel Seltzer nodded and smiled. "Is that because you had only recently arrived home after drinking all night at a social club on 109th Street?"

"Objection!"

"Sustained."

Mel Seltzer nodded soberly at Judge Broom but was smiling again by the time he had turned back to the witness.

"Tell me, Mr. Rios. Is that the equipment with which you recorded the event?" Seltzer indicated a camcorder sitting on the evidence table.

"Jes." Fernando was no longer returning the lawyer's smile. That was bullshit, implying that he had been drunk. Anybody in the neighborhood would tell that fuckin' Jew that no matter how much Fernando Rios drank, he never got drunk.

Mel Seltzer nodded respectfully at modern technology. "Rather impressive," he said. "Is that your hobby, Mr. Rios? Recording events on videotape?"

"Jeah, I guess," grunted Fernando, unwilling to say any more than was necessary. The district attorney shifted again as if some foreign object had found its way on to his chair.

"How long have you been doing it?"

"Doin' what?"

"You know, Mr. Rios. Shooting videotapes."

Fernando paused a moment to deduce. This was a trap of course, but what kind? Then he had it. The Jew lawyer was trying to get him to admit he didn't know how to use the equipment, although for what purpose Fernando did not know. Fernando decided that Seltzer was not as smart as the DA said.

"Long time," replied the witness with a grin. "I like to shoot stuff."

"Oh," nodded Mel Seltzer, "then you have owned other videotape equipment?"

"Objection! This line of questioning is irrelevant."

"Overruled."

Fernando stared at the judge.

"Answer the question, Mr. Rios."

Fernando glared at the overrated defense lawyer. "I don' know wha'jou mean." Now Seltzer must be trying to get him to admit he was unfamiliar with that specific recorder.

"Other recording equipment, Mr. Rios. You must have owned other recording equipment."

"Wha'jou talkin' about. I only owned that one there."

Mel Seltzer shook his head in befuddlement. "I don't understand. You said you've been recording events for a long time and you've always used that recorder . . ."

"Jeah."

Seltzer walked to the defense table and picked up a piece of paper. "But Mr. Rios, according to this police report, the serial number on the recorder that you were using matches one that was reported stolen only five days before. From a Raymond Thoma of East 86th Street."

"Objection!"

"Overruled!"

Fernando sneered at the lawyer. "I don' know wha'jou mean. That police report is crazy."

"Perhaps," admitted Melville Seltzer. Then he continued as if nothing significant had transpired. "Let's change gears a bit, Mr. Rios." But Seltzer did not indicate what he intended to change gears to, rather returning to the defense table to exchange the crazy police report for another piece of paper.

Whatever mysterious substance was causing the district attorney to shift in his seat now communicated itself to the witness chair, causing Fernando Rios to develop the same affliction. Fernando was miffed, being caught like that by some guy who was not as smart as the DA had said. Fernando concluded that the necktie and the prohibition against certain flowery phrases was inhibiting his deductive process and resolved to deduce harder.

Seltzer returned from the defense table. "Let's examine the actual shooting, shall we?"

Fernando did not reply.

"As we have seen, you recorded the entire event."

"Jeah," Fernando grunted, no longer sure that he wished to acknowledge his creation, but sure as hell that he wanted to help convict that fuckin' cop to get even with the Jew lawyer.

"You also stated positively that Lawanda de Bourbon did not have a gun in her hand when Officer Rodriguez confronted her."

"Jeah," snarled the witness. "She didn' have no gun."

"You're quite sure."

"I positive. I jus' say that. No gun." Fernando leaned forward and smiled. Let him try to prove different.

The Jew lawyer seemed unperturbed. "Your Honor, I request that portion of the tape that depicts the actual shooting be replayed."

"Objection," came the cry from the district attorney, although this time lacking some of the righteousness of the previous attempts to protect his witness. "We have just seen the tape."

"Your Honor," replied Seltzer, using a tone that meant to establish a bond between the defense and the bench, "I merely wish to question the witness about the shooting and believe it is only fair to give him every opportunity to have the sharpest recollections."

"Overruled."

Without dimming the lights, (done on the first viewing for effect, the monitor being sufficiently bright to be viewed by all parties), the bailiff cued that section of the tape just before the shot was fired and played it through once more.

Seltzer made sure that the witness paid careful attention, and then, when the tape was completed, continued his questioning.

"Mr. Rios, is the tape the sole criterion upon which you decided that Lawanda de Bourbon was unarmed?"

"Wha'jou mean?"

"Well, it seems to me that Miss de Bourbon's left hand is not visible on the tape."

"So what?"

"So, how can you be sure that she was not holding a gun in her left hand?"

Now it was Fernando's turn. He had anticipated this question and was ready to spring the trap.

"Because," he grinned, "I seen her the whole time. Not jus' on the tape. I seen her. She didn' have no gun."

"I see," nodded the Jew lawyer, not seeming to realize that he had just been suckered. He merely walked calmly to the evidence table and hefted the recorder. Holding the artifact, he returned to the witness.

"Mr. Rios, could you favor the jury by demonstrating the proper technique for shooting some tape? After all, you said it was your hobby."

Fernando refused to dignify the lawyer's sarcasm and took the recorder. Expertly, he hoisted the camera to his shoulder, and with his eye to the viewfinder, pressed the trigger.

"Thank you, Mr. Rios. Is that the way you operated the machine while making the tape in question?"

"Sure," replied the witness, then caught himself. That fuckin' lawyer was trying to trap him again. "Except when I pull away to look across the street."

"Ah," replied Mel Seltzer. "You mean you removed your eye from a zoom lens that placed you right in the victim's . . . lap, to get a less defined view, all the time continuing to record the events across the street with the camera off your shoulder?"

"Objection. Counsel is leading the witness." This time the district attorney's voice had lost all traces of assertiveness, and he had begun to sit even before Judge Broom overruled him.

"Jeah, thas right," snapped Fernando. "Thas what I did. And she didn' have no gun."

"Quite," smiled Mel Seltzer. "One last item, Mr. Rios . . . did you ever attempt to reap financial gain from this tape? Sell it, I mean."

"Objection."

"Sustained."

"No further questions, Your Honor."

The district attorney decided to dispense with redirect, thinking, quite correctly, that Fernando Rios' continued presence on the witness stand would do little to strengthen the People's case. As the witness returned to his seat, somewhat restored by the rigors of cross examination to his usual appearance, Mel Seltzer returned to the defense table with the same sad shake of the head that had preceded his opening remarks.

Under ordinary circumstances, the district attorney would have then asked for an adjournment until the following day, much in the manner of a basketball team asking for a time out to cool an opponent's hot streak. But this trial was no ordinary affair. This trial was a public display of the efficiency and dedication to justice of the district attorney's office and it would not do to end the day on such a disastrous note, thus leaving the media nothing but Fernando Rios on which to report.

The district attorney rose. "The people call Lieutenant Phillip Gagliardi to the stand."

Phil Gagliardi stood up from his seat in the gallery and stepped forward. Unlike the other police witnesses, Gagliardi had made no concession to the presence of courtroom artists and lurking cameras, and had dressed in his usual decade-old sport jacket and open-necked shirt. He moved in the slow rolling gait common to tough cops and sailors and was sworn in wearing the expression of a man who had done this a thousand times before, which, of course, he had.

After some preliminary questions, establishing Phil's duties in the department and his relationship to the case, the district attorney moved closer to the witness to begin the serious questioning.

"Lieutenant, in the course of your internal affairs investigation, did you look for the gun that Officer Rodriguez claimed had been in the possession of the defendant?"

"Yes, sir." Phil knew he must answer the DA's questions straight or risk having just the opposite effect on the jury as he hoped. Any whiff of cops protecting cops would do the kid no good. He just hoped that Seltzer was as good as he had just seemed to be with the Puerto Rican.

"Did you conduct a thorough search, Lieutenant?"

"Yes, sir."

"Did you check the courtyard under the area where Miss de Bourbon was shot?"

"Yes, sir."

"Did you interview the residents of the building to try and determine what might have become of such a gun, if one had indeed existed in the first place?"

"Objection, Your Honor."

"Sustained. Please, counsel, confine yourself to questions of fact."

The district attorney nodded at the judge. "Did you interview the residents of the building, Lieutenant?"

"Yes, sir."

"Did any of them have any knowledge of a gun?"

"No, sir."

"In your experience, do you think that there is any chance that you overlooked any possibilities in your attempt to locate this weapon?"

Phil Gagliardi ventured a glance at the defense table. He wanted to put forward his ledge theory, but now wasn't the time. The jury would think he was fishing for an alibi for Rodriguez. He hoped Seltzer would give him the chance, but the defense lawyer seemed not to be paying much attention to the proceedings.

"No, sir. In my experience, I don't believe there is a chance I overlooked something."

"Thank you, Lieutenant. Your witness, counsellor."

The district attorney looked hard at the jury as he returned to his seat. Perhaps Fernando Rios *was* unreliable, but this decorated police veteran was not.

Unlike his smiling approach to Rios, Mel Seltzer sprang from his chair and approached this witness all business.

"Lieutenant, how long did it take you to prepare your report?"

"Three days." Phil Gagliardi felt better already.

"Was that, in your opinion, an adequate period of time in which to compile the particulars?"

"Objection. Calls for a conclusion."

Mel Seltzer turned to his opponent and stared quizzically. "Certainly, Your Honor, this witness qualifies as an expert whose opinion as to the time it takes to prepare a complete and thorough report is admissible."

"Overruled."

Mel Seltzer smiled. "Answer the question, Lieutenant."

Well, thought Phil Gagliardi, here goes my career. "No, it was not."

"Why not?"

Phil Gagliardi caught the shifting disease, but in his case the affliction was feigned so as to allow the jury to think that he had been trapped by the brilliant defense lawyer.

"Well," he said tentatively, "in this case, only a longer term investigation could determine whether or not a gun had been recovered by a local resident, since it is unlikely that if someone did find a gun, they would turn it over to us."

"So in your opinion, a gun may have been present."

"Objection!"

"Overruled!"

"Who knows? There were indications that *something* was present."

"What indications?"

Phil Gagliardi explained about the dislodged bricks and the possibility that something had been concealed in the structure.

"I see," said Seltzer, as if he had just heard this for the first time. "Did you put that in your report?"

"Of course."

"Did you recommend that the department follow up?"

"Yes."

"Did they?"

Phil Gagliardi shrugged.

Mel Seltzer turned so that he half-faced the jury. "One more question, Lieutenant . . . why did you return a report in three days when you stated that you preferred a longer investigation?"

Phil Gagliardi sighed, kissing his last chance for a decent assignment good-bye. "Those were my orders," he replied flatly.

"Were you given any rationale for those orders?"

"I was told that the heat was on from upstairs."

Mel Seltzer now turned full to the jury. "No further questions."

"Just a moment, Lieutenant." The district attorney had leaped to his feet. "I have a few questions on redirect."

The district attorney walked quickly to the witness box.

"Lieutenant, you stated that your department made a thorough search of the roof, the courtyard and the surrounding areas in search of a gun and that none was found, is that correct?"

"Yes, sir."

"The shooting occurred during a narcotics raid, did it not?"

"Yes, sir, it did."

"And consequently, law enforcement officials were present on the street below, were they not?"

"Yes, sir."

"And they saw no evidence that a weapon was dropped off the roof?"

"No, sir."

"Do you believe in supernatural disappearance, Lieutenant?"

"Objection!"

"Sustained."

"If you searched everywhere and found no gun, what other explanation can you suggest to support the presence of a weapon?"

Phil Gagliardi shrugged again. "The only thing I could think of is maybe the gun fell on a window ledge and one of the locals got it."

"A window ledge, Lieutenant?" The district attorney turned and faced the jury, a look of derision on his face. "A window ledge? How wide are those ledges, Lieutenant?"

"About nine inches."

"Nine inches. And that is at their widest point, is it not?"

"Yes, sir."

"So you are saying that a pistol fell from Lawanda de Bourbon's hand, over the side of a building, landing on a nine inch ledge and not bouncing off?"

"No, sir. I am not saying that's what happened, only that it is the only place a weapon might have come to rest without our finding it."

"A slim chance, Lieutenant, is it not?"

"Objection. Calls for a conclusion."

"Your honor," smiled the district attorney, "isn't this the same witness whom the defense claimed was a qualified expert whose opinion of such matters was admissible?"

"Overruled."

"Answer the question, Lieutenant."

"Yes," agreed Phil Gagliardi. "A slim chance."

The district attorney turned to his opponent. "Your witness."

Mel Seltzer walked slowly to the witness stand. He rested his arm upon the railing so that he actually faced the jury. "Lieutenant, those ledges are surrounded by metal gratings, are they not?"

"Yes, sir. It's to keep kids from falling out of the windows."

"And many of them have flower pots set inside, do they not?"

"Yes."

"So if a gun *did* land on a ledge, it might have been kept there by the grating or a flower pot?"

The district attorney began to speak, but stopped himself. No point being overruled at this juncture.

"Yes, sir. It might have happened that way."

"Rather a far-fetched theory, isn't it Lieutenant?"

Phil shrugged again. "Maybe, but I've seen a lot of far-fetched things in eighteen years."

"Objection!" shouted the district attorney.

"Sustained." Judge Broom leaned toward the jury. "The witness will confine himself to the facts of this case, and the jury will disregard the lieutenant's speculations, which have no bearing on the matter before us." Judge Broom levelled his formidable gaze upon the witness. "You should know better, Lieutenant."

"I'm sorry, Your Honor."

"One last question," smiled Mel Seltzer. "Far-fetched as it may have been, you considered the possibility of a gun coming to rest upon a window ledge and being found and not reported by a local resident sufficient to want to keep the investigation open, did you not, Lieutenant?"

"I did."

"But you were overruled by your superiors, were you not?"

"I was."

"Thank you, Lieutenant. That will be all."

As Lieutenant Gagliardi returned to his seat, he passed the district attorney sitting at the prosecution table, who, due to his being busily engaged in underlining a preposition in his notes, or perhaps it was a punctuation mark, did not bother to look up.

# CHAPTER TWENTY-SEVEN

A Sooner in the Oklahoma Land Rush did not move any faster than did the district attorney in his attempt to be the first to be interviewed at the conclusion of the day's proceedings. He casually sped out of the courtroom into the swarm of reporters waiting in the hall.

Addressing his friends in the media, the district attorney, while remaining totally confident of victory, expressed outrage at his opponent's transparent attempt to turn the case into a sideshow.

"The question here is very simple. Did Officer Rodriguez shoot down an unarmed woman in wanton disregard for her life? Mr. Seltzer is merely attempting to cloud that issue by introducing extraneous matters into the case. Despite this attempt to obfuscate, I believe the People have amply demonstrated that Miss de Bourbon was unarmed at the time of the shooting."

A voice came from the back of the crowd. "But what motive did Patrolman Rodriguez have in shooting Miss de Bourbon, if *not* self-defense?"

"I'm sorry," replied the district attorney, still smiling, "but I cannot comment further until the conclusion of the trial."

The district attorney was joined by his assistant, who had left the courtroom with a bit more reluctance than her boss.

"Miss Lieberman-Smith," they shouted, "do you have any comment on the rumors that you are the assistant district attorney who is reported to have leaked information to Herbert Whiffet?"

The district attorney called Renee Lieberman-Smith to his side and raised his hand for silence. His smile disappeared, replaced by the stern expression of the man in whose charge the rights of the people of New York resided. Although he did not go so far as to put his arm around her, as he might well have done if his beleaguered assistant happened to be male, it was clear to everyone that Renee Lieberman-Smith had his full support.

"This office will not dignify baseless, anonymous charges, delivered as if in the dead of night, vicious innuendo, forsaking responsible journalism for the sake of headlines, sensationalism without substance."

"But what about the report?" came the en masse reply.

"The report, if you could call it that, is completely false. I am confident that no member of my staff has had any unauthorized contact with Herbert Whiffet, Miss Lieberman-Smith here least of all. May I remind you that it was only through her efforts that Mr. Whiffet was persuaded . . ." he grinned slyly, "to relinquish the videotape that allowed us all to witness the killing of Lawanda de Bourbon."

The attention span of the press is remarkably short. As Melville Seltzer exited the courtroom the herd was turned his way.

Mel Seltzer was also smiling.

"Mr. Seltzer, do you think you've got the case won?"

The defense counsel shook his head. "No case is won until the judge dismisses it or the jury returns a verdict of not guilty. But I will say that unless the district attorney has something to add to what he has presented so far, you could describe my mood as confident."

The reporters turned their attention to the defendant, standing at his lawyer's elbow. "What about you, Patrolman? Are you confident?"

James Rodriguez forced a smile. After all, he had promised both Seltzer and Maria. "I have complete faith in Mr. Seltzer. If he says he's confident, then so am I."

"Do you really think the gun fell on a window ledge?" The question was asked by the reporter from WDEF in a 'how long have you been beating your wife?' manner.

James Rodriguez looked the man full on, ignoring his lawyer's squeeze on the wrist. "It had to fall someplace."

Mel Seltzer smiled once more. "That's it, I'm afraid. No more comment for now." Taking his client by the still-attached wrist, Mel Seltzer parted the journalistic sea and ushered Rodriguez into the waiting car. (No limousine for this trial.)

For Herbert Whiffet, although minus his chorus, access to the press remained open. He called a press conference at his office and was pleased that almost every station and newspaper was represented. WRCT even had the good manners to send someone other than Cornelia Pembroke.

"This case is a *travesty*," he began. "I have never *seen* such an example of poor planning and incompetent lawyering as I saw today in that courtroom. It is almost as if the district attorney is intentionally *throwing* the case. If he *loses*, perhaps he won't *offend* any of his *friends*."

But to Herbert's disappointment, the reporters seemed to be there less to hear his theories on the Rodriguez prosecution than to question him about a possible liaison to the district attorney's office.

"I have commented on that contemptible charge all I intend to," he responded angrily. "We can't be sidetracked by such petty vulgarity when *crucial* issues are at stake."

Try as he might, Herbert Whiffet could not turn the interest of the press away from his covert actions. He began to wonder if he would ever be able to discuss anything else. An activist lawyer was of little use if all people could talk about was his sex life. A racy private life might complement a serious public one but should never replace it.

The Reverend Leotis Chestnut had arranged to meet the press on his own. He had invited a number of reporters to the church, where he echoed the assessment of the district attorney's performance given by his former associate.

"Gentlemen . . . and ladies," he said, more operatic than ever, "I believe there are *fewww* prosecutors in the nation who could so adeptly have turned an OPEN-AND-SHUT case, where a murder was *videoootaped*, into a *rout* for the defense. There is *nooo* question that the jury, which, I remind you, was seated with virtually *nooo* objections from the defense, will return a verdict of NOT guilty."

"Are you saying that the case is a fix?" asked one of the reporters.

Ah, love those scandal-mongering journalists, thought the reverend, who was now able to have the charge raised without having done it himself. "*Welll*, I didn't say *that*. But it *isss* a coincidence, wouldn't you say? It was like Mr. Mel Seltzer didn't care *whooo* sat on that jury."

The headline potential of the Reverend Mr. Chestnut calling the Rodriguez trial a fix was such that the reporters almost forgot to ask about the absence of Herbert Whiffet. One did not.

"Well, Miss Pembroke," Leotis Chestnut replied with a sad smile, "Herbert Whiffet had different ideas as to the manner in which the community's outrage at this travesty should be expressed. We both felt that each of us should serve the people in our own way."

"Does this mean that the rumors surrounding Mr. Whiffet may have caused embarrassment to members of your organization?"

"We have no organization, as such, Miss Pembroke. Just an ad hoc group of citizens pressing for the equal rights of our people. And as to any charges that Herbert has become an embarrassment . . . we don't put much stock in rumors."

The district attorney was grateful to Seltzer for showing up when he did. That was the least he could do after beating my pants off all day, he thought. Once in the official car, he had dropped his public pose and looked at Renee Lieberman-Smith, who was staring out the window at the courtroom receding down Centre Street.

Could she have done it? he wondered. Lord knows, she certainly can't get laid a lot. But *Herbert Whiffet*? He debated asking her straight out, then decided against it. She'd probably lie anyway.

As it turned out the question was unnecessary. Upon his return to his office, after sending Renee home in a cab, he entered to find his chief investigator waiting for him. One look at the man's face and the district attorney knew that a particularly shitty day had not yet ended.

Beckoning the detective inside his private office, the district attorney sat heavily in his chair and awaited the bad news.

"Well," growled the chief investigator, "someone is definitely tryin' to get someone. This afternoon we got an anonymous telephone call from the usual 'concerned citizen,' female this time, sayin' that our dear Renee had indeed been banged by one Herbert Whiffet, Esquire, and that in return for such banging she gave him some information . . . among other things."

The district attorney sighed and went to his cabinet to make himself a drink. He did not offer one to the detective.

"Damn," he said. "Can she prove it?"

"Don't know," grunted the investigator, "but she did offer dates and places."

"Damn. I guess it doesn't really matter any more whether it's true or not. Okay, thanks," he nodded, dismissing his subordinate. There was only one thing to do now. After all, there was an almost endless supply of assistant district attorneys.

Supply, as any economist or merchant knows, is the key determinant of price and profit in a thriving economy. In the crack trade, the economy always booms and demand is consistently high, if not rabid. Thus, a decrease in the cost of goods need not be accompanied by a price reduction and, in the parlance of corporate finance, drops right to the bottom line.

So, when Ali Abdul Akbar received the news that a competing supplier was willing to meet his needs at a price that was a full twenty percent below his current cost, he was very interested indeed.

Since the discovery of Psycho Bates in the trash cans of Manhattan Valley, Ali Abdul had returned to the life of selective anonymity that best suited a man in his position. Although he still got the best table in his favorite restaurants and front-row seats for the baseball game or boxing match of his choice, Triple A realized that remaining in the public eye merely made him an irresistible target for those who would pretend to rule his empire. Also, a public figure would never have been offered a deal like this since suppliers, even more than distributors, loathe publicity.

And who would have thought it would be Uzi to make the contact? It just goes to show you, thought Ali Abdul, you never know about people. Uzi Jones, who was a member of the inner circle because of his expertise in baser matters, makes the score of the decade. When he had first showed up with the deal, he was like a pet cat dropping a dead mouse at the foot of his master's bed.

"Ain't it tits, Boss?" he had purred.

"I'm not sure, Uzi," Ali Abdul had replied. "It sounds *too* tits. Might be a set-up. Feds maybe. Or somebody tryin' to whack us."

"Dat's what I thought, Boss," grinned Ralph Jones. "But I checked it all out. Seems they's some heavy shit goin' on in South America. Little war of they own. It ain't no cops. They don' have the bread to operate on dis level."

"What about a whack out?"

Uzi shrugged. "I don' think so. It looks legit." Uzi turned philosophical. "You never know. Gotta take some risks to make a buck."

Ali Abdul Akbar smiled, his gold tooth computing twenty percent windfall profits. Even if it was temporary, that was a lot of money.

"Tell you what, Uzi. These dudes know you, right?"

Uzi nodded.

"Can you run some small deals, say ten, twenty keys? That'll make sure they ain't no Feds. Be careful. Don' want to lose my number one. If it still looks legit, I'll meet the top guys and cut the deal."

"You got it, Boss."

"An' Uzi . . . if this work, you got yo'self an extra ten percent o' the profits."

The preliminary deals had been consummated without a hitch. The stuff was high quality, the weight correct and the transfers made professionally. Most important, the new suppliers seemed to have an inexhaustible source. (Most certainly *not* cops.) And, if someone was planning a whack out, they'd never be that patient. Uzi Jones'd be in pieces by now.

So, on a night when most New Yorkers were amusing themselves watching reports of his attorney, Melville Seltzer, doing his very best to gain an acquittal for the cop who popped his treacherous girlfriend, Ali Abdul Akbar was preparing for a meeting that might well change the face of the drug trade in New York City. A twenty percent increase in the net could buy a lot of fire-power, and fire-power translated into territory.

While Uzi Jones was a superior gunslinger, Triple A did not completely trust him to handle security for a meeting of such significance and danger.

"So let's go over this again, Uzi. You and me go in alone, and they two go in alone. The big boy's Mejias and his number two is Villanueva, right?"

"Right, Boss. Just us four."

The meeting had been arranged for an unoccupied two-story frame house in South Ozone Park. Triple A Akbar had not gotten where he was by trusting Colombians and had assigned both Wrath and the Sheik to stake out the house forty-eight hours in advance of the event. Both had reported that their operatives had noticed nothing untoward during that time except, of course, the Colombians performing similar surveillance.

As confident as possible that the house contained no unpleasant surprises, Ali Abdul, with Uzi Jones at his side, set out in his bullet-proof Mercedes for the rendezvous. Throughout the ride they were in contact with Wrath and the Sheik, using a two-way radio with a frequency chosen only an hour before. The driver took a serpentine route, delivering the two at precisely 11 PM, the agreed time of the meeting. The street was conveniently deserted, residents and users alike having been told to stay home and watch television that night.

As planned, Ali Abdul and Uzi entered the building through the back door, Mejias and Villanueva having chosen the front. Uzi was grinning ear-to-ear as they prepared to enter. Fuckin' Uzi, thought Ali Abdul, he just hopes somethin' goes wrong so he can pop someone.

But nothing went wrong. The two Ghosts entered to find Mejias and Villanueva seated in the front room, just as agreed. At the sight of their future partners the Colombians rose slowly. Mejias, the chief, was short and square, with a pock-marked face and piercing eyes. Villanueva was taller but similarly shaped and stood a discreet step behind his boss.

Mejias stepped forward and smiled, revealing a mouthful of gold teeth. Ali Abdul smiled in return, revealing his one. Quantity don' make quality, he thought.

"Alee Akbar," said Mejias, taking an additional step forward. "Eets a pleasure to meet jou."

Triple A took a step forward as well, matching Mejias. "Señor Mejias," he replied softly, "the pleasure is mine."

Mejias extended his hand, a rare display of politeness in an otherwise impolite business. Ali Abdul smiled once more and accepted the gesture.

As his hand closed around Akbar's, Mejias pushed hard, taking Triple A off guard and sending him a step backwards, just far enough to allow the knife that had appeared in Uzi Jones' hand to make its way across Ali Abdul's exposed throat.

His windpipe severed, Ali Abdul Akbar merely gurgled softly as he fell to the floor, Mejias finally releasing his hand. Uzi, he thought. Fuckin' Uzi. The last guy he'd figure to make a grab. Then, as befits a respected leader in his field, Ali Abdul Akbar died a quick and painless death.

As soon as the king was dead, the new king got on the two-way. "Wrath?" he asked. "You there?"

"Yeah, Uzi. It done?"

"It done here. How 'bout you?"

"Yeah, all finished. Sheik ain't gonna bust anybody's balls no more."

Uzi Jones acknowledged the completion of the unfriendly take-over and signed off. "Okay, boys," he grinned at the Colombians, "let's do some business."

Without bothering to tidy up, Ramon Mejias and Ralph Jones sat down to hammer out the details of the new supply arrangements. The new leader of the Ghosts paused just long enough to consider his good fortune.

Trips always thought he was too dumb. He glanced at the body on the floor, the blood spreading out in a rather nice geometric pattern.

Who be dumb now?

# CHAPTER TWENTY-EIGHT

The discovery on a landfill site of the bodies of Ali Abdul Akbar and Sheik Salaam became the top headline. Following a tip received at midnight, anonymous of course, the police searched the reconstituted garbage and were quickly (to their relief) rewarded for their efforts. It seemed that whoever was responsible for Akbar's death wanted the world to know it. It was only two or three hours more before rumors started to circulate that the notorious drug lord had been the victim of a palace revolt and that Ralph "Uzi" Jones was now in charge. All this in time for the early morning news.

Narcotics details all over the city were put on the alert. The departure of an Ali Abdul Akbar was certain to incite others to make grabs on Ghost territory and the police knew that Uzi Jones was more than capable of making a fight of it. Every experienced cop knew that Akbar and the Sheik would not be the last to die.

What they did not know, what nobody knew, was that Uzi Jones was not relying merely on the membership of the Ghosts to see him through the coming hard times. Ramon Mejias did not do things carelessly, and he had not encouraged Uzi to off his boss merely to see Uzi suffer the same fate. Ramon Mejias had decided from the first that, through Uzi Jones, sales might increase still further, much further, and that the very considerable fire-power available to the Colombian could be put to good use protecting his new distributor. And although the price break was a bit less than the twenty-percent teaser offered to the late Akbar, it was sufficient to provide Uzi the ability to undercut anyone else in the city. Of course, Mejias would have troubles of his own when his brethren in Colombia learned of his new pricing policy, but with the commandant of the Air Force in his pocket, Ramon Mejias was ready to negotiate.

It was in this atmosphere that the fifth day of the murder trial of James Rodriguez began.

The district attorney began with a string of witnesses testifying as to just how slim a possibility it was for a gun to have landed on a ledge or in a flower pot. He had even secured the chairman of the physics department of a branch of the City University, who stated categorically that the chances of such an occurrence were "one in a thousand."

Mel Seltzer had fun with that one.

"Professor," he asked in cross-examination, "how big is a pistol?"

"I don't know," replied the academician, "six inches long perhaps."

"And into how big an area might such a weapon have fallen according to the generally accepted laws of physics?"

The professor shrugged and smiled. "I couldn't say exactly. It would depend on many things: wind direction and velocity, how and where the gun was released, many factors. Certainly a few hundred square feet, at least."

"So," smiled the defense attorney, "we have a six inch pistol capable of falling anywhere in a few hundred square feet. Would you estimate the odds of the gun falling into *any one specific spot* in that area to be a thousand to one?"

The physicist laughed. "Phrased that way, yes."

"Then to a physicist, the chance that the gun may have come to rest upon a window ledge is as great as its coming to rest anywhere else?"

"I suppose that is correct."

"No further questions."

The district attorney jumped to his feet. "Professor, how many other of those locations would have eluded a thorough search by the police?"

"Objection," shouted Mel Seltzer. "The witness is an expert on the laws of physics, not police work."

"Sustained."

And so the morning went, the district attorney attempting to undo the damage done by Gagliardi, his star police witness (Fernando Rios now considered a wash-out) and the defense countering by demonstrating that unusual occurrences are not that unusual in the hazy world of homicide. Finally, as the noon hour approached, the district attorney had exhausted his witnesses.

"The People rest, Your Honor."

Melville Seltzer immediately rose from his chair. "Your Honor, the defense moves for a dismissal on the grounds that the prosecution has not presented a *prima facie* case."

Judge Broom glanced at the defense lawyer. For a microsecond their eyes met and Judge Broom seemed to say, "Not in this case."

"Motion denied," he said. "After lunch, the defense may call its first witness."

Renee Lieberman-Smith couldn't be sure. The district attorney was treating her with the same consideration—he'd been wonderful since Cornelia Pembroke had aired that report—but something was different. Maybe he was being *too* solicitous.

The problem, she decided, was, having committed an indiscretion, she could never be completely sure that evidence would not turn up. For the first time, Renee Lieberman-Smith understood why unindicted felons sometimes walked in and gave themselves up. The reality of punishment was an easier alternative than the constant fear of exposure.

But those felons were often lifetime veterans of the legal system, men for whom the punishment for their crimes was a known quantity. For Renee, the punishment for the crime of collaborating with Herbert Whiffet could not be quantified and was therefore all the more dreaded. That in itself created a desperation in Renee that she keep her job in the district attorney's office, denying to the end any complicity in her sin.

Then, as those under suspicion are wont to do, Renee detailed the many reasons that she would *not* be caught. There was no documentary evidence; Herbert would not admit to something for which he could be disbarred or even imprisoned; even if he did, there was still no proof and Herbert was known for making wild, unsubstantiated charges; she certainly would not say anything; any other accusations could simply be denied.

Having compiled her list of the reasons that it would all be all right after all, Renee Lieberman-Smith went to another floor, ducked into the ladies' room and threw up.

Cornelia Pembroke was now in the unusual position of being news, her exposé of Herbert Whiffet creating a furor sufficient to make her part of the story. Now, in addition to being a reporter she was a target of reporters, and found herself fielding the questions that she usually asked.

"Where did you get your information about Herbert Whiffet?"

"Are you out to get Herbert Whiffet?"

"Is someone else out to get Herbert Whiffet?"

"Are you out to get the district attorney?"

"Did you corroborate your information?"

"Do you expect to be sued?"

"Was your attack on Herbert Whiffet racially motivated?"

"Was your attack on the district attorney's office politically motivated?"

It got so bad that Iserson was forced to issue a statement on behalf of the station that it fully supported both their reporter and her story. Privately he sniffed that the others were just envious that WRCT had scooped them on Whiffet, and 'if you can't get the story first, belittle the one who does.'

At Leotis Chestnut's news conference, her colleagues had treated her like a pariah. One or two friends at other stations had whispered to her that her Whiffet story was a hatchet job, over the line of responsible journalism. Upon her return, Karen had gone to see Iserson.

"Mike," she said glumly, looking into her lap, "I'm not sure I can be effective any more."

Iserson looked up from the copy he was editing. "What the hell is that supposed to mean?"

"Just what it says. The Whiffet story backfired. I thought I was doing a good piece of reporting, but now no one will talk to me. You can't be a very good reporter if you're frozen out."

"Corney," Iserson replied evenly, "that is *bullshit.*" Iserson was subdued, for him, the contrast to his usual bluster striking. Cornelia looked up from her lap. "If you think your effectiveness as a reporter is dependent on your acceptance by other reporters, you're nuts. They are the last people who determine a reporter's effectiveness. You *did* a good piece of reporting and I think you'll find that the people who count, the people out there with news to convey, will talk to you all the more. Not everyone, of course. The Herbert Whiffets of the world may try to freeze you out and your 'colleagues' may sneer at you and hope you fuck up. But if you want to be a *real reporter* . . . don't complain that quality has a price. No decision comes without a certain amount of discomfort. If decisions were so damned easy, everybody would make them."

Karen sighed. "Maybe."

"No maybe about it. You can't just take something whenever you want and think you're not losing something in the process. You may decide that it is a choice worth making, but it is a decision and a choice. You make your decisions honestly and responsibly. That's the best you can do."

"This is kind of funny coming from you, Mike. You're the last person I'd think of as a philosopher."

"Why, because I sit here all day and decide which piece of shit story to air over another piece of shit story? I know the failings of TV news. I was a pretty good reporter, you know. But believe it or not, television reaches enough people that the good we do, the abuses we report, the politicians we jerk off, all help the system run a little better. But if you want to *really* make a difference, you gotta stick your neck out a little. Not just once, but all the time."

"Fair enough."

"Yeah? You want your next assignment?"

Karen smiled "Sure . . . Knute Rockne."

"Find out what's been leaking out of the DA's office. If Renee Lieberman-Smith was doing it, maybe others were too. It sounds like a pretty loose ship over there."

The Rodriguez trial reconvened with the anticipation of Mel Seltzer's counterattack. The consensus was that it wouldn't take much to topple whatever fragile case the district attorney might have made. But Seltzer was known for going for the kill and whatever he had in store promised to be good.

Even Judge Broom seemed caught up in the mood as he took his seat on the bench. "Mr. Seltzer," he intoned, "you may call your first witness."

"Defense calls Patrolman James Rodriguez, Your Honor."

Two raps of the gavel quieted the buzz that had filled the gallery as the first order of speculation was answered. Rodriguez *would* take the stand in his own defense.

The accused stood and walked to the witness stand, his head up. Just before taking the oath, he glanced to the jury box and at one or two of those charged with determining his future. He made eye contact with the foreman and then turned to the bailiff to swear to tell the truth, the whole truth and nothing but the truth, so help him God.

Seltzer let Rodriguez sit for a moment, allowing the jury to fully absorb the defendant's posture and demeanor, something of a contrast to the chief witnesses for the people. Then he stood slowly and walked to the witness box. Standing at a forty-five-degree angle to the witness, which permitted a similar relationship to the jury, Mel Seltzer began the case for the defense.

"Officer Rodriguez, how long have you been a member of the New York City Police Department?"

"Eighteen months."

"And how long had you wanted to be a member of the New York City Police Department?"

The district attorney opened his mouth to speak, but apparently decided against it.

Rodriguez smiled slightly. "Since I was five."

"In the time that you have been a New York City police officer, have you ever accepted a bribe or gratuity, or participated in any activities that ran counter to either the law or the department's regulations?"

"No sir, I have not."

"On the morning of May 18th, did you shoot Lawanda de Bourbon during the course of a joint task force narcotics raid in which you were a participant?"

"Yes sir, I did."

"Why did you do so?"

"Lawanda de Bourbon was armed. There was a pistol in her hand. I felt that my life and the life of my partner were at risk."

"How long did you have in which to make that decision?"

"It was kind of instantaneous."

"And there is no doubt in your mind that Lawanda de Bourbon was holding a gun when you shot?"

"No sir. No doubt at all."

"Thank you Officer Rodriguez." Mel Seltzer turned to the district attorney. "Your witness."

The district attorney started slightly. He hadn't expected to be on so soon. He glared at his opponent for the shabby trick and then rose to cross-examine James Rodriguez . . .

The district attorney's cross examination proceded for the remainder of the afternoon and was continued until the following morning. The prosecutor traced virtually every day of Rodriguez' tenure on the force, and every second of his actions on the roof during the raid. But the more he questioned, the more solid the patrolman's position became. Rodriguez answered each question simply and politely. Mel Seltzer sat at the defense table, allowing the cross-examination to continue without objection, the eloquence of the young patrolman's performance under the pressure of a murder trial the best weapon he had.

By the time Judge Broom adjourned the court for the day, the jury foreman, the cop-hating black advertising executive, was leaning forward, resting his hands on the railing of the jury box. He was staring intensely in the direction of the witness stand, glaring actually. But the cop-hating foreman was not glaring at the cop. He was glaring at the district attorney.

# CHAPTER TWENTY-NINE

That evening there were so many breaking stories on the Six O'Clock News that the usual incidents of random violence, families rendered homeless by fire and rumors of an impending wildcat strike by private haulers could not get more than thirty seconds' coverage each. The owner of one of the local baseball teams fired his manager on that Wednesday in early September. Many barely noticed.

The drama that gripped New York was made all the more compelling by the appearance of the police commissioner warning those so unfortunate as to live in neighborhoods where drug activity was prevalent to maintain an even higher vigilance than usual due to what the department was sure was to be an imminent war among the larger drug gangs. Just that day, in two separate incidents, low-level members of the Ghosts, street dealers, were found dead, various types of punctures doing the damage.

Local politicians hurriedly altered vacation plans to ensure unavailability in the coming weeks and the mayor belatedly accepted an invitation from his Tokyo counterpart to visit the New York of the East, ostensibly to study the Tokyo mass-transit system, something with which the mayor was already totally familiar.

In the almost unprecedented competition for Lead Story, neither Leotis Chestnut nor Herbert Whiffet stood a chance. Their assaults on the district attorney and now-departed mayor were old news and, after an additional day in the Rodriguez trial, there was little to add. It certainly appeared that the district attorney had done all he could to break down Rodriguez on the stand and the only remaining speculation was whether the case should have been brought in the first place. Nonetheless, both activists continued to press the case that the prosecution of Officer James Rodriguez was being conducted in a half-hearted manner because the victim of his act was black.

"And what's more," boomed the reverend, "if the victim of this shooting had been an *eighteen*-year-old . . . *beautiiiful* . . . *white woman, I wonnnder* if you in the press would be so *sanguine* about the prospect of the murderer's *acquittal*."

Herbert Whiffet did not get much of a chance to make a similar accusation. Once again he was besieged by inquiries into his relationship with a certain unnamed member of the district attorney's office.

District attorneys read the papers too and the district attorney currently trying to get James Rodriguez to incriminate himself in the death of Lawanda de Bourbon realized that public sympathy had moved against him. The following morning, when court reconvened, he concluded his cross examination of the defendant in short order, trying only to demonstrate the unlikelihood of a metal pistol disappearing into thin air . . . or someone's flower pot.

As James Rodriguez took his seat, Mel Seltzer slowly stood up and addressed Judge Broom. "The defense rests, Your Honor."

More buzzing and more gavel rapping. Even Judge Broom was taken by surprise at Seltzer's move. "Uh, very well, Counsellor." He turned toward the district attorney. "Any rebuttal?"

The district attorney thought for a moment. There wasn't a whole lot to rebut. The entire defense had consisted of only seven questions. True, he could call Blakemore, Rodriguez' partner, but Blakemore would only confirm what he could of Rodriguez' testimony. In fact, Blakemore had been scheduled as a *defense* witness.

The district attorney glanced at the jury to see if he could read their mood. Christ, it was hard to tell. Finally, he stood up. "No rebuttal, Your Honor."

"Well then," Judge Broom said with a smile, "court will stand adjourned until ten o'clock tomorrow morning at which time we will hear closing arguments and the jury will be charged. I want to thank counsel for the expeditious manner in which this trial has been conducted." Judge Broom cracked his gavel. "Court is adjourned."

The district attorney needed the adjournment. He had only one day to prepare a closing argument that would convince the jury that regardless of how pleasing and entertaining was the counsel for the defense, the facts certainly pointed to a conviction for murder in the second degree, or at least manslaughter. But first there was other business to attend to.

"Tell Miss Lieberman-Smith I wish to speak with her."

The district attorney switched off his intercom and prepared himself. This was the worst kind of conversation to have.

After a moment, there was a knock on the door and Renee Lieberman-Smith entered. The district attorney sized up his assistant once again. It was still hard to believe that this was the woman who carried the germ of sex scandal within the office, his Donna Rice or Jessica Hahn or Elizabeth Ray. There wasn't a single thing about her that he found attractive. That she was frumpy would be that much worse if it all came out. Everyone would laugh and his career as a public servant would be over. How could Whiffet do it? The district attorney tried to imagine Renee Lieberman-Smith naked.

"You wanted to see me?"

"Uh, yes, Renee. Have a seat."

ADA Lieberman-Smith did as requested. She moved with tentative stiffness and the district attorney knew she was not expecting this to be a pleasant conversation.

"Renee, we have a situation here."

Renee sat up a bit straighter and crossed her legs. The district attorney glanced at her exposed knees then looked away. "Renee, an internal investigation has revealed some disquieting information as to your relationship with Herbert Whiffet."

"What information is that?" She spoke firmly but the question trailed off, as if her windpipe would only allow the four words.

The district attorney began to fiddle with his silver dagger letter opener, the memento of the successful prosecution of a serial knife murderer, a gift from his staff ten years before. "I think you know what information, Renee."

He had expected his heretofore meek assistant to back down at this point, perhaps even to throw herself on the mercy of the court. But Renee Lieberman-Smith did not back down.

"No," she snapped, voice recovered, "I have no idea what information."

"Well, Renee . . ." The district attorney fumbled for a way to say it, impromptu remarks not one of his strengths. "Our investigators have uncovered evidence that the charges made in that television report were true."

"What evidence?"

The district attorney looked up. Renee Lieberman-Smith was actually *smiling* at him. Why was she making this so hard? They both knew she was done.

"I'm not at liberty to discuss the nature of the evidence. But it is sufficient for me to ask for your resignation."

"Why should I resign? You don't have anything. You don't have any proof that would hold up."

The district attorney blinked. "Hold up? What are we talking about here, Renee? No one is going to court. You have become an embarrassment to this office at a time when we can't afford another embarrassment. I gave you the responsibility for a key prosecution and you left me with what was, to say the least, a weak case. In addition, you compromised all of us by your relationship with a man who seeks to bring down this office. I think that is an indication of where your sympathies lie. I am offering you the possibility of an honorable resignation, citing, oh, pressures created by the vicious unwarranted attacks in the media and your desire to spare this office any embarrassment. That will kill the investigations into your . . . private life and let you get another job somewhere else. I will give you the highest recommendation. That seems to me to be a more pleasing alternative than ridicule, dismissal, disbarment and, quite possibly, prison."

Renee sat stunned as she listened to the embodiment of all the hypocrisies that had caused her to join forces with Herbert Whiffet in the first place.

"But you have no *proof*," she screamed, amazed at the sound of her own voice. "What about my *rights*?"

The district attorney stared at his soon-to-be former assistant. "What about your rights? We're covering up for you, aren't we?"

With all the furor surrounding the Rodriguez trial and the

protests of injustice by the activists, it was the spontaneous generation of a major drug war that began to dominate the headlines. Four more people died Thursday, bringing to an incredible six the total number of drug-war casualties in the first twenty-four hours of the battle.

Even the most seasoned narcotics officers were shocked at the ferocity with which the Ghosts' fiefdom was being contested. There must be something more to this, they decided, but were unable to confirm their theories. Standard sources of information had dried up, even the most trusted informants refusing to discuss what promised to be the most brutal struggle in the city's history. The police themselves were unwilling to expose undercover operatives to the risk of torture and death that must accompany any effort to ferret out information. So the police contented themselves with wearing body armor and waiting for a break.

Uzi Jones had reacted to the Wednesday murder of his two dealers by kidnapping seven members of rival gangs at random. Early Friday morning, a brightly gift-wrapped hat box was delivered to the headquarters of each of the seven. Inside each box was the neatly severed head of that gang's kidnapped operative.

In addition to the surgical approach, Ghost vans roared down streets belonging to the gang's competitors, spraying automatic weapons fire into store windows and, occasionally, residents. Although the purpose of these drive-bys was to intimidate and not to kill, eight people were slightly wounded.

But the most shocking crime of all in this Fort Sumter of the Ghost War was the murder of the courier.

It was standard practice by the gangs to use under-age members as couriers. These children could not be prosecuted as adults and thus were safe from the long prison sentences that awaited an of-age person caught transporting narcotics. Unfortunately, these mini-couriers were not able to defend themselves with the zeal of their older counterparts and were thus popular targets for those thinking of making a quick score. In wartime, interdiction of this youthful distribution network was an easy and painless way to cause your foe economic hardship.

On that Friday, several unidentified men cornered a twelve-year-old boy on an 'F' train heading from Manhattan to Long Island City. While the frozen passengers looked on, these men calmly shot the terrified boy through the head, took the package he was carrying and jumped off the train at the 23rd Street-Ely Avenue stop. By the time the police were notified, the murderers had disappeared into the housing projects under the Queensborough Bridge.

When detectives arrived to examine the body, they quickly realized that there were no real clues. Although the public would clamor for a solution, the murder of this child would inevitably be just another event that had no resolution but simply trailed off, resurrected every so often by a journalist or writer to illustrate the brutality and caprice of life in New York.

But for now, there was just a child's corpse, growing cold in death, a small boy wearing a Speedy Service jacket. The detectives identified him by the library card in his pocket.

It read 'Matthew Taylor.'

# CHAPTER THIRTY

"The defense may present its closing argument." Judge Broom leaned forward along with the rest of the audience as Melville Seltzer approached the jury box.

Seltzer walked slowly across the silent room. He placed his hands on the rail that divided the jury from the rest of the courtroom and looked into the eyes of each juror before he began.

"Ladies and gentlemen, the district attorney would have you believe that Patrolman Rodriguez was indicted and brought to trial to serve the ends of justice. He would have you believe that this case is no different from any other. He would have you believe that he has demonstrated *beyond a reasonable doubt* that James Rodriguez murdered Lawanda de Bourbon, an unarmed eighteen-year-old. He would have you believe that Patrolman Rodriguez committed this horrible act because of some moral corruption present in the police department and in Patrolman Rodriguez himself. But most of all he would have you believe that a verdict of guilty would serve the people and protect their rights.

"Ladies and gentlemen, I take the same position now as when I addressed you at the outset of this trial, seven days ago. Motive is indeed the crux of this case. And what has the prosecution done to demonstrate what motive this young patrolman may have had to risk his life-long dream and violate everything in which he believed by murdering a woman who was the consort of one drug dealer, the secret lover of a second, and an informant on the side? Was it money? Was Patrolman Rodriguez involved in some dark conspiracy? Was he acting for others to cover *their* crimes? The prosecution would have you believe that one or all of these motives existed . . ."

Mel Seltzer gripped the railing tightly and stared at the

jurors. "*But where is his proof?*" The lawyer relaxed his grip and began to pace the length of the jury box. "*This case is a travesty.* There is *no* indication of Patrolman Rodriguez' motives, not the slightest evidence that the shooting was anything more than it appeared to be, a policeman forced to make a split-second decision, a life-or-death decision. *That is what we pay them for . . . that is the only reason we can walk the streets in what little safety we have.* Without James Rodriguez and those like him, young men who grow up with a desire to serve their neighbors on the front lines, where are we?"

Mel Seltzer stopped again, this time directly across from the foreman. "Yet the district attorney chose to put James Rodriguez on trial for *murder*. Oh yes, ladies and gentlemen, motive is rather important in this case.

"Now let us examine the shooting itself. Patrolman Rodriguez claims Lawanda de Bourbon was armed, yet the prosecution correctly points out that no gun was found, although with police crawling over the entire block, a gun most certainly should have been found. A mystery to be sure. A mystery that the twelve of you must try to solve.

"And what information do you have with which to solve it? We know that Lawanda de Bourbon had fragments of brick under her fingernails and that fragments of her fingernails were on the bricks hurriedly pulled out of the tower housing. Ladies and gentlemen, it is clear that Lawanda de Bourbon was going for *something* as she fled the police officers. *Yet, nothing AT ALL was found*. Whatever it was, a pistol, a knife, or her favorite book, whatever Lawanda de Bourbon pulled from that hiding place *disappeared*. The detective charged with investigating the case for the police department thought that the probability that it was a weapon was sufficient to keep the investigation open, but he was overruled by his superiors. Again, we come back to motive.

"Actually, ladies and gentlemen, the district attorney himself has demonstrated to you how weak this case is. He demonstrated that weakness by relying on an inconclusive videotape, recorded on stolen equipment by a man with a record of convictions dating back to his early teens. Think, each of you, how you would feel, sitting in the place of the accused, having *your* dream, *your* career, *your* chance to become something . . ." Mel Seltzer looked again at the foreman, "*your* life, in the hands of Fernando Rios . . . and the man who chose to make him his star witness.

"Motive and reasonable doubt, ladies and gentlemen . . . that is indeed what this case is all about. And rights. Let us not forget rights. A most interesting word. A word we have tossed about in this case rather casually. The rights of the people, the rights of the accused, the rights of the victim . . . it is almost as if rights could be fabricated at will and dispensed indiscriminately; that we can print new rights like the mint can print new money. That is unfortunately not the case.

"Rights are given to one person or one group at the expense of another. *Always.* That choice, that decision, is the very cornerstone of our system of government. Once we reduce rights to something that we toss around as a substitute for thought and reason and the responsibility for making a decision and living with the consequences, we begin to erode the foundations upon which our freedoms are built.

"And because of the decisions and the choices that are required to safeguard the rights of all of us, today, ladies and gentlemen, today you twelve are the guardians of our rights. You twelve citizens are entrusted with that decision."

Melville Seltzer passed his eyes once again over the jury, then he slowly returned to his seat.

"The People may now present its closing argument."

The district attorney glanced at his opponent as he strode toward the jury. He too placed his hands upon the railing and looked each juror in the eye.

"Ladies and gentlemen, this is a very simple case. This is a case of murder, the violation of our most sacred prohibition. There is only one question in this case—did James Rodriguez take the life of another without the presence of one of the few justifications that our laws provide for such an act?

"We know that James Rodriguez did indeed shoot Lawanda de Bourbon to death on the morning of May 18th. The only question in this case is justification. James Rodriguez has claimed for his justification that his life and the life of his partner were at risk. If true, the shooting may have been justified under our laws. Therefore, ladies and gentlemen, the question seems to be not one of rights, or the motives of this office in bringing the case, or any other smoke screen the defense seeks to send up to obscure the issue. The question seems simply to be, do you believe that Lawanda de Bourbon, running barefoot across a rooftop at 6 AM, pursued by armed police officers wearing body armor, stopped to grab a gun in order to shoot it out? Do you believe that with literally hundreds of police officers on or near the scene, a weapon would not have been recovered?

"Ladies and gentlemen, you are *not* sitting on this jury to decide broad questions about our system of government, although the defense would prefer it. You are here to judge the very narrow question of whether or not James Rodriguez was justified in killing an eighteen-year-old girl, depriving her of perhaps another sixty years of life. The charge you have is a heavy one, for the question of guilt or innocence does not involve sympathy for one party and antipathy for another. It merely involves the weight of the evidence. And the evidence in this case is clear. *There was no gun.* And in the absence of justification, James Rodriguez, the defendant, is guilty of murder in the second degree."

The district attorney turned and strode confidently back to his seat, noting that Renee Lieberman-Smith, still his assistant on this case, had taken their talk to heart. Her hair was done, she was impeccably groomed, the model assistant district attorney for all to see.

Judge Broom cleared his throat and turned toward the jury. "Ladies and gentlemen, now that you have heard the evidence and the closing arguments by defense and the People, I must instruct you on the definitions of the law that will provide the basis for your deliberations . . ."

For the next two hours, Judge Broom painstakingly described the difference between murder in the second degree and manslaughter, applied the evidence and the questions of proof to each statute and detailed the possible verdicts that the jury might return depending on their view of the evidence. The judge cautioned them to take their time, to be thorough and precise, that any piece of evidence or section of transcript was available to aid in their deliberations.

At the conclusion of the charge, the jury was led away, off to a closed and guarded room where they would deliberate and ultimately decide the fate of a young man they had never met, based on recollections and abstractions of events they had not witnessed.

As the jury departed, everyone in the courtroom except the defendant relaxed. No reason to get worked up yet. This promised to be a long haul.

It wasn't.

Only three hours later the foreman sent word to the judge that they had reached a verdict. Court was reconvened and prosecution, defense, spectators and judge awaited the return of the jury. There is little in life to match the drama of those twelve empty seats, soon to be filled by a panel who knows what not one other person in the room knows—whether the defendant has been judged innocent or guilty.

The jury filed in, their faces blank, and filled those chairs. Mel Seltzer never ceased to wonder at a jury's instinctive understanding of the majestic tension that precedes the reading of a verdict. He had never seen a juror, in any case in which he had been involved, tip a verdict before a reading. Never a smile or a glance, no expression of any kind.

Judge Broom leaned forward. "Ladies and gentlemen of the jury, have you reached a verdict?"

The foreman rose. "We have, Your Honor."

As instructed, James Rodriguez rose and faced the jury box.

"And what is your verdict?"

Without hesitation, the black advertising man, the cop-hater, said firmly, "We find the defendant not guilty."

Judge Broom tried to command an orderly adjournment after dismissing the jury, but it was futile. Reporters bolted for the exit to set up immediately outside the courtroom door. Officials of the PBA ran up to congratulate the defendant and his attorney, courtroom buffs came forward to congratulate Mel Seltzer on a masterful defense, and from the back row, Maria Torres, who had been sneaking in to watch the proceedings, ran up to embrace her fiancé. The district attorney and his assistant packed their briefcases and tried to leave unobtrusively although they both knew that the media wolf-pack awaited them just outside the door.

As the losing team left, "Any comment on the verdict?" came out of every reporter's mouth.

The district attorney shrugged and forced a politician's concession speech smile. "We thought we presented a persuasive case, but Mr. Seltzer was obviously successful in convincing the jury that there was some miscarriage of justice going on here. They apparently thought more of the rights of Patrolman Rodriguez than those of Lawanda de Bourbon, who is unfortunately not here to plead for *her* rights in person."

Renee Lieberman-Smith fielded those questions addressed to her, then asked to make a statement.

"I think it is clear," she began, with the serious manner befitting a serious public servant, "that the speculation surrounding my conduct as a member of this office, baseless innuendo though it is, has affected the ability of the district attorney to conduct his business in the whisper-free environment that is required for the dispensation of justice. It may have even affected the verdict in this case. In my years with this department I have felt nothing but the deepest respect for the office and its occupant, and would never allow myself to be the cause of any rumor regarding its integrity. Consequently, with great regret, I have tendered my resignation and will seek a position in private practice."

Before the reporters could press, the district attorney asked to comment. "When Renee told me of her decision, I did my best to dissuade her. She is one of our finest young assistants, as evidenced by the diligence and intelligence she demonstrated in preparing this case . . ." The district attorney paused and smiled once more. "Regardless of the outcome." The reporters laughed politely. "Nonetheless, I am forced to respect Renee's decision. You in the press should stand on notice. It was rumor and idle speculation emanating from your ranks that has resulted in the district attorney's office losing such an able member of the team."

The district attorney surveyed the crowd of reporters, who, from the looks on their faces, bought it. I wish I could have been this good with the jury, he thought.

Despite this compelling and unexpected news, the appearance of Mel Seltzer, that notorious manipulator of juries, also in this case the victor, immediately turned the reporters' attention.

"Any comment?"

"Do you consider this a vindication of the police department?"

"Do you expect any fallout from Whiffet and Chestnut?"
"Did you manipulate the jury?"
Mel Seltzer smiled at the last question. "There was no need to manipulate the jurors. I have just been speaking to members of the jury and each of them, without exception, felt that this trial should not have been brought before them in the first place. As a matter of fact, they had voted for acquittal on their first ballot but the foreman insisted that they spend some time reviewing the evidence and then vote once more. Therefore, I think it is fair to say that it is the district attorney, the politicians and the so-called 'activists' who have been trying to manipulate the jury as well as the public at large. My deepest wish from this trial is that Patrolman Rodriguez gets to return to the career that he has desired since boyhood."
"Patrolman Rodriguez, do you feel vindicated?"
James Rodriguez, standing between his lawyer and his fiancee, felt a big grin cross his face. "Of course I feel vindicated. I will always be grateful to Mr. Seltzer for proving so completely that there was no murder . . . just a cop trying to do his job."
"But you still face departmental hearings, do you not, Patrolman?"
"Yes," Rodriguez nodded soberly, "I do. But I trust the department to treat me fairly. I look forward to a long career on the force."
The questions continued for a few more minutes until the reporters broke away to interview the jurors. When the furor had subsided, James Rodriguez took his lawyer off to the side.
"Mr. Seltzer, I meant what I said. I'll always be grateful to you for proving that there was no murder."
Mel Seltzer looked blankly at the young patrolman. "James, I didn't prove there was no *murder*. I merely proved there was no *case*."

Things had changed for Herbert Whiffet, but not altogether in the ways he had expected. True, he had become an object of vilification and ridicule in the white press as a result of his alleged affair with Renee Lieberman-Smith, a liaison he continued to vigorously deny. But, to his surprise, the very same rumor had the opposite effect in the black community. Many apparently considered it something of a coup to elicit secret information from the white DA by sleeping with a white assistant DA.

Community newspapers lauded his work, church-going women stopped him in the street exhorting him to keep the faith, other local leaders called and asked to meet and discuss strategy, and, in the most sincere form of praise, a tidal wave of new potential clients besieged him for appointments. Leotis Chestnut and those loyal to him, of course, were unrepresented in the new Herbert Whiffet fan club.

Who could have imagined, thought Herbert with a smile, that the two acts in which he had risked the most, defending the late Ali Abdul Akbar and trading sexual favors for information with Renee Lieberman-Smith, would have done so much to increase his stock with his fellows?

Although speculation as to which cause attorney Whiffet would next embrace was as popular in some quarters as guessing the number, Herbert had developed some ideas of his own. He had learned quite a bit in the course of the Lawanda de Bourbon affair. He had learned that when you stick your neck out for a matter of principle you attract a multitude of supporters urging you on, none of whom are willing to share any of your burden or risk. If your head is subsequently lopped off, however, those supporters are right there to scream of the injustice of it all, always from the safety of the background. Herbert Whiffet vowed that his days of riding point had ended. (In fact, when a reporter called to ask for his comment on the de Bourbon verdict, Herbert Whiffet referred him to Leotis. After all, it was his case now.)

No, Herbert Whiffet had other ideas. He would continue to serve his people, of course. It was the thing to which he had dedicated his life. But from now on he would serve his people *by example*. Personal example. He would show young blacks that they too could make it in the white world.

And his new client was just the man to provide the wherewithal.

Herbert Whiffet buzzed his secretary to send the man in. Herbert rose from behind his desk to greet the prominent community leader as he stepped through the door to the private office.

He extended his hand and smiled respectfully. "Mr. Jones, it is a pleasure to meet you."

"You too," the man replied. "But call me Ralph."

It certainly was Leotis' case now. The outrageous but predictable verdict exonerating yet another cop who gunned down yet another unarmed black could not be allowed to recede into the pool of long-term memory, blending indistinguishably with thousands of others. Perhaps Lawanda de Bourbon was not as worthy of the protests of the righteous as Emmett Till or Medgar Evers or Michael Stewart or Eleanor Bumpers, but that was not the point. The point was that the wanton destruction of blacks by whites must be stopped and *any* opportunity to synthesize outrage into political action must be embraced. Thus, not one hour after the jury brought in its verdict, Leotis Chestnut was addressing a protest rally in front of the district attorney's headquarters.

"Now, Brothers and Sisters, *I* didn't raise the specter of FIX in this case. *That* was done by a *whiiite* reporter. *Even theyyy know what's goin' down in this city.* Well *thisss* time they gone *tooo* far. WE AIN'T GONNA TAKE IT NO MORE."

Cries of "Amen," and "Right on, Brother," perfectly punctuated the reverend's words, no voice any more distinct than Mahalia de Bourbon, whose baby, Lawanda, had just been denied justice by a jury that seemed almost to have been revised as white.

"*I* am calling on the *governorrr* to *impeach* this racist district attorney and replace him with a man who will *protect* the people, not *set them up for slaughter*."

As he spoke, the Reverend Leotis Chestnut scanned the rear of the crowd and the full contingent of television and print journalists busily recording his every word.

Thank God for the press, he thought. Without them, we all might still be pickin' cotton for Massah.

Despite pledges of continuity, a change in CEO is inevitably followed by sweeping changes in staff and delineation of responsibility. Every new leader immediately seeks to surround himself with a peerage whose power and position springs from his prerogative and therefore whose loyalty is wedded with self-interest in the new regime.

"I decided right up front that I didn' wan' no white man

representin' *me*," said Uzi Jones. "Dat's bullshit. All dat honkey Seltzer did was take Trips' bread an' watch out fo' hisself."

Herbert Whiffet nodded. "Yes, I've had some dealings with Mr. Seltzer. I can't say that I found him particularly sensitive to black people."

"Exac'ly!" replied Uzi, clapping his hands for emphasis. "Dat's what I'm sayin'. So I figger dat I should get me a black lawyer an' keep the money in the community."

Herbert Whiffet was not about to make the same mistake twice. "As I understand it . . . Ralph, you want me to handle your personal affairs as your counsel. I will not consent to be co-counsel."

Uzi Jones waved his hands. "No way, counsellor. You's it. Number One. You advise me on everythin' . . . any legal bullshit come up, you handle it." Uzi smiled. Without a gold tooth, he looked almost child-like. "So, counsellor, what'cha say?"

Herbert Whiffet considered for only the briefest instant the impending change in his activities. He saw Mel Seltzer and Annie Holdsworth sitting at the defense table in the Rodriguez case, rich and universally respected.

"I think it can be worked out," he said.

"Dat's fine, counsellor. Now what's yo' fee? Wha'cha get by de hour?"

Herbert Whiffet had that very morning raised his fees by fifty percent. "I get one-hundred-fifty dollars per hour."

Uzi Jones laughed. "Make it an even two . . . I don' like to count by halves." He reached inside his jacket and removed two thick envelopes. He tossed them on Herbert's desk. They landed with a resounding smack. "Dat's yo' retainer, counsellor. Dat should cover de first five hundred hours."

In a quirk of modern economics, the cost of giving someone a proper burial is almost the same as the cost of educating them, a fact Clarissa Taylor was forced to confront through the fog of grief. Perhaps if she had had time to consider the alternatives, to appreciate how desperately the money was needed by the living, she might have opted for a less opulent affair.

But the funeral director had been so kind, so understanding, seemed to so appreciate the depth of Clarissa's grief and been willing to shoulder the entire burden of burying a twelve-year-old boy. The funeral director felt it was only right to give proper homage to a promising student, the pride of his family, shot to death protecting what he thought was a trust from his employer, and, put like that, Clarissa Taylor was forced to agree.

It was only later, when the man who took care of everything sent her the bill for his services, that Clarissa Taylor realized that she had buried the family finances along with her son.

# PART III

# CHAPTER THIRTY-ONE

God, how can people do this every day? thought Herbert Whiffet, scanning the lines of traffic queueing up to pay the toll. From this vantage point the automobiles looked almost biblical, Israelites fleeing Pharaoh, rather than the miracle of the twentieth century rendered impotent by its own proliferation.

These commuters, day after day, sitting behind the wheel, eventually years of their lives lost in the daily epic battle to enter and leave Manhattan. It was different for him, of course. Herbert Whiffet had a driver, a young man who was paid specifically to endure these trials so that his employer might not. Thus Herbert could read, take notes, dictate correspondence or memoranda, nap, or merely lean his head back and listen to the music, soft clear tones perfectly rendered by his state-of-the-art sound system.

Today Herbert Whiffet chose the last of those alternatives, because today promised to be a busy one. The United States attorney had hinted that today was the day that indictments were to be handed down in the income tax fraud case which he had been preparing against certain of New York's alleged drug lords. Try though he might, Herbert had been unable to determine whether or not his client, Ralph Jones, was to be included on the list.

The investigation had been two years in preparation and, in the case of the Ghosts, had originally focused on the late Ali Abdul Akbar. That portion of the probe had been rendered moot, of course, by Akbar's still unsolved murder, so it was quite possible that his designated heir and successor might bear the brunt of the U.S. attorney's wrath. In any case, things promised to move quickly.

The Mercedes was only one-quarter mile from the Triborough toll booth now, almost close enough for his driver to move to the 'Exact Change-Tokens Only' lane and thereby save an additional ten to fifteen minutes of waiting. "At least it didn't snow," sighed Herbert. "I'd have been here all day."

"Almost there now, Mr. Whiffet." The driver, a twenty-four-year-old from Brooklyn named Wayne DiNucci, felt the need once or twice in each trip to pass along some obvious bit of information, perhaps to reaffirm his existence to his boss. Herbert had long since decided to employ only whites in service positions.

He did not respond to Wayne's comment; he never responded. He glanced to the magazine sitting on the seat and the caricature on the front cover. It was, he was forced to admit, an extremely well done burlesque. *Inside New York*, founded only one year ago by three former investment bankers, had virtually taken over the hip, urban satire market and was now considered must reading by anyone who considered himself 'in.'

This week's cover story was "Black Defense Lawyers—Equal Opportunity Comes To Sleazeland." The cover pictured a number of prominent white defense lawyers being crushed under the feet of three black men, the largest and most easily recognizable being Herbert Whiffet.

Herbert chuckled softly. In days past, he would certainly have been incensed at such treatment by the white press. Now, however, he could view satire in the spirit in which it should be taken. After all, weren't lawyers always to be the target of the satirist's arrow? It never seemed to bother Roy Cohn or Alan Dershowitz or even Melville Seltzer; they realized that the more they were mocked for their tactics, the more well-heeled clients would flock to their offices. There was only one criterion for a defense lawyer. You had to win, to get your client off.

And these days, no one got their clients off with more regularity than Herbert Whiffet.

What was even nicer, decided the now-prominent defense lawyer, was that the more they attacked him, the more they enhanced his reputation, and that, in turn, only added to his ability to sway a jury. For, as Herbert Whiffet had discovered, it is often the aura surrounding the lawyer that determines his effectiveness. That realization was the one thing that he owed to Mel Seltzer.

Soon the Mercedes was through the toll booth and cruising

the hundred yards before the bottleneck merge to the entrance of the FDR Drive. "Doesn't look too bad today, Mr. Whiffet," chirped Wayne. "Should be downtown in about twenty minutes."

Twenty minutes was fine; it gave Herbert more time to prepare for his meeting with Uzi Jones. That was one client Herbert Whiffet never kept waiting.

The car inched through the merge at 120th Street and entered the highway proper, accelerating to the heady speed of 15 mph. Wayne was right. In twenty minutes they would arrive at the office. Herbert no longer worked in Harlem, just as he no longer lived in Harlem. As the Lenox Terrace apartment had given way to a private home in Scarsdale, the 125th Street office had been supplanted by the bottom of a brownstone in the East 70's. The changes of venue were as much practical as prideful. Clients felt more comfortable with an attorney whose addresses reflected obvious prosperity.

Herbert's mind wandered and soon he was at the entrance to the office. He allowed Wayne to open his door, then emerged from the back of the Mercedes and walked past the scrupulously clean courtyard, leaving the white boy to park the car.

"Any messages?" he inquired of Belinda, his latest secretary.

"Nothing urgent, Mr. Whiffet," smiled the little blond, dimples popping out like rosebuds. Just as well she's engaged, Herbert thought. "Oh yes, Renee Lieberman-Smith called again."

Herbert rolled his eyes heavenward. "What did you tell her?"

Belinda smiled. Herbert suspected that there was something more to that smile than just boss-secretary. "I told her you'd be tied up all day, but would try to get back to her."

"Good." Ever since Renee had begun working for that civil rights law firm, she had continually pestered him to accept *pro bono* assignments. She had some nerve.

As Herbert Whiffet disappeared into his office, Belinda Ryan stared after him. What an asshole, she thought. I wish I didn't need this job so damn much.

This time, Renee Lieberman-Smith's telephone call was not

just to tweak Herbert; this call was business. Unfortunately for the former prosecutor, the assumption of her linkage with Herbert had been responsible for her being designated to attempt to secure a deposition in a case that her new firm was handling.

Upon leaving the district attorney's office, Renee had, as announced, sought a position in private practice. She found, to her surprise and regret that, despite the district attorney's unqualified recommendation, the notoriety that preceded her, coupled with a rather undistinguished record in the public sector, severely limited her appeal to outside firms. Finally, after months of trying, severance pay exhausted along with any illusions, Kravitz and Rotkowitz made her a rather modest offer; junior associate at a salary not even at the level of her civil service rate, and without the generous benefits and vacation *de rigeur* in the public sector. Renee immediately took the job.

At least the work was to her liking. Perry Kravitz, the partner to whom she was assigned, was a sixties refugee, a man who had made his way through that turbulent decade defending the rights of radicals, blacks, chicanos, and those who wished to wear a modified American flag as an article of apparel. His philosophy seemed to be that every American who wished to bring down the system (from the left) was entitled to a defense which took advantage of all the freedoms guaranteed within that system. It was only by protecting the rights of those at the fringes, he argued, that the rights of the rest of us could be guaranteed.

With the passing of the Vietnam War and the rush of many of the most vitriolic protestors to Wall Street and Madison Avenue, Perry Kravitz had lost much of his folk hero status, but continued, despite the loss of fashion, to pursue what radical issues were left. He defended American Indians who were accused of shooting FBI men, blacks who were accused of shooting police officers and solar energy advocates accused of shooting nuclear engineers.

Perry Kravitz had recently taken on a new client, an Hispanic unjustly deprived of his right to work by a scheming and self-serving bureaucracy, a man dismissed to cover the duplicity and complicity of his superiors. The man's name was James Rodriguez.

For, as the cynics had foretold, James Rodriguez had been

dismissed from the police department for his role in the de Bourbon affair. Protests had been unceasing and unmerciful in the wake of his acquittal and the young patrolman's departmental hearing had been little more than a formality. Despite a body of evidence that had caused a jury of his peers to acquit him in a mere three hours, senior members of the police department concluded that, through an inappropriate use of force, James Rodriguez had killed an innocent civilian.

In their ruling, these senior members of the force had cited much the same evidence as had the district attorney in his unsuccessful attempt to persuade twelve civilians: an eyewitness, a videotape, and no trace of the weapon that Officer Rodriguez claimed to have seen in the possession of the victim. It was with much regret, they said, that they were forced to reach the decision they did, but the rights of the public demanded that the police department be impartial in the administration of justice to its own.

So, with much fanfare and an eye cocked toward the Reverend Leotis Chestnut, the police commissioner had excised the bad apple from the ranks of the New York City Police Department. As a result, in what was surely a coincidence, the reverend and his followers ended their calls for special prosecutors, impeachments and investigations by the Justice Department, content to await the next incident of police mistreatment of innocent blacks. The de Bourbon family did, however, file a $20 million damage suit against Rodriguez.

Perry Kravitz had been waiting on the sidelines for just such a decision, and had immediately contacted the ex-patrolman.

"James, you must fight this," he had said, his blue eyes as piercing as halogen headlights on high beam. "Not just for yourself, but for everyone who gets screwed by the system."

James Rodriguez had found that quite funny. "Are you related to Mel Seltzer?"

Perry Kravitz had smiled but did not turn down the beams. "Only by profession. Mel Seltzer takes on cases of notoriety that he can win. I take on cases that I believe in."

"That sounds familiar," nodded Rodriguez. Then he shrugged. What difference did it make now? "Sure, Mr. Kravitz. If you want to press my case, go right ahead. I can't pay you, though."

Perry Kravitz returned the shrug. "So? Who asked you?"

The lawyer continued. "If you get any damages, reimburse me for my expenses only. If not, you don't owe me a cent. That," he added, "does not include back pay. You keep all of that."

James Rodriguez tried to figure out where the loophole was.

"Not only that," Kravitz grinned, putting his arm around his new client, a gesture that Rodriguez found patronizing but oddly comforting, "I have recently hired a former member of the district attorney's staff. Name of Renee Lieberman-Smith."

"Wasn't she . . . ?"

"Yes, James, she was."

"Okay, Mr. Kravitz," sighed James Rodriguez, "here I go again."

"I know how you feel, James. But think of it this way . . . What have you got to lose?"

So, Renee Lieberman-Smith had been put to work full-time preparing a civil rights case on behalf of the now-unemployed James Rodriguez. She hadn't worked this side of the street before, but it did not seem to her that Kravitz had the guns to prove his case. The evidence was inconclusive and there is no requirement that the police department review procedures follow the same rules as a trial. In fact, it was generally accepted that the department must be a good deal more stringent in its standards than the public is in theirs.

"Perhaps we won't win," admitted her new employer, "but we can certainly make it more difficult for them to do it to the next fellow."

Uzi Jones was ushered in as soon as he arrived. Too bad, he thought. If he had been forced to wait a few minutes he might have been able to leaf through the latest edition of *US News And World Report*. Since his ascension to power, Ralph Jones had made a concerted effort to improve his speech, his reading ability and his grasp of politics and economics. He was, after all, a leader in the community and it wouldn't do to seem to be promoting illiteracy.

"Good morning, Ralph," oozed his attorney upon his entry

to the inner office. "I hope you weren't kept waiting."

"No, counsellor," replied Ralph Jones, fiddling with the knot on his Hermes necktie, "not at all."

They sat immediately and got to business. "I'm sorry to say, Ralph," sighed Herbert Whiffet, "that I couldn't get anything from downtown about the indictments."

"Shit," hissed Ralph at no one in particular, although Herbert felt an Arctic wind pass through him. "That be . . . uh, *is* too bad."

"Sorry, Ralph," Herbert offered quickly, "it couldn't be helped. I've never seen such security. I did everything I could."

Uzi Jones smiled at his lawyer although only the bottom half of his eyes were visible under a hooded brow. "I'm sure you did, counsellor." Then he turned up his hands. "Well, can't nothin' be done now . . . *nothing can be done now.* The accountant says they can't touch me, so I'll just have to wait it out."

Uzi Jones had taken to speaking very slowly, as if an emigré in a country with a different language, which perhaps he was. His rush to self-improvement was due in part to the aforementioned civic pride, but also to his sensitivity over his treatment by the media during the Ghost War. He had been called a 'Mad Dog Killer,' 'psychotic' and, worst of all, the man who employed children to carry drugs and be murdered on the subways. Although the killing of young Matthew Taylor had not been solved and there was no direct evidence that the boy *was* carrying drugs at the time of his death and that *everyone* used kids as mules, the press had picked on Uzi.

Well, fuck them, he had decided. He'd show those bastards.

Herbert Whiffet began to breathe normally again after Uzi Jones had left. There was something about that psycho which made him much more fearsome when well-groomed and speaking properly than he had been as a mere street thug. For relief, Herbert decided to return Renee Lieberman-Smith's telephone call. It would feel good to turn her down again.

But Herbert Whiffet was unprepared to be asked to give a

deposition in a civil rights case being prepared on behalf of a killer cop by the woman who had participated in his prosecution for murder.

"Your allegiances are rather easily swayed, aren't they, Renee?" he asked with a chuckle.

"Not at all," came the serious, even cold, reply. "I believe now, as I have always believed, in the rights of those oppressed by the system. And James Rodriguez, I now realize, has most assuredly been oppressed by the system, to say nothing of by you and me."

"Speak for yourself, Renee," retorted Herbert. "I still think he shot down that girl in cold blood. Maybe it wasn't part of any grand conspiracy, but he murdered her all right."

"You're wrong, Herbert. I've talked with him at great length and I believe that James Rodriguez never murdered anybody."

Herbert Whiffet sighed. "I don't see what difference it makes. You've got no case. You'll have to go to the Supreme Court to get any relief and that will take seven or eight years. Tell me, Renee, does your client know that? Is he prepared to work as a security guard in a supermarket for eight years before he even gets a shot? And even then he'll probably lose."

The length of time required for the case to go through the process was the one thing that everyone had neglected to tell Rodriguez.

"Of course he knows," snapped Renee. "He's prepared to fight for his rights."

"Sure he is, Renee," sighed Herbert. "In any event, I have no intention of participating in your case. Subpoena me if you like, but I'll not help a man I believe to be a murderer."

"How's Uzi Jones?" Renee asked icily.

"Don't get holier than thou with me, Renee," growled the former Champion. "Do you really think that Lawanda de Bourbon had a gun and that it fell on someone's goddamn window-sill?"

Show-and-tell is one of the first games children who are old enough to socialize learn to play and it is no different in the ghetto. Except, in the ghetto, frogs, colored stones and lightning bugs are replaced by hypodermics, drug vials, and, occasionally, an implement of violence. As in any session of show-and-tell, the very best and most prized objects cause a good deal of discussion and their origins are vigorously debated.

"That's bull*shit*," sneered eight-year-old Moses Lott with a roll of his eyes. "You 'spect me to fall for that jive?"

"I ain't bullshittin' nobody," protested Moses' playmate, Kenyatta Batson. "I be tellin' y'all the truth."

Moses put his hands on his hips and stared at his friend. "C'mon, Kenyatta," he cajoled. "You done stole it, right? What y'all do, lift it from yo' daddy's closet?"

"I be tellin' y'all," retorted the stung Kenyatta, "I *found* it. Jes like I tol' ya."

"Right," replied Moses, pursing his lips. "You mus' really think I be dumb. You 'spect me to believe you jes' open yo' window and the piece jes' sittin' in yo' mama's flower pot. Like I said, Kenyatta, *bulllsheeiitt*."

Kenyatta Batson secreted the small pistol in his pocket and made to leave. "You b'lieve what y'all like, Moses. You be an asshole anyway."

# CHAPTER THIRTY-TWO

Clovis Buckworth was overworked. The summer had been bad enough, but fall and now early winter had seen enough of an increase in homeless families to convince an observer unfamiliar with the city's demographics that refugees from some terrible war or natural disaster were streaming across its borders. And although homelessness was listed as a top priority by virtually every politician regardless of party affiliation or philosophic orientation, surprisingly little money was actually making its way to the homeless themselves.

In fact, as a symptom of the current rampant prosperity, the burgeoning construction of expensive apartments and the conversion of once-middle-class housing to accommodate the newly-wealthy had actually decreased the housing available to those of modest incomes. They, in turn, put pressure on the limited remaining lower-income housing, leaving those near the bottom of the ladder to compete for whatever dregs were left. (Those on the *very* bottom, traditionally the outlet for the guilt of the rich, were often subsidized, leaving those just above with the rather unpalatable alternative of dropping still further in order to obtain shelter.)

Awareness of the intricacies of this sociological phenomenon was no comfort to those who must marshal what resources were available to try and relieve the misery of the families victimized by it. To deal with a two-hundred-percent increase in the population of homeless families (to say nothing of single men and women) Clovis Buckworth and the Mobilization for the Homeless could only manage a five-percent increase in endowments. Clovis, like his peers, tried to supplant the shortfall in dollars with increased hours, but manpower cannot pay rent.

So, as Clovis Buckworth removed his coat at 7:30 AM, ready to begin another twelve-hour day, the two-inch-high stack of papers, representing that week's new cases, mocked his efforts from its perch on the corner of his desk. Clovis opened his now-room-temperature coffee and sat heavily in his chair. Although it meant keeping the new supplicants waiting, he forced himself to start each morning by getting the paperwork done, so that yesterday's homeless might be duly recorded by the state welfare department and the lucky placed in filthy hotels or assigned to family shelters. Those who for one reason or another did not qualify must return to the streets or the cesspools of the public shelters.

When Clovis Buckworth had started the Mobilization for the Homeless, it had never occurred to him that he would be charged with making the determination as to which families would survive and which would perish. Judging relative worthiness was the most odious aspect of what had become an increasingly odious job. The political process had often reduced him to little more than an executioner.

Clovis made his notes on the three-part forms, occasionally marking one or another 'Priority' or 'Emergency,' indications which he knew were, for the most part, meaningless, although without the notation the referral would have no chance whatever. There just *isn't* any housing available he was always told, except on those rare occasions when a specific family's plight reached the eyes and ears of the public through the news media and shelter for them was miraculously found.

That was why Clovis was so eager to see Karen. He was *always* eager to see Karen, of course, for even though they now shared the same apartment, he didn't feel he saw her much more than when they were merely dating. But today was special. Karen was going to pay a visit, which meant a rare lunch out, but even more important it was a visit from Cornelia Pembroke, who had finally prevailed upon her boss to do a special report on the growing housing shortage.

"Oh, Corney, not *another* report on the homeless," he had wailed until now. "I know it's a problem, but it just isn't *news* any more."

But Cornelia finally convinced Iserson that this problem, old hat though it was, still had all the incendiary potential as the exposé of mismanagement in the district attorney's office that had won her an Emmy and forced the district attorney to announce his resignation when his current term expired.

Well, not convinced him exactly; Iserson had approved the assignment with a grudging, "I owe you one." However it had been achieved, the story was going to happen, and perhaps this time, Clovis sighed, it might do some good.

Before he was halfway through the stack, Karen was at the door.

"Good morning, Mr. Buckworth," she smiled. "May I come in?"

"Of course, Miss Pembroke. Welcome to purgatory."

Karen's smile vanished as she walked in and sat in the chair opposite Clovis' desk. "It really is, Clovis." She glanced in the direction of the hall outside the office. "I don't know how you can take it every day. Those poor families and all those kids . . ."

"Watch that one," he said, indicating the chair. "It's on the verge of becoming three-legged." Then he sat back. "You know, Karen, it's terrible to admit, but I almost don't notice anymore. It's getting so hard to do anything that if I let myself really see those people out there, I'd flip out. I just try to look at them as clients . . . or something."

"Does it work?"

Clovis Buckworth smiled ruefully. "Of course not. Does it sound like it would work?"

"No," Karen replied, wishing, as she had during her last visit, that she had worn older clothes. But this time she had had no choice. She was taping a segment at the Mobilization, so work clothes it must be.

"Well," she continued, gathering steam as she spoke, "maybe we can do something. Iserson's given full backing to this report. I'm going to try to get it all. That everyone talks about doing something but no one wants to spend any money, that no middle-class neighborhood is willing to have decent temporary houses for these people in their backyard, that what little money there is often ends up in the hands of slumlords, and that the politicians who make the most noise about the problem let all sorts of bullshit red tape and little bureaucratic rules maintain a lousy status quo."

"That is a rather ambitious agenda," grinned Clovis. "Good luck."

"Yeah," said Karen, "I'm going to need something. This is one of those neat little problems where everyone blames everyone else. And, conveniently, there are so many regulations, federal, state and city, that they can get away with it."

"Well, my dear," shrugged Clovis, "I hate to cut you off when you are in the grip of journalistic fervor, but I've got work to do . . . especially if I'm going to slip out for a romantic lunch. When do we start?"

"About five minutes. The crew is outside talking with some of the people. We'll start with interviews."

Clarissa Taylor had immediately recognized that pretty television reporter as she strode past heading for the director's office. The reporter seemed to rush by, trying to avoid looking at those waiting without seeming to actually ignore them. I guess I can't blame her, thought Clarissa, surveying the ten or twelve families and partial families that shared the waiting area. We certainly aren't much to look at.

As the reporter had passed, Clarissa had felt a spark of identification—identification with another time. But there was no point in dwelling on the past; the past could make the present unendurable. And the present took all her energy. The present went to finding a place to sleep and thinking no further than one meal ahead. The present was all-consuming. It left no room for a past—or a future.

As Clarissa Taylor fought to hold back her memory, she noticed two men from the station begin talking to some of the others waiting to see the director. So that was it. Another story on the homeless. Interviews shown on television while other folks ate dinner—hot meals in warm dining rooms. Pictures of people who couldn't find a place to sleep to make those who could feel superior or to allow them some cheap charity. "That's terrible," they would say between bites. "Why doesn't anyone do something about those people?"

Clarissa looked around and realized that there was no escape. No, those television men meant to get everybody. Quickly, Clarissa Taylor roused Jeanette and Veronica.

"Come girls. We've got to go now."

"But why, Mama?" wailed Jeanette. "It's warm here."

"No back talk now. I tell you we have to leave."

As the girls struggled to their feet, one of the men from the station noticed. "Hey, Ma'am," he called. "Where you goin'? Don't you want to be on television?"

"Certainly not," replied Clarissa Taylor over her shoulder as she led her children out into the early December morning.

She didn't regret leaving.

After all, she thought, a person has got to have some pride.